BLACK HILLS BLOOD HUNT

Look for these exciting Western series from bestselling authors William W. Johnstone and J.A. Johnstone

The Mountain Man

Luke Jensen: Bounty Hunter

Brannigan's Land

The Jensen Brand

Preacher and MacCallister

The Red Ryan Westerns

Perley Gates

Have Brides, Will Travel

Guns of the Vigilantes

Shotgun Johnny

The Chuckwagon Trail

The Jackals

The Slash and Pecos Westerns

The Texas Moonshiners

Stoneface Finnegan Westerns

Ben Savage: Saloon Ranger

The Buck Trammel Westerns

The Death and Texas Westerns

The Hunter Buchanon Westerns

Tinhorn

Will Tanner, U.S. Deputy Marshal

BLACK HILLS BLOOD HUNT

WILLIAM W. JOHNSTONE

AND J.A. JOHNSTONE

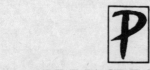

PINNACLE BOOKS
KENSINGTON PUBLISHING CORP.
www.kensingtonbooks.com

PINNACLE BOOKS are published by

Kensington Publishing Corp.
119 West 40th Street
New York, NY 10018

This book is a work of fiction. Names, characters, businesses, organizations, places, events, and incidents either are the product of the author's imagination or are used fictitiously. Any resemblance to actual persons, living or dead, events, or locales is entirely coincidental.

To the extent that the image or images on the cover of this book depict a person or persons, such person or persons are merely models, and are not intended to portray any character or characters featured in the book.

PUBLISHER'S NOTE: Following the death of William W. Johnstone, the Johnstone family is working with a carefully selected writer to organize and complete Mr. Johnstone's outlines and many unfinished manuscripts to create additional novels in all of his series like the Last Gunfighter, Mountain Man, and Eagles, among others. This novel was inspired by Mr. Johnstone's superb storytelling.

All Kensington titles, imprints, and distributed lines are available at special quantity discounts for bulk purchases for sales promotion, premiums, fund-raising, and educational or institutional use.

If you purchased this book without a cover you should be aware that this book is stolen property. It was reported as "unsold and destroyed" to the Publisher and neither the Author nor the Publisher has received any payment for this "stripped book."

Special book excerpts or customized printings can also be created to fit specific needs. For details, write or phone the office of the Kensington Sales Manager: Kensington Publishing Corp., 119 West 40th Street, New York, NY 10018. Attn. Sales Department. Phone: 1-800-221-2647.

First Printing: November 2022
ISBN-13: 978-0-7860-4890-8
ISBN-13: 978-0-7860-4891-5 (eBook)

10 9 8 7 6 5 4 3 2 1

Printed in the United States of America

Dakota Territory, 1885

The trading post belonged to a fellow known in this part of the country as The Dutchman. His last name was Krieger, and he hailed from somewhere in Germany. That was all anybody really knew about him, except for one thing.

Big, bald, and bullet-headed, nobody wanted to mess with him, because he was a dangerous man to cross. He needed that kind of reputation to ride herd on the rowdy bunch of gun-wolves and owlhoots who frequented his place.

On this December night, the wind howled outside, driving thick clouds of snow almost sideways during the strongest gusts. As Dakota Territory blizzards went, it was pretty stout. By morning, the drifts would be piled up several feet high around the sturdy log building. The snow had started only about an hour earlier, so it wasn't too bad yet.

And inside the trading post, the air was nice and warm from the flames in the fireplace and the heat that came from a couple of potbellied stoves tucked in the far corners of the room. The Dutchman wasn't expecting any customers in weather such as this. He leaned on the bar, sipped from a mug of beer, and contemplated the three soiled doves who worked in the rooms off the hall in the back. They were sitting together at one of the tables, and as Krieger's gaze wandered over them, he pondered on which one would warm his blankets tonight.

The way the wind was blowing and the temperature was dropping, this might be a two-whore night, he decided. That brought a smile to his ruddy face.

Then the door opened and brought in cold air, swirling snowflakes, and Gus Greendale and his gang.

Krieger straightened from his casual pose and rested both hands flat on the bar in front of him. He glanced at the shelf below the bar. Two sawed-off shotguns rested there, both loaded, both with the stocks cut down to make good handgrips. Krieger had named the big poppers Hugo and Dietrich after his brothers back in Germany who he hadn't seen or heard from in more than twenty years.

Gus appeared to be in a good mood, though, even jovial, despite yelling, "Shut that door, damn you, you filthy redskinned heathen!" so maybe there wouldn't be any trouble.

Lame Wolf, a Crow warrior who rode with the Greendale gang, leaned against the door and pushed it shut. The wind gave a last howl and spit more snow into the room just before the gap closed. Lame Wolf stomped his feet, encased in high-topped moccasins, to knock off the snow that clung to them.

The other outlaws stomped their feet, too, and came toward the bar with Greendale in the lead. Gus was a hatchet-faced man with bushy blond brows and a tangle of greasy fair hair falling to his shoulders. He wore a thick buffalo coat like the other men, except for Lame Wolf who had a buffalo robe wrapped around him.

The Singleton brothers, Hank and Hubert, followed Greendale. Their long black beards made it difficult to tell them apart, but Hubert, the younger sibling, was taller and heavier. With them were Amos Maddock, gaunt and gray and the oldest of the bunch, and a black man called Tiny because he was anything but. Built like a redwood, he towered over the other owlhoots.

All six of them were killers, Krieger knew. They held up trains and stagecoaches and robbed banks and rustled cattle and ruthlessly gunned down anybody who got in their way. Sheriffs had tried to track them down, and so had U.S. Marshals, but Gus Greendale knew the wild country in Dakota Territory better than just about anybody and always gave the slip to any pursuit.

Krieger didn't like the man, but Greendale's money, stolen or not, spent as well as anyone else's. Like most of The Dutchman's customers, the gang tried to stay on their best behavior when they came here, because they liked having this out-of-the-way place where they could have a drink, gamble, and dally with the soiled doves.

"Howdy there, Dutchman," Greendale said as he came up to the bar and rested gloved hands on the planks. "It's blowin' pretty good out there."

"Ja," Krieger said, nodding. "Didn't expect to see you tonight, Gus . . . or anybody else, to be honest. I figured you'd be holed up somewhere, waiting out the storm."

"That's exactly what we figure on doin' here. Set up beers for me and the boys. 'Cept for Lame Wolf, of course." Greendale let out a bray of laughter. "Can't trust no Injun to guzzle down firewater. He's liable to go loco!"

Lame Wolf had already shuffled over to the trading post part of the building and stopped in front of a counter where a big glass jar full of penny candy sat. He took the lid off the jar, delved into it with his hand, and stuffed several of the sweets into his mouth. Grinning around the candy, which seemed to be his only vice other than being a desperado, he told Greendale what he could go and do to himself, and threw in some references to farm animals, as well. Greendale howled in amusement again.

Krieger drew the beers and set them on the planks in front of the gang. Some places wouldn't serve black folks, but Krieger had never cared about that, so Tiny got just as big a mug as the other men.

The Singleton brothers were already eyeing the girls, who returned the looks a little nervously. Krieger tapped a blunt finger on the bar in front of the black-bearded duo and said sternly, "You take it easy this time, you boys hear me?"

"They're whores," Hubert Singleton growled, "not china dolls."

"You heard what I said. No argument if you want to stay here. You can go back out in the blizzard if you don't like it."

Greendale said, "Hubert, what the hell's wrong with you? You heard The Dutchman. You want him to introduce you to Hugo and Dietrich, real close and personal-like?"

Hank Singleton muttered, "Don't worry, Gus, we won't cause no trouble."

Greendale jerked his head in a nod. "See that you don't." He smiled across the bar at Krieger. "Don't think for a second we don't appreciate your hospitality, Dutchman. Everybody in these parts knows better than to mess with you. Anybody tries, they'll answer to me."

Krieger knew that Greendale's friendly manner was largely a pose. They depended on this establishment not only for entertainment but also for supplies. *That* was why they behaved themselves.

If they ever decided that they didn't need The Dutchman anymore . . . well, then, Krieger held no illusions about his ability to stand up to all six of the outlaws, even with those sawed-offs under the bar. They would gun him down.

But he'd take some of them with him, ja.

Tonight, though, everybody was happy. They drank beer and laughed. Lame Wolf stuffed himself with candy. The Singleton brothers took Daisy and Lucille into the back. Amos Maddock sat and talked with the other whore; Krieger figured at his age, that was about all the old owlhoot could do. Tiny sat by the fireplace, sipped beer, and looked content.

Greendale was at the bar, making small talk with Krieger, when the door opened for the second time since the blizzard started.

Four men came in this time, led by a medium-sized gent in a thick coat and fur hat carrying a Winchester. The three hombres behind him looked like cowboys. Two of them had Winchesters; the remaining man had a shotgun tucked under his arm. He was the one who closed the door behind them.

Greendale turned toward the new arrivals and said, "Whoo-eee! I thought you boys was gonna let half of Canada in here while that door was open."

"Sorry," the leader said in a clear, powerful voice with a crispness that marked him as not being from around here. A brown mustache drooped over both corners of his mouth, and a pair of spectacles attached to a ribbon that disappeared under his coat perched on his nose. "It's a night not fit for man nor beast out there, as the old saying goes."

"You got that right, friend." Greendale waved an arm. "Come on over here to the bar. I'll buy you a drink."

The leader didn't budge. Krieger frowned at him and began, "I know you. You're—"

"Gus Greendale, you're under arrest," the man interrupted him. The three cowboys had spread out behind him, their weapons not pointing directly at the outlaws yet but slanted in their general direction.

Greendale laughed. "What's that you say? Under arrest? Last I heard, mister, you ain't no marshal or sheriff or any other kind of star packer."

"A citizen who has knowledge of a crime is empowered to place the lawbreaker in custody and turn him over to a duly commissioned law enforcement officer. That is what we intend to do."

"You don't have knowledge of a crime," Greendale scoffed.

"Indeed we do. Earlier this afternoon, you and your men robbed the bank in Medora. I and *my* men happened to be in town at the time and followed you here, along with other members of a posse."

Grinning, Greendale said, "I don't see no damn posse."

The man shrugged. "We got separated from them in the storm. But the sheriff mentioned his intention to check out this place, so I'm sure they'll be along shortly. We were simply fortunate enough to arrive first."

"Fortunate," Greendale repeated. "I don't know how you figure that. If there really is a posse, you should've waited for them to get here."

One of the cowboys said quietly, "I hate to agree with a varmint like that, Teddy, but—"

Just then, Hubert Singleton burst through the beaded curtain that closed off the hallway where the whore's rooms were. He wore hastily pulled on boots and trousers but was bare and fish-belly white from the waist up. He swung up a Colt and bellowed, "Die, you four-eyed son of a—"

One of the cowboys snapped his Winchester in line and fired before Hubert could finish his threat or pull the trigger. Hubert stumbled as a splotch of red appeared on his pallid chest. His mouth opened and closed and he tried to lift the revolver again, but the cowboy's second shot drilled through his nose and exploded out the back of his head.

That same slug ripped most of Hank Singleton's right ear off. He was following his brother, and the shot might have missed him entirely if he hadn't jumped up at just the wrong moment, trying to see what was happening over Hubert's shoulder. He screamed and fell to his knees, dropped his gun, and clapped his hand over his suddenly bloody and mangled ear.

Hubert, already dead, reeled back and fell, landing on his brother. Hank squalled even louder.

Tiny sprang up from his seat by the fireplace and lunged toward the knot of men just inside the front door, but he stopped short in his charge and threw his hands in front of him, palms out in surrender, as he found himself looking down the shotgun's twin muzzles.

Amos Maddock wasn't going to give up that easily. He leaped to his feet, reached under his buffalo coat, and pulled his gun with his right hand, while he used his left to grab the girl who'd been sitting at the table with him. He jerked her toward him, clearly intending to use her as a shield as he opened fire.

The other rifle-toting cowboy didn't give him that chance. The Winchester cracked, sending a slug ripping through the side of Maddock's neck. Blood fountained from the torn artery and splashed over the girl's face. She shrieked in horror and tore loose from Maddock's grip. The old outlaw spun in a half-circle and collapsed, folding up into a heap on the puncheon floor.

All that happened in a handful of heartbeats. Gus Greendale had his gun out but hadn't gotten off a shot when Krieger pressed Hugo's twin muzzles against the back of his neck. Greendale froze.

"Dutchman," he breathed, "are you sure you want to get mixed up in this?"

"I don't want any more lead flying around my place," Krieger replied. "Besides, where you're standing, if Mr. Roosevelt shoots you, the bullet's liable to come through and hit me."

He didn't know at the time that something very similar had just happened to the Singleton brothers, but the possibility was a legitimate worry every time gunplay erupted, especially in close quarters like this.

"That's very wise, *Herr* Krieger," the man called Teddy

said. He had his rifle tucked solidly against his shoulder and his cheek nestled against the smooth wood of the stock as he peered through his spectacles at them. Krieger had seen that sort of icy-nerved look before and knew that if Roosevelt had to fire, he wouldn't miss.

Greendale must have known it, too. His hand opened and his Colt thudded to the floor.

"You know who I am?" Krieger asked.

"I've heard talk of this place," Roosevelt replied without lowering his rifle. "I haven't set out to clean it up because that didn't seem necessary. It's said you maintain strict order here. From what I can tell, that appears to be correct."

"I don't want trouble . . . from anybody." Krieger pressed harder on the back of Greendale's neck with the sawed-off popper. "Gus knew not to bring problems here with him, so whatever happened is his responsibility."

Without looking around, Greendale snarled, "You're gonna be sorry you done this, you damn Dutchie."

"Threaten me again and I'll blow your head off your shoulders right now."

"That won't be necessary," Theodore Roosevelt said. "I don't believe Mr. Greendale will cause any more problems."

By the time the sheriff and the rest of the posse from Medora showed up, Gus Greendale, Hank Singleton, and Tiny were tied securely, hand and foot, and sat on the floor, propped against the front of the bar.

Lame Wolf was gone, having disappeared somehow during the shooting. Krieger figured he had gotten into the back and slipped out a window. The Crow was a canny sort and wouldn't hang around. He'd find somewhere else to ride out the blizzard and then likely put this part of the country well behind him.

Either that, or he'd freeze to death before the night was over.

The three cowboys, who rode for Roosevelt's Elkhorn Ranch, had dragged the bodies of Amos Maddock and Hubert Singleton outside so the cold would slow down their decomposition. Krieger didn't want them stinking up the trading post.

Roosevelt stood at the far end of the bar with The Dutchman and said, "You've made yourself an enemy today, *Herr* Krieger."

"You mean Greendale?" Krieger's broad shoulders rose and fell in a shrug. "He was never a friend to start with. Just because a scorpion doesn't sting you one day doesn't mean that it won't on another day."

"It's in their nature, as the fable has it," Roosevelt agreed.

"Besides," Krieger went on, "the way I look at it, I made myself a friend, too."

A wary look came into Roosevelt's eyes behind the spectacles. "Indeed you did," he said, "but you should remember that I'm just a simple rancher now. My political life, such as it was, is behind me, and I harbor no further ambitions in that arena. If you believed that I might be able to perform some sort of favor for you in the future, I fear that you're sadly mistaken."

Krieger scowled and shook his head. "I took a hand in the game because it was the right thing to do. I'm not expecting any favors."

"Then I apologize for considering the possibility. When one spends very much time in Washington, it becomes a habit to distrust everyone's motives."

Krieger grunted and said, "Yeah, I imagine it does."

"That being said . . ." Roosevelt thrust out his hand. "Thank you for your help."

Krieger clasped the rancher's hand, then looked along the

bar to where Gus Greendale sat staring straight ahead, his angular face as hard and cold as stone.

"I think I'm not the only one who made an enemy today."

"In that case," Roosevelt said, "Mr. Greendale will simply have to join the crowd and get in line behind Mr. James G. Blaine and his supporters."

New York City, 1896

That'll do now, that'll do," Inspector Ambrose Neill murmured as he pressed the muzzle of his pistol against the kneeling man's head, just behind the right ear. "No need to carry on so. It'll all be over soon, and we can all rest. Besides, as thick as these walls are, and underground, to boot, no one can hear ye."

The man wailed again in terror anyway, a pitiful sound cut short by the roar of the gun. Neill had taken the time to stuff nice, thick wads of cotton into his ears before tending to this errand, but the blast was uncomfortably loud despite that.

The dead man pitched forward onto his face. Blood ran out of the bullet hole and began to form a pool around his head. The blood was dark, almost black, in the light from the single lamp that burned on a rough table.

Neill turned away from the body and replaced the spent cartridge in the gun before snugging the weapon away in the holster under his tweed coat. He was a dapper, stocky man of middle years with a neatly trimmed mustache. He wasn't wearing a hat at the moment, so his full head of carefully combed, graying brown hair was visible. He took the wads of cotton from his ears and stuck them in a pocket.

"Take care of that, would you, lads?" he said to the two big men who had just looked on stolidly at the execution. Without waiting for an answer from either of them, because he knew they would obey without question, Neill walked toward the stairs that led up out of this basement room underneath a warehouse not far from the docks.

He went to the office tucked in a corner of the huge, cavernous building. The door was open. Light spilled through it, throwing a long, distorted, wavering shadow behind Neill as he approached. He stepped inside, smiled, and said, "Ready to go, my dear?"

A beautiful, elegantly dressed blonde in a dark green gown, matching hat, and fur coat stood up from the chair where she'd been sitting.

"I don't see why we had to come here in the first place, Ambrose," she said as she clutched an equally elegant bag in kid-gloved hands.

"I told you, dear, just a brief business matter to deal with." Neill reached for a homburg hat and thick topcoat hanging on a coat tree just inside the door.

"But you're a policeman. What business would you have *here?"*

"Oh, a policeman's business extends to every corner of the city. We're responsible for maintaining law and order, you know. And you didn't really have to wait that awfully long, did you?"

The blonde made a sour face. "This place is just so grimy and depressing. This whole neighborhood is. And it smells bad. How can people even live in a place like this?"

"People do what they must to survive, Estelle, darling," Neill said as he shrugged into the topcoat and then settled the hat on his head. He offered her his left arm. "Shall we go?"

"Gladly."

She linked arms with him and they left the office through a door that led to the street outside. As they stepped out, a light but chilly wind stirred the feather attached to her stylish hat.

"Were you able to take care of what you needed to do?" she asked, evidently over being annoyed with him. That was one of the things Neill liked about Estelle, she never stayed angry for very long, especially when he promised her dinner and drinks in one of New York City's best restaurants. "I suppose it really *didn't* take all that long."

"Oh, yes," he told her. "I was able to conclude the matter quite successfully."

Alfred Riddle would never again defy his betters and refuse to honor his obligations. And when his body was fished out of the East River with a hole in the head, as Neill would make sure it was, his death would serve as a warning to all the other businessmen in the neighborhood that when they were told to pay up or else, they had damned well better do it. So yes, Neill mused, it was a very successful conclusion.

And Estelle was right: it didn't take long to pull a trigger.

Neill's air of smug self-satisfaction evaporated instantly, however, when he realized that the hansom cab he expected to be waiting at the curb was nowhere to be seen. He stopped short, glared, and said, "Blast it, I told that driver to wait."

Footsteps sounded behind them.

Neill stiffened. He turned his head to look back over his shoulder. Estelle sounded nervous as she asked, "Ambrose, what's wrong?"

Neill realized he was holding his breath. He blew it out in a sigh of relief as he recognized the two men looming up on the sidewalk. Of course, just Jenkins and O'Rourke. A different pair than the two who had been given the task of disposing of Riddle's body, but his men, nonetheless, who were watching over him tonight.

No man achieved the success Ambrose Neill had without making some enemies. Rulers always had to worry about pretenders to the throne, and make no mistake about it, Ambrose Neill *ruled* this kingdom on the east side of Manhattan. So his loyal "knights" were never far away.

"It's all right, my dear," he assured Estelle. "These are associates of mine."

"Other policemen?"

"Not . . . exactly." Neill let go of her arm and faced the two men. "Did you see what happened to the cab?"

"Sorry, boss," Jenkins replied. "I guess we weren't watchin' it close enough. It was there, and then it was gone."

"Yeah," O'Rourke said. "Gone."

Unease stirred again inside Neill. Anything out of the ordinary was cause for concern, and anybody not doing what he told them—like that cabbie—was definitely out of the ordinary. He snapped, "Find another cab."

"Sure, boss," Jenkins began, but before he could move, O'Rourke interrupted him by saying, "Who th' hell's that?"

The street was dimly and intermittently lit by gas lamps set atop iron poles. Fog drifted and eddied from the nearby river and added to the gloom. Because of those things, when Neill turned his head to look where O'Rourke was pointing, at first he could see only an indistinct shape standing in the cone of light cast by one of those street lamps at the end of the block.

Then the figure started toward him with a determined stride that started alarm bells clanging inside Ambrose Neill's head. He recognized that resolute walk.

But it was nothing to worry about, he told himself as he tried to calm his suddenly racing pulse. No one had any evidence against him. Anybody who could have testified against him knew better than to do a foolish thing like that. The ones who were still alive, that is.

"Inspector Neill," the man called. He stopped about twenty feet away and stood with his hands tucked casually in the pockets of his topcoat. He was dressed as dapperly as Neill himself. "I'm glad I found you."

Neill spread his hands and said, "Here I am, Commissioner, at your service. I am, however, off duty and was about to go and enjoy a nice supper with a friend of mine."

He inclined his head toward the blonde.

"I understand, Inspector, but in a larger sense, those of us who serve the public are never actually off duty, are we?"

"You could look at it that way," Neill allowed cautiously. His eyes narrowed. "Did you send my cab away?"

"Indeed I did."

"Why?"

The commissioner ignored that question and asked one of his own as he nodded toward Jenkins and O'Rourke. "Are these two gentlemen your friends as well? Will they be joining you and the lady for supper?"

"As a matter of fact, they will. And we have a reservation waiting for us, so if you'll excuse us . . ."

The commissioner took his right hand out of his coat pocket and raised it. "Not just yet," he said, his voice calm and level but hard as stone. "We have some business to discuss."

"Police business?" Neill was starting to get a little angry now. Who did this man think he was? "It'll have to wait. As I said, I have a previous engagement—"

"Boss," Jenkins said in a low, worried voice. Neill jerked his gaze to the man and saw that Jenkins was staring down the street, toward the circle of light where the commissioner had first appeared.

Half a dozen uniformed men stood in that misty glow now.

"What the hell is this?" Neill demanded.

"Inspector Ambrose Neill, you're under arrest for extortion, conspiracy, grand theft, dereliction of duty—"

"You're just a member of the Board of Commissioners," Neill cut in coldly. "You can't arrest me."

"Those officers can and will."

Estelle clutched Neill's arm and whined, "Ambrose, I don't like this. Make this man leave us alone."

"Shut up, you cow," Neill barked at her. He shook off her hand and, in the process, shoved her back a little.

Jenkins said, "Boss, I can't get arrested again. I ain't goin' back up the river."

"Neither am I," O'Rourke agreed. His hand moved toward the lapel of his overcoat.

"Stop that," Neill said. "They don't have anything on us—"

"Can't take the chance," Jenkins rumbled. He yanked a pistol from under his coat. O'Rourke did likewise.

Estelle screamed as the two big men lunged forward, thrust out the guns, and opened fire.

Neill hit the ground, abandoning the blonde to whatever fate might be in store for her. The commissioner wasn't so callous. He leaped toward her and tried to grab her arm as he shouted, "Get out of the way, ma'am!"

Frightened out of her wits, Estelle darted away from him—right into the crossfire as the uniformed police returned the shots Jenkins and O'Rourke were throwing at them.

The battle lasted only seconds and ended with Jenkins and O'Rourke down on the cobblestones, their bloody forms writhing for a moment before the stillness of death washed over them. A few feet away, Estelle lay on her back, eyes wide but unseeing, blood soaking into her fur wrap, the jaunty little hat with its feather having fallen off her head. As the echoes of the gun-thunder faded in the concrete canyons, the wind caught the hat and tugged it toward the gutter, flipping it over a couple of times.

The commissioner was still on his feet. The bullets had passed close by him, but he hadn't lost his head. Now he bent, closed his hand around Neill's upper arm in an iron grip, and hauled the inspector to his feet.

"I'm sorry about the young woman," he told Neill, "but her blood is on your hands, sir. As I was saying, you're under arrest—"

Neill cut him off with a torrent of curses. His hat had fallen off when he dived to the ground, and his carefully combed hair was now askew. Several strands of it fell over his eyes as he continued spewing obscenities. He didn't stop, even when an officer moved in, jerked his arms behind his back, and snapped handcuffs on him.

Despite the white-hot rage that filled him, part of Neill's brain was still working with cool precision. While reeling off the charges, the commissioner hadn't said anything about murder . . . which meant they probably didn't know anything about Riddle or the other men whose lives Neill had ended in his rise to power. And Riddle's body was gone by now, carried out through another exit in the warehouse, with nothing to tie it to him.

All those other charges, he could beat those, Neill told himself. He was too smart, had too many friends, had covered his tracks too well for any of them to stick, no matter what evidence they thought they had against him.

And if, by some chance, he failed to escape the consequences, he was only looking at a bit of prison time. He wasn't afraid of prison. True, he was a copper and as such would have many enemies behind the walls, but he had friends there as well, men whose families he had seen to while they were locked up. Men who owed him.

As long as they didn't know the truth about the murders, he would be all right, Neill told himself again. But that didn't mean he could allow this outrage to pass unavenged.

He broke off the tirade and stared coldly at the commissioner.

"You're going to regret what you've done here tonight, Roosevelt," he said. "I'm going to make you sorry you ever laid eyes on me. Sooner or later, you're going to be very, very sorry."

Commissioner Theodore Roosevelt sighed. "You mean because of the young woman's death? I'm already sorry about that. Such tragic misfortune."

"What?" Neill frowned. "The woman? Good Lord, I don't

care what happened to that slut! I mean you're going to be sorry you ever dared to come after me!"

"I daresay I'll take my chances," Roosevelt replied. He lifted a hand in a weary gesture to the officers. "Get him out of here. I can't stand the sight of him anymore."

Chapter 1

Big Rock, Colorado, 1902

Conrad Morgan brought the big wagon to a stop in front of Goldstein's Mercantile. In his broad-brimmed Stetson, sheepskin jacket, and denim trousers tucked into high-topped boots, with several days' worth of sandy beard stubble on his face, Conrad looked like a teamster, and acted like one, too, in the experienced way in which he handled the reins hitched to the six mules pulling the wagon.

Nobody would have guessed by looking at him that this tall, well-built young man was one of the wealthiest individuals in the whole country.

That was the truth of the matter, though. Conrad Morgan was the managing partner of the Browning Holdings, one of the largest conglomerations of companies in the nation, if not the world. Conrad had inherited his share of the vast, sprawling enterprise, which had interests in banking, railroads, shipping, steel, mining, manufacturing, and newspapers, from his mother, the late Vivian Browning.

Growing up, Conrad had used the name of his stepfather, Charles Browning, and hadn't met his actual father until he was almost a man. As a youngster who had been raised in the lap of luxury, it was no surprise that Conrad had turned out to be spoiled, pampered, catered to, arrogant, and an all-around horse's behind.

It had taken several encounters with real hardship and danger, plus meeting his real father, the famous gunfighter Frank Morgan, for Conrad to start the painful process of growing up. Frank had saved Conrad's life on more than one occasion, but still father and son had been estranged for several years before Conrad came to understand Frank, respect him, and eventually love him, to the point where he began using the Morgan name himself.

Tragedy had tempered Conrad's steely inner core even more. For several years, he had lived the life of a drifting gunfighter himself, putting all the riches behind him, honing his existence down to life and death on the frontier, which, while fading, could still be plenty wild from time to time.

That part of Conrad's life had come to an end, and he had put aside his guns to return to the business world, to take over the running of the giant operation his mother bequeathed to him. He owned half of it . . . and Frank Morgan owned the other half, although Frank wanted nothing to do with board rooms and financial statements.

Even so, circumstances sometimes compelled Conrad to buckle on a gunbelt and demonstrate the blinding speed with a Colt he had inherited from his father.

In recent months, he had shifted his base of operations here to Big Rock, adjacent to the valley where several gold mines belonging to the Browning Holdings were in operation. Conrad liked this frontier settlement and enjoyed supervising the mines. He had very capable subordinates in offices back in Denver and San Francisco running everything else, so for the time being, he was a mining man, willing to swing a pickax or a sledgehammer or wield a shovel or drive a wagon into town to pick up supplies, as he was doing today.

He had another reason for staying in Big Rock, and as he

looped the reins around the wagon's brake lever, he looked up and down the street, searching for her.

Denise Nicole Jensen, the young lady's name was. Better known as Denny to most folks except her mother Sally. Her father was Kirby "Smoke" Jensen, owner of the highly successful Sugarloaf Ranch. In his earlier years, Smoke had had quite a reputation as an adventurer and gunfighter. Most folks figured he was the fastest man with a gun who had ever lived.

Conrad wasn't sure about that. He figured his own father might be just a hair faster . . .

But nobody knew for sure and nobody ever would, because Smoke Jensen and Frank Morgan were friends and had never drawn on each other, even in fun or the spirit of competition. Some things just weren't done.

Denny, like Conrad, had inherited her father's speed and accuracy with a gun. She wasn't just fast for a girl. She was *fast*. Conrad had seen her in action and knew that. They were well-matched, both of them just a notch below their famous fathers when it came to gun-speed.

Conrad figured they were pretty well-matched in other ways, too.

"Looking for Denny?"

The question came from the mercantile's high front porch that also served as a loading dock. Leo Goldstein, the proprietor, had emerged from the store and stood there with an affable smile on his face and his hands tucked into the pockets of the canvas apron he wore.

"What?" Conrad said. "No. No, I was just, uh . . ." His voice trailed off as he grinned and shook his head. "Shoot, you caught me, Leo. I don't reckon you know if she happens to be in town today, do you?"

Leo shook his head and said, "I haven't seen her, or anybody else from the Sugarloaf. But that doesn't mean she's not around. I've been inside most of the day." He came closer to the edge of the porch. "Are you here for supplies?"

"That's right."

"Then you're bound to have a list. Give it to me, and I'll see that everything's taken care of." Leo chuckled. "That way, you can go down to Longmont's, have a cup of coffee, and ask Louis if he knows whether or not Denny is in town."

Conrad reached inside his sheepskin jacket, which felt good on a cool day at high elevations like this, and stood up on the driver's box to reach across the gap between wagon and porch and hand it to the storekeeper.

"I'm obliged to you, Leo. You'll add it to my bill?"

"Of course."

Conrad smiled. "I'm good for it."

"Yes, I know." Leo started to turn back toward the store's entrance, then paused to add, "Oh, I almost forgot. Somebody's looking for *you.*"

"Who might that be?"

"Eddie from the Western Union office. He came by earlier and asked if I thought you might be in today. I told him I didn't have any idea."

Conrad frowned slightly. "Did he say he has a telegram for me?"

"He didn't say, but he acted like it was important. Said he needed to see you personally."

Conrad scraped his right thumbnail against the stubble on his jaw, frowned slightly, and said, "I wonder what that's all about."

"You can go down to the depot and ask him."

Conrad glanced toward the train station at the far end of town. The Western Union office was located inside the big, impressive, redbrick building.

Longmont's Restaurant lay in the other direction, and *its* proprietor, the gambler and former gunman named Louis Longmont, was one of Smoke Jensen's best friends. As Leo had indicated, Louis was the most likely to know if Denny or any of the other Jensens were in Big Rock today.

"Whatever it is, I reckon it can wait a spell," Conrad decided. He put a hand on the edge of the wagon seat and jumped lithely to the ground on the side away from the mercantile's porch. "I'll take a walk down there before I come back here."

"Suit yourself," Leo said. With a wave of the list Conrad had given him, he went back into the store.

Louis Longmont's establishment wasn't exactly a saloon, but it served the best whiskey in town. It wasn't a gambling hall, either, but high stakes poker games weren't uncommon. It *was* a restaurant, according to the sign outside, and the finest steaks between Kansas City and San Francisco could be found there.

So could Louis Longmont himself, most of the time. He was sitting at a large table in the rear, sipping from a cup of coffee and reading a leather-bound book propped open in his lap. He wore a dark suit with a fancy vest, a snowy white shirt, and a silk cravat with a jeweled stickpin in it. His salt-and-pepper hair and neatly trimmed mustache testified to his late middle age, but he still possessed the vital air of a younger man.

Smoke Jensen was much the same, Conrad reflected as he approached the table where Longmont sat: getting on in years, but you'd hardly know it from the way he looked and acted.

Longmont glanced up, then looked again and smiled as he recognized Conrad. "Ah, Mr. Morgan," he said. "Good morning. It *is* still morning, isn't it?"

"For a while yet," Conrad agreed.

Longmont gestured at one of the empty chairs. "Please, sit down and join me. Would you care for some coffee? Something to eat?"

"Just coffee would be fine," Conrad said as he took a seat.

Longmont signaled to a waiter, who hurried off to fetch the coffee, then asked Conrad, "What brings you to Big Rock today? Developments in the gold mining business?"

"Hardly," Conrad replied with a chuckle. "No, I'm afraid I'm on a totally mundane errand. I came to pick up a load of supplies from Leo Goldstein."

"Ah. Well, the world isn't all drama and high adventure. Those mundane errands, as you call them, have to be taken care of, too. They keep the world turning, after all."

The waiter brought the cup of coffee and placed it in front of Conrad, who nodded his thanks. He sipped the strong black brew and nodded again, this time in approval.

Longmont placed a ribbon bookmark in the volume he'd been reading and set it aside. He looked at Conrad and said, "I imagine you were hoping you'd run into someone else in town today."

"Is it that obvious?"

"The way you feel about Denny? Yes, I'm afraid so, my friend. I think you'd be a good opponent in a poker game and could keep your emotions hidden there, but when it comes to a certain young woman . . . Let's just say you don't exactly have a poker face."

"No point in beating around the bush, then," Conrad said. "Have you seen her?"

"Not today," Longmont replied with a shake of his head. "None of the Jensens, in fact, or any of their crew from the Sugarloaf. I suspect they can all be found on the ranch today."

"Well, I don't really have time to go all the way out there . . ."

Longmont leaned forward slightly in his chair, looking more interested. "Is there some specific reason you're looking for Denny, other than just wanting to see her?"

"Isn't that enough?"

"Of course it is."

Conrad took another sip of the coffee and said, "No, I don't have any particular reason. I've just been pretty busy with the mines lately, and I realized it's been more than a week since I've talked to her. That's why I volunteered to come in and pick up the supplies. I knew there was a good chance she wouldn't be here in town . . . but there was a chance she might be."

"And we don't win any bets we don't make to start with." Longmont nodded. "I understand the feeling."

Conrad lifted the cup and smiled. "But I get a mighty fine cup of coffee out of the deal, and some pleasant conversation, so I reckon I've still come out ahead."

He spent another half-hour in the restaurant, making small talk and catching up on the latest gossip in Big Rock with Longmont. When it came to actually knowing what was going on in a town, no newspaper reporter was ever as well-informed as the man who ran the place where the citizens came to eat and drink. Longmont was a skilled raconteur, too.

But Conrad still had to deal with whatever it was the manager of the Western Union office wanted with him, he recalled, so he drained the last of the coffee from his cup and said, "I suppose I'd better be going."

He reached for his pocket to get out a coin to pay for the coffee, but Longmont stopped him in mid-gesture with a wave of the hand.

"The coffee is on me, of course. Any friend of Smoke's . . . and in due time, you may be more than that."

"I'm his friend, that's for sure," Conrad said with a nod. "He's a fine man. The second finest I know."

"The first being your father, of course."

"That's right."

Longmont leaned back in his chair and said, "I crossed trails with Frank a few times, you know."

"Yes, he's mentioned that."

"Thankfully, we were always on the same side." Longmont smiled. "I'd hate to have to choose between going up against Smoke Jensen or Frank Morgan. I think I know how either encounter would end . . . and it wouldn't be well for me."

"Then it's a good thing that won't ever happen."

"Indeed it will not." Longmont's eyes twinkled as he added, "If I do happen to see Denny, should I tell her that you were asking after her?"

"Sure," Conrad said as he got to his feet. "Why not?"

He left the restaurant and headed toward the other end of town, where the railroad station was located. When he entered the depot's lobby, the Western Union office was to his right. He glanced that direction, then let his gaze take in the rest of the big room, just out of habit. The perilous life he had led under the gunfighter alias Kid Morgan had ingrained in him the habit of always checking out his surroundings, every time he went into a place.

The ticket windows, station manager's office, and freight office were to the left. The area straight ahead of Conrad had a number of wooden benches arranged in it, where passengers could sit and wait for their trains to arrive. The doors out to the platform were also straight ahead, on the far side of the benches. Conrad didn't check the schedule board by the ticket windows, but he could tell that no trains were due to roll in any time soon because the benches were empty.

In fact, the only people he saw were four men standing outside the open door of the freight office. He didn't recognize any of them, but he couldn't really get a good look at them because their hats were pulled down so that the brims partially shielded their faces.

Conrad turned and took a step toward the Western Union office, then stopped abruptly. With a frown, he looked toward the other side of the lobby again. Nothing unusual seemed to be going on, so why had instinct suddenly raised the hair on the back of his neck?

If he had learned anything from the years spent wandering lonely, dangerous trails, it was to trust what his gut told him. He put his hands in the pockets of his sheepskin jacket and strolled, apparently aimlessly, toward the freight office.

One of the men waiting just outside the door stiffened at Conrad's approach. Conrad took note of that reaction. He kept his face bland and expressionless and changed his angle a little to make it look more like he was heading for the ticket windows.

The man who had tensed relaxed again.

Well, *that* was interesting. Something was going on in there, and the men standing around the door, blocking the view, didn't want anybody butting in.

So that was exactly what Conrad intended to do.

Again, he changed course, striding directly toward the freight office now. The man who had reacted before saw that and spoke a low-voiced word to one of his companions. They turned to face squarely toward Conrad, and when he was about ten feet away, one of them held out a hand toward him and said, "Sorry, mister, the freight office is closed right now."

"But I just need to see the man in charge for a minute—" Conrad began.

Then a short, sharp cry came from inside the room, cut off almost instantly by the meaty thud of a fist against flesh. Conrad had slowed down, but when he heard that, he sped up again, striding determinedly toward the men blocking his path.

"That tears it!" the second man exclaimed. He clawed at the gun holstered on his hip, and his companion did the same. Both revolvers flashed into view and lifted toward Conrad.

Chapter 2

But before the guns could come level, Conrad had pulled both hands from his jacket pockets. Each hand held a .41 caliber Remington Double Derringer. He wasn't wearing a gun belt today, but before leaving the mine, he had tucked one of the derringers into a pocket and then decided that he ought to take another one with him, just to keep things balanced properly.

Conrad held off for a second, long enough to give the men an opportunity to realize they had been beaten to the draw and give up on trying to kill him.

When they didn't and the revolvers continued rising, Conrad squeezed the triggers. Both derringers went off with loud pops, the reports blending together and sounding like one.

At this range, the derringers were fairly accurate, and the .41 caliber slugs packed enough punch to knock both men back a step as the shots hit home. Their weapons sagged, unfired. One man clapped his free hand to his chest and reeled against the wall beside the freight office door. Bright blood welled between his spread fingers as he slid down into a sitting position.

The other man's legs buckled and he fell to his knees, then pitched forward on his face.

While that was going on, the remaining two men yelled curses and dived through the open door into the office. One of them kicked it shut behind him. Shots crashed inside the room. Bullets smacked through the closed door, aimed in Conrad's general direction.

He had already shifted swiftly to his right, however, so the shots missed him. He heard the slugs thud into the wall on the far side of the lobby. Thank goodness the room hadn't been crowded with would-be passengers waiting for a train, he thought as he knelt behind one of the empty benches.

"I don't know what's going on in there, but you fellows might as well give up," he called through the door. "There's no way out of there."

Actually, that wasn't true. There was a large storage room on the other side of the office, and a door from it opened onto the platform. But the gunmen might not know that. Conrad hoped that was the case, which might prompt the men to surrender.

Giving up didn't seem to be what they had in mind. A harsh voice shouted, "Back off, mister! You better let us out of here, or we'll kill these two clerks!"

Conrad made a face. He had interrupted some sort of robbery, he guessed, and the thieves didn't want to be captured. Well, that came as no surprise.

He tucked the derringers back in his jacket pockets and then moved forward quickly and quietly to scoop up the two Colts that the dead men had dropped. The station manager was approaching, an apprehensive look on his face. Conrad waved him back, out of the line of fire in case the trapped men sent more shots through the door.

Conrad retreated behind the closest bench, where the station manager joined him.

"I imagine somebody's already reported the shots to Monte Carson," Conrad said to the man, "but just in case, you'd better send somebody down to the sheriff's office."

The station manager nodded. "What are you going to do?"

"Can you use a gun?"

"If I have to," the manager responded grimly.

Conrad pressed one of the Colts into his hand. "Stay here and keep them bottled up. I'll go out to the platform and try to get the drop on them from the storage room."

"Good luck, Mr. Morgan."

"We'll all need it, including those two hostages in there."

With that said, Conrad moved in a quick, crouching walk toward the door to the platform. When he stepped out, he looked around and saw that it was empty. That was good. Still no innocent bystanders to be endangered if gunplay erupted out here.

And it looked like that was about to happen, because the door to the storage room suddenly burst open and one of the men Conrad had seen in the lobby charged out, shoving a frightened-looking young man in front of him. That was one of the freight clerks, Conrad realized.

He had to hold his fire because the hostage was in the way, but the would-be robber didn't have that problem. He cursed as he spotted Conrad and then the gun in his hand spouted flame. Conrad dived to the platform as bullets sizzled through the air above him.

The clerk might have been scared, but he wasn't lacking for sand. He stopped short, half turned, and rammed his elbow into his captor's chest. That knocked the robber back a step and gave Conrad an opening. Lying on his belly, Conrad angled the gun in his hand up and squeezed the trigger. The Colt roared and bucked, and the outlaw doubled over as the bullet punched into his stomach.

But there were still two members of the gang in this fight, emerging from the station hot on the heels of the man Conrad had just shot. One of them fired a round into the clerk who had dared to put up a fight, knocking the young man spinning off his feet.

The other gunman sprayed lead toward Conrad and forced him to roll desperately toward the tracks to avoid the shots. Bullets chewed splinters from the planks of the platform and flung them through the air. Several of them stung Conrad's face.

A rifle cracked somewhere beyond the men who were trying to escape. The one firing at Conrad cried out in pain and stumbled forward. He dropped his gun as he collapsed.

That left only the man who had brutally gunned down the clerk. He leaped from the edge of the platform, landed awkwardly, and tried to run across the two sets of railroad tracks. His ragged gait told Conrad that he had hurt himself somehow in the jump. Conrad surged up and went after him, stopping at the edge and aiming his gun at the man's back.

"Hold it right there!" Conrad ordered. "Drop your gun. It's over, and you can't get away."

The man stopped, but he didn't drop his gun. Instead, he stood there for a long moment, then drew in a deep breath and said clearly enough for Conrad to understand the words, "Damned if I'm gonna hang."

That sentiment was enough to warn Conrad. He was ready when the man tried to swing around suddenly and fire. The gun Conrad was using blasted first. The bullet ripped through the outlaw's torso and dropped him to the gravel of the roadbed on the far side of the tracks.

"Why didn't he just give up?" a familiar voice asked. "He had to know he couldn't beat you and it was over."

Conrad watched the fallen man until he was confident the robber really was dead, then turned to look along the platform at Denny Jensen, who walked toward him with a Winchester carbine in her right hand, holding it so the barrel canted back over her right shoulder. He knew without having to ask that she had fired the shot from the other end of the platform that had dropped one of the gunmen.

And even under the less-than-ideal circumstances, Conrad

was struck by just what a beautiful young woman Denny was, tall and shapely, with the curves of her body displayed to their advantage in denim trousers and a man's checked flannel shirt with a brown vest over it. A brown Stetson was thumbed back on the tumbling waves of Denny's blond hair.

The station manager rushed out of the building and hurried to kneel beside the clerk who had been shot. The young man was sitting up and grimacing, holding his left shoulder. It looked like the bullet had gone clean through him, and while the wound was bloody, it might not be fatal.

Conrad didn't see the second clerk. He motioned to Denny and started toward the door into the storage room.

"Stay behind me," he told her. "There might be another one."

"You don't really think I'll hide behind you, do you?"

"No, but I had to say it. Just be careful."

They went through the storage room with its stacks of crates and piles of canvas bags, holding their guns ready for instant action if need be. No one was lurking in the room, however, and the only person in the freight office beyond was the second clerk, who was lying on the floor in a still-spreading pool of blood with his throat cut.

Conrad sighed at the sight of the body and said, "I suppose that's why the last man wasn't in any mood to surrender. He knew he'd hang for murder if he did."

"I suppose it was quicker, going the way he did," Denny said. She shook her head as she looked at the dead man. "Poor Jonas."

Conrad nodded toward the big safe in the corner. "They must have cut this fellow's throat to try to get the other one to open the safe. I don't know what's in there that they were so eager to get their hands on, but I don't suppose it really matters. This man died for it."

"So did those others."

"Yes, but they were outlaws and killers. That doesn't hardly count."

Denny smiled thinly. "I can't argue with you there."

By the time they returned to the platform, Dr. Enoch Steward was there, tending to the wounded clerk, and so was Sheriff Monte Carson, holding a shotgun that he wouldn't need now.

"Hello, Conrad," he said. "I hear you dealt with these owlhoots before I got a chance to."

"With a little help from Denny," Conrad said.

"It looked like quite a bit of help when you were dodging bullets," she pointed out.

"And I'm obliged to you." He cocked his head to the side. "How come you showed up just in the nick of time that way?"

"I rode in a few minutes ago and heard you'd been looking all over town for me."

"I wouldn't go so far as to say I was looking *all over town—*"

Denny shrugged. "All I've got to go by is what Leo Goldstein and Louis Longmont told me. They both mentioned you were supposed to stop by the Western Union office, so that's where I headed first. Then hell started popping just as I walked up."

"I'm glad you got here when you did," Conrad told her, and this time he was both serious and sincere.

Monte Carson asked, "What was all this shooting about?"

"I don't really know," Conrad answered, shaking his head.

The station manager glanced up from the wounded clerk and said, "I do. There's a payroll for one of the ranches locked up in that safe. Buck Adams is supposed to come into town today and pick it up."

"Adams of the Box A?" Monte asked with a frown.

"Why didn't he get the cash he needed from the bank here in Big Rock?"

"Because he doesn't have an account there anymore," the manager explained. "Evidently he recently had some sort of falling out with the local bank and moved all his money to one in Denver. They sent the payroll on yesterday's train. Adams should have been here to pick it up when it came in, but he sent word that he'd been delayed for some reason."

Monte nodded. "I took a gander at the two dead men inside as I was coming through the lobby and recognized one of them. I'm pretty sure he used to ride for the Box A. He probably knew about the payroll and brought in the other fellas to help him get his hands on it." He turned his attention to the wounded man. "How bad are you hurt, Lester?"

"Oh, it hurts like blazes, Sheriff," Lester told the lawman, "but I reckon I'll live." He sighed. "Not like poor Jonas. The miserable skunks cut his throat right after they came in there and threw down on us! Never even gave him a chance. One of them told me I'd better open the safe, or I'd wind up like him."

Conrad said, "If they were trying to pull off a robbery in broad daylight, why didn't they shut the door into the office?"

"Because it's usually open," Lester replied. "I heard one of them say they didn't want to draw attention by closing it. Four of them just went back out and stood around so nobody could see in while the other one continued threatening me. But then I heard them talking to somebody and I tried to yell for help. The one they'd left inside hit me before I could make much noise."

"You made enough," Conrad told him. "I'm the one they were talking to, and I heard you cry out. I already had a hunch something pretty bad was going on, and that confirmed it."

Dr. Steward had tied bandages in place around the clerk's wounded shoulder. He stood up and said, "Let's get you over to my office, Lester. I'll clean those wounds better and get you patched up properly."

"Will I live, Doc?"

"To a ripe old age," the medico assured him.

Steward and the station manager helped Lester to his feet and then led him into the lobby, bracing him up on each side. As soon as they were gone, the undertaker and a couple of his assistants appeared to load up the bodies of the dead outlaws—and Jonas, the other freight office clerk.

Conrad and Denny were walking back through the lobby when a man in a green vest, string tie, sleeve garters, and black eyeshade hurried up to them.

"There you are, Mr. Morgan," the man said. "I heard about what happened, and I was hoping I could catch you before you left."

"And I heard you were looking for me, Eddie," Conrad said, recognizing the man as the manager of the Western Union office. "Do you have a telegram for me?"

Eddie bobbed his head up and down, visibly excited. "I sure do."

"I'm surprised you didn't just have it delivered to my office here in town or send a rider out to the mines looking for me."

"No, sir, not this telegram," Eddie declared. "This one, I figured it was best if I put it right in your hands, personally."

"It must be an important message," Denny commented with a smile.

"Yes'm, it is." Eddie nodded again. "It's from Washington. The District of Columbia, not the state." He swallowed hard. "From the White House."

Chapter 3

"So President Roosevelt wants you to come to Washington and meet with him?" Smoke Jensen said. The remains of a delicious supper were on the table in front of him in the dining room of the Sugarloaf ranch house. Smoke reached for his coffee cup as he looked to his right where Conrad Morgan was sitting.

"That's right," Conrad replied. "He requested that I travel to Washington as soon as I can and meet him at the White House before the end of the month."

"That doesn't give you much time," Sally Jensen said. Smoke's middle-aged but still quite beautiful wife sat at the far end of the table, directly opposite her husband.

Denny was across the table from Conrad. Her fraternal twin brother Louis, who had a law practice in Big Rock, was next to her, and Louis's wife Melanie was next to Conrad on the right.

"It's not exactly a royal summons," Louis said with a smile, "but I suppose it's about the closest thing we have to one in this country."

"I suppose," Conrad agreed. "I have a great deal of respect for Theodore Roosevelt."

Smoke took a sip of his coffee and placed the cup back on its saucer. "So do I," he said. "He used to have a ranch up in Dakota Territory, back when it was still a territory and not a couple of states, and he worked the cattle with his men just like a regular puncher, from what I've heard. Said to be a good hunter and trapper and a crack shot, in spite of those spectacles he wears."

"Did you ever meet him?"

Smoke shook his head. "No, we never crossed trails. But Falcon MacCallister told me once that he'd met Teddy. He was impressed with him, too . . . and it takes quite a bit to impress Falcon, him having grown up with Jamie Ian MacCallister as his pa."

Denny said to Conrad with a note of impatience in her voice, "Are you sure that telegram didn't give you even a hint of what it's all about? I mean, why would the President want to talk to you?"

Conrad chuckled. "Not even a hint."

Denny's face flushed prettily. She wore a dress tonight, a simple but lovely dark blue gown, instead of riding clothes.

"I'm sorry. I just realized how that sounded. I didn't mean it that way."

"Oh, I'm equally puzzled," Conrad assured her. "I have no political ambition whatsoever, and I can't imagine what Mr. Roosevelt wants with me."

"Half of those politicians up there in Washington are crooks," Smoke said with a frown. "Most of the other ones are moral degenerates, even if they aren't outright criminals. And a bunch of them are dumb as rocks. You can count the ones who are actually trying to do good for the country on your fingers and toes. Lucky for us, Teddy Roosevelt is one of the good ones."

Sally said, "Now, Smoke, you don't truly believe the situation is quite that bleak, do you?"

Smoke snorted. "Maybe not quite. But too many of those men who are supposed to be there to serve the country are only interested in their own power."

Conrad said, "I don't believe most folks outside of Washington itself would argue with you about that, Smoke. But as you said, President Roosevelt seems to be a decent man with the nation's best interests at heart." He shrugged. "All I know to do is go and find out why he wants to talk to me."

"There's an eastbound train tomorrow morning, I believe," Louis said.

"I know. And I intend to be on it."

Later, Conrad and Smoke were standing on the ranch house's front porch, both wearing coats because the high-country air was chilly tonight. They had been chatting idly for several minutes when the door opened behind them and Sally and Denny joined them. Louis and Melanie had already gotten into the buggy they had brought out to the Sugarloaf and driven off, heading back to their home in Big Rock.

Sally linked arms with Smoke and leaned her head against his shoulder. "It's a lovely evening," she said. The air was cold enough to make her breath fog in front of her face. "The stars are incredibly bright and clear."

"You won't find that in towns," Smoke said. "They're getting so bright, with all those gas lamps and those new-fangled electric lights, that the stars just sort of fade out in the skies above them."

Sally laughed. "You remind me of how Preacher used to talk about cities. He never liked them, either."

"Not many of those old mountain men did. Once they had seen what the frontier was really like in those days, nothing else could ever quite match up to it."

"I remember what the frontier was like: primitive and dangerous."

"Yeah, but don't you miss it sometimes, the way it was when we first moved to this valley and were the only ones for miles around?"

Sally sighed. "I have to admit, that *was* pretty nice in some ways. I have many fond memories of those days."

"Why don't we go on back inside and leave the evening to these young folks? I'm about ready to turn in."

"Yes," Sally said, "I think I'd like that, too."

They said their goodnights and went into the house. Once they were gone, Denny rolled her eyes, shook her head, and laughed.

"Those two," she said. "The way they act, you'd never think they were old."

"Maybe the way they act is *why* they don't seem old," Conrad said. "Older, I should say. Neither of them is exactly decrepit, you know."

Denny laughed again and said, "No, that's for sure."

She had pulled on a jacket over her dress. Soft gloves were on her hands. She rested them on the porch railing and leaned forward to look up.

"It *is* a pretty night."

"Very pretty," Conrad agreed, but he was looking at Denny, not the stars. He put a hand on her shoulder.

She turned and came into his arms. Their lips met in a soft kiss that gradually grew in urgency.

When Conrad had first arrived in Big Rock, Denny had been involved in an on-again, off-again romance with Brice Rogers, a young Deputy U.S. Marshal who was assigned to this region, but Conrad was confident that Denny and Brice had settled into being friends, not sweetheart and beau any longer.

Besides, Brice had gotten mixed up with Blaise Warfield, a fiery young woman who owned a saloon in Big Rock, and they seemed to be a better match than Brice and Denny had ever been, even though so far their relationship had struck a number of sparks both good and bad.

"I'm glad you invited me out here tonight," Conrad told Denny as they broke the kiss.

He had gone to the room he maintained at the hotel in Big Rock and cleaned up before riding out to the Sugarloaf, after making arrangements with Leo Goldstein to have one of Leo's clerks drive the wagonload of supplies back out to the nearest Browning mine.

"I always enjoy spending time with your parents and your brother and sister-in-law," he went on. "They're fine folks."

"That's the *only* reason you like coming out here?" she teased him.

"Well, maybe not the *only* one . . ."

They kissed again, and then Denny settled against Conrad's side with his arm around her shoulders. She sighed in satisfaction, and then a moment of companionable silence went by.

Finally, she said, "Actually, I had an ulterior motive."

Conrad turned his head and brushed his lips against her fair hair. "Oh? What might that be?"

"Well, I know you're leaving for Washington tomorrow . . ."

"What are you angling for, Denny?" he asked with a slight frown.

"Take me with you!"

Conrad pulled his head back a little in surprise. "To Washington?"

"That's right. I've been there before, of course, but I wouldn't mind going again."

Denny had spent most of her younger years in Europe, living on an English estate owned by her mother's parents. Louis had been very sickly as a child, and everyone had decided that he would get the best medical attention from doctors in England and on the Continent. But the twins had traveled back and forth many times to visit the Sugarloaf, before returning there permanently a couple of years earlier. Louis's heart was still a concern, but living a somewhat more active and outdoor life had strengthened him quite a bit.

During those trips, the twins had visited all the great

cities in the American East, including Washington, D.C. And Conrad, during *his* childhood, had also lived a cosmopolitan existence, residing in Boston most of the time. That was another reason the two of them were well-matched.

Their breaths fogged and intermingled as he looked at her now. "I don't think that would be a very good idea," he said. "I realize that both of us have spent a lot of time in places where the bounds of propriety aren't quite as tight, but this *is* still the West, and your parents are both Westerners."

"My mother was born back east," Denny pointed out.

"Maybe so, but she's lived here on the Sugarloaf for almost three decades, and she was up in Idaho before that. If we go off to Washington together . . . well, your father's liable to be waiting for me with a shotgun when we get back. And I *don't* want an angry Smoke Jensen waiting for me."

"You're saying he'd force you to marry me, and you don't want that?"

"I'm not saying anything of the kind. But we've never talked about getting married—"

"If you're worried about sullying my honor and stealing my innocence, you don't have to—"

This time it was Conrad who interrupted, holding up a hand to stop her.

"Whatever you're about to say, Denny, I'd just as soon not hear it. And it's sure not that I don't *want* you traveling to Washington with me. That sounds mighty pleasant, in fact. But I just don't think it's a good idea." He paused, then when she didn't say anything, he went on, "For one thing, I don't have any idea what the President wants to see me about. It could be something that would *keep* me in Washington for a while."

"If that were the case, I could just get on a train and come back here any time."

"That's true, I suppose. But your mother and father—"

"I'm a grown woman," she broke in. "I can do what I want."

A grown woman who was better with a gun than ninety-nine percent of the men she would ever run across, Conrad thought. Not to mention rich. So yes, on a practical basis, Denny Jensen could do just about anything she wanted to.

His shoulders rose and fell slightly. "You're right," he told her. "If you want to hurt your folks' feelings and disappoint them, not to mention turning them against me, nobody's going to stop you."

She drew in a sharp breath and then stared at him for a long moment, her eyes narrowing. Finally, she said, "Damn you, Conrad Morgan. Why do you have to be so . . . so blasted decent?"

"Just unlucky, I guess," he said, shaking his head. "Both of us."

"Yeah. Well, I suppose there'll be another time."

"That's right. We can go to Washington later. We can go wherever you want."

After they were married, he thought. He could tell that she had the same thing in her head right now. Without any sort of official proposal, they had come to an unspoken understanding about their future together.

As for the proposal . . . he could take care of *that* later, too. He hadn't really lived a traditional sort of life, but he valued tradition enough to want to do that. *After* asking Smoke for Denny's hand in marriage, of course.

But first, there was that trip to Washington to take care of, and finding out what the President wanted with him. And that was almost as intriguing as the thought of living as husband and wife with Denny.

Almost . . . but not quite, Conrad told himself as he drew her into his arms again and brought his mouth down gently on hers.

* * *

Conrad wore a gray tweed suit, complete with vest, and a black, flat-crowned hat as he waited on the depot platform the next morning. The hat, with its band of silver and turquoise conchos, was his only concession to the Western garb he preferred these days. Other than that, he might have been any successful businessman from New York or Philadelphia.

Well, there were the Remington Double Derringers, too, one of them in each vest pocket. And the Colt .45 revolver and the broom-handle Mauser C96 semi-automatic pistol in the carpetbag at his feet. And the sheathed Bowie knife with its blade honed to razor sharpness, also in the carpetbag. And the Model 1892 lever-action Winchester wrapped up in oilcloth with twine tied neatly around it that a porter would load into a baggage car with the rest of Conrad's things when the eastbound train rolled in.

But other than all that, he might have been a typical businessman.

He and Denny had said their goodbyes at the Sugarloaf the night before. He had asked her not to come into town today. He preferred to remember her as she had been on the ranch house porch, soft and warm in his arms, her lips sweet and tender.

It appeared that he wasn't going to depart with no one to bid him farewell, however. Sheriff Monte Carson strolled up alongside Conrad on the platform and gave him a friendly nod.

"You can thank me, you know," the sheriff commented.

"Thank you for what?"

"Well, once word got around about who you're going to see, the newspaper editor wanted to come and interview you before you set off on what he called your momentous journey. I even heard some talk about having a brass band see you off."

Conrad winced. "And you talked them out of it?"

"I did. Told folks you wouldn't want all that hoopla."

"Then I do indeed thank you for your efforts, Sheriff." Conrad thought about what Monte had just told him and added, "You know, there was a time when Conrad Browning would have been quite pleased to be the center of attention like that. A brass band and everything. I would have loved it."

"But you're not Conrad Browning anymore," Monte pointed out. "You're Conrad Morgan, and while I won't pretend to know everything about you, I reckon you've changed a heap since those days."

"Yes," Conrad agreed dryly. "A whole heap."

"And whatever the President wants you for, he'll be getting a good man for the job."

Conrad frowned. "You think he's going to offer me a job?"

"Well, that was just a figure of speech . . . but think about it. Why else would he want you to come to Washington?"

Conrad lifted his head as he heard the train whistle's shrill, keening cry in the distance.

Suddenly, he was even more eager to find out what President Theodore Roosevelt wanted with him.

Chapter 4

Washington, D.C.

Given the squalid nature of this alley, it was difficult to believe that the White House, the Capitol, and the other buildings housing the government of one of the greatest nations on earth were not much more than a stone's throw from here.

But that was common in cities: squalor and splendor practically side by side, poverty and desperation existing cheek-to-cheek with wealth and power. Perhaps the contrast was a little sharper than usual here in Washington, but it could be found in plenty of other places, too.

A figure wrapped in both a topcoat and a cloak scuttled furtively along the alley. The man's soft felt hat was pulled far down, shielding his face. He was glad for the heavy garments, because the air was cold and dank. Rain had fallen a short time earlier; puddles still glistened in the occasional stray beam of light that penetrated through the shrouding gloom.

The man paused before some rickety wooden steps that led up to a door with paint peeling from it. He went up the steps, grimacing a little as he felt the rotting planks sagging under his feet. The landing at the top was a little more solid, thank goodness. He stood on it and raised a hand to rap quietly on the door. What was that blasted signal the note had told him to use? Three and then two?

That worked. The door swung open, spilling some flickering light from a candle in a brass holder lifted by the man who had answered the summons.

"Conestoga?" the man with the candle asked.

"Studebaker," the visitor replied. He reined in the impatience and annoyance he felt. This whole business of secret knocks, passwords, and clandestine meetings was like something out of a dime novel.

The man with the candle stepped back and said curtly, "Come in. It's cold out here."

"Indeed it is," Ambrose Neill said as he stepped into the room and heeled the door closed behind him.

The candle's soft glow revealed a room as squalid as the neighborhood. The lone window was so grimy that no one could see in or out—which was a good thing, of course, since neither man wanted anyone to know about this meeting. The floor was dirty, too, and so were the pair of ragged rugs thrown on it. A crude table and chair sat in the center of the room. Beyond them, on the far side of the room, was a bunk with a narrow, sagging mattress. A couple of empty liquor bottles lay on the floor under the bunk. The air was thick with an unpleasant mixture of alcohol, tobacco, sweat, vomit, and urine.

"Couldn't you have found a better place to get together than this?" Neill said.

The man with the candle set the holder on the table. He said, "No one is going to expect either of us to be found in a hovel like this. Besides, I don't see why you should be complaining. You spent most of the past five years in prison, correct?"

Neill's already ruddy face warmed and flushed darker with anger. Who did this man think he was, anyway? Neill wasn't armed, but he had no doubt he could deal with his host with fists and feet alone if he needed to.

The man was a little above medium height, narrow-shouldered, with a small pot belly, clearly no physical threat. His egg-shaped head was mostly bald, a fact that a few lank strands of black hair combed over it couldn't conceal. He had a weasel-like face and a prominent Adam's apple. His dark suit was expensive, but it didn't make him any less ugly. Add in a smug, self-satisfied expression, and he was one of the most unappealing specimens of humanity that Neill had ever come across.

Which meant that P.T. Barnum had been correct in his statement that you can fool some of the people all of the time. Warren Pulsipher had fooled enough people that he'd been elected to the United States Senate.

Neill answered Pulsipher's question by saying, "That's right, I've been in prison. And now that I'm out, I don't want to go back to spending time in places like this. I did enough of that when I was on the force in New York."

Pulsipher nodded, his smile oily. "Of course. You were an inspector, I believe. A detective."

Neill took off his hat and shook some lingering drops of moisture from it. "I was. What's your point?"

"But you were actually a criminal," Pulsipher went on. "You were sent to prison for corruption and graft, but I have it on good authority that you also committed several murders. You didn't mind getting blood on your own hands when you needed to."

Neill's eyes narrowed as he said in a menacing tone, "If you think you're going to blackmail me—"

Pulsipher interrupted him with a wave of a well-manicured hand. "Nothing of the sort," he said. "We're on the same side, Mr. Neill. Or Inspector Neill, whichever you prefer."

"My inspector days are over," Neill snapped. "And I don't

know what *side* you're talking about. Why did you send word you wanted to meet me?"

Pulsipher's smirk got even bigger. "I believe the man primarily responsible for your arrest, conviction, and incarceration was none other than Theodore Roosevelt, is that correct?"

"That damned Roosevelt! Yes, he was to blame for what happened to me."

"The man who is now president of the entire country."

Neill drew in a sharp breath. "I couldn't believe it when we got the news in prison. It was bad enough that he became a damned national hero with that charge up San Juan Hill."

"But he *is* a hero, and he *is* the president," Pulsipher said. "But you're not the only one who holds a grudge against him, Mr. Neill, or the only one who'd like to see him taken down a notch . . . or two."

"That's what this is about?" Neill asked. "You're going to get even with Roosevelt?"

"That's right."

Neill smacked his fist down on the table, making the candle flame jump a little.

"Then count me in!" he declared. "Whatever you want done, I'll be part of it . . . as long as it means hurting that damned Teddy Roosevelt!"

The journey from Big Rock to Washington took the better part of two days, which meant it was early morning when Conrad stepped off the train in the capital city. Despite the hour, the station was busy. People came and went all the time in Washington.

Before leaving Big Rock, Conrad had wired a response to Washington, accepting the President's invitation. So he wasn't surprised when a man in a brown tweed suit, brown hat, and wire-rimmed spectacles approached him and asked, "Are you Mr. Morgan? Mr. Conrad Morgan?"

"That's right," Conrad replied.

The man extended his right hand. "My name is Lowell Hammersby. I work for President Roosevelt. He sent me to meet you."

Conrad shook hands with the man, who appeared to be in his middle thirties, although there were already traces of gray in his sandy hair. Working in the political morass of Washington, D.C., probably aged a man, Conrad thought. It would certainly have that effect on him.

"Glad to meet you, Mr. Hammersby. I don't suppose you'd care to tell me what it is I'm doing here."

Hammersby looked shocked by the very suggestion. "Oh, no, sir, I couldn't do that. I'll leave it to the President to explain everything to you, since it was his idea."

Well, that was a little more information, Conrad mused. Whatever it was that had brought him here, it was Roosevelt himself who had come up with it.

"We've booked a room for you in one of the finest hotels in the city," Hammersby went on as he led Conrad across the railroad station's crowded lobby. "I'm sorry that we can't offer you accommodations at the White House, but if we did that, the press might get wind of it, and the President would prefer discretion. I've already arranged to have your bags delivered there." He gestured at the carpetbag Conrad carried. "I can have that taken to the hotel, too, if you'd like."

"I'd rather keep it with me, if that's all right."

Conrad didn't explain that he didn't want to be separated from the guns and the knife in the bag. He wouldn't need the weapons at the White House, of course, but old habits were hard to break.

"Of course, that's fine," Hammersby assured him. "There'll be plenty of room for it in the cab."

That cab was waiting right outside the station. Conrad

suspected the vehicle was given a special place at the curb, since it was bound for the White House with a visitor personally summoned by President Roosevelt.

"Have you been to Washington before, Mr. Morgan?" Hammersby asked as the cab pulled away and began rolling through the busy streets.

"Yes, on a number of occasions. My mother had to visit here on business from time to time, and I accompanied her on some of those trips."

"Ah, yes. Mrs. Vivian Browning. I never had the pleasure of meeting her, but I'm told she was perhaps the most astute businesswoman this country has ever known."

"Thank you," Conrad said.

"Of course, it's not often you find a woman in charge of such an enterprise as the Browning Holdings."

"My mother was quite a strong person."

"I'm sure she was. From what I've heard, you've done an excellent job of continuing her efforts."

Conrad shrugged. "I do the best I can."

"I believe that, at the moment, you're personally involved in some sort of . . . mining operation, is it? In Colorado?"

Conrad suspected that Hammersby was just making small talk, that he knew quite well all the details of Conrad's current projects. He struck Conrad as the sort of man who would always be well-prepared. That would be a good habit for anyone who had to navigate the choppy, treacherous waters of politics.

"Yes, I've reopened some gold mines in a valley near the town of Big Rock. Using new techniques, we've been able to make them profitable again."

Conrad didn't add that getting those mines back in operation had caused a lot of conflict, including a considerable amount of bloody gunplay. That open warfare had been brief but violent, and Conrad was glad he and the citizens of the valley—including the Jensens—had been able to put that behind them.

The cab rolled up Pennsylvania Avenue and came to a stop in front of the famous edifice where the President resided. The driver hopped down from the box and opened the door. Hammersby disembarked first and then held the door for Conrad.

They passed through a gate where some soldiers were standing guard. Quite a few people were strolling along the sidewalk, bound on some errand or other, but surprisingly few of them paid any attention to the White House. Conrad supposed that when you lived in a place, you grew accustomed to what you saw every day, even a world-famous dwelling like this one. Having the President for a neighbor wasn't anything unusual for these people.

He felt himself tightening up inside, though, as he and Hammersby approached the porch with its impressive entrance. Hammersby led the way inside and turned toward the West Wing.

"The President is waiting for you in his office," he said. "It's in the Yellow Oval Room upstairs."

"It's early enough that I thought he might still be having breakfast," Conrad commented.

"Oh, no, Mr. Roosevelt likes to get an early start to the day. He always says there's more to get done than there are hours in the day."

Hammersby pointed to a bench sitting against the wall underneath a large painting of a group of men in powdered wigs, long, fancy coats, and tight white pants. Conrad recognized some of them as men who had been instrumental in the founding of the country.

"You can leave your bag there," Hammersby went on. "I can promise you that no one will bother it."

"All right," Conrad said as he placed the carpetbag on the bench.

He still had the Double Derringers in his vest pockets. He wasn't sure what he'd do if Hammersby or somebody else searched him and took those away from him before he was allowed in to see the President. Theodore Roosevelt had assumed the office of the presidency after an assassin shot President McKinley, and nobody had forgotten what had happened to Abraham Lincoln. Some precautions had to be taken to protect a man as important as the President.

Hammersby made no move to search him, though. He just led Conrad up to the second floor, where he opened one side of a pair of double doors and ushered Conrad through it into the President's office.

President Theodore Roosevelt sat behind the big desk, frowning as he peered down through his pince-nez spectacles at some papers spread out in front of him. He wore a gray suit and vest and a sedate black tie. Despite the fact that he was sitting down, he had an air of power and vitality about him. Conrad recalled reading that Roosevelt had been sickly as a child, much like Louis Jensen, but had built himself up with vigorous exercise and an active, outdoor existence that had led to him owning and operating that ranch in Dakota Territory Smoke had spoken of.

His background also made him exactly the right man to head up the cavalry unit known as the Rough Riders during the war with Spain a few years earlier. Laying eyes on the man now for the first time in the flesh, Conrad had no trouble believing that Roosevelt was capable of leading that famous charge up San Juan Hill in Cuba.

If Conrad had been there, he would have followed Teddy up that hill, too.

Abruptly, Roosevelt slapped a hand down on the desk, grunted, and said, "Professors and politicians. Never use one or two words when ten or twenty will suffice." He came to his feet and extended that same hand across the desk. "You must be Conrad Morgan. I'm very happy to meet you, son."

Conrad clasped the President's hand and said, "It's my pleasure, sir, and my honor, too."

"Give your hat to Lowell there and sit down," Roosevelt said, waving to a leather-upholstered chair in front of the desk. He gathered up the papers into a sheaf, tapped them on the polished wooden surface to square them up, and then set them aside.

Conrad handed his hat to Hammersby, who carried it over to a coat tree in the corner. He hesitated until Roosevelt had resumed his seat, then sank into the visitor's chair.

"I like that band on your hat," Roosevelt commented. "Very Western-looking. I thought perhaps you might swagger in here wearing buckskins, with a gun belt drooping about your hips."

"That wouldn't have been very respectful, sir."

"Wouldn't have bothered me. I dressed much like that when I was running my ranch. Nor was I completely sure who would answer my summons. Conrad Morgan, the businessman . . . or Kid Morgan, the gunfighter."

Conrad frowned. "That part of my life is over, Mr. President, and it's not exactly common knowledge to start with."

"But it's not actually a secret, either, is it? And I hear that Kid Morgan not only rode again, but also invaded Mexico a year or so ago."

"My father needed my help," Conrad responded tightly. "You're well-informed, sir."

Roosevelt grunted again. "Of course I am. I'm the President of the United States. There are a number of people out there"—he made a shooing motion, to indicate the world outside his office—"whose only job is to make certain that

I remain well-informed." The President laced his fingers together over his thickening stomach. "But I'm aware that you've been concentrating on your business dealings in recent months, so that's really the man I expected to see today. The mining magnate."

"It might be a bit of a stretch to call me a magnate—"

"Not at all. You've taken mines that were deemed too low-yielding to be profitable and made them pay off by employing the new hydraulic mining processes."

"We use hydraulics to a certain extent," Conrad said, "but we also employ more conventional methods in the Browning mines."

"And why is that?"

"Because unchecked use of hydraulics damages the landscape, fouls the water supply, and makes life difficult, if not impossible, for the cattle ranches and farms that share the valley with us."

"I see," Roosevelt said, nodding. "And avoiding those things is important to you?"

"Yes, sir, it is."

"Why?"

The President's short, sharp questions came as no surprise to Conrad. Roosevelt had a reputation for getting right to the point. He might not be a Westerner by birth, but he shared certain qualities with the frontiersmen Conrad had come to know, including his own father.

"I want those mines to be profitable, but not at any cost. There's no reason why I can't make plenty of money without hurting a lot of other people."

"Admirable, very admirable. As you may know, I have an interest in the land myself. I've been called a conservationist because I want to protect it, and I wear the name proudly."

"Nobody's called me a conservationist," Conrad said, "but I agree with you about protecting the land, sir."

"Good." Roosevelt unlaced his fingers, sat up straight, and leaned forward. "Because that tells me I was right in my assessment of you, Mr. Morgan. I think you're exactly the man I need."

"The man you need for what, sir?" Conrad asked bluntly.

"To serve as my Assistant Secretary of the Interior."

Chapter 5

Conrad sat there for a long moment. He wasn't stunned, exactly, but he was too surprised to respond. He had expected Roosevelt to ask something of him, perhaps even to offer him a job, but he hadn't anticipated that it would be something that high up in the ranks of power.

On the other hand, Conrad mused, he didn't know how high up an Assistant Secretary of the Interior actually was.

Roosevelt was waiting for him to say something. A trace of impatience appeared in the President's expression. Before Roosevelt could demand an answer, Conrad said, "I'm honored that you'd consider me for such a position, sir."

"That's not an answer, my boy. That's a stall."

Conrad shook his head. "No, sir. I'm just surprised. But it actually *is* an honor. I never thought anybody would want me to work for the government. I'm just a businessman."

"You're more than that, and you know it. You've lived a varied life and traveled the entire country, have you not?"

"I've been most places," Conrad admitted. "Not everywhere, but close to it, I suppose."

"You've been a businessman, as you said, and a very successful one, at that. So you have experience dealing with negotiations at the highest level, in the most exclusive boardrooms, with hundreds of thousands, if not millions, of dollars at stake. You understand that sort of pressure."

Roosevelt stood up, hooked his left thumb in his vest pocket, and pointed his right index finger at Conrad, stabbing it forward to emphasize his next statement.

"But you've also wandered the lonely trails, the dark trails, just you and a horse and a gun. You've faced men who did their best to kill you, and you've survived. You've given assistance to the Texas Rangers, leading them to try to recruit you to join their ranks, as well as helping other law enforcement agencies from time to time. You know what it takes to deal with long odds, and you have a grounding in reality that, let's face it, many here in Washington do not. To put it simply, Mr. Morgan . . . Conrad . . . you're a man to ride the river with, as the men who worked for me in the Dakota Territory would have phrased it, and I want you riding for *my* brand."

Again, Conrad was speechless. As Roosevelt settled down in his chair behind the desk, the only response Conrad could manage was, "I don't know what to say, Mr. President."

"Of course you don't. This has come out of the blue, I realize that."

Roosevelt leaned back and clasped his hands over his stomach again. A moment earlier, he had been fiery and persuasive, as if he were trying to talk a group of senators into passing legislation he wanted. Now, he was relaxed again, a stern but friendly uncle.

"You don't have to give me an answer today, son. I know you probably want to think it over. That's why we booked a room for you in a fine hotel. Rest up from your journey, partake of some good food, take in the sights, if you want, although I understand that you've been to Washington before."

"Yes, sir, I have."

"It's still a magnificent city. But while you're enjoying your stay here, I want you to ponder my offer, as well. I won't be leaving Washington until the end of the month, so you have a few days to make up your mind." Roosevelt smiled. "I hope you'll decide to accept."

"Well, sir . . . what exactly does an Assistant Secretary of the Interior *do?"*

The President let out a bark of laughter. "An excellent question! Bully for you, son. Talk to Lowell. He'll be glad to explain to you what your duties would be."

Hammersby, who had faded into the background even though he was still in the room, stepped forward now and said, "Of course, I'll be more than happy to answer any of your questions, Mr. Morgan. In fact, we can start while I'm escorting you to your hotel, if you'd like."

"Yeah, I think that's a good idea," Conrad said, nodding slowly, still feeling a little overwhelmed.

"At least you didn't turn me down flat," Roosevelt said with a slight smile. "I'll take that as a good sign."

Roosevelt could take it however he wanted to, Conrad thought, but the only reason he hadn't flatly rejected the offer was because he hadn't figured out how to say no to the President of the United States without insulting him.

As soon as the reality had sunk in, something inside Conrad had rebelled instinctively. He didn't want to be an assistant secretary or anything else that involved living and working in Washington, D.C. He wanted to go back to Colorado, supervise the mining operation, and marry Denny Jensen . . . the latter being the most important of those things.

But he supposed it wouldn't hurt anything to be polite, talk it over with Lowell Hammersby, and wait a day or two before giving Roosevelt his decision.

Then he could get back to the things he really cared about.

Conrad was waiting for Roosevelt to stand up and signify that the meeting was at an end. Before that could happen, he gave in to an impulse to satisfy his curiosity. He said, "You mentioned you're leaving Washington at the end of the month, Mr. President?"

"That's right. I'm going west, in fact. To the Black Hills."

Conrad's eyebrows rose a little in surprise. "In Dakota Territory? I mean, in South Dakota?"

Roosevelt chuckled. "It was Dakota Territory when I first knew it," he said. "A part of me will always think of it that way. An old friend of mine has invited me to Deadwood for some sort of celebration they're having to commemorate the founding of the town. You might even know him. Seth Bullock?"

Conrad shook his head. "No, sir. I've heard of Mr. Bullock, but we've never met. My father might know him, though."

"I wouldn't be surprised. At any rate, I'm taking advantage of the opportunity to get out of Washington and treat the journey as a vacation of sorts. That's why we've tried to keep it out of the newspapers. Eh, Lowell?"

"That's right, sir," Hammersby responded. "I'm sure there'll be a large number of journalists in Deadwood for the actual event, but so far we've managed to maintain secrecy about you being in attendance, too."

"My wife and children have already departed from Washington and will be spending a few days in Deadwood prior to my arrival," Roosevelt went on. He chuckled. "My boys are quite excited that they'll be walking the same streets Wild Bill Hickok and Calamity Jane did in the old days. Like most boys, they dream of the Wild West." For a moment, the President's eyes got a faraway look in them. "Those of us who experienced that time and place first-hand have a slightly less glamorous perspective on those days, I imagine, but still . . . there is much to celebrate in the settling of the West, too."

"Yes, sir, I agree," Conrad said.

"It will be good to see Seth again, too," Roosevelt mused.

"Despite the fact that no one ever wrote dime novels about him, I'm not sure the town would have survived those wild, early years without him . . ."

Deadwood, South Dakota

The place was a real town now, not a crude mining camp that turned into a boomtown almost overnight. There were brick buildings and paved streets. There were electric globes on posts to light those streets. Deadwood was actually one of the first towns in the country to have an electric power plant, something that Seth Bullock never would have dreamed of the first time he laid eyes on the settlement.

Back then, in August of '76, the streets were muddy swamps half the time, and the other half they were so dry a man could almost choke to death on the clouds of dust kicked up by horses, mules, and wagon wheels. Tents lined the streets. The few buildings were constructed of raw, splintery planks hammered together in haphazard fashion, roofed with tin, tar paper, or canvas. The air was full of noise around the clock: people yelling, cursing, crying, laughing; tinny piano music; the occasional flurry of gunshots. You could say a lot of things about Deadwood in those days. Life was dirty and grindingly hard and often cut short.

But it was never boring.

Bullock stood on the front porch of the three-story hotel he had built on the site of the original hardware store he and Sol Star had established in Deadwood more than a quarter of a century earlier. Some years back, a fire had claimed that store, and instead of rebuilding, Bullock had put up the hotel instead. He believed it was the finest hostelry in this part of the country, and not many folks would argue with him.

He wore a dark gray suit and vest and a flat-crowned black hat. He had always figured that a respectable man should dress in a respectable fashion, so he wore a suit most of the time and had even when he was the marshal of Deadwood in its rowdy days. His face was stern but still handsome in middle age. Gray streaked the impressive mustache that swooped over his mouth. He seldom wore a gun belt—not many men did, these days—but a small pistol was tucked into his waistband at the small of his back, hidden by his coat tails.

Seth Bullock had always been a forward-looking man, a trait he deemed the main reason for his success as both a businessman and a public servant. But more and more these days, if he paused to look around the town as he had just now when he stepped out of the hotel, his mind strayed back into the past . . . the bloody past.

Bullock himself had never killed anyone during his time as the law in Deadwood, but he had been perfectly willing to if that was required to keep order and deliver justice. Folks knew that about him, so the many confrontations he'd had with lawbreakers all ended with the other men either backing down or surrendering, if Bullock was trying to perform an arrest.

He had seen plenty of death in those days, though. Deadwood had been a dangerous place. A lot of that had centered around the Gem Saloon, run by Al Swearingen, a man with whom Bullock had had numerous run-ins.

Despite that, Bullock had come to hold a grudging respect for Swearingen, a feeling that he believed Swearingen returned. The man was completely immoral, of course, but sometimes Bullock thought that he deserved a better ending than the ignominious one he had gotten, run over and killed by a beer wagon in Denver.

The Gem was gone now. So was the Bella Union. The Number 10 Saloon, where Jack McCall had shot Bill Hickok in the back of the head just two days before Bullock and Sol Star arrived in Deadwood, was still there, an attraction of sorts although most of Deadwood's current citizens preferred to downplay the town's violent past.

All of it would come flooding back in another week and a half, though, with the Founders' Day Celebration.

Hell of a time to hold such a fandango, Bullock mused. Deadwood had been founded in the spring, not the fall, and twenty-six years had passed since then. Seemed like the twenty-fifth anniversary would have been a more appropriate one to celebrate. But nobody had gotten around to doing anything in the summer of '01, and once the idea took hold in the minds of some of the town's leading citizens, it had taken this long to get everything organized.

Like most things in life, celebrations didn't just happen. Folks had to get up off their rear ends and actually *do* something to get the ball rolling.

Bullock's lips curved a little under the thick mustache. People were going to be surprised when they found out what he was contributing to Founders' Day.

None other than the President of the United States was going to be on hand for it.

It would be good to see Teddy again. They had known each other for almost two decades. Bullock hadn't seen Roosevelt since Teddy had become President following McKinley's assassination. Roosevelt had put Bullock in charge of the Black Hills Forest Preserve, but that had been done through correspondence and telegrams.

Bullock had never met Roosevelt's second wife and their children, but he would soon. They would be arriving later today on a Chicago & North Western train, and Teddy had asked his old friend to look after them, keep their real identities to himself, and help them enjoy their visit without all the commotion that would ensue if folks knew who they really were.

Bullock figured he was up to that job. He went down the steps and started walking leisurely toward the train station.

He knew it would take him a while to get there, since he would have to stop, say hello, and chat with almost everybody he passed in the street. Everybody knew Seth Bullock. Everybody was friends with Seth Bullock.

Even though he was in good health and figured on being around a good while longer, that wasn't a bad legacy to have, he reflected.

"I hate that damned Seth Bullock."

The snarled words came from a man resting his hands atop the batwings in a saloon entrance as the well-dressed, mustachioed figure passed in the street outside, smiling and glad-handing folks as usual. He watched until Bullock was out of sight, then shook his head and turned away from the entrance, headed back to the table where he'd been sitting before he spotted Bullock through the place's grimy front window.

"What was that all about?" the other man sitting at the table asked.

"Saw somebody I know. Well, I don't really know him, but I know *of* him, and I don't like him. Damn swell-headed law dog. Thing of it is, he got a big reputation for bein' the marshal of Deadwood, and from what I've heard, he didn't hold the job for even a year! But that don't keep people from thinkin' he's some sort of hero."

The man leaned over and spat into a corner. Nobody seemed to notice. It was that sort of place.

"That's what I think of Seth Bullock and every other son of a buck who packs a badge."

"I used to carry a badge, you know," the man's companion said dryly. "That was a long time ago, though."

His accent made it clear that he wasn't from these parts. Back east somewhere. Maybe a hint of Irish. He was muffled in a thick coat and had a soft felt hat on his head. His face held the natural flush of a habitual heavy drinker, but his dark eyes were still keen and clear. Whiskey had begun taking its toll on him, but it hadn't yet muddled his mind.

The man who had cursed Seth Bullock was lean, with long gray hair framing his hawkish features. The brim of the brown hat he wore was pinned up in front. A long duster had swung around his legs when he paced to the entrance and back. The walnut handle of a Colt stuck up from a cross-draw rig on his left hip as he swept the duster back and stretched his legs out. He reached for a glass on the table that still had an inch or so of whiskey in it.

"I'm surprised you'd sit that way," he said to the other man.

"Sit what way?"

The Westerner threw back the drink. "With your back to the door. Don't you know you're in Deadwood?"

"Of course I know where I am," the Easterner said impatiently.

"Then you shouldn't be sittin' with your back to the door. That's how ol' Wild Bill got a bullet in the brain. I wasn't around here in those days, but I've heard plenty about it."

The Easterner shook his head and said, "Nobody would want to shoot me. No one in Deadwood has a reason to or even knows who I am."

The Westerner's eyes narrowed. "*I* don't know who you are, mister, or why you wanted to talk to me. I just ain't in the habit of sayin' no when somebody offers me a drink." He pushed the empty glass aside and leaned forward. "So if you've got somethin' to say, you'd best go ahead and say it."

Anger flared in the Easterner's gaze. They sat there for a couple of heartbeats, the tension between them growing, but then the Easterner shrugged and said, "Very well, but first

I have to make sure . . . Your name *is* Augustus Greendale, is it not?"

The man across the table grimaced. "It's Gus," he snapped. "Nobody's called me Augustus since my pa." Greendale grinned. "And I killed him before I lit out on my own."

The Easterner didn't know if that was true or just a boast. Greendale seemed capable of patricide.

"I don't give a tinker's damn about anything you might have done in the past. My only concern is what we might achieve together in the future."

"Me work with a stuck-up Yankee dandy like you?" Greendale shook his head. "Why would I want to do that?"

"Because we have a mutual enemy. I know you were released from prison last year after serving fifteen years behind bars . . . and I know the name of the man responsible for putting you there."

"You mean—"

"I mean, Mr. Greendale, that you and I both have scores to settle with the President of the United States," Ambrose Neill said.

Chapter 6

Washington, D.C.

Lowell Hammersby proved to be an amiable, informative companion, Conrad discovered over the next couple of days in Washington.

During lunch at the hotel and dinner that first evening at a nearby restaurant, Hammersby filled him in on the duties of an Assistant Secretary of the Interior, which, as far as Conrad could tell, consisted mainly of sitting in endless meetings and listening to the Secretary of the Interior drone on about laws and regulations and policies to an assortment of other politicians and businessmen.

"I'm sure there would be some public appearances, too, where the Secretary would send you to be his representative, so some traveling would be involved," Hammersby explained.

"You mean I'd have to go out and give speeches," Conrad said, the ominous tone of his voice indicating what he thought about that.

"Well, yes, but nothing too elaborate. Most likely, you would just need to smile and wave at an assemblage of citizens and make a few remarks about how happy you were to be in . . . whatever particular place you happened to be. Shake hands with the local dignitaries. Things like that."

"Sounds like political glad-handing to me."

"Well . . ." Hammersby shrugged. "Part of politics is convincing people to like you, isn't it? They generally won't do what you want them to do unless they like you." He smiled. "And the goal is to persuade them to do what you want but believe it was their own idea."

"President Roosevelt mentioned how my company has been using hydraulic methods to make mining pay off without causing too many problems for the other folks in the area. I thought maybe I'd be talking to other mining men about that."

"And I'm sure you will be, once you've settled into the job. But these things have to be taken one step at a time. Politics is the art of compromise, you know."

They talked at length about that and about how the Department of the Interior operated while they were strolling around Washington the next day. The weather was sunny and pleasant, the air crisp but not as damp as it often was in Washington, Hammersby observed.

"I don't know if you've ever been here in the summer, but it can be quite oppressive at times," he said.

"I haven't been," Conrad said. "And to be honest, Lowell, if you were supposed to convince me to accept the President's offer, I'm not sure how good a job you're doing of it."

Hammersby chuckled. "President Roosevelt instructed me to answer all of your questions fully and honestly, Conrad, and that's what I've been doing. He wouldn't want you to accept the position if any deception was involved."

"He's a straight shooter, all right," Conrad said with a nod as they paused before the Washington Monument. "That's one thing everybody seems to agree on, his friends and enemies alike."

"He's asked that you have lunch with him tomorrow. I suspect that he'll want your answer then."

"And I'll give it to him," Conrad said.

Hammersby looked intently at him. "You already know what it's going to be, don't you?"

"Unless something happens between now and then to change my mind . . . yeah, I do."

"I don't suppose you want to tell me—" Hammersby stopped short and held up a hand. "No, please disregard that. What you have to say in respect to that matter should be for the President's ears first. In the meantime, there's an orchestra performance tonight that I think you might enjoy."

"Sounds good," Conrad said, even though a large part of him wished that he was already back in Big Rock.

Deadwood

Seth Bullock made it to the train station before the big locomotive pulling the Chicago & North Western train arrived from Rapid City. He stood on the platform watching the passengers disembark until he spotted a woman herding a brood of children out of one of the cars. She was well-dressed—they all were—and while she wasn't exactly beautiful, she was what folks referred to as a handsome woman. Bullock figured she was about forty years old. That matched up, and so did the half-dozen kids. Bullock approached the group and took off his hat.

"Mrs. Johnson?" he said, using the false name that had been agreed on.

"That depends on who's asking," the woman responded coolly.

"Seth Bullock, ma'am. Your husband, ah, Mr. Johnson, asked me to meet you and your family and look after you while you're in Deadwood."

"In that case . . ." The woman smiled, which relieved what seemed to be a naturally stern expression and made her prettier. "I am indeed Edith Johnson. These are my children."

Bullock recalled that the oldest one, a girl in her late

teens, actually wasn't Edith Roosevelt's child. She was named Alice, after the mother who had died two days after giving birth to her, before Bullock ever met Theodore Roosevelt. Teddy had married Edith a couple of years later, though, so she was the only mother Alice had ever actually known.

The other five youngsters were Edith's, and Bullock suspected that keeping up with them, *and* serving as First Lady, was more than enough to fill anybody's plate. She introduced them: Theodore and Kermit, also in their teens; Ethel, around ten or eleven; and Archibald and Quentin, both under ten years old and both full of vinegar, if Bullock was any judge of little boys.

They were all using their real given names, their father having decided it might be too much to expect from children for them to keep up with aliases. They might even have trouble remembering that their last name was supposed to be Johnson instead of Roosevelt. They wouldn't have to keep up the masquerade all that long, however, and if they were anything like Teddy, they were smart enough to do it.

Bullock put his hat back on and said, "I'll make arrangements to have your bags delivered to my hotel. That's where you'll be staying. And then I'll see to getting a carriage to take you and the children there."

"Can't we walk?" Kermit asked. "Is it too far?"

"We want to see the town," Theodore added. He looked the most like his famous father, a sturdily built, brown-haired youngster wearing a pair of rimless spectacles.

"Some of us do," Alice said. She was a tall, pretty girl with dark hair pulled behind her head in an elaborate arrangement of braids, but Bullock had a hunch she was inclined to sulkiness. Of all the children, she was the one who looked the least like she wanted to be here.

"Well, it's a few blocks to the hotel," Bullock said, "but it's not too far to walk if you want to. The weather's pretty nice today. This time of year, it can range anywhere from pleasant like this to a howling blizzard."

Edith smiled again and said, "I'm certainly glad we didn't arrive in the middle of a blizzard, then. We'll wait here for you, Mr. Bullock, until you've made arrangements for the bags, and then we'll take a stroll through Deadwood."

Bullock pinched the brim of his hat. "Yes, ma'am."

"Can't we wait in the lobby, at least?" Alice asked. "The smoke from that train smells bad."

"We'll be in the lobby," Edith told Bullock, who nodded and went to find some porters to take care of the visitors' baggage.

Gus Greendale and Ambrose Neill stood at the far end of the platform, not calling attention to themselves as they watched the meeting between Seth Bullock and the family from back east.

"You're sure that's them?" Greendale asked quietly.

"I'm certain," Neill replied. "I've seen their photographs in the illustrated weeklies. Besides, no other middle-aged woman and six brats got off the train, now did they?"

"No, I reckon not." Greendale hitched up his gun belt and twisted it so the cross-draw holster was a little easier to reach. "When do we grab 'em?"

Neill had explained the plan to Greendale while they sat together in the saloon, finishing off the bottle the Easterner had bought. Greendale didn't fully trust the former policeman from New York City; he would never be able to put all his faith in anybody who'd ever packed a badge. But once Neill had said that the real target of the plot was Theodore Roosevelt, Greendale was sure as hell willing to listen.

"We're not going to kidnap all of them," Neill had said, leaning forward and keeping his voice down so nobody in the saloon could overhear. "We want to get our hands on

Roosevelt's wife and perhaps two of the children. Any more than that might prove too difficult to manage once we get away from town. And that will be plenty to force Roosevelt to pay up."

"That's what we're after? Money?" Surprisingly, Greendale had felt a little disappointed when he thought about that.

"That's what everyone is going to believe. But we're going to insist that Roosevelt deliver the ransom himself, and when he does . . ."

Neill had allowed his voice to trail off, and as he did, a surge of excitement had boiled up inside Greendale.

"We're gonna kill the son of a—"

Neill had held up a hand to stop him and motioned for Greendale to keep his voice down.

"We want that ransom money, true enough. But we want Roosevelt to suffer, too." Neill's lips had peeled back from his teeth in a savage smile. "I can't think of anything that would make the man suffer more than to see his wife and children killed right before his eyes . . . just before we put a bullet in his own brain."

"You might want to think again about that part of the plan."

Neill had frowned. "You don't want to kill him?"

"I don't want him to die that quick and easy. I got a friend . . . a redskin name of Lame Wolf . . . who used to ride with me back in the old days. He knows all sorts of Injun tricks to make a man suffer while keepin' him alive for a long time. I don't reckon he'd mind doin' the same to a woman and some kids before turnin' his attention to ol' Teddy."

Neill had gazed at him with something akin to respect, Greendale thought, then said, "You really *are* a vicious brute, aren't you?"

Greendale had thrown back another drink. "You never killed anybody?"

"I most certainly did, but always for business reasons. I never got any great joy out of it. Those deaths were expedient and efficient, that's all."

Greendale didn't believe that. He'd been able to tell that Neill had a mean streak and got some pleasure out of those killings, as well, whether the man wanted to admit it or not. But it didn't really matter.

"You'll enjoy seein' Roosevelt suffer."

Neill had shrugged. "Yes, you're probably right about that. I became part of this because of a desire for justice—"

"Revenge."

"Yes, damn it, revenge, too. Whatever happens, Roosevelt has it coming. The man ruined my life."

"Mine, too. Sent me to prison for fifteen long years. Only reason I didn't wind up on the gallows was because they couldn't prove I actually ever pulled the trigger on anybody. I blamed all the killin's on Hubert Singleton and Amos Maddock, a couple of fellas who rode with me. They was both dead, so they couldn't argue. Hubert's brother Hank and another one of us called Tiny were more than happy to back up my story, because that meant they didn't hang, either. They both got twelve years in the pen." Greendale had scratched his jaw and made a face. "I got fifteen 'cause the prosecutor said I was the boss of the gang. Well, that's true, I was. Fifteen years stole outta my life on account of that damn Roosevelt."

"So you'll help me carry out the plan?"

"You damn betcha I will."

Now, as they watched Mrs. Roosevelt and her brood go into the station lobby while Bullock walked along the platform in the other direction, Neill said, "We can't just go in there and grab them, as you put it. It's broad daylight, and there are too many people around. We want to be careful enough about this that we can get away and put some distance behind us before any alarm is raised. I want to be well hidden in the hills when the inevitable posse comes after us."

Greendale nodded slowly as he thought. "We're gonna need help," he said. "We can't pull this off with just the two of us."

"I agree. You already mentioned some Indian—"

"Lame Wolf."

"Yes, Lame Wolf. Do you know where he is?"

"Matter of fact, I do. And I know where Hank and Tiny are, too. They're the other fellas I said rode with me in those days."

"Yes, I remember. You believe them to be dependable?"

"I sure do."

"How soon can you get them here?"

Greendale smiled. "Lame Wolf's right here in town. Hank and Tiny ain't far off. I can probably round 'em up today."

Neill raised a finger and said, "One thing. Whatever you offer them comes out of your share."

Greendale flushed angrily. "Now, that don't hardly seem fair."

"Nevertheless, that's the arrangement. Two partners are all I'm willing to split with."

"What do you mean, two?" Greendale demanded. Then a look of understanding came over his face and he went on, "Oh, I get it. You didn't come up with this plan all by yourself, did you?"

"In fact, I was brought in on it by someone else, just as I'm bringing you and your friends in."

"This other fella, he's somebody Roosevelt done wrong, too?"

"I don't know his motive," Neill said, "and I didn't question him. As soon as I heard that the target is Theodore Roosevelt, that was all I had to hear."

"Yeah, me, too. Should I go after Lame Wolf, Hank, and

Tiny? If I can get ’em here in time, we might could make our move tonight.”

“I see no reason to wait. The sooner Roosevelt pays for what he did to us—”

“The better,” Greendale finished.

Chapter 7

"Wake up, damn it."

Lame Wolf grunted as a hand prodded hard against his shoulder. For a second, he didn't know what was going on. In his mind, he was back in his village, a young man being shaken awake in the misty hours of dawn. Angry shouts and terrified screams came from outside the lodge. Hoofbeats thudded on the earth.

The Blackfeet! Lame Wolf thought. The hated Blackfeet were attacking again, raiding his village to steal horses and women and kill as many Crow warriors as they could. With a furious cry, he snatched the tomahawk from where it lay beside him on the buffalo robe, sprang to his feet, and rushed out of the lodge, his breath fogging in the chilly air as he brandished the weapon and looked around for his enemies . . .

"Damn it, Chief, stop wavin' that tomahawk around, or I'll brain you, I swear I will!"

This time, Lame Wolf recognized Otis McPherson's voice. He realized he wasn't outside at all. He was in a small, gloomy room, standing next to a bunk with a thin mattress and tangled, threadbare blankets that stunk of unwashed flesh and, to be honest, a number of unfortunate accidents when Lame Wolf hadn't been able to hold his water.

He stared at the tomahawk in his hand and then looked at Otis, a medium-sized young man with a rust-colored mustache and a derby hat crammed down on a thatch of equally rusty hair. Otis wore a fancy vest over a white shirt and had a carefully knotted string tie around his throat. His fingers were stained from the chemicals he used to develop the photographs he took in his studio.

This tiny room where Lame Wolf lived was in the rear of Otis's studio. Otis let him stay here in return for helping out around the place.

"I need you for a picture," Otis said. "Straighten yourself up and bring the tomahawk, but for heaven's sake, don't go waving it around like you're fixing to scalp somebody."

"Uh," Lame Wolf said. He swatted and tugged at the buckskin shirt and trousers he wore until they looked better. He glared for a second at his feet, encased in tight leather shoes scavenged from some trash behind one of the mercantiles rather than moccasins. That didn't matter, he supposed. His feet probably wouldn't show in the photograph.

After scrubbing a hand over his face, he retied the strip of rawhide that gathered his long hair together at the back of his neck.

"Well, you look sort of presentable," Otis said. "Come on."

He led Lame Wolf through the developing room and into the studio's big front room with its assorted backdrops standing around. A well-dressed couple waited there, the man in his thirties, the woman probably still in her twenties, with fluffy blond hair tucked up under a fancy hat with a feather attached to it. When she caught sight of Lame Wolf, she clutched her husband's arm as if frightened . . .

But who could really be scared of a drunken old Indian?

"Folks, this is Chief Lame Wolf of the Crow tribe," Otis told them with a big smile on his face. "He'll be glad to have his picture made with you. You can stand right over there"—he pointed to a backdrop made to look like a Crow lodge—"and you can tell folks that you visited the chief right there in his village and that he made you honorary members of the tribe."

"Nobody's going to believe that," the man said. "It's clearly just a picture painted on canvas."

Otis's smile never wavered. "Oh, you'd be surprised what folks will believe, sir . . . when they want to."

Like these two believing he was a chief, Lame Wolf thought. He had never been a chief. A warrior, yes. A fierce warrior. And after that, an outlaw, a member of the Greendale gang, which, if it hadn't exactly been the James boys, or the Youngers, was still pretty well-known and even feared for a while.

But now he was just a fake, like that backdrop. Instead of spending his days stealing horses from the Blackfeet or robbing banks, he used a broom or a cleaning rag and sucked firewater from a jug just so he could sleep at night . . . or sometimes, like now, during the day.

He shuffled forward, and the woman acted even more frightened of him. Was she actually scared, or was it just an act?

"Are you sure this is safe, Robert?" she asked her husband. "I mean . . . he's a savage . . ."

"It's perfectly all right, my dear," he assured her. "I'm right here with you. I'll protect you. This heathen wouldn't dare try to harm you."

And if I raised this tomahawk and acted like I really was going to use it, you'd wet yourself and cry like a baby, Lame Wolf thought. For a second, he visualized what that would be like, crashing the tomahawk down on this dandy's head and splitting his skull like a melon, brains and blood everywhere, the woman screaming . . .

"All right, if you folks would just step right over here, and Chief, if you'll move in behind them," Otis said.

Lame Wolf lifted his chin and looked as dignified as he

could as he got into position. Other than the husband casting a scornful glance over his shoulder, the couple acted as if he weren't even there. He was just part of the backdrop.

Otis got his camera ready and bent to put his eye to the lens as he draped the shroud of black cloth over his head and shoulders. "Stand very still," he told his customers. "This won't take long at all."

Even though Lame Wolf was accustomed to it, when the flash powder went off, it blinded him for a moment. He blinked and tried not to rub his eyes. When the bright, floating spots finally went away and his vision cleared up, he saw that someone else had come into the studio.

Gus Greendale stood there, leaning against the wall near the door, arms crossed over his chest, a smile on his lean face.

"When will that be ready?" the male customer asked Otis.

"Give me a week, and I'll have it mounted and framed real nice for you," Otis said. "Don't you worry, it'll look really good."

"I hope so, for what you're charging us." The man smirked at Lame Wolf again and added, "Especially with a phony backdrop and a ratty imitation Indian."

Lame Wolf sighed and looked down at the floor, but he raised his eyes when he heard a sound he hadn't heard in a long time: the metallic ratcheting of a gun's hammer being drawn back.

"Imitation Indian?" Gus Greendale rasped as he prodded the barrel of his Colt against the soft underside of the man's chin. The woman cried out in genuine fear, and Otis McPherson blurted out a shocked curse.

Greendale went on, "That man right there is a genuine Crow warrior and one of the fiercest fighters ever to stalk the Black Hills, strikin' terror into the hearts of everybody who crossed his path. You damn fool, if he wanted to, he could split your skull in the blink of an eye and spill your brains all over this floor."

That was exactly what he had been thinking a few moments earlier, Lame Wolf mused. He wondered how Gus had known that.

"You better just get on outta here right now while you still can," Greendale went on. He leered at the woman. "You can leave this pretty little gal with me and the chief, though, if you want. I reckon we probably know how to treat her a whole lot better than you do."

"C-Come along, Sylvia," the man stammered out. He grabbed his wife's arm and started to edge toward the door.

"Hold on just a minute," Greendale said. "Before you go, you tell that warrior how sorry you are that you insulted him."

The sharp motion of Greendale's revolver made the man turn. Lame Wolf felt a moment of satisfaction when he saw the dark stain on the crotch of the man's trousers.

"I . . . I'm sorry, Chief. I meant no offense."

Still holding the tomahawk, Lame Wolf folded his arms over his chest and glared solemnly at the frightened man for a long moment before he grunted, "Umm."

That was enough to make the man whirl around and grab his wife's arm again. The two of them practically stampeded out of the photographic studio.

Greendale cackled with laughter and slapped his thigh with his free hand. Lame Wolf allowed himself a faint smile.

"What . . . what the hell was *that*?" Otis demanded.

Greendale's amusement ended abruptly. His gun came up again.

"Be careful with your tone of voice, boy," he grated. "When you get right down to it, you're the one responsible for humiliatin' my friend here."

Otis swallowed hard and took a step back, his eyes fixed on the gaping maw of Greendale's gun muzzle.

"I . . . I was just trying to help him out," Otis said. "I gave him a place to get out of the weather and a job to do—"

"A job that ain't fit for a real man. A real warrior."

Lame Wolf said quietly, "It's all right, Gus. Otis has treated me well."

"Nowhere near as good as you deserve." Greendale gave Lame Wolf a shrewd look. "You ready to take on a real job again?"

Lame Wolf cocked his head to the side. "Like in the old days?"

"Well, not exactly, but the money promises to be good and it'll be a hell of a lot better than *this.*"

Greendale's lip curled scornfully as he said the last word and looked around at the phony backdrops.

"Count me in," Lame Wolf said as he stepped past Otis and went to join Greendale. He didn't know what he was getting into, and he didn't care.

All he knew was that he suddenly felt like he had when he and the other young men set out to raid the Blackfeet, and it was good again.

Spearfish, South Dakota

Unlike Deadwood, which had steep, heavily wooded slopes looming above it on all sides, Spearfish sat in a small but relatively flat valley between ranges of hills. Nearby, Spearfish Creek emerged from Spearfish Canyon and meandered through the valley. Those early settlers back in the Gold Rush days must have been mighty fond of the name Spearfish, Gus Greendale told himself as he and Lame Wolf rode toward the town, although he was damned if he could see why.

Spearfish was only about ten miles from Deadwood in a straight line, but the rugged terrain meant that the two men had had to ride nearly fifteen miles to get here. Even so, it was still only early afternoon. There was enough time to get back to Deadwood by nightfall, assuming they found Hank and Tiny quickly enough, and Greendale had a good idea where to look for them.

Lame Wolf was riding a horse Greendale had bought for him, since he'd long since sold his own pony and hadn't had any need of a mount. Greendale had used money Ambrose Neill gave him to buy the horse for the Indian. Neill had some cash he was allowed to use for expenses, no doubt provided by that mysterious partner of his, but the big payoff was still ahead. Greendale wasn't sure exactly how much ransom they would ask for. He supposed it depended on how many of the Roosevelt brats they managed to snatch, along with that horse-faced wife of Teddy's.

No matter how much it was, though, it wouldn't match the sheer satisfaction of putting Roosevelt through hell and then watching Lame Wolf torture him to death. Of course, they'd still take the money . . .

"I'm sorry you had to see me like that, Gus," Lame Wolf said, out of the blue as they approached Spearfish.

"What? Oh, hell, don't worry about that. Everybody falls on hard times sooner or later." Greendale made a face. "I know I should've come to see you before now, once I heard you was workin' in that place."

"I am happy you did not. You would have had to witness my shame that much sooner."

Greendale shook his head. "Ain't nothin' for you to be ashamed of. Don't forget, me and Hank and Tiny went to prison, and Hubert and Amos wound up dead."

"Yes, but I abandoned you, there at the Dutchman's. Perhaps if I had stayed to fight—"

"Then those punchers from the Elkhorn probably would've killed you, too, or else you'd have ended up goin' to prison like the rest of us. You reckon you could've survived ten or fifteen years behind bars, Lame Wolf?"

The answer came slowly. "No. I could not have. I would have gone mad and forced them to kill me."

Greendale grunted and said, "Don't think I didn't consider doin' that a time or two myself." He grinned. "But that's all behind us now, boy. We're on our way up again. With the loot we make from this job, we'll be able to put together a bigger and better gang than we ever had in the old days. We'll have everybody in the territory afraid to close their eyes at night because the Greendale gang might be lurkin' around!"

"It is not a territory now. It is two states."

"Hell, I know that. We're in South Dakota. Spearfish, South Dakota." Greendale reined in and looked at the town. Beside him, Lame Wolf did the same.

Like Deadwood, Spearfish was an actual city now, with a lot of substantial buildings, a good-sized central business district, and several residential areas sprawling around it. Greendale had been here before, but not for many, many years.

The place had actual sidewalks, too, not just rough plank boardwalks. Greendale hailed a man walking along one of them.

"Hey, partner, come here a second."

The man, who looked like a store clerk of some sort, hesitated and poked a thumb in his chest as if to say *Who, me?*

"That's right." Greendale waved him over and said, "My friend and me are lookin' for a place called Madame Wilma's. You happen to know where that is?"

The man frowned and looked like he was about to puff up a like a frog. "I beg your pardon?"

"Madame Wilma's. It's a—"

"I know what it is. It's a vile den of iniquity, that's what it is. I'll have you know, sir, that I'm a married man—"

"Wasn't for married men, I reckon at least half the whorehouses in the world'd go outta business," Greendale drawled. He grinned. "Ain't that right? You know what I mean, I'll bet."

"No, I don't," the townsman said stiffly.

Greendale's grin went away. "Well, whether you do or not, it don't matter. Do you know where it is, or don't you?"

As he asked the question, he shifted his hand a little toward the butt of the Colt in the cross-draw rig.

The townsman saw that and swallowed. "I know where it is," he muttered.

Greendale understood him but said, "What was that again?" He raised his voice. "I asked you if you knew where the whorehouse is."

The man glanced around, as if afraid that somebody else on the street might have heard, which had been Greendale's intention.

"Yes, I know where it is," he repeated hastily. "A man doesn't have to . . . to patronize an establishment to be aware of its location." He sniffed. "I daresay most people in Spearfish know where Wilma's is whether they've ever been there or not."

"Then how about daresayin' where it is. This is gettin' tiresome."

The man sighed and pointed. "Go on through town. Another half-mile or so, and you'll see a large grove of trees on the right, perhaps fifty yards off the road. The house is there, among those trees." He paused. "It's actually rather a nice-looking house. A mining man built it as a home for him and his family, back in the boom days, before it became a . . . a . . . what it is now."

"See, that wasn't all that hard, was it?" Greendale didn't offer the man any thanks, just heeled his horse into motion. "Come on, Lame Wolf."

"They won't let him in, you know."

The townsman's comment made Greendale stop again. "What was that?" he asked, half-turning his horse.

"They won't let him in." The townsman made a vague gesture in Lame Wolf's general direction. "Your friend. They don't cater to his sort."

Lame Wolf said, "What about darkies, Chinks, and greasers?"

The townsman looked a little surprised to hear the question come from the Crow. He nodded and said, "Yes, they'll accommodate men like that, as long as they have the money and the girls they choose don't object. Just not Indians."

Greendale said, "You seem to know a lot about the place for somebody who's never been there, mister."

The man flushed. "I've heard stories, that's all."

"Sure, sure." Greendale jerked his head. "Come on, Lame Wolf. They'll let you in, all right . . . or we'll burn the damn place down around their ears!"

They rode off, leaving the townsman staring after them, pale-faced and nervous.

Chapter 8

Madame Wilma's was right where the man had said it was. As the two riders approached along the hard-packed dirt lane leading to it from the main trail, Greendale studied the place.

As the townie had said, it was a nice-looking house, two stories, white-washed, with dark green trim around the windows. A small portico stood over the front entrance. Big trees surrounded the house. In the back was a coach house with an attached stable and corral.

Greendale could imagine a mining tycoon living here. Something must have happened to the man's mine. A cave-in, maybe, or else the vein of gold had just petered out. It was difficult to predict such things. But in the Gold Rush days, according to what Greendale had heard, a man could make a fortune overnight . . . and then lose it just as quickly.

Several saddled horses milled around in the corral. Greendale spotted a few buggies and buckboards parked back there, too. He grinned and pointed them out to Lame Wolf.

"The respectable citizens, like the one we talked to back yonder, don't want anybody knowin' they're payin' a visit to a house of ill repute," Greendale said. "So they hide their horses and buggies behind the place."

"They're not hidden very well," Lame Wolf pointed out. "We can see them."

"That's because it's all just for show. Folks know what's goin' on out here. They just pretend they don't. Say the fella who owns the hardware store pays a visit to Madame Wilma's to have hisself a little slap-and-tickle with one of the doves. The banker might know about it, but he dassn't say anything because the hardware man knows that *he's* been out here, too. So when they meet in town, they shake hands and talk about what the minister had to say in his sermon last Sunday, when what they're really thinkin' about is what they done last Friday and Saturday night."

Lame Wolf nodded slowly and said, "You are a deeply cynical man, Gus."

"If that means I know how the world really works, you're damn-tootin' I do." Greendale drew rein at an empty hitch rack in front of the house. "And I don't give a rat's behind who knows I'm here, neither, so we'll just tie our horses here."

The two men dismounted, looped their reins around the hitch rack, and went to the front door. Greendale had just raised his hand to knock on it when a loud crash sounded inside.

Shouted curses and a woman's scream immediately followed the crash. Footsteps stomped, men grunted, and fists thudded against flesh. Greendale grinned and said, "Sounds like they're havin' theirselves a high ol' time in there. Maybe we'd better see what's goin' on."

Lame Wolf just grunted and looked resigned to more trouble.

Greendale twisted the glass doorknob, which was cut in glittery facets, and shoved the door open. He stalked inside with Lame Wolf right behind him, only to come to an abrupt halt and duck hurriedly as a chair flew toward him from the left.

The chair struck Greendale's upraised left shoulder and staggered him, but it was only a glancing blow, so he didn't lose his footing. The impact made him angry as well as curious. He spotted the man who had flung the chair and lunged toward him, yanking his gun out as he did so.

The man saw Greendale drawing and clawed at his own holster, but he hadn't cleared leather before Greendale's Colt smashed into his head and knocked him to the floor. The man sighed and went still all over. The blow had knocked him out cold.

Greendale swung around to take in the chaotic scene in the house's big parlor. Knots of men battled here and there, slugging wildly at each other. The groups surged back and forth, knocking over chairs and spindle-legged tables. Several pieces of furniture were already in ruins. One man caught a fist to the jaw and flew backward to trip over a bench and fall onto a piano's keyboard, landing with a discordant crash of clashing notes.

On the other side of the room, a staircase led up to the second floor. Arranged along the stair railing, almost like a row of ducks in a shooting gallery, were half a dozen soiled doves displaying a considerable amount of flesh in an assortment of camisoles, bustiers, silk stockings, and near-transparent wraps. Some of them looked frightened, but others yelled encouragement to the battling men in the parlor.

At the bottom of the stairs stood a woman who was somewhat more decorously dressed in a long gown, but it was cut low enough that most of her heaving, ample bosom was right out there in the open for anybody to see. She screeched, "Stop it, you men! Stop it!" but none of the brawlers paid any attention to her.

Then, like a moving mountain, a huge man appeared in a hallway that led toward the rear of the house. His bald, black head shone in the light from the crystal chandeliers as he strode into the parlor. He wore a black suit and a collarless white shirt. A bright red flower was stuck in the buttonhole of his coat's left lapel.

Greendale had moved back alongside Lame Wolf. He grinned and nudged the Crow's ribs with an elbow as he said, "Here comes Tiny! He'll put a stop to this!"

But instead of interfering in the battle, the massive former member of the Greendale gang headed for the far side of the room. He broke up a couple of fights just by casually shouldering men aside, but clearly, restoring the peace wasn't his intention.

"Betsy!" he bellowed. "Betsy!"

Greendale looked in the direction Tiny was going, thinking that maybe one of the doves had gotten stuck on that side of the fight without him noticing her. But no woman was over there, he realized.

Only the piano.

"Betsy!" Tiny roared again, and when he reached the musical instrument, he laid his hands atop it as gently as if he were indeed caressing a woman.

A storm of profanity made Greendale look the other way again. Another familiar figure had appeared. Hank Singleton was blowing through the brawl like a whirlwind, lashing out right and left with the short, thick bludgeons he held in both hands. Every time Hank struck, a man fell, either knocked senseless or unable to keep fighting with a broken arm. Hank was only medium height, but he packed a lot of power in his wiry frame. The streaks of gray in his dark beard testified that prison life had aged him, but he was still extremely dangerous in a fight.

Hank had grown his hair long, Greendale noted, to hide the damage to his bullet-mutilated right ear.

While Hank broke up the fight, Tiny picked up the bench in front of the piano that had been knocked over, and set it upright. He put a toe under the unconscious man on the floor and rolled him out of the way like a child kicking aside a toy that no longer held any interest. Tiny sat down on the bench and brought his fingers to the keyboard.

The tune that floated up from the piano was beautiful, even counterpointed by the continued thuds as the clubs wielded by Hank knocked out the battlers.

After a moment, both sounds stopped. The brawl was over; Hank Singleton was the last man standing, except for Greendale and Lame Wolf. At the piano, Tiny heaved a sigh of relief and said, "Thank heavens she's all right."

Hank stared at Greendale and said, "Gus, is that you?"

"It dang sure is," Greendale replied. He let out a whoop. "Boy, howdy, you went to town on those fellas! Let me get this straight . . . *You're* the bouncer here, and not him?"

Greendale nodded toward Tiny, who ran his fingers over the piano's keys again and produced a cascade of pretty notes.

"Shoot, Tiny never did like to fight," Hank said. "I was born for it! And once he started workin' here, he found out that he's good at plunkin' away on that pi-anny. Even gave the damn thing a name!"

Hank stuck the clubs behind his belt and threw his arms around Greendale to slap the outlaw on the back.

"Damn, it's good to see you again, Gus!" He turned to Lame Wolf and greeted the Crow in the same fashion. "You, too, you filthy redskin!"

"And it is good to see you, as well, even though your ugliness still knows no bounds," Lame Wolf said.

Hank grinned, turned his head, and called, "Hey, Tiny, look who's here!"

Tiny stood up from the piano bench and came toward them. The grin on his face matched Hank's.

"Gus! Lame Wolf!" He wrapped his arms around both of them at the same time and drew them into a hearty embrace. "My old friends!"

"Ease up a mite," Greendale told him. "You're squeezin' so hard, I'm having a little trouble gettin' my breath."

As Tiny let go of them, except for resting a ham-like hand on their shoulders, the big-bosomed woman in the low-cut dress approached tentatively and said, "You know the Indian can't be in here, Hank."

"You mean Lame Wolf? But he's an old friend of mine."

The woman, who evidently was Madame Wilma, shook her head and said, "I'm sorry, but rules is rules."

"And rules was meant to be broken, especially among friends," Greendale said as he gave her a cold, angry stare.

Lame Wolf held up a hand. "It is all right. I will wait outside." He looked at the woman. "Is that all right, ma'am?"

"Yeah, I reckon. While you're goin', how about you help Hank and Tiny haul out some of these riff-raff?"

"Well, of all the nerve!" Gus exclaimed. "Kick you out and put you to work at the same time."

"I do not mind," Lame Wolf said. "It will be good to work with old friends again."

Showing that the dissipated life he had led the past few years hadn't sapped all his strength, he caught hold of two unconscious men by the ankles and dragged them out of the parlor. Tiny did likewise, followed by Hank with one of the brawlers. They deposited the senseless men to one side of the portico.

Greendale herded the men who were injured but still ambulatory out of the house and told them, "Climb on your horses and light a shuck, but not before emptyin' your pockets. You got a whole heap of damages in there to pay for."

"What about them other fellas?" one man protested with a wave toward the unconscious men. "They was fightin', too!"

"Leave them to me," Hank growled. "I'll go through their pockets and make sure they pay their fair share. For now, hand over what you got! Lame Wolf, you want to collect it?"

"Of course." Lame Wolf took off his hat and passed among the men. With great reluctance, they took coins and greenbacks out of their pockets and dumped the money in the Crow's hat. While that was going on, Hank began emptying the pockets of the men who'd been knocked out. They would come to broke and with headaches, but that was better than not coming to at all.

As the men struggled onto their horses and rode off, Greendale pawed through the loot in Lame Wolf's hat and said, "Just like old times, ain't it, boys?"

"Yeah, except we won't be keepin' this money," Hank said. "It's goin' to pay for what those hombres busted up in there."

"Yeah, but if there's some left over . . ."

"It still goes to Wilma," Tiny said. "She's been mighty good to Hank and me."

Greendale held up his hands, palms out. "That's fine, that's fine," he assured them. "Anyway, we'll be makin' a whole lot more money soon."

"How do you figure that?" Hank asked. "When we heard that you was outta prison, we thought you might come look us up, Gus. You know, get the bunch back together again. But you never did."

"I was gonna," Greendale said. "Just hadn't gotten around to it yet. I heard where you boys were, and I planned to come see you. I was just waitin' for the right job, though." He nodded emphatically. "And now I've found it."

That wasn't exactly true, he thought. Ambrose Neill had

come to him. He hadn't actually found anything. But the others didn't have to know that. They had always trusted his leadership, and there was no reason for that to change now.

"What is it?" Tiny asked.

"You're gonna like it." Greendale smiled. "We're about to get rich, boys, and even better, it's gonna come at the expense of the man who ruined everything for us in the first place."

"You mean . . . ?" Hank began.

"That's right," Greendale said. "Teddy Roosevelt his own damn self!"

Chapter 9

Deadwood

The Roosevelt family seemed to enjoy their walk from the train station to the Bullock Hotel, Seth thought. The town's hustle and bustle were infectious. Even Alice lost some of her sulkiness and peered around at the buildings and the people with interest.

Theodore, who everybody called Ted, and Kermit were the most caught up with excitement. "Can we see where Wild Bill Hickok was shot?" Kermit asked with a breathless note in his voice.

"Well, we're not going by the Number 10 Saloon right now," Bullock told him, "but I'll make sure you get to take a look at it later."

"What about Calamity Jane?" Ted asked. "Is she still alive? Will we run into her on the street?"

Bullock shook his head. "She's still alive, but she's not here in Deadwood right now. She's off performing in Bill Cody's Wild West Show. She comes back to Deadwood now and then, and I hear tell that when she passes away, she wants to be buried up in the Mount Moriah Cemetery, next to Wild Bill."

"That's appropriate," Alice said, "since they were lovers, I mean."

"Alice," her stepmother said sternly, "we didn't come all this way to discuss such scandalous things."

"Yes, ma'am," Alice said meekly, but Bullock could still see the interest glittering in her eyes.

Based on her comment, Alice, like her younger brothers, seemed to have gotten most of her information about Deadwood's notorious history from dime novels, Bullock reflected. He hadn't been here during Wild Bill's time in Deadwood; he and Sol Star had arrived to establish their hardware store just two days after Jack McCall's infamous ambush in the Number 10.

But he had been well-acquainted with plenty of people who had known both Hickok and Martha Jane Cannary, such as Colorado Charley Utter, and he was convinced that Bill and Calamity were never lovers. There was no doubt that Calamity Jane had admired Hickok and would have welcomed his attention and affection, but in all likelihood he hadn't returned the feeling and might not even have been aware of her existence. Calamity Jane had loved him from afar . . . or as far as one could get in the fairly small confines of the boomtown Deadwood had been in those days.

Bullock wasn't going to say anything about that to Alice Roosevelt or her little brothers, though. Once events were far enough in the past to take on a patina of history, most folks no longer had any interest in the truth. They didn't care how it really was; they just wanted the *stories*. And since that was what made them happy, Bullock didn't see any reason to shatter their illusions. Let the dashing gunman and the rough-around-the-edges but beautiful female scout be lovers. What did it hurt?

"While you're here, we'll be sure and go up to pay a visit to the cemetery," Bullock told the youngsters. "Lots of famous people buried there."

"And you know all the stories about them, don't you, Mr. Bullock?" Kermit asked.

"Most of them, son. Most of them."

Since they took their time strolling through town, the family's bags arrived at the hotel before they did. Bullock's staff knew to expect them, even though they weren't aware of the visitors' true identities, so the bags already had been taken up to the two suites the Roosevelts would occupy during their stay in Deadwood. Bullock saw to it that the visitors were all settled in, then told Mrs. Roosevelt he would return later and have dinner with them in the hotel dining room.

"I assure you, that's not necessary, Mr. Bullock," she said. The smile she gave him took any potential sting out of the words. "I don't want you to feel that you have to spend every waking moment catering to us. I'm sure you must have matters in your own life that need looking after."

Hat in hand, Bullock said, "As a matter of fact, ma'am, everything runs so smoothly around here that I'm pretty much at loose ends a lot of the time."

"I'm sure things run smoothly because of your supervision."

"Well, maybe. But your husband has been a good friend of mine for many years, and if there's anything I can do to make the visit here better for you and your family, I sure don't want to neglect it."

"All right. I'm certain we'll enjoy your company at dinner. I warn you, though, those two older boys of mine may talk your ear off with all their questions."

"That's all right, ma'am," Bullock assured her. "I enjoy talking about the old days."

Even though the stories he told might have to be cleaned up and embellished a mite, he cautioned himself wryly as he took the woman's gloved hand and bid her farewell for the time being.

* * *

"Do you think Mother would allow me to have a six-gun?" Kermit Roosevelt asked his older brother.

Instead of answering the question, Ted frowned and said, "Have you lost your mind?"

"We're in the Wild West, aren't we?"

"I'm not sure how wild it is anymore," Ted said. "Didn't you look around while we were walking over here? They have electric lights in Deadwood, and gas heat, and paved streets and brick buildings! Why, we might as well be back in Washington."

"Washington doesn't have hills and forests like are all around here."

"I suppose not," Ted allowed.

Kermit went to the window and pushed the curtain back. This second-floor room overlooked the main street, and a good view of the surrounding landscape was visible as well.

"Just look at it," Kermit said, waving a hand to indicate the steep, wooded slopes. "There could be anything hiding up there. Outlaws or savage Indians or grizzly bears."

"There aren't any hostiles in this area any longer, and I believe that by this time of year, most of the bears are either already hibernating or about to, so there shouldn't be any of them roaming around."

"What about outlaws, then? There could still be outlaws!"

"Not likely," Ted said with an older brother's smugness as he stuck his hands in his pockets and rocked back and forth on the balls of his feet. "Wild Bill Hickok ran them all off while he was here, and any he missed would have been taken care of by Mr. Bullock when he was sheriff."

"Those days were a long time ago," Kermit argued. "New outlaws could have moved in."

Ted shook his head and said, "You need to face it, little brother. I like seeing historical places, too, but those dime novels aren't real. Despite what happened in the past, Deadwood is a civilized, perfectly modern town."

Kermit sighed and said, "I suppose you're right." He remained there at the window a moment longer, holding back the curtain. A man standing on the other side of the street caught his attention. The man wore a topcoat and soft felt hat and was stockily built. He puffed on a cigar he had clenched between his teeth beneath a neatly trimmed mustache. Clearly, he wasn't a cowboy or a prospector or anything like that.

In fact, the man looked like dozens of men Kermit had seen on the streets of Washington and New York and Boston and other big cities he had visited. He was a businessman of some sort, nothing glamorous or exciting about him.

But he must have sensed someone watching him, because he raised his head and peered up at the windows on the hotel's second story. For a moment, his gaze locked with Kermit's. Something about it made the boy uneasy.

Then the man smiled, raised his hand, and flicked a fingertip against his hat brim in a salute of sorts. He spat out the cigar butt, which landed in the street, then stuck his hands in his overcoat pockets, turned, and walked away.

Kermit let the curtain fall shut. He was just being silly, he told himself. There had been no need for him to feel uneasy. The fellow had smiled at him, after all.

"All right," he said to his brother as he turned away from the window, "if you don't think Mother will allow me to have a six-shooter . . . how about a Bowie knife?"

The roast beef with all the trimmings in the hotel dining room was very good. Seth Bullock insisted on quality all the way around at his establishment. All the Roosevelts enjoyed it, as did Bullock.

When the meal was over, he and Mrs. Roosevelt lingered

over cups of coffee. The younger boys, Archibald and Quentin, yawned sleepily, as did the girl Ethel. Alice, Ted, and Kermit all seemed to be wide awake, however. As Mrs. Roosevelt had predicted, the older boys had spent most of the time asking Bullock questions about Deadwood's past.

Now Ted said, "I've heard that my father helped capture rustlers and other outlaws on several occasions. Is that true, Mr. Bullock?"

"He wrote a book about those days, didn't he?" Bullock responded with a smile. "I expect you've read it."

"I have . . . but I think there must have been other stories. Stories that Father left out of his writings because they were too lurid and violent."

"What we want to know," Kermit said, "is how many men he killed."

"Kermit!" Mrs. Roosevelt exclaimed. "That's hardly a suitable subject to discuss at the dinner table. Or anywhere else, I might add."

Bullock sipped his coffee and then said, "Boys, I reckon if there was something your pa wanted to talk about, he would've put it in his book. So if you want to know anything beyond that, you'll just have to ask him." He paused, then added, "I will say, though, that I never knew him to do anything that wasn't honorable . . . or necessary."

"So he *did* kill people," Ted said.

"Not what I said at all. You just talk to him about it when he gets here in a few days."

"That can't be too soon to suit me," Alice said. "I'll be happy to see him again."

"We all will, dear," Mrs. Roosevelt said.

Bullock looked down into his coffee cup again. Rumor had it that Alice Roosevelt didn't always get along with her stepmother. The two of them seemed cordial enough in the way they treated each other in public. What went on behind the walls of the White House—or any other house, for that matter—was none of his business.

"Mother . . ." Kermit said, clearly wanting something.

"What is it?"

"Do you think it would be all right if I bought a Bowie knife? I've saved up my own money for it!"

Mrs. Roosevelt stared at him in surprise. "Why in the world would you need a Bowie knife?" she asked after a moment.

"Well, you never know. There might be trouble. This is Deadwood, after all. The Wild West."

"Mr. Bullock."

"Yes, ma'am?"

"Do you believe there will be anything about our visit that would require my son to possess a deadly weapon such as a Bowie knife?"

Kermit turned an eager face toward Bullock. He hated to disappoint the boy, but he answered honestly, "I don't think it's very likely, ma'am."

"That's what I thought." Mrs. Roosevelt turned to Kermit. "No, you definitely may *not* purchase a Bowie knife, or any other sort of knife. Or a weapon of any kind."

Ted leaned closer to his younger brother, smirked, and said, "Told you."

Kermit looked down at the table and muttered, "Oh, shoot."

"What was that?" Mrs. Roosevelt asked sharply.

"I just said, uh . . . very well, Mother, dear."

She gazed at him narrow-eyed for a moment but didn't say anything else. Bullock saw the younger children hiding smiles behind their hands as they enjoyed Kermit's discomfiture.

Shortly after that, Mrs. Roosevelt got the youngsters up and, with Alice's help, ushered them out of the dining room. Through the arched entrance, Bullock watched them climb the stairs in the lobby, heading for their suites on the second floor. Their first day in Deadwood had been a success, he thought. The visitors from Washington were all enjoying themselves. He was glad he had thought to invite Teddy and his family.

But as he sat there, a sense of unease stole over him. He couldn't see any reason to feel that way. Everything was going fine so far. Whatever was bothering him, his gut was just wrong this time, he told himself.

He wished he could bring himself to believe that.

Chapter 10

The faint glow from a lantern hung on a nail driven into a post didn't reach to the far corners of the cavernous stable. The yellow circle of light was large enough to encompass the seven men who stood in the stable's wide center aisle, though.

Gus Greendale had Tiny to his left, Lame Wolf and Hank Singleton to his right. They had ridden back here to Deadwood from Spearfish, arriving around dusk. That had given Greendale enough time to meet briefly with Ambrose Neill and then round up the three men who stood before him.

He studied them now, hoping that he had picked good enough men to do the job. John Perry was the oldest of the trio, a weathered, gray-haired man who had been a road agent back in the days when the Deadwood stagecoach got held up on a pretty regular basis. Next to him was Nate Poore, a scrawny gent with a blond beard on his angular jaws. Rounding out the group was Oscar Sheehan, a black-bearded Irishman who seemed about as broad as he was tall. None of them had ever been very successful at any of their endeavors, ranging from freighting to prospecting to being outlaws.

Greendale didn't need all that much from them tonight, though.

"That's the job," he said. "You fellas reckon you can handle it?"

"We're just supposed to start a fight?" Perry said. "That's all?"

Poore pointed at Tiny and whined, "With him? Hell, he's as big as an ox! As two oxes put together!"

"I won't hurt you, little man," Tiny rumbled. "At least, I'll try not to."

"It won't be a real fight," Greendale explained patiently. "It's just got to look good enough to make people think it's real and come a-runnin' to see what's going on."

"That's three to one odds," Sheehan said. "Might not be much of a fight if it was real."

Lame Wolf surprised them by laughing. "Did you ever see a bear set upon by wolves?" he asked. "The bear is many, many times larger than the wolves, but it cannot strike in all directions at once. Three wolves can defeat a bear, if they are swift and diligent enough."

"None of that matters, damn it," Greendale said with irritation creeping into his voice. "You ain't wolves, Tiny ain't a bear, and it ain't a real fight I'm talkin' about. All I want is for you to cause enough of a ruckus to serve as a distraction. Get it now?"

Perry nodded and said, "I understand." Sheehan's head bobbed in agreement, too.

Poore still looked confused, but he said, "If my pards here think it's a good idea, I'll go along with it."

"It pays fifty bucks apiece," Perry said. "It's a good idea."

Sheehan grunted his agreement.

"Remember," Greendale said. "This happens right across the street from the Bullock Hotel." He pulled a turnip watch from one of the pockets of his canvas trousers and flipped it open. "One hour from now at nine o'clock. Got it?"

Perry, Poore, and Sheehan all nodded.

Nine o'clock would be late enough to make their move, Greendale and Neill had decided during their hurried meeting. The businesses in town would all be closed down except for the saloons. And by then, their quarry ought to be sound asleep in their beds in the hotel.

"You gonna pay us now?" Perry asked.

"What kind of numbskull do you take me for?" Greendale snorted. "If I give you that money now, you'll just go get drunk on it, and when I need you in an hour, you'll be passed out in some alley."

"But if you don't pay us now, you're liable to run off and never pay up, even after we done your dirty work for you," Poore complained.

Greendale dug some coins out of his pocket and flipped a double eagle to each man, the coins glittering in the lanternlight as they spun through the air. Perry and Sheehan caught theirs, but Poore fumbled his double eagle and dropped it in the dirt at his feet. He scooped it up like a starving man going after a morsel of meat.

"You just be where you're supposed to be and do what you're supposed to do," Greendale warned them. "If you don't . . . if this whole scheme falls through because of you . . . I'll hunt you down and kill you, every damned one of you. You got my word on that."

"Don't worry, Gus," Perry said. "You can count on us."

"You meet up with Tiny here, after the fight, when enough time's past for all the hullaballoo to die down. He'll give you the rest of your money."

Tiny nodded to confirm Greendale's words.

With that, the meeting was over. The trio shuffled out the barn's rear door. As Hank Singleton watched them go, he said, "*Can* we count on them, Gus? You know them better than any of us do."

"Yeah, I think we can," Greendale said. "Nate Poore's dumber than dirt, and Sheehan ain't much smarter. But John Perry's a canny old fox, even if he's ridden in hard luck most of his life. He'll keep the other two in line."

Greendale wasn't the praying sort, but he sure hoped that turned out to be the case.

"And you want me to take it easy on them?" Tiny said. "Not bust them up too bad?"

"That's right. Mostly we just need the fight to be loud and attract a lot of attention. That way nobody'll notice when we ride off with whoever we grab from the hotel."

"That Alice gal," Hank said. "She's the one we want. She's a looker, Gus. Her ma ain't bad for an older lady, neither. Them's the ones we need to grab."

Greendale knew that Edith Roosevelt wasn't actually Alice's mother, but he didn't bother correcting Hank. For their purposes, it didn't really matter.

"They have two suites, with two bedrooms each," he said. "I know which one the gals are in. Roosevelt's wife is in one of the bedrooms, and the two girls are in the other. Takin' them makes the most sense. With any luck, the boys won't even realize their ma and sisters are gone until morning, and by then we'll be a long way from Deadwood."

Hank rubbed his hands together. "We're gonna be rich, boys. Rich!"

Lame Wolf asked, "How will we get word to Roosevelt and demand the ransom?"

"My partner will take care of that," Greendale said without naming Neill. The former inspector from New York wanted his connection to remain a secret for the time being, although if everything went as planned, he would join them later, after the kidnapping was successful and the message to Roosevelt had been delivered.

Neill, like the rest of them, certainly wanted to be on hand when Teddy finally got his comeuppance. At that point, it wouldn't matter if the others knew who he was.

Tiny frowned and said, "I'm a little worried. It'll just be the three of you, to keep three prisoners under control. Can you manage that?"

"One of 'em will be a little girl, and Teddy's wife's an older lady. They won't give us any trouble. The only one liable to raise a real fuss is the older girl."

Hank licked his lips. "Leave her to me, Gus," he said. "I can handle her."

Greendale pointed a finger at him and said, "Not too rough, you understand? Nothin' too bad happens to any of them, Miss Alice included, until we got Teddy and the money in our hands and it don't matter anymore."

"Yeah, sure, Gus. Don't worry."

Despite that, Greendale knew that he *was* going to worry. He would worry until the three Roosevelt gals were their prisoners and that wire demanding the ransom was winging its way to Washington.

The ransom to be delivered by Teddy Roosevelt his own self . . . with death waiting for him.

Greendale opened his watch again, studied its face, and said, "All right. Time for us to start gettin' ready."

Deep in the shadows of the alley that ran between the Bullock Hotel and the next building, Greendale stood with Hank Singleton and Lame Wolf, watching as Tiny strolled along the street. He was so big and so thickly covered with muscles that his arms stuck out a little from his sides. Greendale had checked his watch just a few minutes earlier, angling it so that a stray beam of light penetrated the gloom and touched its face, and he knew that the other three men should be showing up any time now.

"Where in blazes are they?" Singleton muttered. "Tiny can't just keep paradin' up and down the street like that all night. Somebody's bound to notice sooner or later and realize that somethin' funny is goin' on."

"They'll be here," Greendale said, but he wasn't sure if he was trying to convince Singleton of that . . . or himself.

"There," Lame Wolf said. He pointed. "They're coming."

Greendale leaned forward a little so he could peer farther along the street. The Crow was right. Perry, Sheehan, and Poore were walking along the street toward Tiny. They were a little unsteady, telling Greendale that they had spent some of the advance money on whiskey, despite his warning. But at least they weren't falling down drunk, and it didn't really matter if they were a little soused. That would just make the brawl more believable.

Tiny had to adjust his course a little to make sure the three men intercepted him. He did so, and a moment later, Sheehan bumped heavily into the big man's chest.

Sheehan was a good-sized hombre himself, but he bounced off the massive obstacle that Tiny formed. As he staggered back a step and caught his balance, he said in a loud, angry voice, "Hey! Watch where you're goin', you damn—"

He launched into a tirade of obscenities and slurs regarding Tiny's ancestry, eyesight, and general demeanor. Perry and Poore joined in, urging their companion on in his verbal abuse. The rant was offensive enough that no one would see anything unusual about it provoking a fight, and loud enough that most of the people on the street heard it and looked in that direction.

Tiny stood it for several moments, then, without warning, snapped a short but powerful punch into Sheehan's face. The blow lifted him off his feet and dumped him on his back.

"Damn, he hit him too hard!" Singleton exclaimed in the alley. "He knocked him out!"

"No, Tiny pulled his punch," Greendale said. "I could tell. Look, Sheehan's gettin' up."

That was true. Perry and Poore had shouted more curses already and lunged at Tiny, swinging punches as they attacked. Sheehan clambered to his feet, shook his head, and dived into the fracas, too. Tiny started bellowing at the top of his lungs, adding his voice to the clamoring commotion.

Along the street, other men yelled in excitement and hurried toward the scene. Deadwood might be civilized these days, at least in comparison to its boom years, but a fight would always draw eager spectators, no matter how settled down a place was supposed to be.

Greendale grinned and said, "That's it! Let's go!"

The three would-be kidnappers hurried through the shadows toward the hotel's rear entrance and the narrow staircase just inside.

Ted was sound asleep, snores coming from his bed, but Kermit was still awake, staring up at the darkened ceiling and brooding. All he'd wanted was a six-gun, maybe the same kind that Wild Bill Hickok had carried. Although in the end, those guns hadn't saved Wild Bill, had they? Of course, he'd been ambushed from behind by a craven coward, so he never really had the chance to defend himself . . .

Kermit supposed he could understand why his mother had forbidden him to have a firearm. But a knife wouldn't have hurt anything. He *needed* something to protect himself, and to protect his mother and sisters, if need be. Ted was big and buff and hearty, like their father, but Kermit was on the slender side. He took more after their mother. He wasn't likely to win many fistfights.

What was the old saying? *God created all men, but Colonel Sam Colt made them equal.*

His mother ought to be smart enough to understand that, Kermit thought.

Then, out on the street, men began to shout. Kermit heard a lot of words he wasn't supposed to know, even though, actually, he had heard them before. Most of them, anyway. It sounded like somebody was really scrapping out there.

Kermit swung his legs out of bed and hurried to the window, which had been raised an inch or so to let in fresh air despite the chilly weather. His father was a firm believer in the strengthening qualities of fresh air. Kermit pushed the curtain aside and peered out.

He was right. There *was* a fight going on. Although it was a bit difficult to make out the details in the poor light, it appeared that three men had another man surrounded and were hammering punches at him. The target of those blows, who was the largest man Kermit had ever seen, shrugged them off and swung arms that were as thick as the trunks of small trees. He battered his attackers, causing them to fall back, but they always relaunched their assault.

It was epic, Kermit thought. A battle of giants. Of titans. He had to get a better view.

But instead, the view suddenly got worse as the knot of combatants shifted farther along the street.

He could get a better look at what was going on from the window in the sitting room of the other suite, he realized. Without hesitation, barefoot and wearing his nightshirt, Kermit whirled away from the window, hurried out through the sitting room, where a gas lamp still burned with the flame turned very low, and went out into the hall.

He didn't knock on the door of the next suite. If he did, his mother would just answer the summons and order him back to bed. She wouldn't understand if he told her he wanted to watch a fight in the street. She'd just say that such things were beneath him.

Kermit twisted the knob and was relieved to discover that

it wasn't locked. Most Western folks didn't lock their doors, he knew from his dime novel reading. He went inside, eased the door closed behind him, and hurried across the sitting room to the window. A gas lamp burned with a low flame in this room, too.

He was right, he saw as he pushed the curtain back. The brawl was still going on, right in front of him now. He leaned forward, watching avidly, close enough to the window that his breath made the glass fog a little. He lifted his arm and wiped that way with the sleeve of his nightshirt.

A hand fell on his shoulder. "Kermit, what do you think you're doing? I heard somebody sneaking around out here, and I should have known it would be you."

Kermit jumped in surprise but controlled the reaction quickly. The voice that demanded an answer was female, of course, but he knew even before he twisted his head to look around that it belonged to his half-sister, not his mother.

"There's a big fight out in the street, Alice," he told her. "Look."

"Why would I care about such a thing?" she asked. But she leaned forward, too, and looked over Kermit's shoulder. She wore only her nightdress, and her feet were bare like his. Her thick, dark hair was loose and down around her shoulders, tousled somewhat from sleep.

"See?" Kermit said. "They're whaling the tar out of each other."

"Don't speak so uncouthly," she told him. "Merciful heavens, that man is *large*. I'm not sure I've ever seen a man quite that big before."

"Yeah, but he's outnumbered. It's three to one."

"I'm not sure that's going to make any difference. He almost seems to be toying with them—"

Before Alice could say anything else, they both heard a door open quietly behind them and glanced over their shoulders, thinking that their mother was about to emerge from her bedroom and put an end to their observation of the pugilistic spectacle in the street.

It wasn't the door to Edith Roosevelt's room that had opened, however. It was the one leading to the hall, and coming through it were three men: an evil-looking one wearing a hat with a turned-up brim, one with a black beard who looked like a villain from the drawings on those yellow-backed dime novels Kermit read, and an Indian with his hair in braids, wearing a round-crowned black hat with a feather stuck in the band.

As soon as Kermit laid eyes on them, he realized they were up to no good, and so did Alice. She opened her mouth wide to scream.

Chapter 11

Gus Greendale bit back a curse as he instantly took in the scene in the dim light from the lamp in a wall sconce.

The oldest Roosevelt girl, Alice, stood at the sitting room window with an arm raised in surprise and fear in front of her. One of the boys was beside her. Greendale didn't know which one he was, right off hand, but whichever of the brothers he was, he wasn't supposed to be in here.

In fact, no one was supposed to be in the sitting room. The three Roosevelt females should have been sound asleep in their beds, so that Greendale and his companions could slip in, grab them and make sure they didn't holler, and then spirit them out of the hotel through the back.

That part of the plan was shot all to hell.

But that didn't mean things couldn't be salvaged. Those thoughts flashed through Greendale's brain in an instant, while he was already moving across the sitting room toward the two youngsters as fast as he could.

The girl had her mouth open to scream, but she flinched back from Greendale's charge and that kept her quiet for a vital second. All she managed to get out was a short yelp before his outstretched hand clamped over her mouth. He grabbed her around the waist with his other arm to pull her away from the window.

The boy hauled off and punched Greendale in the ribs. He was fourteen or fifteen, but not very big, and he didn't pack much power in the punch. Still, it was enough to throw Greendale off his stride. As he stumbled, the girl tried to twist free of his grip. He couldn't help but be aware of the supple body under the nightdress, unencumbered by the usual stays and corsets and foofaraws high-class women wore, but there was no time to think about that now.

He gasped in pain as she sunk her teeth into the ball of his hand.

He jerked that hand back, and as he saw the smear of blood on it from her bite, fury welled up inside him. She was Teddy's daughter, he reminded himself. So she had a lot worse coming, he thought as he closed the hand into a fist and slammed it into her jaw, knocking her head to the side. She sagged in his grasp, stunned by the blow.

By now, Hank Singleton had swooped in, grabbed the boy around the chest from behind, and jerked him up off his feet. Singleton's other hand closed cruelly over the boy's mouth, muffling the outcry he tried to make. Singleton backed into the center of the room so that the boy's flailing kicks couldn't hit anything.

"Damn it, Gus, *now* what do we do?" he asked in a harsh whisper.

Alice moaned. Greendale was tempted to hit her again and knock her out cold, but he wouldn't do that unless he had to. He might hurt her worse than he intended, and he didn't want that to happen until they had her father, too.

"The woman?" Lame Wolf asked with a nod toward the door of Mrs. Roosevelt's bedroom.

Greendale thought quickly. "Leave her," he said, reaching an abrupt decision. "The other girl, too. We've got these two. They'll be enough to make Teddy do what we want."

For a second, Lame Wolf and Singleton both looked unconvinced. But then Lame Wolf nodded and said, "The girl made enough noise that her mother may have heard her. We should leave undetected while we still can."

"Yeah, I reckon," Singleton said. He put his mouth close to the boy's ear and growled, "Quit wigglin' around, you damn little tadpole! I'll break your damn neck if you don't settle down."

The youngster's eyes were wide with terror, but the threat must have penetrated his brain. He stopped fighting.

Greendale yanked a bandanna out of his pocket and hurriedly stuffed it between Alice's lips as a gag as well as to keep her from biting him again as he put his hand over her mouth. He tightened his other arm around her waist and nodded toward the door, saying to Lame Wolf, "Take a look and make sure the hall's empty."

The Crow checked the corridor and returned Greendale's nod. "No one out there."

So, luck might have deserted them briefly, but now it was on their side again, Greendale told himself as they hustled the prisoners out of the sitting room and into the hallway.

They didn't encounter anyone as they took Alice and the boy down the back steps and out into the alley where their horses waited. They had three extra mounts, since they had intended to take three captives with them when they fled Deadwood, but getting the prisoners on their own horses could wait. For now, Greendale and his men needed to hang on to the captives. Lame Wolf could lead the extra mounts.

Greendale and Lame Wolf lifted Alice onto Greendale's horse and Greendale swung up in the saddle behind her. Lame Wolf and Hank Singleton did the same with the boy. From the glances Greendale had gotten at Singleton's face, he could tell Hank was disappointed that it wasn't him with the girl pressed up against him. But that was just too damn bad. They had more important things to worry about now.

Lame Wolf grabbed the lead ropes of the extra horses, mounted up, and led the way through the alleys to the edge of town. They could hear shouting from the main street that told them the staged fight was still going on. That part of the plan had worked, anyway.

And so would the rest of it, Greendale told himself. He remained tense, ready to grab a gun and shoot his way out if necessary, but the three of them and the two captives made it out of Deadwood without a hitch.

Greendale called a halt atop one of the hills overlooking the town, not far from the cemetery. This was the rendezvous he and Neill had arranged.

Sure enough, the man from New York was waiting for them. Mounted on a horse, he moved out of the shadows to meet them, his sudden appearance prompting Singleton to curse and Lame Wolf to reach for a gun.

"Take it easy, boys," Greendale said quickly. "This fella's our partner."

At least, he hoped the shadowy figure was Ambrose Neill. If it wasn't, they might all be in bad trouble . . .

"What happened?" The question came in a familiar Eastern accent tinged with a hint of Ireland. "You were supposed to have three prisoners. And that's not the little girl."

Greendale sniffed and said, "Things changed. But it's all right. As a hostage, the boy's just as good as the girl, and maybe it's a good thing we didn't bring their ma. She'll just put that much more pressure on Teddy to go along with what we want."

For a long moment, Neill didn't respond. Then he grunted and said, "I suppose. Anyway, it's too late to do anything except make do with what we have, isn't it?"

"That's right."

"We'll meet at the place you told me about? The one you drew the map to?"

"Yeah." Greendale laughed. "It's the best place I can think of to finally settle the score."

"Very well. Be careful with them. We don't want anything happening to them until they've served their purpose."

"Don't you worry about that. Just send that telegram to Washington."

"I'll send it as soon as I reach Rapid City tomorrow," Neill promised. A vicious, hissing tone crept into his voice as he added, "And we'll be one step closer to our revenge."

Nate Poore groaned and complained, "I'm gonna be stove up for a week. Every time that big varmint hit me, it felt like I'd been walloped by a two-by-four."

"Shut up," John Perry said. "You keep flappin' your gums that way, he's gonna hear us and know that we're followin' him."

The three men rode at a slow, careful pace through the darkness. For one thing, even though they knew this part of the country pretty well, the ruggedness of the terrain made caution important. A misstep could send both horse and rider tumbling down a steep slope. The area was crisscrossed with gulches and ravines, too, and falling into one would be fatal.

Not only that, but they didn't want to close in too much on their quarry, either, and alert the massive black man that somebody was trailing him.

Perry was the one who had come up with the idea, after they had met Tiny in the deserted livery barn and collected the rest of the money Gus Greendale had promised them. About an hour had passed since the fight had ended in a stand-off. Perry, Sheehan, and Poore were all battered, bruised, and bloody. Tiny didn't have a mark on him and hadn't even been breathing hard when they finally stopped fighting.

He paid them off, though, which was all Sheehan and

Poore cared about. They were already thinking about all the bottles of whiskey this windfall would buy for them.

Perry was the only one of the trio who took a longer view of things. Fifty bucks was a good payoff, to be sure . . . but there might be something even better waiting for them on down the trail, if they played this right.

"Hold on, boys," he'd said as the other two were about to make a beeline for the nearest saloon. "I been thinkin'—"

"Oh, hell, John, there's no time for that," Sheehan said. "We're gonna have us a real bender, and we need to get started on it."

"Is that all you want to do?" Perry snapped. "Just go from bender to bender?"

Poore chortled. "Sounds like a pretty good idea to me!"

"Maybe we could make ourselves some real money," Perry said. "Enough to maybe take us all the way to Mexico."

Going to Mexico was a dream the three of them had worked up during their friendship. They had never been south of the border, or anywhere close to it, to be honest, but they'd heard about how the weather was warm there, and the girls were warm, too, and mighty willing, and they had a drink there called tequila that would set a man plumb on fire from gizzard to gullet. It sounded like a hell of a place.

"All right, John," Sheehan had said after a moment. "You was always the smartest one of the bunch. Tell us your idea."

"You think I'm smart, but Gus Greendale's a hell of a lot smarter. Whatever he's up to, whatever reason he had for payin' us to get in that fight with the big fella, I figure it's got to be something that'll pay off mighty good for him. I mean, he just gave us a hundred and fifty bucks tonight like it was nothin'."

Sheehan muttered and nodded as if Perry's words made sense, and Poore followed suit as he always did, since that was easier than straining his brain trying to think for himself.

"I figure Tiny's gonna meet up with Greendale and them

other two boys," Perry went on. "Whatever they were gonna do while we had the whole town watchin' us, they've gone and done it by now. So if we follow Tiny until he joins back up with 'em, maybe we can talk Gus into cuttin' us in on the deal. I mean . . . we helped him out, didn't we? For all we know, he couldn't have pulled off the job unless we done what we did."

"You know, that makes sense," Sheehan said, sounding astounded that anybody had been able to think through such a complicated matter. "What if Greendale won't cut us in, though?"

"They're bound to have the loot, whatever it is, with them. Maybe we'll just take the whole jackpot for ourselves."

"I don't know," Poore said. "Gus Greendale's a bad hombre to cross, from everything I've heard."

"And I don't want to tangle with that Tiny again, and sure as hell not in a real fight," Sheehan added.

"Greendale can't do a thing to stop us if he's got a bullet in his head," Perry declared, "and if a few rounds from a Winchester will bring down a grizzly, they'll sure as hell cut Tiny down to size."

"You're talkin' about ambushin' 'em."

"You got a problem with that?"

Sheehan considered and then said with a shrug, "No, not really. We'd need to make sure we didn't leave any of 'em alive, though. I don't want any of that bunch on my trail, even that ol' drunk Indian."

"Maybe it won't come to that," Perry had said. "We'll try to strike a deal with them first. Unless, of course, the right chance comes along . . ."

"If we're gonna follow Tiny, hadn't we better do it?" Poore suggested.

Out of the mouths of idiots, Perry had thought at the time. But Poore was right. They had hurried off in the same direction Tiny had gone and were lucky enough to spot him on horseback, heading out of Deadwood. Even at night, it was hard to miss anybody that big. Quickly, they had saddled their own nags and set off after him.

Now it was long after midnight, and they were miles north of Deadwood. They had been tracking Tiny by the sound of his horse. Nate might not be very smart, but he had mighty good ears when it came to hearing.

"Hold it," Perry whispered as he reined in. He had just spotted an orange glow up ahead. It appeared and disappeared when he moved his head, telling him that there were a lot of trees between him and the fire. That was good, because the growth would serve as cover.

At his low-voiced orders, they dismounted and went ahead on foot, taking extreme care now not to make any more noise than was necessary. A chilly wind blew out of the north. That was good, because it wouldn't carry the scent of their horses to the other mounts and cause them to react.

Finally, they were so close that Perry didn't trust his companions to keep going without giving away their presence. He put his head close to theirs and breathed, "You boys stay here. I'll crawl on ahead and try to get a look."

"You think it's them?" Sheehan rumbled.

"It's almost got to be. I don't know who else'd be out here."

In truth, there were several other possible explanations for coming across a campfire here in the Black Hills. Hunters, maybe, or woodcutters. Maybe even prospectors. Even though the gold rush was long over and the mines all belonged to big corporations these days, there were a few old-timers who still roamed the hills in search of the precious metal.

Perry's gut told him otherwise, however. That fire belonged to the men they were after. He was sure of it. He wanted to slip up close enough to confirm that and maybe even eavesdrop, if anybody was still awake to talk, and find out what was really going on.

He set off on his belly, pushing himself along on elbows and knees. Following the flickering light from the flames and the smell of woodsmoke, he closed in and at last was able to carefully part some brush and peer through the gap he created.

The camp belonged to Greendale and the rest of his bunch, sure enough! There was no mistaking the huge shape of Tiny, wrapped up in a buffalo robe, asleep near the fire. Hank Singleton sat on a log on the other side of the fire, not far from a big slab of rock that jutted up to overhang the camp. Singleton was standing guard, Perry figured. Those blanket-wrapped shapes on the other side of the fire had to be Greendale and the Indian . . .

But if that was true, then who were the *other two* stretched out and covered with blankets? There were four shapes over there, not two. Were the others asleep, or were they . . . dead?

No, not dead, Perry thought as he watched raptly, because one of the shapes moved as whoever it was inside the blankets shifted around. The blankets fell away in one place. Perry saw bare arms with the wrists held together as if they were tied. They *were* tied, he realized a moment later, lashed together with strips of rawhide. And when he followed those bare arms up, he saw . . .

Hank Singleton saw, too, and stood up to move around the fire, cat-footing so he wouldn't wake any of the sleepers. He hunkered next to the gal, grasped the edge of the blanket, and moved it back a little farther, revealing thick dark hair pillowed on a rolled-up blanket and more of a bare, creamy shoulder where her nightdress had slipped down.

Singleton gazed at the young woman with undisguised lust, but he didn't try to touch her. He might have given in to the temptation to do that anyway, but just then, the ominous sound of a pistol being cocked filled the night air.

"Get away from her, Hank," Gus Greendale ordered from where he lay propped up on one elbow, the other hand holding the revolver he aimed at Singleton. "You know I don't want to shoot you, but I'll damn sure do it if I have to."

Gus Greendale was a light sleeper. Always had been. He'd had to be in order to survive, first on the owlhoot trails and then, later, during all those years in prison where trouble could slip up on a fella without any warning.

So he wasn't surprised that he had roused from his slumber when Hank Singleton started creeping around. Nor was he all that surprised to see Hank kneeling next to the sleeping Alice Roosevelt and leering at the flesh her shifting around had exposed.

Hank knew better than to be doing that, of course; Greendale's orders to leave the girl alone had been clear. But Hank didn't have much willpower when it came to such things. He was drawn to females like a moth to flame . . . and if he wasn't careful, he'd end up like that damn moth, consumed by his own instincts.

Greendale drew his gun quietly and pointed it at Hank, who never noticed until Greendale eared back the revolver's hammer. That sound was ominous enough to penetrate even Singleton's lust-fogged brain.

His head snapped around as Greendale ordered him to get away from the girl. Singleton's mouth opened and closed. He said, "What . . . Damn it, Gus—"

"You heard me," Greendale said. "Stand up and move away from her."

"All right, all right," Singleton muttered sullenly. "I'm goin', blast it."

He rose to his feet. By now, the talking had stirred Alice Roosevelt from the sleep that exhaustion had forced on her.

Her eyelids fluttered open, and when she saw Singleton looming over her, she gasped, cringed, and tugged at the blanket to wrap it tighter around her.

"Take it easy, Miss Roosevelt," Greendale said. "Hank ain't gonna hurt you."

"What . . . what is he doing?" she managed to say.

"Just checkin' on you, that's all. You're all right, and so's your little brother."

Alice's gaze darted over to where Kermit slept. By now, Greendale knew the boy's name. He had questioned Alice while they were riding and found out that the desire to get a better look at the fight in the street had lured the youngster into the other suite.

There was no way he could have predicted that, Greendale told himself. It was just another of those twists of fate that challenged any man who dared try to grasp what he wanted from a world stubbornly determined not to give it up.

Singleton walked back around the fire and, with a sigh, sat down on the log again.

"Put your gun up, Gus," he said. "You don't need it."

"You sure about that?"

"Yeah, I'm sure."

"Don't forget it, then." Greendale lowered the Colt's hammer and slipped it back into the holster attached to the coiled shell belt on the ground beside him.

Alice glanced back and forth between them, clearly suspecting that more had gone on here than Greendale was willing to admit. She didn't press the issue, though, as she clutched the blankets around her throat.

After a moment, she said, "It's cold. If you're going to force my brother and me to go with you, you're going to have to give us some clothes, at least."

"We gave you socks to keep your feet warm," Greendale said. "What more do you want?"

In a way, he liked the idea of keeping the prisoners in

their nightclothes. That would make them less likely to try to escape, because they'd surely freeze out here with nothing more to protect them than that.

But such a move also meant that Hank Singleton would continue to be tempted even more by the pretty girl, and it was possible the captives might catch the grippe and die of it, which would be inconvenient if it happened too soon.

Alice was still glaring at him in the firelight. Greendale said, "All right, damn it. Come mornin', we'll rustle through our gear and see if we can find some things for you and the boy to wear. Don't get the idea that you're the boss around here, though. You're still our prisoners, missy."

Alice sniffed and said, "I don't think I'm liable to get confused about that, seeing as how you have us tied hand and foot. You're going to have to do something about *that*, too. Wherever we're going, if we have to ride horseback the entire way, you'll have to cut us loose."

"Could just sling you belly-down over the saddle and tie you in place," Singleton said. "I wouldn't mind doin' that."

"Hank . . ." Greendale said warningly.

Singleton held up his hands, palms out in surrender, and didn't say anything else.

"We'll make sure you can ride without bein' too uncomfortable," Greendale told the girl. "From what I hear, you're pretty smart. You know there's no place for you to go out here. If you try to run off, you'll just wind up freezin' to death or fallin' in a ravine or gettin' eaten by a grizzly or a mountain lion. The Black Hills are no place for a couple of kids on their own."

Alice looked down and muttered, "I know that."

"On the other hand," Greendale went on, "if you just come along with us and do as you're told, there's a mighty good chance that you and your brother will come outta this whole thing just fine."

That was a flat-out lie, of course. Greendale intended for

both of the captives to die . . . but not until their father was there to witness the deaths and suffer accordingly.

Telling the girl wouldn't serve any purpose, though. It would just make things worse. Let the two of them have a shred of hope to cling to . . .

"Where is it we're going?" Alice asked.

The question took Greendale a little by surprise, and he blurted out the answer before he stopped to think about it.

"A place you've never heard of," he said. "A place that's a hell of a long way from anywhere. Back in the old days, folks used to call it The Dutchman's . . ."

CHAPTER 12

Deadwood

Seth Bullock sat at one of the tables in the hotel dining room, sipping from a cup of coffee and reading a copy of that morning's newspaper. He didn't live at the hotel; he and his wife Martha had their own house, so he nearly always took his breakfast there, as he had today. But he liked to come here fairly early, sit in the dining room or the lobby, and get a sense of what the day was going to be like.

Today seemed promising. The newspaper was full of stories about the upcoming celebration. Bullock smiled. The stories would be even more breathless and exciting if the reporters knew who was going to be in attendance. It wasn't often that Deadwood welcomed a visitor as famous as Teddy Roosevelt.

As if Fate knew what Bullock was thinking, Edith Roosevelt hurried into the dining room at that moment and paused just inside the entrance to look around as if searching for someone.

Bullock frowned slightly. Mrs. Roosevelt was fully dressed, of course, but her clothing seemed a bit disarrayed. She appeared to have thrown it on quickly and carelessly. Likewise, her hair was pulled back and pinned into place, but it wasn't neatly combed and as carefully arranged as it normally would be.

The feeling Bullock suddenly experienced in the pit of his stomach told him that maybe the day wasn't going to be as pleasant as he had thought it would be, after all.

He stood up, and at that moment, Mrs. Roosevelt spotted him and came toward him. He could tell from her expression that she was upset about something.

"Good morning," he said as she walked up to the table.

She didn't bother returning the greeting. She just said, "Have you seen my children?"

"No, as a matter of fact, I haven't. Do you mean all of—"

"Alice and Kermit," she broke in. "They're gone."

That ball of worry rolling around in Bullock's guts got bigger. "Maybe they're out looking around the town," he suggested. "That Kermit, his eyes were really full yesterday while I was showing you folks the sights."

"If it were Kermit and Ted who were missing, I might agree with you," Mrs. Roosevelt said. "But Alice has never been enthusiastic about this trip. She's not really interested in history like the boys are."

"Kermit could have dragged her out anyway—"

Again, Mrs. Roosevelt interrupted him. "None of their clothes are gone, not even their shoes." Her expression grew even more bleak. "They wouldn't be wandering around Deadwood barefoot, in nothing but their nightclothes."

"No," Bullock agreed, "I don't reckon they would."

He stepped around the table and risked lightly putting a hand on her elbow to steer her out of the dining room. She might be his old friend's wife, but she was also the First Lady of the United States. She had to be treated carefully, and with the utmost respect. He left the half-drunk cup of coffee and the newspaper on the table behind them, completely forgotten now. "Let's go back up to your suites."

"We must notify the authorities," Mrs. Roosevelt said with

a note of hysteria creeping into her voice. From everything Bullock knew about her, she was a strong, level-headed woman . . . but when a woman's children were missing or threatened, how she was at all the other times didn't mean a damned thing.

He didn't want her having a breakdown right here in the crowded dining room, though, so he kept his own voice as quiet and calm and reassuring as he could as he said, "I'm sure they're around here somewhere. We'll get to the bottom of this very quickly, don't you worry about that."

His words didn't do much good, but maybe a little. She allowed him to guide her out of the dining room, into the lobby, and toward the stairs.

"Tell me exactly what happened," he said as they started up to the second floor.

"Ethel woke me a short time ago," Mrs. Roosevelt explained. "She said that Alice wasn't in their room."

"But her bed had been slept in?"

"Yes, they were both in there when Ethel went to sleep. She was sure Alice was asleep, too."

"What did you do?"

"I thought she might be in the other suite with her brothers, so I went there. But Ted had just awoken, as well, and discovered that Kermit was gone. He swore to me that he had no idea when Kermit had gotten up or where he might have gotten off to. When I woke the younger boys, they knew nothing about it, either."

They had reached the second-floor corridor. Bullock paused with his hand on the gleaming brass knob of the door that opened into the suite shared by Mrs. Roosevelt and the two girls.

"What did you do next?"

"I checked to see if any of their clothes were missing. Like you, Mr. Bullock, my first thought was that they had left the hotel early for some reason unfathomable to me. But when I realized that wherever they had gone, they had to be in their nightclothes, I knew something had to be dreadfully wrong."

"No offense, ma'am, but it doesn't pay to jump to conclusions."

"It doesn't pay to doubt a mother's instincts, either," she said sharply.

"Uh, no, ma'am, it sure doesn't. Is your younger daughter in here?"

"No, she's over with her brothers. I've charged Ted with watching the younger ones. He's quite capable."

"Yes, ma'am." Bullock twisted the knob, then looked at her. "Were these doors locked last night?"

"No, I don't believe they were. Theodore has always talked about how hospitable and trustworthy Westerners are, so I didn't believe it was necessary."

Bullock didn't allow his face to show how he felt about that. Instead he went into the suite's sitting room and started looking around.

"It was like this when you got up? Nothing out of place, no signs of a disturbance?"

"No, none." Mrs. Roosevelt frowned. "There *was* one thing a bit unusual. The curtains over the window were pushed back, and I'm sure they had been drawn closed before we went to bed last night. Does that mean anything?"

Bullock examined the window. The pane was closed, but the curtains were definitely open.

"Don't know," he said in reply to Mrs. Roosevelt's question. He went to the doors that led into the bedrooms. "Which one is the girls'?"

She pointed it out. He opened the door and looked into the room. The covers on the bed were thrown back and rumpled, but other than that the room looked as neat as Bullock insisted that all the rooms in the hotel be kept.

Bullock turned away from the bedroom, then stiffened as

something caught his attention that he hadn't noticed before. He had spotted a small, dark spot on the polished wooden floor near the window. He didn't want to examine it more closely while Mrs. Roosevelt was in the room, but it looked to him like a small drop of blood.

Better one small drop than a lot of blood, he told himself, but still, it was quite concerning.

"Let's go talk to the boys," he said.

The first thing he did when he stepped into the sitting room of the other suite was to look at the window. The curtain was pushed back on this one, too. The window was raised a couple of inches, as if to let in fresh air. That made sense.

The four youngsters were sitting on a sofa and a couple of chairs, looking as hastily dressed and worried as their mother. Bullock said to the oldest boy, "Ted, do you remember if the curtain was closed on this window last night?"

Ted frowned in apparent confusion at the question, but he said, "Yes, sir, I'm pretty sure it was."

"But it was open when you got up this morning?"

"Yes, sir."

He moved to the window and peered out. The sitting rooms of both suites had good views of the street outside.

"Mr. Bullock," Mrs. Roosevelt said, "I simply must insist that the authorities be notified immediately. A search must be mounted with no further delay."

"Yes, ma'am, I agree with you. I'll take care of that. In the meantime, I want all you folks to stay here for the time being. I'll have breakfast sent up."

"You mean we can't go anywhere?" Ted asked.

"That's right. Just for right now, until we figure out what happened and where your brother and sister are."

None of them looked happy about it, but that drop of blood he'd spotted convinced him that whatever had happened, it had taken place in the ladies' suite. He didn't want them disturbing any evidence that might be in there.

He left them there after Mrs. Roosevelt promised that they wouldn't go anywhere. He went into the other suite again and moved quickly to the window, where he knelt and lightly touched the tip of his right index finger to the small spot on the floor.

It was almost dry but still just the slightest bit sticky. Blood, all right, Bullock thought as he rubbed his fingertips together.

Not wasting any time, he went downstairs and said to the clerk on duty at the desk, "Who was working last night, Henry?"

"Jerry Hamilton," the man replied without hesitation.

"He still stay at Mrs. Tipton's boardinghouse?"

"Yes, sir."

Bullock jerked his head in a curt nod and went out. Three minutes later, he was pounding on the door of a room in the Widow Tipton's boardinghouse.

A young man in a nightshirt answered the urgent summons. His eyes were bleary with sleep, and his hair was tangled. He gulped, stood straighter, and made a visible effort to wake up more as he recognized his boss.

"Mr. Bullock," he said. "Something wrong?"

"You're not in any trouble, Jerry. I just want to know if anything unusual happened last night, probably sometime after ten o'clock."

"In the hotel, you mean?"

"Actually, I was thinking more like in the street out front."

"Oh." The young man nodded. "You mean the fight."

"What fight?" Bullock snapped.

"There was a big, knock-down, drag-out fight in the street sometime around one o'clock, I reckon. Three fellas started whaling away on the biggest black man I ever saw. I mean, he was almost like a giant. It was a sight to see, let me tell you, Mr. Bullock."

"And you watched it, did you?"

"Well, when I heard the commotion, I went to the front door and took a look . . ." Realizing he might be straying close to admitting he'd neglected his duties, Jerry added, "Just to make sure nothing was going on that might cause trouble in the hotel."

"Uh-huh," Bullock said. "But the fight stayed out in the street."

"Yes, sir."

"Drew quite a crowd, did it?"

"Yes, sir. Most everybody who was still up and about at that hour, I'd say. The way those fellas were yellin' and carrying on, they must've woke up a lot of folks."

Including a youngster who pushed back the curtain to watch the fight from the sitting room of his suite, then went next door to the suite where his mother and sisters were staying to get a better look at the fisticuffs. Bullock could visualize that scene playing out in his mind as clearly as if he were watching it in a theater.

Alice must have been roused from sleep when her brother came in and joined him in the sitting room. They hadn't been at the window for long, Bullock reckoned, when somebody else came in. Just long enough for these unwelcome visitors to come in the back of the hotel and up the rear stairs . . .

"What's wrong, Mr. Bullock?" Jerry asked.

"Nothing," Bullock answered. "You go on back to sleep, Jerry, so you'll be good and rested for your turn on the desk tonight."

"Yes, sir. I'm, uh, not in trouble, am I?"

"No, you're not." Bullock couldn't blame the young man. The intruders probably had been in and out of the hotel so quickly and quietly that their crime wouldn't have disturbed anyone, other than their victims.

Bullock wondered for an instant whether they had actually targeted Alice and Kermit, or if they'd been content to just grab whoever they could get their hands on. He pushed that thought away. The intent didn't matter; the fact did.

And now he had to figure out how to tell his old friend, the President of the United States, that two of his children had been kidnapped.

Rapid City

Rapid City, lying just east of the rolling, thickly wooded Black Hills, was a popular place for people to visit, especially during the summers. During the winter, it was subject to the same sort of extreme weather, including blizzards, as the rest of this area of the country, so there weren't as many visitors.

Even so, it wasn't uncommon for strangers to pass through at any time of year, so the telegrapher in the Western Union office wasn't surprised when a man stepped up to the counter and spoke to him in an accent that indicated he wasn't from around these parts.

"I need to send a telegram," the man said.

"That's what we're here for, my friend," the telegrapher responded in a cheerful voice. He liked to think of himself as something of a cosmopolitan, even though he'd never been east of Sioux Falls, so he added, "I'll bet you're from New York, aren't you?"

"That's right," the customer said.

"I could tell by your accent. And maybe a touch of the Ould Sod, as well?"

The man ignored that and said with a crispness that could have been the beginnings of impatience, "I need a wire sent as soon as possible."

"Oh, sure, of course. I'll get it right out." The telegrapher pointed. "There are blank forms and pencils right over there on that counter against the wall."

The man gave him a curt nod and turned away from the window. He went to the other counter, took a form and a pencil, and printed out his message without any hesitation. Clearly, he'd worked out what he wanted to say and didn't have to search for the words.

When the man brought it back to the window, the telegrapher counted it out with an experienced look and quoted the price, which the customer paid without hesitation.

"How long will it take to get there?" he asked.

"Well, we're not busy, so I can send it right now, like I said. Can't say as for how long it'll take to be delivered on the other end, though. But your"—the telegrapher glanced at the words printed on the form—"cousin Jeremiah ought to have it within a couple of hours."

"Very well. Thank you."

"You're quite welcome, sir. And you have my deepest condolences."

The man just nodded with a solemn expression on his face and turned to leave the office. Once he was gone, the telegrapher started whistling to himself and sat down at his key. After all this time, tapping out a message was a process that didn't require much thought, and he paid little attention to the words he was sending.

COUSIN JEREMIAH REGRET TO INFORM
YOU GRANDPAP PASSED AWAY STOP
TELL COUSIN MILLIE AND COUSIN ALFRED
FUNERAL ARRANGEMENTS PENDING
ARRIVAL UNCLE FRANKLIN STOP

Chapter 13

Washington, D.C.

The door of Senator Warren Pulsipher's office opened. His secretary stuck his head in.

"That telegram you've been waiting for just arrived, sir," the young man said. When Pulsipher lifted a hand and crooked it, the secretary came all the way into the room and crossed it to hand a small envelope over the desk.

Pulsipher took it without standing up. He didn't look at the secretary as he said, "Thank you, Jeremiah. And thank you for allowing me to use your name for this."

"Of course, sir," the young man replied. "Political matters often require discretion."

Pulsipher just grunted.

"Is that all, sir?"

"Yes."

"If you need anything else—"

"I'll summon you," Pulsipher said with a trace of annoyance in his voice. The young man was ambitious and eager to please his employer, not necessarily a bad thing under the right circumstances, but now wasn't the time or place.

Once the secretary was gone and the door was closed,

Pulsipher tore open the envelope. His fingers trembled slightly as he did so.

So much was riding on this message.

He slid the yellow telegraph flimsy out of the envelope and smoothed it on the desk. His eyes devoured the words in their block printing, instantly grasping the hidden meaning in them. Then he sat back, breathing a little hard.

Clearly, not everything had gone according to plan. The code names Ambrose Neill had used told him that much.

But close enough, Pulsipher assured himself. Close enough.

He read the message again and then again, committing it to memory and making sure he hadn't misinterpreted anything in it. Then he slid a cigar from his vest pocket, rolled the telegram into a cylinder, and lit it with a match he took from the center desk drawer. Using the burning telegram to light the cigar pleased him, and as he dropped the last bit of curling, blackening paper into the large glass ashtray on the desk, he sighed in relief and satisfaction.

He needed to write a message of his own now, a note that would be delivered through a series of messengers so convoluted that it could never be traced back to him . . . but first he was going to take a moment to bask in the glory of success.

He had Theodore Roosevelt right where he wanted him, and soon now, very soon, the most powerful man in the United States of America would be Senator Warren Pulsipher from the great state of California.

Conrad Morgan came down the stairs to the hotel lobby and found Lowell Hammersby waiting for him, hat in hand.

"Good morning, Mr. Hammersby," Conrad greeted the president's aide.

"And to you, as well, Mr. Morgan," Hammersby replied. "I hope it *is* a good morning."

"It is for me."

"But will it be for the president?" Hammersby held up a hand to forestall any answer. "Never mind, I withdraw the question. I said that I'd allow you to deliver your decision to Mr. Roosevelt, and so I shall. Or are you still contemplating his offer?"

"No, I've made up my mind," Conrad said. He didn't add that his mind had been made up almost from the very moment Roosevelt had offered him the cabinet position. The only reason he had delayed was for appearance's sake.

"Very well. He told me to bring you into the office as soon as we arrive at the White House, and he'd put everything else aside for the moment. You can't imagine how many different things a president has to deal with all the time."

"No, I can't," Conrad agreed. And that constant pressure, although it had to be less for an Assistant Secretary of the Interior, was one reason he had decided to decline the president's offer.

Hammersby went on, "Plus, with this trip to South Dakota coming up, he's trying to get even more done than usual. Clearing the decks, I suppose you could say."

Hammersby offered to get a cab as they left the hotel, but it was a pleasant day and Conrad suggested they walk. When they arrived at the White House, Hammersby led the way to the second-floor office and ushered Conrad inside. Theodore Roosevelt sat at his desk, which was covered with neatly arranged stacks of papers. He stood up, grinned, and waved his hand at the documents.

"It's difficult to believe that one government can generate such a multitude of reports, isn't it, Mr. Morgan?" he said by way of greeting.

"Well, there's a lot to take care of." Conrad grasped the hand that Roosevelt extended across the desk.

"Indeed. And that's why I need all the good help I can get." He gestured toward the visitor chairs. "Have a seat, have a seat. Have you come to tell me something, young man?"

"Yes, sir, I have." Conrad waited until Roosevelt sat down again, then settled himself on one of the comfortable chairs in front of the desk. "I—"

Before he could tell the President his decision, the door into the office opened and a man stepped inside to whisper urgently into the ear of Lowell Hammersby, who was standing behind Conrad. Roosevelt glanced in that direction, clearly annoyed by the interruption. Conrad turned his head to look and saw the newcomer press an envelope into Hammersby's hand.

"What is it, Lowell?" Roosevelt snapped. "I gave orders that Mr. Morgan and I weren't to be disturbed unless some matter of vital importance arose."

"I . . . I don't know, Mr. President. Evidently this sealed letter was just delivered—"

"A letter for me?"

"Yes, sir, and the man who brought it said . . . well, he said that you needed to read it right away." Hammersby, normally a little on the pale side, was even more pallid than usual as he swallowed hard and added, "The man claimed that . . . that the lives of your family depend on it."

"Good heavens!" Roosevelt said as he bolted to his feet. "Give that to me!"

Hammersby hurried forward and skirted around Conrad's chair. He handed the envelope to Roosevelt, who tore it open and pulled out a single folded sheet of paper. The President unfolded it and read the message, squinting through the pince-nez perched on his nose as he did so.

Then he gasped and let go of the letter. The paper fell to

the desk, gliding back and forth a little as it did so before settling down on one of the stacks of reports.

Roosevelt sat down, but it was more like he fell back in his chair. His face had gone gray. He looked for all the world like a man stricken with apoplexy or a heart seizure.

"My darling girl," he said. "My poor lad."

Conrad forgot all about protocol and reached forward to pick up the sheet of paper. Roosevelt didn't try to stop him, but Hammersby said, "Mr. Morgan, you shouldn't—"

It was too late. Conrad was already reading the message that had been delivered to Theodore Roosevelt.

By the time he was finished, he understood why Roosevelt was so shaken. He placed the letter back on the desk and said, "I'm sorry, Mr. President."

"Good Lord!" Hammersby burst out. "What in the world has happened?"

Roosevelt sat up straighter, drew in a deep breath, and squared his shoulders. Conrad could see that the President's resolute nature was asserting itself. Roosevelt had been faced with trouble and tragedy plenty of times in his life, and he was a fighter. His instinct was to battle through whatever problems were assailing him.

"Two of my children have been kidnapped, Lowell," he said. "Alice and Kermit."

"K-Kidnapped?" Hammersby repeated. He looked and sounded stunned. "But . . . but how . . ."

Roosevelt shook his head and said, "I don't know. The letter doesn't explain that. It simply sets out the fact that my children have been taken and demands that I pay a ransom of $100,000 to ensure their safe return."

"That's a lot of money," Conrad said.

"I can pay it," Roosevelt snapped.

"I was just going to say that if your personal resources weren't adequate, I could help you out, Mr. President."

Roosevelt looked as if he were about to respond angrily,

but instead he gave Conrad a curt nod and said, "Thank you, Mr. Morgan, but I assure you, I can muster that amount . . . although it *is* quite large."

"What do the kidnappers want you to do?" Hammersby asked. "Where are you supposed to send the money? To Deadwood? I assume that's where the children were taken."

"That's right. From the hotel of my old friend Seth Bullock, I assume. But the letter makes it clear that I'm not supposed to *send* the ransom money." Amazingly, a grim smile tugged at Roosevelt's lips. "I'm supposed to *deliver* it. Personally."

Hammersby's mouth opened for a second, then closed, as he struggled to find words, finally blurting out, "But that's preposterous!"

"Is it?" Roosevelt waved toward the letter. "I know the West, after all. I spent a number of years there. It's reasonable for the kidnappers to assume that I know my way around."

Conrad leaned forward in his chair. "They say they'll contact you again once you're in Deadwood and let you know exactly where to take the money. They can't expect you to do that alone. You're the President of the United States!"

"But that is exactly what they expect. Or, at least, what they specify that I must do." Roosevelt placed his hands flat on the desk. "If that's what I must do to have my children returned safely to me, then it's exactly what I *shall* do."

"That's not all they want, sir, and I think you know it." Conrad leaned forward and tapped a finger on the letter. "Whoever took your children, they have a grudge against you. If all they wanted was the money, they wouldn't have demanded that you bring it to them personally. They want to get *you* there in the Black Hills so they can settle some sort of score against you."

"You can't possibly know that," Hammersby argued. "And I don't see how you even get that from a . . . a ransom demand written by criminals."

"Because I've dealt with that sort of men before," Conrad said flatly.

Roosevelt looked intently at him and said, "That's right. You were kidnapped by outlaws as a young man, weren't you?"

"That's right. They demanded that my mother deliver the ransom. But someone else got involved when she turned to him for help."

Roosevelt smiled again, but this time the expression was a bit less bleak. In fact, there was even a touch of something that might be hope in his eyes as he asked, "Do you know where to find that gentleman, Mr. Morgan?"

"As a matter of fact," Conrad said, "I do."

Chapter 14

Silver Creek, Texas

"Riders coming, Frank."

Frank Morgan didn't look up from the piece of wood he held in his left hand while his right used a folding knife to whittle shavings off it. The curled shavings fell on the porch at his feet. The wood had already taken on the shape of a horse, and it would look even more like one by the time Frank finished with it.

"I know that, Bob, but it'll still be a few minutes before they get here," he said. "Figured I might as well put the time to good use. I plan on giving this to your boy Jimmy for Christmas in a couple of months."

He sat in a ladder-back, cane-bottomed chair on the front porch of the small house he'd been renting here in Silver Creek for the past few months. His legs were stretched out in front of him and crossed at the ankles.

The man called Bob had taken off the canvas apron he usually wore while running the town's general store and put on a coat against the cool autumn air while he was delivering a crate full of groceries to Frank Morgan's house. Once a week, he brought supplies to Frank's place. Frank was perfectly capable of walking the quarter-mile into town and going to the store, of course, but he preferred to keep to himself.

He didn't want a bunch of people gossiping about how Frank Morgan—called by some The Drifter and by others The Last Gunfighter—was living here in Silver Creek, enjoying a quiet, peaceful, day-to-day existence. A well-deserved retirement, Frank thought of it.

And that was something most men in his line of work never got to experience.

Unfortunately, the faint prickling he felt on the back of his neck warned him that it might be about to come to an end.

Bob was one of the few people in Silver Creek who knew who he really was. So did the local marshal, a man named Roy Thurgood, and the sawbones, Axel Hoffman. To everybody else in town, he was just Frank, a ruggedly built, soft-spoken man getting on in years who minded his own business.

No one would guess that he was one of the fastest, maybe *the* fastest, to ever strap on a gun belt, nor that he had sent countless men across the divide during the long years he had spent wandering the West.

He was still fast, and he made sure he stayed that way by practicing every day in the dry wash behind the rented house. Most of the enemies he had made along the trail were dead, but not all of them. And some of the dead ones had relatives who hadn't forgotten . . . or forgiven.

So Frank wasn't going to be a bit surprised if the three men riding toward his house were looking for trouble. But he wasn't going to get ahead of himself, either.

"You'd better be getting back to your store," he went on now. "You don't want to miss any customers."

"I've got a clerk there handling things," Bob said. "I can stick around for a while—"

"No offense, Bob, but I'd rather you didn't."

The storekeeper looked at him for a long moment, then nodded. "If that's what you want, Frank."

"It is."

Bob glanced at the approaching riders again, then gave Frank another nod and stepped down from the porch. He headed for town, not running but not wasting any time, either.

Frank continued whittling. Earlier, when he'd come out here on the porch, he had placed a Colt .45 on the cane seat of the chair next to him. Then he had draped his coat over it, since he'd decided that it wasn't quite cool enough to need the garment.

When the three riders were a hundred yards away, Frank picked up the coat, set the whittled horse and the knife on the other chair, picked up the Colt, and tucked it into the waistband of his trousers on the left side with the butt facing forward. He stood up and put the coat on. It hung so that it hid the revolver.

Frank stayed where he was, behind the porch railing, as the three horsebackers rode up. His left hand rested easily on the railing. His right thumb was hooked in his waistband so that hand wasn't far from the gun under his coat.

"Afternoon, gents," he said with a nod as the three men reined in. "Something I can do for you?"

The man in the center nudged his horse slightly ahead of the other two. He was somewhere in late middle age, not much younger than Frank, with white hair under a black Stetson and a seamed, weathered face.

"Your name Frank?" he asked in a gravelly voice.

"Haven't checked lately, but I reckon it still is. Has been all my life."

"Funny old pelican," the man on Frank's right said. He was younger, with a round, florid, beard-stubbled face.

"Thinks he is, anyway," the man to the left said. He was

younger, too, with red hair under a thumbed-back hat and a quick, smug grin.

The white-haired man rasped, "Frank Morgan?"

"You know who I am," Frank said, tiring quickly of this banter. "What do you want?"

"My name's Ethan Sanders. That mean anything to you?"

"Can't say as it does," Frank replied honestly.

"I had a boy named Charles. Chip, we called him. How about that?"

Frank shook his head and said, "Sorry."

"You ought to be," Sanders said. "You killed him ten years ago."

That news came as no surprise to Frank, even though he genuinely had no memory of ever facing off against anybody called Charles, or Chip, Sanders. But there had been too many young men over the years, young men eager to make a reputation for themselves and prove that they were as bad as they thought they were. There was no way Frank could remember all of them.

"Ten years is a long time. Why are you just looking me up now?"

"Because my wife begged me not to, and I loved her enough to swallow the pain, for her sake." Sanders turned his head and spat to the side. "I put her in the ground a month ago. Consumption. And then I started looking for you."

"So you found me," Frank said heavily. "You may not believe it, Sanders, but I'm sorry for your loss."

"Which one?" The words came from Sanders like they were being carved out of him with a knife.

"Your wife. If I killed your boy, it was because he was trying to kill me, or because he was trying to hurt or kill somebody else."

"You never shot anybody who didn't have it comin', is that what you're sayin'?"

Frank nodded and said, "Pretty much. But for what it's

worth, I wish Chip hadn't put me in a position where I had to draw on him."

Sanders' lips drew back from his teeth in a grimace as he leaned forward. "Don't you dirty his name with your mouth, you damn killer! He was just a boy. You had no right—"

Suddenly the memory burst on Frank's brain. The memory of a hot, dusty day in a western Kansas town where he'd met Charles "Chip" Sanders for the first and last time.

"He was a grown man," Frank's voice lashed out, "and he took a razor blade to a girl's face because he mistook her for a soiled dove and she turned him down. He was about to kill her when I stepped in and told him to stop."

"That's a lie! Chip never would've—"

"Yeah, he would, and you know it." Frank nodded. "Inside, you know it. You know he went for his gun, too, instead of backing down. You probably taught him never to back down, and never said anything about whether he was right or wrong."

"You son of a—"

Sanders didn't finish the epithet as he clawed for the gun on his hip.

He hadn't even come close to clearing leather before Frank had swept his coat aside and palmed out the Colt.

Years ago, Frank had learned how to tell which one was the fastest when he faced multiple men. Part of it was instinct, part was observation. He had seen that the man to Sanders' left, his right, licked his lips eagerly. He wanted this fight, believed he was fast enough to take down the legendary Drifter. The other man, despite his smirk, had an uneasy look in his eyes. He wasn't sure he was going to come out of this alive, so he would put everything he had into his draw.

Frank went for him first, and sure enough, the man to Sanders' right beat the cocksure one to the draw. He was fast but not fast enough. Frank's Colt boomed, and the man went backward off his suddenly skittish horse with a bullet in his chest.

Frank swung the Colt back to his right. The cocky one got a shot off, but he'd rushed it a hair too much. The bullet went past Frank's right shoulder and thudded into the wall behind him. The slug from Frank's gun punched through the tag hanging from the sack of tobacco in the man's shirt pocket and drove on into his heart.

That left Ethan Sanders. He actually managed to jerk the trigger of his gun twice, but both shots went high. Frank lined the Colt's sights on him and called, "Give it up, Sanders! No need to die!"

"Yeah, there is," the man rasped as he tried to bring his gun down from where the recoil of the previous shots had forced it up.

Frank shot him in the chest, too.

Sanders sagged back in the saddle and dropped his gun. Spooked by the shots and the smell of powdersmoke and blood, his horse crow-hopped across the little yard in front of the house. Sanders toppled off and landed in a bloody, huddled heap that didn't move again.

The echoes of the gunfire rolled away across the Texas plains. The fight had taken less than a handful of heartbeats. All three men were down, and none of them stirred. Frank didn't put the Colt away, though. Instead, he held it ready as he slowly descended the steps from the porch and checked on all three men.

Dead, all right.

A shame and a waste, he thought, considering what had prompted this showdown.

Not only that, but now his respite in Silver Creek was ruined, too. When he looked toward the settlement, he saw several townspeople hurrying in the direction of his house, led by Marshal Roy Thurgood.

By the time the folks got there, Frank had taken three

fresh cartridges from his pocket and thumbed them into the Colt's cylinder, replacing the rounds he had fired. As the men came to a stop, panting from the run out here, Thurgood asked, "Are you all right, Frank?"

"Yeah. I think there are a couple of bullet holes in the house I'll have to patch before I leave, though."

"You're leaving?"

"I reckon it'd be best."

Bob said, "But this was self-defense. I was watching, and I could tell that much even from town."

"Maybe so, but word of what happened will get around anyway. I won't draw more trouble to you folks here in Silver Creek. You deserve better than that."

Roy Thurgood grunted and said, "I don't know if it's a matter of what we deserve or don't deserve. A fella rode out here from Sweetwater and gave me a telegram to deliver to you."

Frank's forehead creased in a frown. "A telegram?" he repeated.

"Yeah. Addressed to Frank Morgan, Silver Creek, Texas. When you told me who you are, you said there was only one fella who knew where to find you: your son."

One of the men who had tagged along exclaimed, "Wait! You mean old Frank is really Frank Morgan, the famous gunfighter?"

Another man said, "I heard he killed more men than John Wesley Hardin!"

Thurgood reached under his vest and took a small envelope from his shirt pocket. He held it out to Frank, who took it and opened it.

"Am I right?" Thurgood asked after Frank had had time to read the wire. "You've got another reason for leaving town, don't you?"

"Yeah," Frank said as he stuck the telegram in his own

pocket. "My boy Conrad needs my help. Or rather, a friend of his does."

Frank didn't offer any explanation of who that friend was. The good folks of Silver Creek probably wouldn't believe it, anyway.

"What about these fellas?" Thurgood asked with a wave at the dead men.

"I'll leave enough money behind to cover putting them in the ground."

Thurgood shook his head and said, "That's not your responsibility, Frank."

"Things happen in this world," Frank said, "and a lot of the time they're nobody's fault. But they still have to be taken care of."

Chapter 15

Washington, D.C.

There was a telegraph line right into the White House, with its terminus in a special room where an operator was always on duty. So Conrad didn't have to leave in order to send the wire to Frank, addressing it to him at the Western Union office in Sweetwater, Texas, the nearest town of any size to the small settlement of Silver Creek.

Conrad asked Frank to meet him as soon as possible in Deadwood. The way the railroads had spread out across the entire country, if Frank got a fast start, he might even beat them there. Or maybe not, since the railroad companies would do everything in their power to accommodate the President and clear the lines ahead of his special train.

Either way, Frank ought to be there about the same time Conrad and Roosevelt arrived.

Roosevelt wouldn't be persuaded not to go. The letter from the kidnappers demanded that he deliver the ransom payment himself and come alone. He had argued vehemently that that was precisely what he ought to do.

"No offense, Mr. President," Conrad had said while he and Roosevelt were alone in the office, Hammersby having been sent to summon the Secretary of State, John Hay, "but when you're dealing with men like this, it's never a good idea to do exactly what they tell you to do."

"But they've threatened to kill my children!"

"And if they were trustworthy, they wouldn't be mixed up in something like this. To put it bluntly, sir, those children are the bait in the trap. *You're* the real target."

Roosevelt had waved a hand impatiently. "I know, I know. We've discussed this already, Mr. Morgan. What would *you* suggest that I do?"

"Let them *think* that you're playing along with them. Obviously, you're not going to travel from Washington to Deadwood without an entourage. But once you get there, insist to the authorities that you're going to deliver the ransom by yourself, just the way you've been instructed. The kidnappers said they'd get in touch with you once you're there and let you know what you're supposed to do next. Go ahead and do it."

Roosevelt stopped the pacing he was doing to snap, "But you just told me *not* to cooperate with them!"

"Wherever you're supposed to go, my father and I will be trailing you," Conrad said. "We won't be far off, but we'll be careful enough that the kidnappers won't spot us."

Roosevelt peered intently at him. "Do you actually believe you can do that?"

"Yes, sir," Conrad replied without hesitation. "I also believe that we can get Miss Alice and young Kermit away from those varmints safe and sound."

"If you can do that . . ." For a moment, Roosevelt was too overcome with emotion to go on, something rare in this sturdy, strong-willed man. He took a deep breath. "If you can do that, Mr. Morgan, I'll be in your debt . . . and eternally grateful to you. More so than if you'd agreed to that damned Assistant Secretary of the Interior position!"

Conrad had smiled. "I'm not really cut out for that, Mr.

President. But *this* job . . . that's more the sort of trouble I'm equipped to handle."

"You mean Kid Morgan is equipped to handle it. Especially with The Drifter on hand, too."

Conrad shrugged. "Frank and I do seem to hunt up trouble pretty often. Or rather, it usually hunts us up."

That was when Hammersby had come in with the Secretary of State. At the moment, John Milton Hay was the second-most powerful politician in the country. Roosevelt had been serving as William McKinley's vice-president when McKinley was assassinated, so that left the vice-president's position vacant when Roosevelt took the reins as the chief executive. It would remain empty until the next election. That left Hay as the next in the line of succession if anything should happen to the President.

Roosevelt had greeted Hay, a fellow Republican, and then said to Hammersby, "Lowell, take Mr. Morgan to the telegraph room so he can send that wire."

"Yes, sir."

They left the Yellow Oval Room and turned right, past the Lincoln Bedroom to the Lincoln Sitting Room, where the telegraph office was housed. The room was comfortably furnished with an overstuffed sofa and matching chairs, but its real function at the moment centered around the desk where a telegraph key rested. Mounted on the wall beside the desk was a telephone.

Hammersby explained that the telegraph room would soon move to the newly constructed West Wing, along with the President's office and other offices, but for now this small, unobtrusive room served as the hub for communications going in and out of the White House.

Conrad had printed out his message, and the operator had sent it. "Will there be a reply, sir?" he asked.

"More than likely," Conrad said.

"And will you be remaining in the White House?"

Hammersby took it upon himself to answer that. "For the time being, Mr. Morgan will be here. If there's a reply, check first with me in the President's office."

"Yes, sir."

They had just stepped back out into the hall and the door in the Lincoln Sitting Room was still open when the telegraph key began to chatter.

"My goodness," Hammersby said as he and Conrad paused. "That was fast."

They turned back into the room, where the telegrapher was writing swiftly on a pad of paper with a pencil. Despite the speed with which the pencil moved, the printing was extremely clear and legible.

The rapid clicking came to an end. The operator wrote another couple of words to finish the message, then looked up at Conrad and Hammersby and told them, "This isn't a reply to your message, Mr. Morgan. It's a wire for the President. I'll transcribe it onto a form—"

"No need for that," Hammersby said. "He can read your original."

The telegrapher shrugged, tore the sheet off the pad, and folded the paper in half before he handed it to Hammersby. Conrad noted that Hammersby didn't read the message as the two of them went back along the hall to the Yellow Oval Room. Whatever it was, Roosevelt would see it first—other than the telegrapher, of course—and decide whether or not to share it.

Roosevelt was pacing again when Conrad and Hammersby entered the office. Secretary Hay, a distinguished-looking man with dark hair parted in the middle and a Van Dyke beard heavily streaked with gray, appeared frustrated and confused as he watched Roosevelt striding restlessly back and forth.

Hay turned to the two younger men and said, "Ah, Mr.

Hammersby, perhaps you can help me make sense of this. The President informs me that he's leaving Washington and has no idea when, or even if, he will return. The government cannot be left without its leader!"

Roosevelt stopped and pointed at the secretary. "That's why I summoned you, John, so you'd be aware that you may be called upon to lead this nation."

"But Mr. President, I'm hardly qualified—"

"Nonsense," Roosevelt barked. "You've been a fixture in Washington for forty years. You were Abraham Lincoln's personal secretary. You stood at his bedside while he was dying."

"That doesn't mean I'm suitable to take over the entire country, sir."

Roosevelt stopped pacing and summoned up a smile from somewhere. "Well, I'll certainly allow you to hope that it never comes to that, John, but even so, know that I have full confidence in you if it does."

"But you haven't even told me where you're going or why you believe there's a chance you might not be coming back."

Roosevelt shook his head and said, "Nor can I explain those things to you at this moment in time, my friend. I can only ask that you honor my wishes and prepare yourself in case the worst comes to pass."

Hay regarded Roosevelt intently for a moment and then drew a deep breath.

"My life has been devoted to serving this country," he said. "If I'm called upon to serve it in a . . . greater capacity than heretofore, I shall certainly endeavor to do so, to the best of my ability."

Roosevelt clapped a hand on Hay's shoulder and exclaimed, "Bully for you! I knew I could count on you, John."

Hay said, "Theodore, I don't know what's wrong, but if there's anything I can do . . ."

"You're doing it, old friend, simply by letting me know that I can rely upon you to do what's best for the country."

"Always."

Roosevelt shook hands with the Secretary of State, and then Hay left the office. As soon as the door was closed behind him, Hammersby stepped forward and extended the folded sheet of paper to the President.

"A wire came for you, sir, while Mr. Morgan and I were in the telegraph room."

Roosevelt practically snatched the message out of Hammersby's fingers. He unfolded it and squinted at the printed words through his pince-nez.

"It's from Seth Bullock," he announced. "Confirmation that Alice and Kermit have been abducted by persons unknown. He says that he can organize a search party, but he awaits word from me before proceeding."

"He doesn't know about the other message you received this morning," Conrad said.

Roosevelt shook his head. "How could he? I have to respond to this immediately. Lowell, take this down."

"Yes, sir." Hammersby grabbed a pencil and another piece of paper from the desk.

"No search party. Stop," Roosevelt dictated. "Have received ransom demand. Stop. Am departing Washington immediately. Stop. Will arrive Deadwood soonest. Stop. Take no action until I am there. Stop. TR. Have that sent to Seth Bullock in Deadwood right away, Lowell."

"Yes, sir, I will."

"Then contact the railroad and make arrangements for a special westbound train with my personal car attached to it. I'll gather my gear and be ready to depart in an hour or less." Roosevelt looked at Conrad. "Will that give you enough time to get together whatever you need, Mr. Morgan?"

"I have my personal weapons at the hotel, Mr. President, as well as some better traveling clothes. I can pick up a horse and saddle and Winchester once we get to Deadwood."

Roosevelt grinned despite his obviously distraught state. "A good horse and a good gun, eh? When you get right down to it, what else does a man need in times of trouble?"

"Those things will solve a lot of problems, sir," Conrad said, "as long as it's a good man using them."

Chapter 16

Conrad made it back to the White House in less than an hour, carrying the carpetbag he had brought with him from Colorado. Inside it were coiled gun belts with attached holsters for the Colt .45 and the Mauser C96, along with a change of clothes and a few other personal belongings. He was dressed in dark gray whipcord trousers tucked into high-topped black boots, black coat over white shirt and gray vest, and his flat-crowned black hat with the silver conchas on the band. He was no longer a businessman or a potential politician.

In the language employed by the dime novel scribblers, Conrad thought wryly, Kid Morgan was ready to ride again.

As soon as he arrived somewhere he could get a horse, of course.

He wasn't the only one who had changed clothes—and attitudes—he discovered when he reached the White House. Theodore Roosevelt was decked out in fringed, high-topped moccasins, brown corduroy trousers, and a fringed buckskin vest over a flannel shirt. A wide-brimmed brown hat with a Montana pinch in its crown sat on the presidential desk. The outfit might have looked gaudy on some men, like something from one of Buffalo Bill's Wild West Shows, but Roosevelt's grim, resolute expression didn't permit him to be taken as anything less than serious. Deadly serious.

Lowell Hammersby was in the office, too, and looked back and forth between the two men before saying, "Good heavens. I feel like I'm going to be traveling with Colonel Cody and Wyatt Earp."

"You're coming with us, Lowell?" Conrad asked.

"Of course. The President might need my assistance."

A knock sounded on the office door. It opened to reveal another of Roosevelt's secretaries. The man said, "Excuse me, Mr. President. Senator Pulsipher would like to see you."

"Pulsipher!" Roosevelt's booming voice dripped with contempt as he repeated the name. "I've no time for that . . . that preening sycophant right now! What does he want?"

"I don't know, sir."

Roosevelt scowled. "Tell him I'll speak to him when I get back to Washington, whenever that is. Whatever he wants will just have to wait."

"Yes, sir." The secretary closed the door.

"Give him a minute to get rid of that damned Pulsipher," Roosevelt said to Conrad and Hammersby. "The man's quite irritating. Vaulting ambition combined with fuzzy-headed thinking and sheer ignorance, like so many others in this city! But utterly insignificant in the big scheme of things, of course. Lowell, check and see if they're gone."

"Yes, sir." Hammersby looked out into the corridor and reported that there was no sign of the visiting senator, then added, "I hope he didn't overhear your comments."

Roosevelt shook his head. "I don't care if he did. Trying to be diplomatic with idiots is a losing game in the end." He picked up his hat from the desk and clapped it on his head. "Come along, gentlemen."

Before they left the White House, they checked in the telegraph room and found that there hadn't been a reply to the telegram Conrad had sent earlier.

"As soon as one comes in, I'll wire it on to the next station where your train will be stopping, sir," the telegrapher assured Roosevelt.

"Good man."

They left the White House through a rear entrance. Roosevelt had put on a topcoat over his Western garb and pulled his hat down so the brim obscured his face. Conrad and Hammersby weren't well-known enough for anyone to recognize them as they got in a closed carriage with the President. The vehicle pulled away and rolled toward the train station with no one taking notice.

Roosevelt sat on the rear seat facing forward. Conrad and Hammersby shared the front seat.

"Once we get to Deadwood," Conrad said, "I'll stay on the train for a while after you've gotten off, sir. It's likely the kidnappers may have at least one accomplice in Deadwood, waiting and watching for you, and we don't want them to know that you and I are connected. That way if they spot me and my father later on, they might not realize that we're trailing you."

Roosevelt nodded. "That sounds like a good plan, young man. I put myself in your hands when it comes to such things. It's been a long time since I took part in a manhunt!"

"You helped chase down outlaws and rustlers several times, didn't you, sir?" Hammersby asked.

"That's right. I've experienced the sharp bite of powdersmoke in my nostrils on numerous occasions. It makes the blood flow faster."

"And the, ah, bowels get more nervous, I expect."

Roosevelt laughed. "That's true, Lowell. But don't worry. I very much doubt that you'll be involved in any gunfights during the course of this expedition."

"I hope we can all avoid that, sir, and that your children can be rescued without any violence."

Roosevelt nodded and said, "We can certainly hope so."

Conrad saw the look in the President's eyes, though. Roosevelt was expecting trouble . . . and so was he.

That was in the future. For now, all they could do was try to get to Deadwood as quickly as possible.

Deadwood

"No search party?" Edith Roosevelt repeated what Seth Bullock had just told her. "What do you mean, no search party? Has my husband lost his mind?"

"I sincerely doubt that, ma'am," Bullock said. "I'm sure he has a good reason for telling me that."

"Two of my children are out there somewhere in the wilderness, in the hands of desperate men."

"I'm aware of that."

"Allowing them to suffer and languish in such danger for one more moment is unacceptable!"

They were in Bullock's office in the hotel. A clerk from the telegraph office had brought Roosevelt's reply to him a short time earlier, and he had summoned Mrs. Roosevelt from her suite immediately so he could tell her what her husband said.

Bullock had posted a couple of good men upstairs, outside the doors to the suites. They were well-armed, and while they didn't know exactly *who* they were guarding, Bullock was confident they wouldn't allow any harm to come to the other Roosevelt children.

Bullock put a finger on the yellow telegraph flimsy that rested on his desk. "The President says that he's received a ransom demand, which confirms what we suspected about those youngsters being kidnapped. You can rest assured that even though they're captives, the men who took them won't allow anything to happen to them."

"Because they won't be worth anything if they're dead, is that right?" Mrs. Roosevelt asked bluntly.

"Well . . ."

"But if we have no way of *knowing* whether they're alive or not, does it actually matter?"

Bullock had no real answer for that. He said, "I just don't think they'd dare hurt the children."

"You've dealt with desperadoes in the past, have you not, Mr. Bullock?"

"Yes, ma'am, many times."

"And they were not gentle, caring individuals, were they?"

Bullock managed not to grimace, but it took an effort. He sighed and said, "No, ma'am, they were not."

Mrs. Roosevelt changed tacks. "Are there men here in Deadwood who are capable of finding the tracks left by the kidnappers and following them?"

"Possibly," Bullock allowed. "But the problem is that we don't know what direction they headed. I've got men out now, talking to everybody they can find around town, trying to find out if anybody saw anything that might put us on the trail, but unless they turn up something . . ."

Bullock's voice trailed off. He didn't need to say anything else.

After a moment, Mrs. Roosevelt said hollowly, "It's hopeless, isn't it?"

"No, ma'am, not at all." Bullock glanced at the telegram again. He had been thinking about what Roosevelt had said in the message. "If your husband got a ransom demand from the kidnappers, then they must have told him what to do next. If I know Teddy . . . I mean, the President . . . he'll already be taking action. He's probably on his way here by now, and I'd bet a brand-new hat that he's got a plan to recover your children and deal with the miscreants who took them."

"Well . . . Theodore *does* tend to act decisively. If he *has* already started in this direction, how long will it take for him to get here?"

"Considering that the railroads will do everything they can to speed up the trip, I'd say he should arrive by the day after tomorrow, ma'am."

"That long?" Mrs. Roosevelt had a handkerchief in her hand. She clutched it tighter and held it to her bosom. "Two days for my children to spend as prisoners, probably cold and uncomfortable and terrified."

"I reckon we'll just have to, uh, hope for the best."

Even as he spoke, Bullock realized how empty and hollow those words sounded. The futility of them gnawed at him, too. He had always been a man of action, and it was torture knowing that there was nothing he could do about this right now.

He hoped Teddy wouldn't waste any time getting here. And when he went after the varmints responsible, Seth Bullock intended to be right there beside him.

Washington, D.C.

Warren Pulsipher stalked back and forth in his office, seething with fury. How dare that bombastic clown Roosevelt say such things about him! If it had been possible, he would have wired Ambrose Neill and told him to order his accomplices to kill those brats immediately.

But if he did that, it would ruin his plan. His *real* plan. Neill and the men he'd recruited believed that Pulsipher shared the same goal they did: simple revenge on Theodore Roosevelt. They didn't know that he had something bigger in mind, something that would not only change the course of his own life but that of the entire country, as well.

Pulsipher stopped pacing. He was behind his desk, so he leaned forward and rested his hands on it, standing there like that for a long moment while he breathed deeply and brought his raging emotions under control.

He had planned to issue new orders to his allies once things were in motion and it was too late for them to back out, but he couldn't afford to take any chances, he realized now. So far he had left the execution of the plan to Neill and his subordinates, but there was too much at stake to continue in that risky manner. He needed to be there, to be on hand himself, to make certain everything was carried out as it needed to be. That would mean placing himself in a situation and surroundings that would be completely new to him, but there was no other way he could be sure of achieving his goal.

He straightened, took another deep breath, and called, "Jeremiah!"

The young secretary stuck his head in the door immediately. "Yes, Senator?"

"Get me on a westbound train as soon as you possibly can."

Jeremiah looked confused but said, "Of course, sir. Uh, what destination other than 'westbound'?"

"I'm going to Deadwood," Warren Pulsipher said. Those words sounded very strange to him, coming out of his mouth, but as he spoke them, he knew in his heart that was where his destiny awaited.

Chapter 17

Deadwood

The train wasn't far from Deadwood now. It would arrive in less than half an hour, Conrad knew. Outside the presidential car's windows, dusk was settling down over the rugged, thickly wooded hills.

It was the evening of the second day since Conrad, Theodore Roosevelt, and Lowell Hammersby had left Washington, D.C. They had made better time getting here than Conrad had expected. He had thought it might be the next morning before they arrived. But the railroads had gone all out to assist the President, shunting trains out of the way, expediting the stops to take on water and coal, and generally doing everything they could to keep this special express barreling on its way.

Conrad felt sure that his father hadn't arrived in Deadwood yet, but he knew that Frank was on his way. His reply to Conrad's wire had been waiting for them in Chicago. He had promised to get there as quickly as possible. If he *hadn't* shown up by the time Roosevelt set out to deliver the ransom money, Frank would just have to follow along as best he could, because Conrad would already be on the President's trail, watching out for Roosevelt and waiting for the kidnappers to make their move.

Roosevelt was in his sleeping compartment at the moment, although Conrad doubted if he was taking a nap this close to Deadwood. Probably gathering his strength for the upcoming meeting with his wife. Conrad and Hammersby were in the special car's sitting room. Hammersby fidgeted nervously with the watch chain looped across his midsection from one vest pocket to the other.

"If you don't mind, Conrad, can we go over the plan one more time?"

"Sure," Conrad said. "In a few minutes, before we get to Deadwood, I'm going back to the caboose to wait there while you and the President get off the train. Seth Bullock will be waiting to meet you at the station, and he'll escort you to his hotel where Mrs. Roosevelt and the children are staying. I'll stay in the caboose until I'm sure none of the kidnappers' accomplices are still watching the train, and then I'll slip off. It'll be good and dark by then, so that'll help keep anybody from noticing me. As far as folks in Deadwood are concerned, there won't be any connection between me and the President. I'll be just another drifter who happened to show up at about the same time."

"A drifter called Kid Morgan," Hammersby said.

Conrad smiled. "Well . . . I'm not going to go around introducing myself to people. If anybody wants to know who I am, I'll just use the name Morgan. I need to get a horse and saddle and rifle so I'll be ready to ride when Mr. Roosevelt heads out on the trail, whenever that is. I'll go ahead and take care of that this evening, although I don't think it's likely the kidnappers will get in touch with the President until tomorrow, at the earliest."

"This must be a large, well-organized gang we're dealing with," Hammersby said. "Not only were they able to abduct two of the President's children, but they also got in touch with Washington in a matter of less than twelve hours to deliver their demands. That's swift action, even in this era of modern communication."

"It is," Conrad agreed with a nod. "But I think I can handle them."

"Have you given any thought to letting me come with you?"

Conrad frowned in surprise. "You, Lowell? No offense, but you don't seem the type to go riding across the Black Hills, chasing down outlaws."

"Oh, I'm not, make no mistake about that!" Hammersby declared. "I've been on a horse, but I'm not exactly comfortable on one. However, the President has been very good to me and placed a great deal of trust in me where delicate matters are concerned, and I feel as if I owe him. I've always been loyal to him, and I see no reason to change that now."

"I'm sure he appreciates that, but being loyal to him doesn't mean you ought to go charging into something that might get you killed." Conrad knew his words were blunt, but he wanted to be sure that Hammersby understood. "You're not equipped for a job like this, Lowell."

"Actually, I am." Hammersby reached inside his coat and, to Conrad's surprise, produced a pistol. Conrad recognized it as a .32 caliber Smith & Wesson. Hammersby fumbled it a little as he tried to hold it out and display it for Conrad.

"Take it easy there," Conrad said as he stood up quickly. "Don't drop that thing. It's not likely to go off if you do, but you don't want to take a chance."

"I just want you to see that I'm armed."

"Have you ever fired that gun?"

"Of course I have." Hammersby looked a little embarrassed. "Once. When I bought it. The fellow at the store took me out behind the place and let me fire a few shots into some hay bales he had set up for target practice."

"And how did you do?"

"None of the shots went over the fence behind the bales," Hammersby said, "so no one was endangered."

Conrad managed not to shake his head in dismay. He said, "Well, that's good, anyway."

"I thought so. And there's no danger of it going off accidentally, because it's not loaded at the moment."

"Let me see."

Conrad held out his hand. Hammersby gave him the .32. He checked the five-shot cylinder. Hammersby was right; the gun was unloaded. Conrad gave it back to him.

"So you see, I'm not unarmed."

"Having a gun and being able to use it are two different things," Conrad said. "And shooting at some hay bales is a hell of a lot different than shooting at a man . . . especially when that man is liable to be shooting back at you."

Hammersby sighed and nodded. "I know. I just feel so helpless! The President is going through a terrible ordeal, and there's nothing I can do to assist him."

"I'd say you've assisted him a lot already. He counted on you to set things up so he could get here in a hurry, and you did that, didn't you?"

Hammersby said, "Anyone could have done that—"

"No, not anyone," Conrad said. "And you've been right there, every time he wanted to talk about things. That can be worth a lot, too."

Hammersby nodded slowly and said, "I suppose I *was* being unrealistic."

"I'm certain he's expecting you to look after Mrs. Roosevelt and the other children while he's gone. That'll be a real load off his mind, knowing that they're being taken care of, and he won't be distracted while he needs to be concentrating on what he's doing."

Hammersby stood up a little straighter. "I suppose there's something to what you're saying, Conrad. Perhaps I *am* helping. Thank you."

"For now, you'd better put that gun away. You have cartridges for it?"

Hammersby patted his coat and said, "A box of them in an inside pocket."

"Well, keep them handy. It's not likely you'll need to start blazing away at anybody, but if you do . . ."

"I'll be ready," Hammersby declared.

Conrad wasn't sure how accurate that statement was, but he didn't say anything else about it.

For one thing, he was distracted a moment later when the conductor stepped into the presidential car.

"We're five minutes out of Deadwood, Mr. Morgan," he said. "You told me to let you know."

"Yes, thank you. I'll go on back to the caboose now."

"I'll join you in a few minutes," the conductor said.

Conrad shook hands with Hammersby. "Good luck, Lowell."

"And to you, too. There's a great deal riding on you, Conrad. Isn't that what you Westerners say?"

"Sums it up pretty well," Conrad agreed. Roosevelt still hadn't emerged from his sleeping quarters, but Conrad didn't want to wait any longer. He nodded to Hammersby and stepped out onto the platform at the rear of the car. There was another car between it and the caboose, which was empty. Conrad walked through it quickly and then went into the caboose. He wasn't visible for more than a few moments as he crossed between cars, and the shadows were thick now. Night fell quickly in the Black Hills once the sun was down.

The conductor came in a couple of minutes later. "I let the President know we're almost to Deadwood," he said. "I don't know what this is about, Mr. Morgan, but I sure hope it works out all right."

"So do I," Conrad said.

"And I'm glad the railroad could help."

The conductor didn't know it, but the Browning Holdings actually owned a chunk of this railroad, so in a way, Conrad was his boss . . . although Conrad had kept that information to himself. Unlike the arrogant young man he had once been, he usually conducted himself in an unassuming manner these days. That was something he had learned from his father. One of the *many* things he had learned from Frank Morgan.

Conrad lifted his head a little as he heard the locomotive's whistle blow. The train lurched slightly as it began to slow.

"That'll be Deadwood coming up," the conductor said. "Whatever brings you and the President here, Mr. Morgan, I wish the both of you luck."

"Thanks," Conrad said. "More than likely, we'll need it."

Seth Bullock was waiting on the depot platform when the train rolled in. Big clouds of smoke and steam rolled out from the Baldwin locomotive as it slowed and shuddered to a halt.

Now that the sun had gone down, the air had taken on a considerable chill. The wind blowing on the platform magnified it. Bullock tugged his hat down tighter and shoved his hands in the pockets of his overcoat.

He had a short-barreled, .32 caliber Colt New Line revolver in the right-hand pocket. It wasn't accurate except up close, and some folks claimed that you could do more damage by throwing a .32 at somebody than by shooting them with it, but Bullock liked the little gun and felt better when he closed his palm around its checkered grip. He squared his shoulders, lifted his head, and strode toward the rear of the presidential car, where a porter was putting a set of steps in place.

Theodore Roosevelt appeared at the top of those steps, dressed like a Westerner, other than the pince-nez. Not many hombres out here wore fancy spectacles like that.

"Teddy," Bullock said as he let go of the gun and pulled his hand from the pocket to extend it toward the President. "Mighty good to see you again. I wish it was under better circumstances."

Roosevelt came down the steps with the spryness of a younger man. He gripped Bullock's hand hard and summoned up a smile, weary and worried though it was.

"I echo your sentiments, old friend. I always welcome your company. But these are hardly the ideal circumstances, as you say." Roosevelt looked around the empty platform. "How in the world did you manage this? I thought the arrival of a train is always of great interest in Western settlements. Where are all the people flocking to see what's going on?"

"I have men posted around the station to keep folks away," Bullock explained. "People will be curious, but I'll just spread the word that some special guests arrived for the celebration. We've managed to keep all this other business quiet, so when all goes well and you have your son and daughter back, we can carry on with the fandango just like we planned and nobody will ever have to know what really happened."

"I devoutly hope you're correct, Seth." Roosevelt's features hardened even more. "Regardless of the outcome, we must keep knowledge of this dreadful affair between ourselves and a select few. It would never do for criminals to start thinking they can threaten the President of the United States by threatening his family. This perfidy must be crushed!"

"I couldn't agree with you more, Teddy. I mean, Mr. President."

Roosevelt waved that off and said, "Don't worry about propriety. For right now, and until I get my children back safe and sound, I'm just Teddy Roosevelt, father."

"Sounds good to me. Now, I know there's someone waiting to see you . . ."

"Edith," Roosevelt said with a sigh. "I tell you, old friend, I'm not sure but what I'd rather face is a rampaging horde of rustlers!"

Conrad watched through a tiny gap in the curtains over one of the windows in the caboose as Roosevelt stood on the platform and talked with a man who had to be Seth Bullock. After an obviously heartfelt greeting and a few minutes of conversation, the two men disappeared into the train station.

Conrad waited fifteen more minutes, then opened the door at the rear of the car and stepped out, moving quickly so he wouldn't be silhouetted against the glow of the lamp for more than a second or two. He dropped to the ground on the side of the tracks away from the platform and walked alongside the train until he could slip around the front of the engine and move quickly into the thick shadows of an alley between two nearby buildings.

He had never been in Deadwood before, but he had spent time in plenty of other frontier settlements and he trusted his instincts to guide him. Cutting through alleys and across narrow streets, he came to a stretch of businesses several blocks long. An icy wind tugged at his coat. He buttoned it around him and pulled his hat down tighter as he looked up and down the street.

Spotting a sign that announced the establishment was a livery stable and wagon yard, Conrad headed for it and found that the office was still open. Yellow lamplight glowed through its single window. Conrad went inside and found a young man in overalls sitting behind a desk with his work-booted feet propped up on it. He was reading a dime novel. Conrad managed not to smile when he caught sight of the title: *Smoke Jensen Battles the Valley Vultures.*

He'd have to tell Smoke about that when he got back to

Big Rock, Conrad thought. Smoke would either grin amiably or make some caustic comment about the degenerate scribblers who penned such fanciful tales, depending on what kind of mood he was in.

Right now Conrad was in need of doing some business, so he said, "Excuse me?"

The young hostler, who had a round face and shaggy hair, sat up and placed the dime novel on the desk. "Yes, sir," he said. "What can I do for you?"

"I need to rent or buy a good horse and a saddle."

"How long you needin' the critter for? We rent by the hour or the day." The young man looked a little confused. "It's a mite late to be ridin' out, not to mention chilly."

Conrad shook his head and said, "I won't be needing the horse until tomorrow, more than likely. And I don't have any idea how long I'll need it." He thought about it for a second and went on, "It might make more sense for me to buy the horse and tack. Can you sell me a good mount and then leave it stabled here until I need it?"

"So you're gonna buy the horse and pay rent on a stall, too?" The hostler stood up and shrugged. "If that's the way you want to do it, mister, I sure as shootin' won't argue with you. Come on in the barn and I'll show you the stock we have on hand."

The stable had only three horses for sale or rent, and after looking at the first two in the light of a lantern the hostler carried, Conrad was starting to think he might have to seek out some other livery. The horses were older, and he could tell they didn't have the sort of strength and stamina he might well need.

But then the hostler spilled lanternlight into a stall where a big bay tossed his head as if annoyed at being disturbed. "This varmint's proddy as all get-out," the young man said. "The boss took him to pay the feed bill for the gent who owned him, who got hisself killed a while back in a fight over a card game. Or was it over a whore? I sort of disremember which. The horse is for sale, but the boss won't rent him out. Says he's too wild for that and might hurt somebody, and then we'd be in trouble."

Conrad stepped past the garrulous hostler and reached through the bars on the stall's gate.

"Careful. He's liable to bite you."

Conrad had seen something in the bay's eyes. He said, "No, I don't think he'll bite me."

In fact, the horse came up, butted its nose against Conrad's hand, and then snuffled it affectionately.

"Well, I'll be hornswoggled!" the young man said. "With everybody else, it's like he hates 'em on sight! But he took to you right away."

"Maybe he was just waiting for somebody he was sure could handle him."

"If you say so, mister. The boss is askin' seventy-five for him. For a hundred and twenty-five, we'll throw in a good saddle and the rest of the tack. Nothin' shoddy, either. Good quality stuff."

"It had better be," Conrad said. "Let me see it."

The hostler showed him the saddle, and while there was nothing fancy about it, Conrad agreed it was perfectly functional.

"We don't have to settle this deal tonight, you know," the young man said when they were back in the office. "Don't you want to come back tomorrow and ride that critter before you make up your mind?"

"I saw what I needed to see." Conrad counted out six double eagles and a five-dollar gold piece, stacking them on the desk. "I don't want somebody else coming in and snatching that bay out from under me."

The hostler stared at the coins and gave an involuntary whistle. "Mister, you must be rich!" he declared.

"Not hardly," Conrad lied, "but if there's something I want and I can afford it, I don't like to let it get away from me."

"All right, you got a deal. Anything else I can help you with?"

"Point me to a good hotel," Conrad said, then smiled and added, keeping up the pretense of being just an anonymous drifter, "Not anything too fancy or expensive, though. I seem to have spent most of my money on a horse . . ."

Chapter 18

"Father!"

The three younger children rushed to hug Roosevelt. He gathered them into a wide embrace. Ted hung back, a solemn, serious look on his young, bespectacled face, but after a moment he hurried forward, too, and hugged his father.

Mrs. Roosevelt stood a little to one side, hands clasped in front of her, looking even more serious than her oldest son.

Bullock waited by the door, hat in hand, more than a little embarrassed to be present for this family reunion. As soon as he could, he would make his excuses and get out of here, leaving the Roosevelts alone to say whatever they wanted to say in the privacy of this suite.

On the way here to the hotel from the train station, Roosevelt had explained to Bullock how fate had supplied him with an unexpected ally in the person of Conrad Morgan. Bullock had listened in surprise as the President told him about Conrad's plan . . . and also how Conrad had enlisted the help of his father, Frank Morgan.

"The Drifter," Bullock had said. "I've met him. Never had any real dealings with him, but folks say he's just about as fast on the draw as anybody who's ever strapped on a gun.

A good man to have on your side. And he's on his way here to Deadwood, you say?"

"That's right. I'm not certain when he'll arrive, but Conrad believes his father will make all due haste and join us within a day or two."

With that cold wind blowing, not many people were on the street tonight, and none of them paid much attention to the two men striding along determinedly. Even so, Bullock felt like they had eyes on them, although that might have been his imagination. But the kidnappers had said they would be in touch with Roosevelt again once he reached Deadwood, so they had to have *somebody* keeping an eye out for him.

"I know Frank Morgan's supposed to be a square shooter," Bullock had continued as they walked to the hotel. "But are you sure you can trust his son? There's no chance he might be in on this . . . this scheme, whatever it is?"

A bark of laughter had come from Roosevelt. "I'm the one who invited him to Washington in the first place, so I don't see how that's possible. Besides, he's one of the richest young men in the country, in the same league as Vanderbilt, Rockefeller, Carnegie, and that *other* Morgan, the one with all the steel mills. In fact, it wouldn't surprise me if he has business connections with all those other fellows. Not to mention, I'm a good judge of character, and that young man's is sterling, I tell you. Sterling!"

"Well, if you vouch for him, Teddy, I'm glad he's on our side."

The plan Conrad Morgan had come up with resembled the same one that Bullock had put together in his head. There was no way in hell he was going to allow the President of the United States to go traipsing across the Black Hills by himself in search of kidnappers and outlaws . . . but it might be vital to the safety of those youngsters that the villains *believed* that was going on.

In order to do that, Roosevelt would have to run some risks. There was no getting around it. But the man who had led the charge up San Juan Hill wouldn't shrink from any danger if it meant rescuing his children. Seth Bullock knew that.

Just like he recognized the slightly apprehensive frown on his old friend's face as Roosevelt turned to face his wife, here in the hotel suite.

"Edith," Roosevelt said.

"Theodore," she replied coolly.

Roosevelt was a demonstrative man by nature, but from what Bullock had heard about his wife, Mrs. Roosevelt was normally rather reserved and dignified. She had had a little time to recover from the initial shock of what had happened, so it was no surprise that she didn't throw herself in her husband's arms, weeping and wailing.

Bullock figured it was time for him to get out of here. He spoke up, saying, "I'll be going now, Mr. President, but I'm staying here in the hotel tonight. If you need me, ring down to the front desk." Bullock pointed to the telephone sitting on a small table near the door. "I'll be here right away."

"Thank you, Seth," Roosevelt said with a distracted nod. He told the children, "You fellows go in the bedroom now, so that I can speak with your mother privately."

They filed out of the room obediently as Bullock slipped into the hall and eased the door closed behind him. He put his hat on and headed for the stairs.

He wondered where Conrad Morgan was right now. Since it looked like they were going to be working together to help foil the kidnappers, they ought to have a talk about how they were going to manage that. But he had no idea where Conrad was, and he had promised Roosevelt that he would remain in the hotel tonight.

He would find Conrad Morgan later, Bullock decided,

and maybe by that time, Frank Morgan would have reached Deadwood, as well.

The first time Frank Morgan had come to Deadwood was in the summer of 1876. He was still a relatively young man as far as the years went, but a decade spent with a reputation as a fast gun hanging over his head had aged him, at least on the inside. Or maybe he had been born with an old soul; Frank was never sure which. But all he wanted to do was check out the rumors he had heard about the gold strike and maybe do a little prospecting up the gulch from the crude, wild mining camp.

Besides, Deadwood already numbered one famous gunfighter among its citizens. Frank had heard that Wild Bill Hickok was there, so that was all the more reason for him to keep his head down and not let folks know who he was. If word got around that the notorious Drifter was in Deadwood, too, people would start clamoring for a showdown between the two pistoleers. Frank had no desire to challenge Hickok. He didn't know which of them was faster . . . and didn't care.

The ambition to be known as the fastest draw just wasn't part of Frank Morgan's personality. His speed with a gun was a tool he was forced to use from time to time; that was all.

As it turned out, by the time Frank reached the settlement, Wild Bill had been dead for more than a week, shot from behind in one of the squalid saloons. And prospecting for gold was tedious work, so Frank didn't stick with it for very long. He didn't mind hard physical labor, but being bored gnawed at him. Or maybe he had just picked up the habit of being fiddle-footed during the past ten years. Either way, he didn't stay long before riding out, bound for no place in particular, as usual.

In the quarter of a century since then, his rambling ways had taken him back to Deadwood a few times, so he was aware that it had grown into an actual city. When he swung down from one of the passenger cars in the regular Chicago & North Western train from Rapid City the next morning, he wasn't surprised by the sight of paved streets, sidewalks, and gas streetlights. Deadwood had entered the twentieth century willingly, unlike old pelicans like Frank who had to be dragged into it.

The sky was overcast and the air had a bite to it. The sheepskin coat Frank wore felt good. He glanced at the clouds as he walked across the depot platform with a carpet-bag in his left hand and a Winchester in his right. With the seasoned eye of a veteran frontiersman, he judged that those clouds didn't have any snow in them, but a man could never be sure about things like that. The weather had a mind of its own.

A young man leaned against the lobby's outside wall, arms crossed over his chest and his head down. Despite the casual pose, Frank knew he was watching everybody who got off the train. The young man straightened and walked toward the steps at the end of the platform, apparently paying no attention to Frank.

Frank let the young man get ahead of him, then went down the steps, too, and walked along the train to a stock car. A couple of railroad hostlers opened it and lowered a ramp, then one of them led a saddled golden sorrel horse out of the car.

"Here you go, mister," the man said to Frank. "This is a mighty fine-looking animal. He have a name?"

"I call him Goldy," Frank said, then chuckled and added, "Not very original, I know, but it fits him."

Goldy was the only one of Frank's regular trail partners he had brought with him. He had left his other horse, Stormy, and the big cur called Dog with Salty Stevens, the bearded old-timer who had also shared a number of adventures with Frank. Salty was stove up with the rheumatiz and had retired from gallivanting all over the countryside getting into all sorts of dust-ups, and Stormy and Dog didn't get around as well as they once had, either, so it made sense for Salty to look after them.

"When are you gonna stop all this trouble-huntin' and hell-raisin', Frank?" Salty had asked during their brief visit on the horse ranch Salty had started. "You may not look it, but you're pert' near as old as I am!"

"I'm trying to settle down, Salty," Frank had replied with a grin, "but those ruckuses keep coming along and dragging me in!"

Frank took Goldy's reins from the hostler and led the horse away from the railroad tracks. He started walking along the adjoining street but hadn't gone very far before a tall, lithe shape fell in step alongside him, the same one that had been awaiting the train's arrival.

"You made good time getting here," Conrad said.

"Figured you needed my help, or you wouldn't have sent for me."

"It's a friend of mine who needs the help."

"Yeah, so you said in your telegram. But you didn't say *who.*"

"That's because I didn't want to write it down," Conrad replied. "I'm talking about the President of the United States."

It was a tribute to Frank's calm demeanor and steady nerves that he didn't break stride at that news, even a little. He let out a low whistle of surprise, though, and said quietly, "Teddy Roosevelt his own self? That must be one heck of a story you have to tell me."

"Let's take Goldy to the stable where my horse is, and I'll fill you in on the whole thing."

* * *

Seth Bullock was in the hotel dining room, finishing up his breakfast, when a young man came in and looked around. Bullock recognized him as one of the clerks from the Western Union office, and every instinct in his body told him the boy was looking for him. He was about to raise a hand so the youngster would notice him when the clerk spotted him anyway and hurried across the dining room. Bullock saw that he had a small envelope in his hand and knew there had to be a telegram inside it.

"Mr. Bullock, I got something odd here," the clerk said as he came up to the table. "We found this message a few minutes ago."

"Found it?" Bullock repeated. "You mean it didn't come in over the wire?"

"No, sir. It's on one of our telegram forms, in one of our envelopes, but somebody left it on the counter. Somebody here in Deadwood. Had to be."

"You didn't see who it was?"

The young man shook his head. "No, sir. Several people have been in already this morning. It could have been any one of them, I reckon. Or maybe somebody slipped in that we didn't notice."

"How easy is it to get hold of one of those forms and an envelope?"

"They're sitting out on the counter," the clerk said. "Anybody could've done it."

Bullock nodded slowly and said, "This message is addressed to me?"

"Well, no, sir, not exactly. But it's addressed *in care of* you."

"That means I can read it, I reckon." Bullock held out his hand.

The youngster still hesitated. "I don't know," he said.

"My boss told me that if you know who it's really intended for, I should give it to that fella, instead. It may not be a regular telegram, but it was sort of entrusted to us, you know?"

The clerk turned the envelope so that Bullock could read what was printed on the outside of it: *An Important Man, Care of Seth Bullock.*

"I know who it's intended for," Bullock said, "but you need to let me give it to him, son. No offense, but things are going on that are none of your concern." He smiled thinly. "Don't worry, I give you my word I'll deliver it unopened and unread."

The youngster swallowed hard and said quickly, "Oh, golly, Mr. Bullock, I didn't mean to make it sound like I don't trust you. Gosh, there's nobody who's done more for Deadwood than you have—"

Bullock held out his hand again, and this time the clerk gave him the envelope. With his other hand, Bullock slid a silver dollar across the table within reach of the young man.

"Thanks, son. You've done more than you know."

"Yes, sir. I mean, thank you, sir." The clerk snatched up the coin and hurried away.

Bullock sat there for a moment, gently tapping the envelope's edge against the table beside his empty coffee cup. A part of him was tempted to open the blasted thing and read the message inside, but whatever was written there, it was meant for Teddy Roosevelt and Bullock's old friend had the right to read it first.

He stood, picked up his hat from the table where it lay, and headed upstairs to the President's suite.

Roosevelt himself answered Bullock's discreet knock. The President wore a tightly belted robe over his pajamas. His hair was slightly rumpled from sleep. But as usual, he was alert and intense and looked as if, with a few minutes of preparation, he could be ready to address a joint session of Congress.

"Is there news?" Roosevelt asked crisply.

Bullock glanced past him, saw that the sitting room was otherwise empty. He nodded and held out the envelope. Roosevelt took it from him and motioned for Bullock to come in.

The envelope's flap was only lightly fastened. Roosevelt opened it while Bullock was closing the door. He slid out the yellow piece of paper and peered at it through his pince-nez. He drew in a deep breath. Bullock saw Roosevelt's fingers tighten on the telegram, and for a moment he thought the President was going to crumple the paper.

But then Roosevelt got control of his emotions. He extended the telegram form to Bullock and said, "At least I know now who's responsible for this atrocity, although I doubt if he wrote this message himself. I don't believe he was ever that literate."

Bullock read the printed words:

BRING THE AMOUNT WE TOLD YOU TO THE LAST PLACE YOU SAW ME OR RUE THE DAY STOP GREENDALE.

Looking up from the telegram, Bullock said, "Greendale? That old rustler? What was his first name?"

"Gus," Roosevelt said. "Gus Greendale. And yes, he was a rustler and outlaw. Many years ago, while I was running my ranch, I helped the law track down him and his gang. As far as I know, he's been in prison for the past fifteen years. I had no idea he was out."

"Looks like he's been carrying a grudge for you all that time," Bullock said.

Roosevelt took the telegram back and nodded. "Indeed. But as I said, I don't believe Greendale wrote this himself. Nor was he the sort of man who could put together such an audacious scheme. He has allies, and they're the ones who are truly to blame for what's happened."

"That makes sense," Bullock admitted. "I never crossed trails with Greendale, but I remember hearing about him. He was no Jesse James, never more than a small-timer. But that doesn't make him any less dangerous now."

"No, it certainly does not." Roosevelt squared his shoulders. "But at least we know the next step."

"And that is . . . ?"

"I'm going to the Dutchman's," the President declared.

Chapter 19

Somewhere in the Black Hills

One man rode out of the trees, reined in, and spent several minutes looking around at the rugged, thickly wooded slopes. Several hundred yards away, at the bottom of this hill, an old, sprawling log building stood near a creek that meandered through the narrow valley. Off to the side was a pole corral in poor repair. Part of the enclosure had collapsed. All the building's walls were still standing, and the roof hadn't fallen in, but an air of neglect hung over it anyway. No smoke rose from the stone chimney. On a cold day like this, there ought to be a fire in the fireplace if anybody was here.

Hank Singleton hipped around in the saddle and nodded. A moment later, Gus Greendale rode out of the forest, leading the horse on which Alice Roosevelt was mounted. Tiny came next, riding alongside Kermit Roosevelt. Lame Wolf brought up the rear, riding with his head cocked sideways so he could listen and make sure nobody was coming up on their back trail.

Alice shivered as the chilly wind swept through the valley and along this slope. The men didn't have any spare coats, but they had given her two shirts to wear, along with a pair of denim trousers and some boots that were too big. She had to wear an extra pair of socks to make the boots even come close to fitting, and the clothes were pretty baggy on her, but the extra garments they had given Kermit practically swallowed the slender youngster.

Greendale had complained about having to dress the prisoners, grousing that he hadn't planned on needing to do that. Alice thought that was just one more indication how stupid the outlaw was. If you were going to kidnap someone in the middle of the night, wouldn't it make sense that they would be dressed for bed, not for traveling?

That was more proof, as if she needed it, that Gus Greendale wasn't the mastermind behind the kidnapping. That man they had met on the hill just outside of Deadwood, the one with the Eastern accent, perhaps *he* had planned the whole thing. Alice didn't know . . . and of course, it didn't really matter.

She and her brother were helpless captives, scores of miles from anywhere, in the clutches of brutal men who were ruthless, if not overly smart. All things considered, *not* a good situation for them to find themselves in. That was what was important.

Greendale smirked over at her and said, "I told you that if you'd just be patient, missy, we'd get to some place more comfortable."

"Yes, that squalid hovel appears to be the veritable lap of luxury," Alice replied in a voice as cold as the wind.

"You'll see," Greendale insisted. "Once we get inside and build up a fire, it'll be plumb cozy in there. I know that for a fact because I've been there plenty of times."

"Not in recent years."

Greendale frowned. Alice knew that he had spent the past decade and a half in prison, and he knew she was jabbing at him about it.

"I'd think that after four nights on the trail, you'd be happy to spend a night indoors for a change," he snapped.

Alice took a deep breath. "I am," she said. Even though she had a rather tart tongue by nature, she couldn't see the value in annoying him at this point, so she knew she ought to try to control it. "I'm grateful for any consideration you show to my brother and myself, Mr. Greendale. Thank you."

Greendale said, "Hmmph. That's better."

Alice was trying to mollify him, but her words held some truth. This long, arduous trip through the Black Hills had been a very unpleasant ordeal. In addition to the sheer discomfort of unsuitable clothing and long hours in the saddle, the ever-present fear of being killed or molested had hung over her and, to a lesser extent, Kermit. She was confident that none of these men were deviants who would do anything depraved to a boy, but she had no doubt that any of them would put a bullet through Kermit's head if the situation dictated the need for such violence.

And the one called Hank made no secret of the animalistic lust he felt toward her. She had seen the others looking at her in that manner from time to time as well, even the old Indian. But she had to give Greendale credit for being true to his word: none of them had laid a finger on her in that fashion. The only times they touched her were to tie her up at night so she couldn't try to escape. They did the same thing to Kermit.

And Alice *would* have tried to escape if she got the opportunity, even though they were in the middle of a wilderness, days away from civilization, with winter coming on, and no doubt she would die from exposure or be mauled and eaten by wild animals if she were on her own. She would attempt it anyway, just to keep these filthy outlaws from getting what they wanted.

The little group was halfway down the hill now, with Hank

Singleton still riding ahead of the others. He half-turned in his saddle to look back with a grin on his bearded face.

"I sure do remember some of the good times we had at the Dutchman's, boys," he called. "Sure, everything went bad that last time, but before that, I always enjoyed comin' here—"

The sharp, sudden crack of a rifle interrupted him. Singleton cried out, and as his horse reared, he toppled out of the saddle.

Greendale yelled a curse, yanked his revolver from its holster, and jabbed his heels in his horse's flanks as he hauled on the reins with the same hand that held the lead rope of Alice's horse. Greendale's mount turned and jumped in front of Alice's. The outlaw was shielding her with his own body, Alice realized, somewhat to her surprise.

Although he just wanted to protect his investment of time and energy, she told herself. She was worth something to him as long as she was alive. She might or might not be, dead.

"Get back!" Greendale called to Tiny and Lame Wolf. "Back to the trees!" They reined in, wheeled their mounts, and headed for the cover of the thick forest. "Hank! How bad are you hit?"

Singleton was lying facedown as his spooked horse skittered away. He lifted his head and gave it a shake as if he were trying to clear cobwebs from his brain. After a second, his vision focused and he peered blearily at Greendale.

"What happened?"

"Somebody down there at the Dutchman's shot you outta the saddle!"

Alice had seen the spurt of powdersmoke from one of the windows, just as the shot rang out. But no more reports had sounded. It appeared that whoever was down there in the old trading post was waiting to see what Greendale and the others would do.

"I don't think I'm hit!" Singleton said. Without getting up, he patted himself all over as best he could and went on, "I can't find no bullet holes. I just whacked my head pretty hard when I landed."

"I see some blood on your horse's hip," Greendale said. "Looks like the slug grazed him. That's what made him buck you off." He glanced over his shoulder. "You all right back there, missy? That wild bullet didn't hit you?"

"I'm fine," Alice told him. "Or as fine as I can be, under these circumstances."

"Somebody just took a potshot at us," Greendale snapped. "Don't go gettin' mouthy." He looked down the hill again and raised his voice. "Hello, the Dutchman's! Hold your fire! We're friendly!"

The response came in a thin, querulous voice. "Ain't got no friends! That shot was just a warnin'. Come any closer and I'll drill you, you *verdammt* scoundrel!"

The voice trailed off in a spate of guttural language that Alice recognized as German, although she wasn't able to make out any of the words. From their general tone, however, she suspected they were obscenities.

Greendale stared at the old building in amazement for a moment, then shouted, "Krieger? Krieger, is that really you, you damned old Dutchman? I heard tell you died ten years ago!"

"I live," the hidden rifleman replied. "Who are you?"

"It's me, your old pal, Gus Greendale!"

The rifle roared again. Greendale yelped and ducked his head instinctively. So did Alice, behind him, even though she heard a whining sound that she was pretty sure came from the bullet passing high overhead.

"You are not *mein freund,* Greendale," the man called Krieger replied while the shot still echoed over the Black Hills. "You never were."

"You never turned down our money, damn your hide!"

Greendale yelled back. "It was good enough for you then, and it oughta be good enough for you now."

Lame Wolf had emerged from the trees again when it became obvious the man holed up in the old building wasn't actually trying to kill them. He moved his horse up alongside Alice's mount and said quietly, "It might not be wise to antagonize him, Gus. If that really is Krieger—and it certainly sounds like him—he's probably been up here by himself for a long time. He may be a bit mad by now."

"I don't give a damn how loco he is," Greendale said. "That old tradin' post is where Neill was gonna tell Roosevelt to meet us. That's where we've got to be."

"The Dutchman probably believes you have a grudge against him," Lame Wolf pointed out. "He *did* side with Roosevelt, that night when we were captured."

Greendale rasped fingertips over his beard-stubbled chin as he thought about what Lame Wolf said. Finally, he nodded.

"You're right. I got to convince him he ain't in no danger from us." Raising his voice again, Greendale went on, "Hey, Krieger, listen to me! Me and the boys don't hold no grudge against you. We want to let bygones be bygones. So put that rifle away and let us ride on down there. For old time's sake, pard. There ain't many of us old boys left from those days."

Silence met Greendale's words. Seconds dragged by. Then Krieger called from the trading post, "You have not come to settle the score with me?"

"Shoot, no! We've done forgot all about what happened back then. Besides, you didn't have no choice but to back that four-eyed varmint's play. If you'd tried to help us, they'd have just sent you to prison, too, or put you six feet under like they did poor Hubert and Amos."

From where he lay on the ground, Hank Singleton growled, "I ain't forgotten what happened to Hubert."

"That wasn't the Dutchman's doin'," Greendale told him,

tight-lipped. "I'm startin' to convince him, so keep your trap shut, Hank."

Singleton glared, but he didn't say anything else.

Greendale lifted his voice again. "How about it, Krieger? You gonna hold your fire and let us ride on down there?"

After another moment of silence, Krieger responded, "*Ja*. Come ahead. I will not shoot."

"Get on your horse, Hank," Greendale ordered. He nudged his mount ahead and rode past Singleton, still leading Alice's horse.

The door opened and a man stepped outside, holding a rifle. He was tall but stooped, indicating that he had been even taller at one time, and he had a shrunken look about him, as if time had stolen flesh from his bones and turned a much bigger man into a scrawny one. He wore canvas overalls over a faded red, long-sleeved union suit. The sun gleamed on his bald head, which reminded Alice uncomfortably of a skull.

The man watched the new arrivals warily as they rode up to the old trading post. Greendale brought his horse and Alice's to a stop and chuckled.

"Damn, Krieger, you got old," he said.

"So did you," Krieger said.

"Well, prison ages a man, they say, and I can't argue with 'em."

Krieger studied Alice and Kermit. His mouth twisted as if he had bitten into something sour.

"These children, they are prisoners?"

"That's right. We got no intention of hurtin' 'em, but we can't take a chance on them gettin' away."

"You are kidnappers." Krieger sounded like he wanted to spit.

"Back in the old days, you did business with fellas who were a lot worse than that," Greendale reminded him. "So don't go gettin' all high an' mighty on us. You never turned away an owlhoot because you were next thing to bein' one yourself."

Krieger's chin, covered with silvery stubble, jutted forward. "I ran a business," he said. "It was not my job to ask questions of my customers."

"Yeah, you look at it any way you want, if it makes you feel better."

Hank Singleton said, "Why'd you shoot at me, you old buzzard?"

"If I had shot at *you,* you would be dead. As I said, I wished only to warn you."

"Well, my hoss has got a bullet burn on his hip, and it probably hurts."

Krieger's shoulders, no longer brawny, rose and fell. "My apologies . . . to your horse. Perhaps I creased the wrong dumb animal."

Singleton glared and moved his hand toward the gun on his hip. Krieger shifted his grip on the rifle.

"Stop it, the both of you," Greendale said. "Hank, I've got some liniment that'll fix your horse right up. Krieger, if you'll cooperate and let us stay here for a few days, there's a hundred bucks in it for you."

"How much ransom have you demanded for these children?" Krieger asked coldly.

"That's none of your business. I'm offerin' to cut you in for a hundred bucks, and you don't have to do a thing but put up with us for a few days."

"Who are their parents?"

"You don't need to know that, either." Greendale rested his hand on the butt of his gun. "Now, are you takin' the deal, or leavin' it?"

Krieger looked from Greendale to Singleton to Tiny and Lame Wolf. Four against one odds were clearly too much for him to buck. He said, "It seems I have no choice—"

"Our father is the President of the United States," Alice said.

Greendale cursed and twisted toward her. For a second, Alice thought he was going to lean over in the saddle and backhand her. She glared at him defiantly. Let him do his worst.

Well, maybe not his absolute *worst* . . .

"This is true?" Krieger said. "You demand ransom from the leader of this nation?"

"What if it is?" Greendale snapped.

"This man Roosevelt, he commands an army. Eventually, they swept the Indians from the plains and the hills and the mountains. What will they do to a small band of desperadoes?"

"Not one damned thing, if Roosevelt wants these kids to live," Greendale said. "That's the deal, and he knows it."

Slowly, Krieger's head went up and down, nodding. He said, "Five hundred."

"For just lettin' us stay here for a few days?"

"For risking the wrath of the entire nation," Krieger replied. His mouth curved into a grin that made him look more like a death's-head than ever. "It is worth that much, *ja*?"

Greendale blew out a breath and said, "All right, you've got a deal."

Krieger's rifle had remained aimed in their general direction. He pointed it toward the ground and said, "Come in. I will build a fire. At my age, I never feel warm anymore, so it is a waste of firewood when I am here alone."

Singleton licked his lips and asked, "What happened to the whores who used to work here?"

Krieger shook his head. "Long gone. Almost certainly dead by now, in that line of work. And no others were willing to come all the way out here."

"Well, that's a shame. A damned shame."

Singleton looked at Alice, and a shiver ran through her.

She worried that it was just a matter of time until Greendale couldn't control the man anymore.

But right now, Greendale just said, "Come on. I want to get in outta the wind. Tiny, Lame Wolf, see to the horses. Looks like you'll need to put some of those corral poles back up."

High on the slope overlooking the old trading post, well hidden in the trees, three men watched as Greendale and Singleton took the prisoners off their horses and marched them inside. The black man and the Indian set poles back in place in the corral, tied them with strips of rawhide, and then led the horses in and unsaddled them.

"John, they got a fire in there," Nate Poore whined as smoke began to rise from the stone chimney. "I been freezin' to death since we've been sleepin' outside the past few nights. Can't we go down there and warm up?"

John Perry took off his hat and wearily scrubbed a hand over his weathered face. He put the hat back on and sighed.

"Nate, I've told you, we can't let those fellas know we've been following them. I don't trust Greendale. He won't cut us in on the deal just because we show up and tell him we want him to. We have to wait for the right time, when Greendale and his bunch actually need us, or when we can move in, take them by surprise, and grab those kids for ourselves."

"And kill Greendale and them others?" Oscar Sheehan rumbled.

"I expect we'll have to, if it comes to that," Perry replied with a solemn nod. "So we need to make sure everything's set up the way we want it before we run that risk."

"Yeah, I reckon that makes sense," Sheehan said.

"Yeah, I reckon," Poore added, agreeable now that Sheehan had declared himself first.

Sheehan sounded proud of himself as he went on, "We

done some good trackin', managin' to stay close to that bunch without them ever figurin' out we were on their trail. I halfway expected that redskin to realize we were behind 'em."

"Redskins are sneaky," Poore said.

"No sneakier than us," Perry said, and he sounded pretty satisfied with himself, too. They didn't know exactly what they had gotten themselves into yet, but if they played their cards right, they would wind up rich. Perry could feel that in his bones.

And after the hardscrabble life he'd led, he didn't care how many people had to die to make that dream come true.

Chapter 20

Deadwood

Frank had gotten himself a room at the Black Hills Inn, the same saloon/hotel where Conrad was staying, and they had been talking together this morning in Conrad's room when a knock sounded on the door.

Father and son had glanced at each other, then stood up and drawn their guns. Old habits made them approach the door warily, with Frank moving slightly to the left so he would be behind the door when it opened.

"Who's there?" Conrad called through the panel, then took a quick step to the right, just in case anybody tried blasting through the door with a rifle or shotgun.

Instead, a voice came from the corridor, saying, "Seth Bullock."

Conrad had never met Bullock, didn't know the man's voice, so he looked at his father. Frank nodded, confident the visitor was who he said he was. And it seemed unlikely that anybody could force Bullock into betraying friends, even with a gun on him, so Frank remained silent but gestured for Conrad to open the door.

Conrad did so with his left hand, keeping the Colt ready in his right. The man in the hall, dressed in a dark suit and hat, was alone. Conrad recognized him as the man who had met President Roosevelt at the train station. He stepped back to let Bullock enter the room.

Bullock did so, pausing just a couple of steps in and smiling. He said, "I reckon you can come out from behind the door now, Frank."

"How'd you know I was there?" Frank asked as he stepped into sight and lowered his gun.

"That's where I would've been, if the situation was turned around." Bullock stuck out his hand. "It's good to see you again."

Frank pouched the iron he held and clasped Bullock's hand. "Pleased to see you, as well." He nodded toward Conrad. "This is my son Conrad."

"It's an honor, Mr. Morgan," Bullock said as he shook hands with Conrad. "Teddy tells me you were almost the Assistant Secretary of the Interior."

"Well, not exactly," Conrad said. "But he did offer me the job."

"You would've been one of my bosses if you'd taken it. I'm the supervisor of the Black Hills Forest Reserve. Not that there's all that much to the job. It sounds more impressive than it really is."

Frank shut the door and asked, "How's the President doing?"

"He's getting ready to ride out."

"He's heard from the kidnappers?" Conrad said.

"That's right. A note from them showed up at the telegraph office this morning. Not an actual telegram, mind you, but a message for them to deliver, left there by somebody who managed to slip in and out without being seen."

"More proof that the kidnappers have at least one accomplice here in Deadwood," Conrad said.

"That's right."

"What did the message say?" Frank asked.

"Teddy is supposed to deliver the ransom money to a place called the Dutchman's."

"The Dutchman's!" Frank repeated.

"You know it?" Bullock asked.

"An old outlaw hangout. I've been there. Not that I was on the dodge," Frank added quickly, "but I roamed around so much that I wound up visiting most places, sooner or later." He shook his head. "I heard that the German fella who ran the place died, so I figured it had been abandoned for years."

"That may well be the case. But that's where the kidnappers told the President to bring that money, anyway."

"And he's going to do it," Conrad said.

"Of course he is. He's not going to take a chance on his children's lives. But he's not going to let those varmints get away with what they've done, either." Bullock looked back and forth between Frank and Conrad. "That's where we come in, gentlemen."

Conrad and Frank went in the rear door of the Bullock Hotel and up the back stairs to the second floor. It was later that morning, but not much later. The two of them, along with Bullock, had spent some time going over the plan, but it hadn't required a great deal of discussion. Even before the President arrived in Deadwood, Bullock had figured on trailing him to the rendezvous with the kidnappers, then playing it by ear from there. Now, he would have allies in that effort, in the persons of the Morgans, father and son.

The door of the suite opened to Bullock's knock. Theodore Roosevelt let them into the sitting room. Frank wasn't the sort to be in awe of any man, but the knowledge that he was in the presence of the leader of the United States—and such a vital leader as this one—made him look at Roosevelt with genuine respect.

Evidently the feeling was mutual, because when Bullock said, "Teddy, this is Frank Morgan," the President held out his hand and smiled broadly.

"This is quite an honor," Roosevelt declared. "For myself, I mean. I've heard a great deal about you, Mr. Morgan, not only from your son but also from the days when I lived in these parts and operated a ranch."

Frank gripped his hand and said, "It's an honor for me, as well, Mr. President."

"Please, call me Teddy. We're old campaigners, you and I."

"All right, Teddy. Make it Frank."

"Bully! Bully, I say! That miscreant Greendale doesn't know how much trouble he's let himself in for, eh?"

"We can hope so," Frank said. "It's always better to take hombres like that by surprise."

"And the men who are working with him," Conrad put in. "That's why we were very careful coming over here. Nobody's going to know that we have any connection to you, Mr. President, so when we ride out later today, if any members of the gang are watching, they won't know that we'll be on your trail."

Bullock said, "We'll be close by and keeping an eye on you the whole way, Teddy."

"Not too close," Roosevelt cautioned. "We don't want to tip off the enemy."

"I hear you're headed for the Dutchman's," Frank commented.

Roosevelt looked at him with interest. "You know the place?"

"I do," Frank nodded. "Been a long time since I've been there."

"That's true for myself, as well."

"Are you sure you can find your way to it?"

"I have no doubt of it," Roosevelt declared. "I have a good memory for trails and landscapes, gentlemen, and the

Black Hills haven't changed much since the last time I visited the Dutchman's. The terrain is so rugged that it *can't* change much."

"True enough," Frank agreed. He squinted in thought. "You figure a three or four day ride from here?"

"That's what I make it, yes."

Bullock said, "We'd better hope the weather holds. The last thing we need to deal with, on top of everything else, is a blizzard."

"Whatever it is . . . weather, wild animals, evil men . . . nothing will stand in the way of me rescuing my children, gentlemen," Roosevelt said. "Nothing."

Frank heard the utter determination in the President's voice and saw it on Roosevelt's face.

Roosevelt took a deep breath and went on, "I'll be leaving within the hour, as soon as I've said my farewells to my wife and the other children. You've made all the arrangements, Seth?"

"That's right. You'll have three saddle horses so you can switch among them, as well as a pack mule. Four Colt revolvers, two Winchesters, and a shotgun, along with plenty of ammunition for each." Bullock smiled. "You're loaded for bear, Teddy."

"And I won't hesitate to use those weapons if I need to. But, if by some chance, Gus Greendale will honor his word and is willing to turn Alice and Kermit over to me unharmed in exchange for the money, I'll make that trade. If I can get those children out of his hands without any violence, that will be the best outcome."

"Of course," Bullock said. "We'll follow your lead and won't step in unless we have to."

"Very well. May good fortune follow us all."

They shook hands all around, then Bullock, Frank, and Conrad left the suite so that Roosevelt could say goodbye to the rest of his family. Out in the corridor, Bullock said to

Frank and Conrad, "I'll meet you fellas a mile up the gulch in an hour."

"We'll be there," Conrad said.

As they went down the rear stairs, Frank said, "What do you think the chances are that this fella Greendale will keep his word, like Teddy was talking about?"

"I don't think there's any chance of it at all," Conrad replied bluntly. "Greendale wants revenge on the President, and if that's not enough, I'm convinced that he's mixed up with a bigger gang, one that's after something else. This isn't just about money, Frank."

"I think you're right," Frank said. "In fact, I'd bet a hat on it."

In addition to Goldy and the big bay Conrad had bought, they also had a pack horse with enough supplies to last a couple of weeks. They didn't expect to be gone that long, but on a mission such as this, you never could tell exactly how long it would take. Frank and Conrad could live off the land if they had to, but that would be more difficult with the three Roosevelts along.

Seth Bullock had brought a pack horse loaded with supplies, too, they saw as they rendezvoused with Bullock a mile up Deadwood Gulch from the settlement. The former sheriff smiled as he saw the packsaddles that Frank and Conrad had loaded on their extra horse.

"Great minds think alike, or so they say," he commented. "We oughtn't to go hungry."

"Yeah, all we have to worry about is being bushwhacked by kidnappers," Frank said with a grin. He grew more serious as he went on, "The gang's liable to have somebody trailing the President, so we'll need to keep our eyes open."

"I'll be mighty surprised if they're *not* following him," Bullock said. "I kept a sharp eye out while I was riding up the gulch, though, and didn't see anybody. Still, we need to be careful, so that's why we're not going to follow Teddy, exactly."

Conrad frowned. "We're not? I thought that was the plan."

"That was before we knew what the destination is. I know how to get to the Dutchman's, so once we're out of this gulch, we're going to veer off to the south a ways and parallel the most direct route, which is the one Teddy will be taking. That way anybody watching for him will be more likely to miss us."

"What if he runs into trouble?"

"From the gang?" Bullock shook his head. "I don't think that's very likely. They want him to get there with that ransom money. But if they *do* try to pull some kind of a double-cross, or if he encounters any other kind of problem, Teddy knows to fire three shots. We'll still be close enough we ought to hear that signal, and we can come a-runnin'."

"Sounds like it ought to work," Frank said with a nod. "Let's go."

The three men nudged their mounts into motion and rode up Deadwood Gulch, leading the pack horses. The next few days would be tense ones, with a bloody showdown quite possibly waiting at the end, but none of them were the sort to back down from something like that.

In fact, if the truth were to be told, all three of them were looking forward to facing off against the varmints who had dared to kidnap the President's children.

Chapter 21

Deadwood

A couple of days had passed since the President left town, but Lowell Hammersby still felt just as tense as he had when Roosevelt first rode out.

He tried to keep that anxiety well hidden. Mrs. Roosevelt and the other children were counting on him to look after them. The President had given Hammersby that assignment, and Lowell Hammersby had never let Mr. Roosevelt down. He didn't intend to start now.

So he maintained an optimistic attitude and kept a smile on his face as he knocked on the door of the suite shared, at the moment, by Mrs. Roosevelt and her younger daughter Ethel. This was where the family had been gathered most of the time, although the boys still slept in the other suite.

Ted opened the door and said, "Oh, good morning, Mr. Hammersby. Come in."

Hat in hand, Hammersby stepped into the sitting room. A dining table had been set up, so that the Roosevelts could take all their meals here. It still wasn't common knowledge that the President's family was in town. In fact, with Seth Bullock and the Morgans gone, Hammersby thought he might well be the only one who knew the truth. Mr. Bullock had provided guards, but those men knew only that they were protecting someone important, without being aware of the details.

The Roosevelts, except for Ted, were sitting at that dining table now, with what was left of breakfast spread out before them. Ted's empty seat was at the head of the table. With his father gone, he was the nominal man of the family, although there was no doubt that his mother, seated at the other end of the table, was really in charge here.

"Good morning, Mr. Hammersby," Edith Roosevelt greeted him. "Would you care to join us for breakfast?"

"No, thank you, ma'am," Hammersby replied. "I've already eaten. If there's any coffee left in that pot, though . . ."

He gestured toward a gleaming coffee pot sitting on a tray on a sideboard. A pair of empty cups were still upside down on saucers with it.

Mrs. Roosevelt smiled politely. "Help yourself, by all means."

"Have you heard any news about my father?" Ted asked while Hammersby poured coffee into one of the cups.

"No, I'm afraid not. But there really hasn't been time. Where he's going, he's not likely to find any way to communicate with us before he's able to return to Deadwood, and he expected to be gone at least a week."

Ted resumed his seat. He looked down glumly into his plate and said, "I suppose I knew that. I'm just worried about him, and about Alice and Kermit."

"We all are," Mrs. Roosevelt said. "But dwelling on those worries serves no purpose." She looked at Hammersby. "I take it the preparation for the festivities that brought us here are proceeding as if nothing has happened?"

"As far as the folks in Deadwood are concerned, nothing *has* happened," Hammersby replied. "So yes, they're definitely going ahead and getting ready for their celebration. In fact, earlier I saw men on ladders putting up some sort of banner that stretches all the way across the main street. I wouldn't be surprised if they start hanging bunting on the buildings pretty soon."

"But there's still time for Father to get back before then, isn't there?" Ted asked.

"Yes, there is." It was going to be a close thing, though, Hammersby thought. He didn't see any point in saying that. And of course, the most important thing was that the President return with his two kidnapped children, safe and sound, no matter when they got back to Deadwood.

He sat with the family for a while, chatting and trying to keep their minds off the trouble. The two younger boys were easily distracted, but Hammersby could tell how worried Ethel and Ted were. And of course Mrs. Roosevelt, although her usual air of calm control and reserve remained unshaken, had to be feeling it worst of all.

When everyone was finished with the meal, Mrs. Roosevelt sent the children into Ethel's bedroom. She said to Hammersby, "I'm keeping them all together now, as much as possible. It seems safer that way."

"Yes, ma'am, I understand. That's a good idea."

"I never expected to have such a thing happen." Her cool façade slipped for a second as she went on, "I was under the assumption that Deadwood was . . . was a civilized place now."

Hammersby said, "Based on things your husband has told me and that I've read about, Deadwood is much more civilized than it once was, but unfortunately, that's no guarantee of safety, ma'am. I mean, Washington is completely civilized, and bad things happen there sometimes."

A tiny smile passed briefly over Mrs. Roosevelt's lips as she said, "I believe if you asked Theodore, he'd say that Washington often isn't civilized at all."

"Yes, ma'am, more than likely."

Mrs. Roosevelt pushed her chair back. Hammersby hurried to hold it for her as she got to her feet.

"I believe I'll go and read for a bit. Try to take my mind off the circumstances. If you hear any news . . . any news at all . . . you'll come and tell me immediately, won't you, Mr. Hammersby?"

"Of course, ma'am. You can depend upon that. But really, I wouldn't expect to hear anything for several days yet, at the earliest."

"You're probably right." She sighed. "It's just that . . . the days are awfully long."

She retired to her bedroom, leaving Hammersby alone in the suite's sitting room. He drank the last of the coffee in his cup, put his hat on, and stepped out into the corridor. After nodding to the two men who sat there holding shotguns, he went to the stairs and descended to the hotel's lobby.

Several men stood at the desk on the other side of the room, evidently checking into the Bullock Hotel. Hammersby didn't pay much attention to them as he started toward the entrance, but then one of the men spoke to the clerk and something about his voice made Hammersby pause. With a slight frown, he turned his head and took a better look at the men.

A shock went through Hammersby as he recognized the profile of the man who was speaking to the clerk in a haughty tone. Even with a hat on, there was no mistaking the rounded head with the weak, receding chin, or the arrogance with which the man spoke and carried himself.

But what in the world was Senator Warren Pulsipher of California doing in Deadwood?

The three men with Pulsipher all wore dark suits, like the senator, and derby hats. They were brawny, hard-faced types, one clean-shaven and the other two sporting mustaches and bushy sideburns. They certainly didn't look like secretaries or any other sort of assistant who might be traveling with a prominent legislator.

The poor clerk, cowed by whatever Pulsipher was haranguing him about, turned the registration book around and offered Pulsipher a pen. When Pulsipher had signed in, the clerk took two keys from the board on the wall behind him and slid them across the desk.

While that was going on, Hammersby sidled over next to a potted palm and got behind it enough to obscure him if Pulsipher happened to glance in his direction. Carefully, he moved one of the fronds so he could see better as Pulsipher took the keys and handed one of them to his clean-shaven companion.

Hammersby couldn't imagine Pulsipher sharing a room with a subordinate, so he was confident the senator was keeping one of the rooms for himself and forcing the other three men to share. Pulsipher then turned to one of the mustachioed men and said something to him that Hammersby couldn't hear. The man nodded and headed for the doors. Pulsipher was sending him on some sort of errand.

Hammersby didn't want to look suspicious, but it was difficult not to do so while lurking behind a potted palm. Keeping his head averted, he stepped over to a writing desk and picked up a piece of paper lying there. He pretended to look at it until the man who was leaving had walked out of the hotel, and Pulsipher and the other two were going up the stairs.

They didn't have any bags with them, Hammersby noted. More than likely, porters were bringing them from the railroad station. Hammersby just assumed that Pulsipher and the other men had come in on that morning's train, which, come to think of it, he had heard whistle a short time earlier while he was in the Roosevelt suite. He hadn't thought a thing about it at the time.

For a moment, Hammersby stood there in the lobby,

conflicted as to what he ought to do next. Pulsipher and the other two men must have gone up to their rooms, but that left the other man, and Hammersby was curious about him. Making up his mind, he went quickly to the door and stepped out of the hotel, then paused to look in both directions.

The tall, broad-shouldered man was easy enough to spot, even a block off, walking away. Somewhat baffled at himself for doing this, Hammersby began following him, almost as if he were Nick Carter or Sexton Blake or some other dime novel sleuth.

The man went to a livery stable and disappeared through the open double doors. Hammersby increased his pace and hurried up to the doors, then stopped short just outside where he could eavesdrop without being seen.

At least, he hoped he could accomplish that. This was the first time he had ever tailed anyone, so he didn't know if he was doing it right or not. Nor would he have been able to explain why he had felt the impulse to follow the man.

"... could be gone as long as a week," a man was saying inside the big barn.

"I don't have four saddle mounts I can rent you, mister, nor a pack horse, neither."

That would be the man who operated the stable, Hammersby thought. So the first man he'd heard was the one he had followed here. In comparison to the liveryman's drawl, it was easy to recognize his Eastern accent.

"I suppose I'll have to go somewhere else, then," the man said.

"Hold on, hold on, mister. There are other livery stables here in Deadwood, and the fellas who run them work together sometimes, when they don't have what a customer needs. Give me an hour or so, and I'll round up those four mounts for you, and a good pack horse or mule, too. Will that work?"

"Maybe," the man from the east replied grudgingly. "We'll need supplies for a week, too."

"Well, you just let me handle all of that for you," the liveryman said, his voice hearty now that he sensed he was close to making a deal. "I've outfitted plenty of huntin' parties headed out into the Black Hills. Are you and your friends goin' huntin'?"

"You could say that."

"What're you after? Elk? Moose? Bear?"

The man didn't reply for a moment. Then he laughed, an unpleasant sound, and said, "I suppose you could say we're going after bear."

"Let me take care of everything for you. You have rifles, ammunition, things like that?"

"Just get the horses and enough provisions for a week," the man from the east snapped. "How long until everything is ready to go?"

"Well, let's see . . . it's nearly ten o'clock now . . . ought to have it all ready for you by noon or a little after. Of course, if you and your friends would rather wait and get a fresh start first thing in the morning—"

"No, we're riding out this afternoon, if at all possible."

"Of course, we ain't actually settled on a price yet . . ."

"I don't want to waste time dickering. Name your best price." The man's voice hardened. "And if I find out you're trying to cheat us—"

"No, sir, no sir, I'd never do that!"

They wrapped up the negotiations quickly. "We're at the Bullock Hotel for right now," the man from the east said. "My boss wanted to rest for a bit after that train ride. So you can get in touch with us there once everything is ready."

Knowing that the man would be leaving the livery stable any minute, Lowell Hammersby walked away with a frown putting deep creases on his forehead.

Senator Warren Pulsipher was riding out into the Black Hills with three men who looked for all the world like some sort of hired toughs? That was insane! Pulsipher wouldn't do something like that. The senator was fussy, arrogant, and devoted to creature comforts, from everything that Hammersby knew of him. The President couldn't stand Pulsipher and did his best to avoid him, which meant that Hammersby did likewise. Why would Pulsipher mount such a bizarre expedition as this one, heading out into the Black Hills to hunt for . . .

Bear.

Hammersby stopped short, his eyes widening, and let out an audible gasp. No one on the street appeared to notice his shocked reaction. He had to be mistaken, he told himself. Pulsipher wouldn't dare . . .

But that was the only explanation that made sense. Hammersby swallowed hard and looked around. He had to find one of those other livery stables he'd heard mentioned.

Even though it would mean going against the President's orders to stay in Deadwood and look after the rest of the Roosevelt family, he needed to rent a horse, too.

CHAPTER 22

Somewhere in the Black Hills

Frank Morgan felt an unmistakable sensation on the back of his neck. In a quiet voice that barely rose above the hoofbeats of their horses, he said to his two companions, "Somebody's following us."

Frank had spoken so that only Conrad and Seth Bullock could hear him. Conrad replied, "Yeah, I feel it, too."

"And me," Bullock added. "Kind of like I've got a target painted right between my shoulder blades."

Conrad grunted in agreement with that sentiment.

The three of them had been riding through the rugged, thickly wooded landscape for two days after leaving Deadwood. Frank and Bullock knew where they were going, although from time to time they had to stop and discuss which route would be the best for them to follow. Those discussions never turned into arguments, but they got a mite emphatic now and then. Like most frontiersmen, Frank and Bullock were both convinced that they knew the best way to get from one place in particular to another place in particular . . . in this case, the old trading post/saloon/whorehouse known as the Dutchman's.

Despite that, they had made good progress and expected to arrive at their destination late the next day, if nothing happened to delay them. So far, they hadn't even seen another human being other than President Theodore Roosevelt, who they had watched from a distance of half a mile or more at times as he rode alone through the wilderness. Frank and Bullock both had telescopes they used to keep track of the President, being careful to shield the front lens with a hand so sunlight wouldn't glint off it when they peered through the instrument.

All three men suspected that the kidnappers had someone following Roosevelt, too, but whoever it was stayed out of sight and proceeded cautiously, just like they were doing.

At least no one had tried to bushwhack the President, and even though they didn't expect that to happen, they were grateful that it hadn't.

The smooth sailing they had experienced so far might be about to come to an end, though. Frank said, "All three of us can't be wrong about what our guts are telling us. Somebody's dogging our trail, and I'm betting they're up to no good."

"I agree," Bullock said, "but what are we going to do about it?"

Conrad said, "The trail goes through a pretty thick stand of trees up ahead. Once we're in there, whoever's following us won't be close enough to see me if I grab one of those low-hanging branches and pull myself up out of sight. He'll still hear all of our horses and won't have any idea that I'm waiting to get the drop on him."

"You can hope he won't spot you," Frank said. "But if you're wrong and he knows you're there, hidden among the branches, you'll be a sitting duck. He can stop a little ways off and empty his gun at you."

"Well, if he does that, you two can come back and kill

him," Conrad replied with a reckless smile. "Might be a good idea to ask him first why he's been following us, though."

"It's not a bad plan," Bullock said, "but why don't you let me or Frank be the one to jump the hombre?"

"Because I'm a lot younger than either of you," Conrad replied bluntly. "If anybody's going to be clambering around up in a tree, it needs to be me."

Frank sighed. "Hate to say it, but the boy's right, Seth. This is a young man's play."

"All right," Bullock agreed with obvious reluctance. "Reckon it'd be a waste of time to tell you to be careful."

"Where Conrad's concerned, it always has been," Frank said.

Conrad laughed and said, "You wouldn't know about when I was younger. I was pretty cautious back then. Timid, actually. But since I met you, too much of you has rubbed off on me."

"Life's got a habit of being that way with fathers and sons, I suppose."

The three men rode on, and a few minutes later they followed the trail into that thick stand of pines Conrad had mentioned. The way the path twisted and weaved among the trees, it was hard to see more than a few yards in any direction.

Conrad spotted a likely looking branch ahead and silently pointed it out to his companions. Frank and Bullock both nodded in agreement. Frank was already leading the pack horse, so Conrad nudged the bay forward a little, close enough that he could lean forward and hand the saddle mount's reins to his father, as well. Frank gave him a curt nod of encouragement.

Conrad slipped his feet out of the stirrups, lifted his arms above his head, and watched the branch as they drew closer to it. The branch was thick enough to support his weight, but not so thick that he couldn't clamp his hands around it when the bay passed underneath it. He hung on tightly as the horse walked out from under him and left him dangling by his hands.

With a grunt of effort, Conrad chinned himself up, hooked an arm over the branch, and kicked up with his right leg to catch a grip with it, too. In a matter of seconds, he was lying on the branch, which sagged a little toward the ground under his weight.

He reached up, caught hold of a higher branch, and pulled himself to his feet. Again he lifted a hand and gripped a branch. Most kids climbed trees when they were young, he reflected, but being raised in a mansion in Boston, he hadn't had any opportunities to do that. He had climbed a few since then, during his years of drifting as Kid Morgan, usually to look for someone pursuing him. That necessity had been a good teacher.

He didn't climb very high, just enough that he was nestled behind several boughs that were heavily laden with needles. As long as he remained still, he would be difficult to spot up here, but when he parted the growth slightly with one hand, he was able to see a short distance back up the trail.

The hoofbeats from the horses ridden by his father and Bullock were already fading. The dense growth muffled sounds. After a few minutes, Conrad couldn't hear them at all, and silence cloaked this forest. The passage of human beings through their domain had caused all the small animals to be quiet. Conrad heard his own pulse in his head, and a soft sighing of a breeze moving through the trees.

Then the faint *clip-clop* of more hoofbeats, these coming from the east. That would be the rider who had been trailing them for the past few hours.

Conrad leaned forward slightly, eager to catch a glimpse of the man. Before the horse and rider came into view, however, he heard something else, a rapid pattering that, for a second, he couldn't place.

Then he realized it was the sound of an animal running, and as that understanding came to him, a gray, furry form flashed into view. A dog—no, a *coyote!*—dashed along the trail, heading the same direction as Frank and Bullock were going. Conrad caught only a glimpse of the creature before it went out of sight, but he heard it run under the place where he was concealed.

What in blazes was a coyote doing here? Conrad thought of them as belonging more in Texas and the Southwest, but he knew they actually ranged over most of the frontier. Was the rider chasing the animal? Was he just some innocent hunter, not trailing Conrad and the other two at all?

From the deliberate sound of the approaching hoofbeats, though, the rider wasn't in any hurry, as he likely would have been if he were a hunter in pursuit of some quarry. Indeed, when the man came into view, he was riding at a steady pace but not rushing at all.

Conrad squinted to get a better look at him. The first impression the man gave was one of size. Even on horseback, it was obvious he was tall, broad-shouldered, deep-chested. Thick, fair hair fell around his head to his shoulders. A mustache drooped over his wide, expressive mouth. Stubble covered his cheeks, jaws, and chin. Even though the stranger wore a broad-brimmed brown hat and an open sheepskin coat over denim trousers and a buckskin shirt, Conrad immediately noted the man's resemblance to pictures of Vikings he had seen in books.

Conrad saw the man for little more than the blink of an eye, and then he was out of sight, following the coyote along the trail. Conrad shifted his stance and looked down. He could see the trail directly below him, and as soon as the rider passed, Conrad planned to drop down behind him with the Colt in his hand. Then he could order the man to stop and demand an answer to the question of why he was following them.

That plan might have worked if the horse's saddle hadn't been empty when it trotted underneath the branches where Conrad was hidden.

Conrad knew as soon as he saw the empty saddle that the rider had spotted him somehow. A split-second after that realization, a gun roared below him. The bullet clipped through the branches well away from him, which meant it was probably a warning shot, but the next one might not be. Conrad swung down to a lower branch. As he did, the man called, "Get down here with your hands up, mister, or I'll shoot you out of that tree like a damn possum!"

Conrad was coming down, all right, but that didn't mean he was surrendering. He swung again, launching himself feetfirst out of the pine tree. The sudden attack took the big stranger by surprise. The man tried to twist out of the way and swing his gun to bear, but Conrad's boot heels drove into the broad chest and knocked him off his feet. The gun boomed again, louder this time, as Conrad and the stranger both sprawled in the trail. Conrad knew he wasn't hit. He rolled, slapped both hands against the ground, and powered to his feet.

The impact had jarred the man's hat off, but he'd managed to hang on to his gun. He came to his knees and tried to lift the weapon. Conrad kicked it out of his hand with a move he had learned from a Frenchman who had taught him the art of *savate*. The next instant, Conrad crashed into his opponent in a diving tackle that forced him over backward.

Conrad knew the man was taller and probably outweighed him by forty or fifty pounds. But Conrad was betting that he was quicker. He proved that by peppering a couple of swift jabs past the hands that the man clumsily threw up to try to block the blows. Both punches smacked into the man's face.

Conrad had hoped that would be enough to stun the man, but instead he seemed to shrug off the punishment as if it were nothing. With an angry bellow, the man grabbed the front of Conrad's shirt and heaved. In a heartbeat, Conrad went from having the advantage to flying through the air, out of control.

He landed hard enough to knock the breath out of his lungs. Momentum rolled him over. As he came to a stop, he gasped for air and looked up to see the big stranger charging at him. The man drew back his right leg and swung a kick aimed at Conrad's ribs. Conrad twisted desperately, caught hold of the man's foot, and did some heaving of his own. With a startled yell, the man toppled backward and crashed onto his back.

Still breathless, Conrad scrambled up. He reached for his Colt and grimaced as he pawed at an empty holster. The revolver had fallen out during the fight. He spotted it lying in the trail, a good ten feet away.

It might as well have been a mile, because the big man was up again already, lunging toward Conrad with a fist like a ham swinging at his head.

Conrad couldn't let that roundhouse punch land. It would end the fight immediately if it did. He ducked and felt the wind of the fist as it passed over his head. Stepping in, he hooked a right, a left, and another right into the man's belly and ribs. That didn't do any more good than punching him in the face had done. It was like hitting a washboard.

Conrad realized he had gotten too close when the man threw both arms around him and caught him in a bear hug. The man growled like a bear, too, as he jerked Conrad against him and started trying to squeeze the stuffing out of him. Conrad's feet came off the ground.

With his arms trapped, his options for fighting back were limited. He pulled his head back as far as he could, pinioned like this, and drove it forward, smashing his forehead into the middle of the man's face. Blood spurted hotly from the man's nose into Conrad's face. The man roared in pain, but his grip slipped a little, enough for Conrad to writhe until he had his right arm free. He caught the man under the stubbled chin with the ball of his hand in a vicious upward strike. That rocked the man's head back and allowed Conrad to break free the rest of the way. Conrad lowered his right shoulder, bulled it into the man's chest, and forced him to stumble back a couple of steps.

That gave Conrad room to club his hands together and put all the strength he could muster into a double-fisted blow that landed squarely on the big man's chin. The man flew backward off his feet, but Conrad fell, too, victim of his own momentum. His strength deserted him as he lay there in the trail. He was done. The short but brutal fight had taken everything he had out of him.

Luckily, the same appeared to be true of his opponent. The big man sprawled on his back. He tried to push himself up and actually got his head and shoulders off the ground, but then he groaned and slumped down again.

Conrad didn't have time to congratulate himself for this victory, half-hearted though it was. Suddenly, a furry gray shape flashed around him, growling and snapping and slashing with sharp teeth that Conrad barely avoided. Ten seconds earlier, he might have said that he was too tired to move. It was amazing how quickly that changed when a man found himself with a crazed coyote in his face, trying to rip his throat out.

"Buddy! Back!"

The powerful shout of command made the coyote pause in his attack. The beast slunk back a little, still snarling and baring his teeth at Conrad, who looked over and saw that the big man had succeeded in pushing himself up on an elbow this time.

"Hold, Buddy," the man ordered. "Better not move, mister, or he's liable to be more than you can handle."

"Somebody ought to . . . shoot that crazy beast," Conrad said.

"Anybody who tries will answer to me."

The man had fallen within reach of the gun Conrad had kicked out of his hand earlier. He picked it up and pointed it at Conrad, who recognized it as a LeMat, an odd hybrid weapon with a thicker barrel that fired a shotgun shell underneath a regular revolver barrel. That louder boom he had heard had been the shotgun going off, he realized. But even though that chamber was empty now, the gun was still dangerous.

The LeMat's barrel never wavered as its owner struggled to his feet. He gestured with his other hand for Conrad to get up, too, but added, "Slow and easy-like. Move too fast and Buddy won't take it kindly."

The man didn't have to worry about Conrad moving too fast. Conrad didn't think he was capable of that right now. But he made it to his feet and asked in a tone of disbelief, "That coyote has a name?"

"Well, why shouldn't he?" the man responded, sounding offended.

"Most wild animals don't."

"Who says he's wild? Buddy's my friend. Although, to be honest, he *is* still pretty wild, too."

Now that he wasn't caught up in the desperate combat, Conrad could see that the man was considerably older than he had thought at first. His skin was weathered and there were deep creases around his mouth and eyes. He was in his fifties, Conrad estimated. Maybe even his sixties. But the years hadn't shrunk his powerful frame and he had battled with the strength and speed of a much younger man. That reminded Conrad of somebody, and it didn't take him long to realize that he was thinking about his own father. Frank hadn't aged as much as most men, either.

That was the way of the frontier. It broke some men. Others, it made ageless.

"Why the hell were you lurking up in that tree?" the stranger asked. His voice had a hint of a Southern accent, as if he were originally from the other side of the Mason-Dixon line but had left those environs behind a long time ago. "You were fixin' to bushwhack me, weren't you?"

"You're the bushwhacker," Conrad shot back. "You've been following me and my friends all day, and we know who you are." Maybe it was unwise to blurt any more out, but Conrad was angry enough that he added, "You're part of the gang that kidnapped those children."

"What the *hell* are you talking about?"

At that moment, hoofbeats sounded nearby, approaching quickly. A look of alarm came over the man's face. He glared at Conrad and went on, "Those friends of yours better take it easy, or they'll be digging you a grave before the day's over, mister."

The coyote looked up the trail and growled. "Steady, Buddy," the big man told him.

Frank and Seth Bullock swept around the nearest bend in the trail. They both held guns, but they reined in quickly and kept the weapons pointed down when they saw that the stranger had the LeMat aimed right at Conrad's head.

"Drop those guns, fellas," the big man called, "or I'll let daylight through this youngster's noggin."

Seth Bullock's eyes widened. "Hunter?" he said. "Hunter Buchanon, is that you?"

Chapter 23

The name Hunter Buchanon was vaguely familiar to Conrad, but he couldn't place it at all. He thought maybe he had heard mention of it during his wandering years as Kid Morgan.

Seth Bullock obviously knew the man, though, and the recognition was mutual. A grin broke out on the rugged, Viking-like face as Buchanon said, "Howdy, Bullock. Been a while. You still in Deadwood?"

"Where else would I be? Are you still running that ranch with that pretty, redheaded wife of yours?"

"Where else would *I* be?" Buchanon laughed. "Yeah, Annabelle's still stuck with me."

"I need to get by there and pay a visit sometime."

"You're always welcome." Buchanon's eyes narrowed. "Or maybe I should say, you used to be, before you took to running around with bushwhackers."

He jerked his head in a curt nod toward Conrad.

"I wasn't going to bushwhack you," Conrad protested. "I just wanted to get the drop on you so I could find out why you've been following us."

"Why wouldn't I be following you? I'm a curious sort of hombre, and in case you haven't noticed, there aren't that many pilgrims roaming around these parts. When I spotted you boys earlier, I figured I'd trail along and see what you were up to."

"I reckon you still regard the Black Hills as your own private stomping ground, don't you?" Bullock said.

Buchanon let out a disgusted snort. "It hasn't been that way for a long time. Not since Shep and Tyrell were still alive, and the three of us traipsed all over these hills looking for trouble." A bitter edge came into his voice. "We found plenty of that, all right."

Bullock nodded. "I remember hearing about it, all those years ago. Your brothers were already gone by the time I met you, but I reckon losses like that never really stop hurting."

Buchanon waved his free hand and said, "I can't complain overmuch about my life. I've had Annabelle all these years, and plenty of excitement."

"And you still have a coyote tagging along with you."

That put a grin back on Buchanon's face. "Yeah, I like to think that Buddy is Bobby Lee's great-great-grandson or some such. He seems like Bobby Lee come back to life most of the time, that's for sure. Smart as he can be." The big man shook his head. "But enough reminiscing and palavering. I still don't know what's going on here. Who's this young buck and the other old-timer you're riding with?"

Frank said, "Old-timer, is it? I don't figure I've got *that* many years on you, mister. And if you want to know my name, you can ask me. It's Frank Morgan."

Buchanon's jaw tightened. Clearly, he couldn't help but stare for a second.

"Frank Morgan," he repeated. "The gunfighter? Some say . . . the Last Gunfighter?"

"Some may say it. Doesn't mean it's true. Plenty of men who are good with a gun still on this side of the divide." Frank pointed at Conrad. "There's one of 'em. My son. Conrad Morgan."

"Sometimes called Kid Morgan," Bullock added dryly. "So you see, Hunter, you're in the presence of famous men."

"Yeah, but I'm the one with a gun in my hand," Buchanon said.

"Not the only one," Frank pointed out.

Bullock suggested, "Why don't we all pouch these irons and talk civilized. We're not enemies."

Conrad said, "How do we know that? Buchanon explained why he was following us, but can we believe him?"

"I'm not in the habit of lying," Buchanon said coldly. "And accusing me of it is no way to start a friendly talk."

Bullock slid his Colt back into its holster and said, "We can believe him. In his younger days, Hunter Buchanon was quite the hell-raiser, but he's always been an honest man."

"Thanks, Seth. I think."

Bullock smiled. "You said yourself that you used to roam the Black Hills looking for trouble."

Buchanon's broad shoulders rose and fell. He lowered the LeMat and then holstered it. Frank put his Colt up, as well, and then he and Bullock swung down from their saddles.

"All right if I pick up my hat and gun?" Conrad asked. "Or will that just start the ball all over again?"

"Go ahead," Buchanon told him. "I recall hearing about Kid Morgan. You're not as famous as your pa there, Kid, but maybe that's because nobody knew you like to clamber around up in trees like a monkey."

Conrad glared at him for a second but then walked along the trail to retrieve his hat and gun. Buddy, the coyote, watched him warily while he did so, and lifted his lip to bare a tooth when Conrad returned the look for too long.

Buchanon's had followed Frank and Bullock when they hurried past it to find out what the shooting was about. All of the animals stood and cropped at the grass along the edge of the trail as the four men gathered to talk.

"You know who we are, Buchanon," Frank said, "but except for Seth, we don't know a blasted thing about you."

"Fair enough," Buchanon allowed. "I'm not all that fond of talking about myself, though."

Bullock said, "I'll vouch for Hunter. Most folks who have been around the Black Hills for very long know him or have at least heard of him. He used to drive the stagecoach in these parts and rode shotgun on it sometimes, too, before the railroad came to Dakota Territory. He wore a badge for a while—"

"Packing a lawman's star never really suited me," Buchanon interrupted. "Not like it did you, Seth."

"And rounded up his share of outlaws and rustlers," Bullock went on, "whether it was official or not. Even tangled with a killer grizzly one time, didn't you, Hunter?"

Buchanon closed his eyes and shuddered. "Don't remind me of that unholy beast. I'm still not sure if it was really a bear or a devil or both."

"Hunter's done some scouting for the army, tangled with Indians and gunrunners, and built himself a fine ranch with his wife Annabelle," Bullock continued. "And from the looks of things, he still goes roaming from time to time. You're a ways from your spread, Hunter."

Buchanon shrugged again and said, "You're right, sometimes I get a mite restless." His shaggy eyebrows drew down in a frown. "Now, what's all this about kidnapping some children? Is that who you're after, Seth? Some skunks who'd be low down enough to do a thing like that?"

Conrad, Frank, and Bullock looked at each other. From what Bullock had said so far about Hunter Buchanon, it sounded like the man would make a good ally in their mission. Frank nodded to Bullock and said, "It's up to you, Seth. You know him a lot better than Conrad and I do. If you trust him . . . ?"

"With my life," Bullock said with a firm nod. "Maybe

what we ought to do is boil up a pot of coffee. Then we can tell you all about it, Hunter."

"The *President?*" Hunter Buchanon said a short time later. "Teddy Roosevelt his own self? The Rough Rider?"

"One and the same," Bullock confirmed with a nod.

Hunter was sitting on a log next to the small campfire they had built, the blaze just big enough to heat the coffee pot sitting at its edge. He had a tin cup in his hand, filled with the strong black brew, and he took a sip of it to hide the surprise he felt at the story he had just heard from the lips of his old friend Seth Bullock.

After a moment, Hunter went on, "Why would they take those kids? For the ransom money?"

Bullock shook his head. "I'm sure the money's part of it, but Gus Greendale and the men from his gang have a grudge against Teddy. Years ago, he and some riders from his ranch killed a couple of Greendale's bunch, rounded up the rest of them, and turned them over to the law. Greendale wound up spending fifteen years in prison. He wants to settle that score. I'm convinced that's why he picked the Dutchman's as the spot where Teddy's supposed to deliver the money. That old abandoned trading post is where Teddy caught up to Greendale's gang, all those years ago."

"Makes sense," Hunter said, nodding slowly, "except for one thing. The Dutchman's isn't a trading post anymore, but it isn't abandoned. Krieger's still alive and squatting there by himself, like a lonesome old toad."

"Alive? I thought Krieger died years ago! That's the story I was told, anyway."

"I saw him there with my own eyes, about ten months ago. No telling what's happened since then, of course, but I'll bet he's still around. He's too poison-mean to die."

Bullock shook his head. "The old pelican must be a hundred."

"He looks it, but really, he's not that much older than us, Seth. Too much whiskey and too many whores. Believe it or not, a life like that ages some men."

Frank said, "If the Dutchman is still there, will he cooperate with Greendale?"

"If Greendale promises him some of the loot, he will," Hunter answered without hesitation. "He was never an owlhoot himself, but he never seemed to believe there was anything wrong with looking the other way and selling booze and women to any long riders who came his way. I'm sure he'd regard letting Greendale have his little reunion there as just another business deal."

Conrad said, "So we're talking about Greendale and the three or four men he'll have with him, plus this man Krieger, plus whoever was working with the gang in Deadwood and is now following the President. That makes the odds two to one against us, minimum, if you throw in with us, Mr. Buchanon. Could be a lot worse. Are you sure you want to do that?"

Hunter grinned. "Two to one odds?" he scoffed. "I've faced a heap worse than that. And it's been a while since I've had any excitement. Besides, if I'm helping out the President, then in a way I'll be helping out the whole country, right?"

"I suppose you could look at it like that," Bullock said.

Hunter downed the rest of the coffee in his cup and then said, "So try and stop me from playing out this hand with you boys."

"We won't be doing that." Frank leaned over from the rock where he was sitting and extended his hand to Hunter. "We're glad to have you with us, Buchanon."

Hunter clasped Frank's hand and returned the famous gunfighter's firm grip. "Call me Hunter," he said.

* * *

With their group now numbering four instead of three, they set off a short time later, after putting out the fire and covering the ashes with dirt. Hunter quickly proved to be a worthwhile addition to the party, because he knew the Black Hills better than just about anyone, including Seth Bullock. He led them onto a high ridge from which they had an excellent view of the rugged hills and valleys rolling off to the north.

The ridge dropped off to their right in a towering cliff of red sandstone. Its top was covered with pine, fir, and spruce. The growth was thick enough that the four men could ride up here without any fear of being skylighted because the tall trees were behind them. Also, the forest came up almost to the edge of the cliff, so Frank and Bullock were able to step back into the shade of the trees and use their spyglasses without having to worry about any reflections from the lenses.

After they had ridden along the ridge for a while, Bullock called a halt and dismounted to look for Roosevelt. Frank did likewise. After slowly scanning the landscape for several tense minutes, Frank announced, "I've got him. He's riding along a hillside about a mile from here. Your eight o'clock, Seth."

Bullock adjusted where he was looking and after a moment said, "I see him, too. But look back to the east, Frank. Maybe three-quarters of a mile behind Teddy."

Frank swung his telescope in that direction and slowly played it across the distant view. At first he didn't have any luck, then suddenly, a rider seemed to spring into sight in the round tube of the spyglass. Frank focused on him: a stocky man in an overcoat, wearing a soft felt hat above a beefy face with a closely clipped mustache. From the way the man sat the saddle, Frank could tell that he wasn't an experienced rider.

"An Eastern dude, I'd guess," he said.

"That's what he looks like to me, too," Bullock agreed. "Ever seen him before?"

"Never laid eyes on him." Frank lowered the spyglass and held it out to Conrad. "Take a look and see if you know him."

"I don't know every crook east of the Mississippi, you know," Conrad commented. "In fact, I haven't spent much time back there for quite a while."

He lifted the telescope to his eye and looked where Frank pointed. After a few seconds, he spotted the distant rider.

"No, I never saw him before, either. I agree, though, he's not from around these parts." Conrad lowered the spyglass. "I don't think a man who looks like that would have any business all the way out here, this far from anywhere, unless he *is* following the President, as we suspected."

Bullock closed his telescope. "At least it's just Hammersby and not a whole gang," he said. "I don't mind being grateful for any good luck we can get."

"Only one man we can see right now," Hunter pointed out. "He could have a whole gang following him, though. But now that we know where he is, we can keep an eye on him, too."

That was what they did for the rest of the afternoon, stopping periodically to check not only on President Roosevelt but on the man trailing him, as well. The follower never got closer than half a mile and usually stayed farther back than that.

Late in the day, Roosevelt halted and made camp in a small clearing next to a huge boulder. Conrad, Frank, Bullock, and Hunter stopped, too.

"I'm glad we had that coffee earlier, boys," Hunter said, "because we'll need to have a cold camp tonight. Up high like this, a fire would be too easy to spot . . . and I'm assuming you don't want anybody to know you're around."

"That's right," Bullock said. He looked up at a crystal clear blue sky. The low gray clouds that had lingered for the past few days had broken up during the afternoon and the remnants had drifted away. "Without those clouds, it'll be mighty cold by morning, too. Well below freezing, I imagine." He shrugged. "But we all have good bedrolls."

Hunter grinned. "And I've got a coyote to curl up next to me and help me keep warm. Want me to see if Buddy can sing a mite and call some of his cousins?"

"Thanks, but I'd just as soon not share my blankets with a coyote," Bullock replied dryly. Then he grew more serious as he added, "I just hope that wherever Miss Alice and young Kermit are, they're able to stay warm tonight."

Chapter 24

The Dutchman's

Drafts whistled through the old building night and day. Some of the chinks in the log walls had fallen out, leaving gaps, and Krieger hadn't taken the time and effort to replace them. As he had said, he never warmed up anyway, so why bother?

Because of those drafts, it stayed very cold inside even when a fire was burning in the fireplace. A person had to stand pretty close to the hearth to get much warmth from it. By the time the heat traveled a few feet away, the wind snatched it with vicious claws and blew it right on out.

Krieger had some old buffalo robes, though, and he allowed Alice and Kermit to use them. They shook as much of the dust and as many of the vermin out of the robes as they could, and wrapping up in the thick, shaggy, smelly things certainly kept them warmer. Alice was convinced that she and her brother were still sharing the robes with quite a few crawling creatures, though. She tried not to allow herself to think about that.

So far Hank Singleton had kept his distance from Alice, but his lustful gaze focused on her most of the time he was awake, making shivers of apprehension go through her. She could tell that Singleton was afraid of Greendale and didn't want to go against his orders not to touch her, but she wasn't sure how long that restraint would last.

She wished her father would get here. She was well aware that she and Kermit were the bait in a trap and that these men intended to harm her father. She knew she ought to be selfless and wish that he would stay away, so he'd be safe, but she just wasn't that strong. She was scared, and she wanted him to come and get her and Kermit and take them away from this awful place and those evil men.

She sat on the hard-packed dirt floor in a corner with her brother snuggled up against her, both of them covered by one of the buffalo robes. The wall was relatively intact here, with only a few small gaps, so not as much wind got through. Alice wouldn't go so far as to say it was *warm*, but at least it wasn't as frigid as it might have been.

The corner was also fairly dim. A lantern sat at one end of the bar, and another hung from the ceiling in the far corner. The flickering yellow glow they cast didn't reach very well to where Alice and Kermit sat. Earlier in the evening, they had eaten some of the beans and elk steak Krieger had dished out, then retreated to what had become as close to a sanctuary as they had.

The Dutchman sat on a stool behind the bar now, taking nips from a flask and looking like he was almost drunk enough to fall face forward onto the planks and start snoring.

Greendale *was* snoring. He sat at one of the tables, slumped over it with his head resting on his crossed arms as he slept. His hat had fallen off, revealing the tangle of long gray hair on his head.

Tiny was at another table, reading a tattered, yellow-backed dime novel, holding it close to his face and squinting so he could make out the small, dense print on the pages. The Dutchman had a stack of the books behind the bar.

Lame Wolf and Singleton sat at yet another table, playing

blackjack with a deck of greasy cards. They weren't betting, but rather just playing to pass the time. As the latest hand ended, Singleton yawned and pushed the cards away, signaling that he was done with the game. He looked around, his eyes turning toward the corner where Alice and Kermit huddled. He pushed himself to his feet.

"What are you doing?" Lame Wolf asked, his tone wary.

"It's late, so I reckon I'll turn in," Singleton replied. "And it's mighty cold tonight and'll be a heap colder before morning, so I figured I could use somethin' to keep me warm."

"We have blankets and buffalo robes," Lame Wolf said. "And I will go build up the fire more."

"There ain't enough firewood in the world to keep me as warm as that gal right over there can."

Lame Wolf placed his hands flat on the table. "Gus said to leave the prisoners alone."

"I ain't gonna bother the boy. And I ain't gonna do anything to the girl that'll do her any harm. She won't have to do nothin' but warm my blankets a mite."

"You know that is not how it will go," Lame Wolf said with a scowl on his face.

Tiny looked up from his book and said, "It's too late for a bunch of arguing. Hank, do what you were told."

"I'm tired of doin' what I was told," Singleton snapped. "Gus is the boss, but that don't mean he gets to decide everything."

"Actually, it does," Lame Wolf said.

"Well, he's asleep. Hell, the way he put away the Who-Hit-John this evening, he probably ain't gonna wake up until morning. So that means he ain't in charge anymore. I've been with this bunch as long as either of you boys have, so that means I got just as much say over what I do."

He shoved his chair closer to the table and turned to walk toward Alice and Kermit.

Alice had heard the whole conversation clearly. Terror

welled up inside her as Singleton stalked toward her and her brother. She knew, just as certainly as Lame Wolf did, that Singleton wouldn't stop at forcing her to curl up in his blankets with him. He would try to push things beyond that, even with all the others in the room.

She was about to scream, in the hope that would wake up Greendale, but as she opened her mouth, Kermit threw the buffalo robe aside and stood up, planting himself squarely in Singleton's path.

He was a ridiculous, scarecrow-like figure in multiple layers of too-big clothing, but as he clenched his fists and confronted Singleton, Alice felt her heart swell with pride in her little brother.

"You stay away from my sister," Kermit said, his voice not showing any of the fear he had to be feeling. "Don't you touch her. Just leave us alone."

Tiny and Lame Wolf watched. Even Krieger roused a little from his half-drunken stupor behind the bar. Gus Greendale continued to snore, however.

"Get outta my way, kid," Singleton said. "I'm ain't gonna hurt your sister."

"Damned right you're not, because you're not going to lay a single finger on her."

If Kermit's mother had been here, she might have scolded Kermit for cursing, Alice knew. Propriety was of supreme importance to Edith Roosevelt. But their father probably would have been proud of the boy, just as she was.

Not that Kermit's valiant stand was going to do any good. He wasn't capable of stopping Hank Singleton from doing anything he wanted to do. Only the other men could do that, and they didn't seem inclined to interfere.

"I'll give you one more chance to step aside—" Singleton began.

Instead of complying, Kermit did the unexpected. He lunged forward and punched Singleton in the belly.

Kermit was slender and didn't weigh much. He wasn't as athletic as his older brother Ted. The blow couldn't have packed much power.

But it took Singleton completely by surprise. The outlaw went "Oooff!" and bent forward at the waist.

Before he could straighten up, Alice leaped to her feet and lashed out. She didn't really know how to throw a punch, but sheer luck guided her fist to Singleton's jaw. It landed with enough force to rock his head to the side. Alice cried out in pain and jerked her hand back. It felt like she had broken every bone in it.

Kermit lunged at Singleton again, but this time he didn't try to hit the man. Instead, he reached out with both hands and closed them around the butt of the gun holstered on Singleton's hip. He pulled the heavy revolver free and leaped back, struggling to thrust the gun in front of him and hold it level.

"Alice, run!" he yelled.

Run? Run where? Out into the freezing night? Out into the wilderness, a hundred miles or more from civilization?

Those questions flashed through Alice's brain, but before she could even try to answer them, Kermit succeeded in using both thumbs to haul back the revolver's hammer. It clicked into place, and he jerked the trigger.

The gun went off with a deafening boom that made Alice cry out in shock. Kermit was trying to shoot Hank Singleton, but the gun barrel was shaking so much that the bullet zipped right past the man, flew the length of the room, missed Lame Wolf by several feet, and smashed into the lantern hanging from the ceiling, not far from where Tiny sat with his dime novel.

Kerosene splattered, catching on fire as it sprayed through

the air. Tiny bellowed and leaped to his feet. Some of the flaming stuff had landed on his book and caught it on fire, too. He dropped it on the table and backed away, swatting at the smoldering patches on his coat.

The gunshot jolted Gus Greendale out of his sleep. He surged to his feet, looking around wildly and shouting, "What? What is it?" as he clawed at the gun on his hip.

Kermit tried to cock the gun again, but Singleton had recovered from the initial shock of getting punched and shot at. He snarled a curse and swung a brutal backhanded blow that cracked against Kermit's right cheek and knocked the boy off his feet.

"Gimme that gun, you little pissant!" Singleton roared.

Behind the bar, Krieger shrieked, "*Feuer! Feuer!* The *verdammt* place is on fire!"

Indeed it was. Some of the blazing kerosene had splattered on the wall, and now those logs were burning. Flames crawled rapidly along them and leaped up, level by level, toward the roof.

The thought of being caught in here as the place burned down around her increased Alice's terror that much more. She glanced at the door and thought about making a dash for it, but she couldn't leave her brother behind. Kermit writhed around on the dirt floor while Singleton tried to get the gun away from him. Alice cried out in anger as Singleton kicked Kermit in the side.

Greendale's frantic gaze finally focused on what was happening long enough to prompt him to yell, "Hank! Leave that kid alone! Don't hurt him!"

"The little son of a buck *shot* at me!" Singleton shouted back. He made another grab for the gun.

Just at that moment, Kermit finally succeeded in drawing the hammer back again. He jerked the trigger and the gun went off a second time. Singleton screamed as the bullet ripped a path along his forearm.

Instead of running toward the door, Alice lowered her shoulder and rammed into Singleton from the side. Preoccupied with his wound, he never saw her coming. She crashed into him and knocked him down.

"Kermit, come on!" she said as she bent over and extended a hand to him.

Kermit kept hold of the gun with his left hand but grabbed his sister's wrist with his right. She hauled him to his feet as smoke from the burning wall began to fill the room. No matter what sort of trouble they found themselves in next, they had to get out of here.

Lame Wolf suddenly blocked their path, arms spread out to keep them from darting around them. Behind them, Singleton still rolled on the floor and hugged his bleeding arm. Tiny had grabbed a blanket and was swatting at the flames with it, trying to put out the fire. Krieger stood not far away, dancing around in agitation but not actually doing anything to help.

With Lame Wolf between them and the door, Alice and Kermit turned the other direction, but Greendale was there to block them again. He leaped forward and chopped at Kermit's wrist with the side of his hand. Kermit cried out as the blow knocked the gun loose from his fingers. Greendale grabbed the boy and lifted him from the floor.

"C'mere, you little—"

Kermit kicked him in the groin. Greendale groaned and doubled over, but he didn't let go.

Alice leaped back and forth in an attempt to get around Lame Wolf. The warrior might have been old, but he wasn't slow. He didn't fall for Alice's feint and got hold of her arm, instead.

"We need to get out of here, now!" Tiny shouted.

Alice looked around and saw that the trading post's far wall was completely ablaze. Tiny hadn't been able to put out the fire. Krieger scuttled to the door, threw it open, and charged out into the frigid night.

Through teeth gritted against the pain in his groin, Greendale told Tiny, "Grab Hank and drag him outta here if he won't come along!"

Tiny turned toward Singleton to follow that order while Greendale stumbled toward the open door, still holding the struggling Kermit. Greendale's back was hunched in pain, but he wasn't doubled over anymore.

With Lame Wolf's hand clamped around Alice's arm in an iron grip, he pulled her out the door into the night ahead of Greendale and Kermit, who followed closely behind them. Tiny came last. He had picked up Hank Singleton and was carrying the outlaw in his arms. They had just emerged from the building when the fire reached Krieger's supply of whiskey behind the bar.

The liquor exploded in a fireball that threw Tiny and Singleton forward onto the ground.

The racket was so loud that at first none of them heard the gunshots coming from the riders who galloped down the nearby slope toward the trading post, orange tongues of muzzle flame licking out into the darkness from their guns.

Chapter 25

A short time earlier, John Perry, Nate Poore, and Oscar Sheehan had been hunkered around a tiny fire built in a hollow surrounded by trees, so the glow from the flames couldn't be seen. Those flames leaped and danced as the wind blew. As small as the fire was, it didn't give off much heat.

"We're gonna freeze to death tonight," Nate Poore said. "I just know it."

It was rare for Poore to venture any opinion of his own. Usually, he was content to parrot whatever one of the other men said. The fact that he had spoken up was a good indication of just how miserable he really was.

"You said we were gonna freeze to death last night, and the night before that," Sheehan pointed out. "And we're still here, ain't we?"

"Yeah, but it's gonna be colder tonight. I can feel it in my bones."

"What do your bones think we ought to do? Go waltzin' down there to that old tradin' post and demand that they let us in? I'm sure they'd be willin' to do that. They wouldn't just up and shoot us or somethin' like that."

Sheehan's scornful tone made it clear he believed that was *exactly* what the men holed up at the Dutchman's would do.

Poore said sullenly, "You don't have to make fun of me, Oscar. I'm just cold, that's all."

"We're all cold," John Perry said. "Sometimes you have to put up with things you don't like to get the things you want."

The trading post was about half a mile from their current position. Ever since they had followed Gus Greendale and the others here and it became obvious that the gang wasn't going anywhere else, Perry and his two companions had lingered in the vicinity, waiting to see what was going to happen. They had stayed hidden but were close enough that they could keep an eye on the trading post during the day. Perry thought it was unlikely that anything important would take place at night. In the Black Hills, at this time of year, most folks stayed inside, close to a fire, once the sun went down.

The three of them hadn't been able to do that, of course and Perry knew that Sheehan was running out of patience. If Sheehan gave up, Poore would, too. And if they rode off, Perry wouldn't have any choice other than to go with them. He couldn't risk tackling Gus Greendale's gang on his own. It would be dangerous enough as it was, with him and his friends being outnumbered four to three.

Greendale didn't have any idea they were close by, though, and surprise counted for something. Perry kept telling himself that, and he hoped he was right.

He said, "I reckon I'd best check on the horses," and started to climb to his feet. He had just gotten up when he heard something that made him lift his head and frown. The sound was faint, as if muffled by distance or something else, but he thought he recognized it.

"Was that a gunshot?"

"Was what a gunshot?" Sheehan rumbled. "I didn't hear anything."

"Neither did I," Poore said.

Perry listened intently for several moments, but the sound wasn't repeated . . . if he had actually heard it at all. Maybe it had been his imagination.

"Don't worry about it," he told the other two. He started toward the horses.

He had taken only a couple of steps when he heard it again.

"Damn it, I know that was a gunshot, and it sounded like it came from the Dutchman's!"

Sheehan stood up. "Yeah, maybe I heard it that time, too. You reckon we ought to go and see what it's about, John?"

"I don't think it'd hurt anything." Perry smiled in the darkness. "Maybe they're having a falling-out over those prisoners, and they'll kill each other off."

"That'd sure be some good luck for us," Sheehan said.

"Yeah, good luck," Poore added.

They hurried to where their horses were picketed, threw saddles on the animals, and rode toward the Dutchman's as quickly as they dared in the darkness. Part of the way there, Sheehan exclaimed, "I smell smoke!"

"So do I," Perry agreed. "And it's not just from their fireplace."

As they neared the top of the hill that overlooked the trading post, the hill from which they spied on the place during the day, Perry saw an orange glow in the sky up ahead. Something big was on fire, all right, and it almost had to be the trading post itself. An old building like that might go up in a hurry if it ever started burning. He urged his companions on.

They had just reached the top of the hill when a large ball of flame burst inside the trading post. It wasn't an explosion, exactly, but pretty close. Perry figured it came from whatever liquor the old-timer had stored in there.

The three men hauled back on their reins and brought their horses to a halt as they stared at the incredible scene below them. The trading post was on fire, all right. It looked like flames were consuming everything inside it, and the roof was blazing now, too.

Two people were lying on the ground not far from the door through which the hellish light of the inferno spilled. That glare revealed another group nearby. Perry recognized Gus Greendale holding the little boy. Close by, the Indian gripped the young woman's arm, and a wizened figure who was probably the Dutchman hopped around agitatedly.

Perry had no idea what had caught the place on fire, but he *did* know a stroke of luck when he saw one. Everybody down there was staring at the burning building. They weren't paying attention to anything else, and after looking into those flames so intently like they were, they wouldn't be able to see much of anything else until their eyes adjusted.

Perry yanked his gun from its holster and said, "Now's our chance to grab those youngsters! Kill Greendale and his bunch, but whatever you do, don't shoot those kids!"

With that, he jabbed his boot heels into his horse's flanks and sent the animal bounding down the slope. He figured on killing the two men lying on the ground first, so he aimed his gun at them and opened fire.

One of them scrambled up, shaking his head like a bull buffalo. He was as big as a bull buffalo, too. Perry recognized the massive black man he and his friends had staged the fight with in Deadwood. Perry triggered two more shots and saw the man stagger backward.

At the same time, Poore and Sheehan were shooting at the others. Perry thought that he might have acted too hastily in his excitement. He couldn't really count on those two not to ventilate the prisoners. Perry still didn't know who those kids were, but he figured they would be worth less—or nothing at all—if they were dead.

So far, though, all of the shots Poore and Sheehan had fired seemed to be going wild, which also had its disadvantages.

Gus Greendale got his gun out and returned the fire. Muzzle flame stabbed from his revolver. A few yards away, the Indian did likewise.

With both of them occupied like that, they couldn't maintain their grips on the captives. The boy and the girl both broke free. The girl grabbed the boy's hand and shouted something to him that Perry couldn't make out over the roar of gunfire and the drumming hoofbeats. They started running away from the burning trading post, toward a line of trees along the nearby creek.

That might be another break for him and his friends, Perry realized. He jerked his horse to the left and yelled, "Nate! Oscar! Let's get those kids!"

Without looking back to see if Poore and Sheehan were following him, Perry pounded after the fleeing children.

Alice had no idea who those men were, but she was grateful to them anyway, for giving her and Kermit a chance to escape.

That gratitude vanished in a heartbeat as she realized that the strangers were pursuing her and her brother. Alice's instincts told her those men had bad intentions toward them, too.

"Come on, Kermit!" she called as she tugged him toward the trees. "We'll get away from them in the darkness!"

She didn't know if they could do that, and even if they did, they would still be in a bad fix. But anything would be better than being held captive by Greendale's gang, she thought.

Alice hoped she was right about that.

The too-large clothing and boots they wore made running difficult, but fear made them fleeter of foot than they might have been otherwise. Alice heard the swift rataplan of hoofbeats coming closer behind them and ran harder, urging

Kermit to try to keep up. She might have outdistanced the men on her own. But that didn't matter, because she wasn't going to abandon her brother.

The line of trees wasn't far off now. Alice thought that if she and Kermit could reach the thick shadows under them, they might be able to slip away.

But the riders closed in too fast. Suddenly they were practically on top of the fleeing youngsters. Alice screamed as one of the men reached down from his saddle and grabbed Kermit's other arm. The man ripped Kermit away from her and hauled him upward off the ground. Alice was afraid Kermit would fall and land under the slashing, steel-shod hooves of the running horse.

She didn't have a chance to see what happened to her brother, because at that moment one of the other riders leaned down and wrapped an arm around her, too. She felt herself being lifted and then the dizzying sensation of abruptly having empty air under her feet.

The next instant, she slammed belly-down across the back of the horse, in front of the rider's saddle. The impact knocked the breath out of her and left her stunned. The man's strong hand rested on her back and pinned her to the horse. Even if her muscles had been able to cooperate, she was too scared of falling to move.

Instead of turning back toward the burning trading post, the riders kept going, plunging between trees, across the creek bank, and then into the stream. Water splashed up around them. It was so cold that when drops of it landed on Alice's exposed face and hands, they felt like tiny daggers of ice plunged into her flesh. She gasped.

Then they were through the creek and still moving at a dead run through the darkness. Alice began to worry that the horse carrying her would step in a hole or trip over something and collapse, either throwing her with bone-shattering force or rolling over and crushing her.

The mount stayed upright, though, and after a few moments Alice recovered her wits and enough strength to lift her head. She couldn't see the man who had grabbed Kermit, but she heard his horse, galloping off to her captor's right. To the left was another man, riding alone and urging his companions on with waves of his arm.

Behind them, popping sounded. Those were gunshots, Alice realized. Greendale and the others were shooting after them, and clearly, the outlaws didn't care all that much whether any of the bullets struck the prisoners, because they had to be firing blindly after the riders.

Alice almost groaned in despair, but she held it in. She had wanted to get away from Greendale and his men, but obviously, she and Kermit had just traded one set of kidnappers for another. She figured they weren't the least bit better off now than they had been.

A deep voice rumbled above her as the man holding her on the horse called, "John, that bunch'll be comin' after us. What do we do now?"

"Keep riding," the man called John replied. "Their horses were really spooked by that fire and were charging around inside the corral. They're liable to stampede when Greendale and the others try to get them out. It'll take 'em a while to round up those nags and get saddles on them. If we put enough distance between us and them, they'll never find us in this darkness!"

The third man, the one who had grabbed Kermit, shouted, "But what'll we *do* with these kids?"

"I don't know," John said, "but if they know what's good for 'em, they'll tell us why Greendale kidnapped them in the first place. It's got to be something that'll make us rich, boys!"

This time, Alice actually did groan. An hour earlier, she would have said that things couldn't get any worse.

But as usual, fate had found a way to make the situation deteriorate even more, she realized as her new captors galloped on into the night.

Chapter 26

Conrad came awake instantly and completely as a hand touched his shoulder. That hand tightened its grip as a familiar voice whispered, "It's just me."

Conrad relaxed as he recognized his father's voice. He pushed aside the blankets, sat up, and asked, "Is something wrong?"

Even though they didn't expect to run into any trouble until they reached the Dutchman's, they had been taking turns standing guard every night, just in case. It never hurt to be careful. Frank had taken the first shift tonight while the other three men rolled up in their blankets, so obviously the hour was still fairly early. The temperature had dropped quite a bit already, though. The air was calm, crystal clear, and bitingly cold.

"I just spotted something interesting," Frank said. "Thought you might want to take a look."

If his father believed something was worth looking at, it probably was, Conrad thought as he reached for his boots. He pulled them on, then shrugged into the thick sheepskin coat. He wore a heavy flannel shirt, but that wasn't enough to keep a man warm on a night like this.

The two of them walked to the edge of camp, which was also the edge of the ridge they had been following since

Hunter Buchanon led them to it. Frank pointed to the west, where Conrad saw a faint but definitely ominous-looking orange glow, low down in the sky.

"Something's burning," Conrad said. "A forest fire, maybe? That might really complicate things."

"Most forest fires are started by lightning. The sky's clear and was all day. That's something else on fire. I can't see any flames from here, but to cast that much of a glow, something pretty good-sized must be burning." Frank paused, then added grimly, "Like an old trading post."

"The Dutchman's," Conrad whispered.

"It could be. We don't know that, but it could be."

A new voice said from behind them, "It sure could. That fire's four or five miles from here, and that's about where the Dutchman's is located, all right."

Conrad and Frank looked back over their shoulders and saw Hunter Buchanon standing there, looming massively in the shadows. Conrad hadn't heard the big man come up behind them, and judging by his reaction, neither had Frank. Hunter had to be pretty damned light on his feet to sneak up on either of them that way, let alone both of them. Especially for such a large hombre.

"What do you reckon it means?" Hunter went on.

"I don't know," Frank replied. "But if that fire *is* coming from the Dutchman's, I don't think it's very likely those kidnappers would burn down their own hide-out, at least not intentionally."

"So we're dealing with *two* gangs?" Conrad speculated.

"Or one that split up, maybe."

"What about Indians? They liked to burn down settlers' cabins, didn't they?"

"They did plenty of that, all right," Hunter said, "and I can't blame 'em too much since these hills are sacred ground to them and we just waltzed in and took over. On the other hand, they killed a lot of innocent folks who just wanted to get along with them, so it's hard to feel too sorry for them. But that hasn't happened for a good while around here. Unless something's gone on that I don't know anything about, Indians wouldn't go around setting fires like that."

"Maybe we ought to wake up Seth and see what he thinks about it," Frank suggested.

Hunter chuckled. "No, let the old-timer sleep. When you get to be his age, you need your rest."

"Again, you're not that much younger than Seth and me," Frank said.

"It ain't the years, it's the miles. I've stayed pretty close to home ever since my pap and my brothers and I come up here from Georgia, after the war. I didn't traipse around too much, looking for trouble."

"From what Mr. Bullock said, *trouble* never had any trouble finding *you,"* Conrad pointed out.

Hunter's broad shoulders rose and fell. "Maybe not." He yawned. "Whatever happened, we can't do a blasted thing about it until morning. We're all headed in that direction, including President Roosevelt, so I reckon it won't be too awful long before we find out the truth about it."

"I still say we ought to go after those thievin' varmints right now!" Hank Singleton insisted as Lame Wolf finished tying a bandage around his arm by the orange light of the still-smoldering ruins.

"Tiny's in no shape to travel right now," Gus Greendale replied, "and with that wounded wing of yours, I'm not sure you'd be any good in a fight."

"I can shoot left-handed!"

"Hmmph," Lame Wolf said. "Not very well, as I recall."

"But after everything we've done, we can't just let them get away with those kids!"

Greendale frowned in thought and rasped his fingertips

along his angular jaw. A few yards away, Krieger stood staring at the smoking rubble and muttering in German.

"I ain't sure we actually need the kids," Greendale said. "What we want is for Roosevelt to show up here, so we can settle the score with him and get that money he's bringin', and that can still happen whether we've got the young'uns or not. Roosevelt won't know that we don't."

Lame Wolf nodded slowly and said, "This is true. I mean, we were never actually going to turn them over to him, anyway."

"As long as he *thinks* they're our prisoners, he's got to go through with the deal," Greendale went on. "By the time he finds out we don't have 'em anymore, it'll be too late to do anything about it."

Singleton scowled, cradled his wounded arm against his body, and said, "Well, maybe . . . but what if the fellas who stole the kids find Roosevelt first? Then *they'll* get the money, and we'll be left with nothin'. No ransom, no revenge, nothin'!"

Greendale shook his head. "That's not likely to happen. Did you see who they were?"

"No, I never got a good look at them," Singleton admitted.

"I did. It was those three idiots from back in Deadwood. The ones we paid to start that fight with Tiny."

Tiny sat with his back propped against a couple of saddles that were stacked up. Under his coat showed the lighter color of the cloth that Lame Wolf had wrapped around his barrel chest to serve as a bandage. The bullets had passed on through, and Tiny insisted that they hadn't hit anything vital and he wasn't really hurt too badly, but Greendale wasn't sure if that was true. The big man had lost quite a bit of blood.

Now Tiny spoke up, saying, "Gus is right, those three didn't seem very bright. And they took off from here riding west, *away* from where the President's coming from. Roosevelt ought to be here tomorrow. They won't have time to figure out some way to interfere with us."

"Maybe so," Singleton said, "but I still don't like lettin' them get away with it. And I'd sure as hell like to get my hands on that boy again. The little skunk shot me!"

"We'll track them down once we're finished with their pa," Greendale promised. "You've got my word on that."

Krieger turned away from his contemplation of the burned-down trading post and stomped toward Greendale and the others. He shook a bony fist at them and said, "You destroyed my home, you *dummkopfs*! What am I supposed to do now? Where am I supposed to go?"

"You can go to hell for all I care," Greendale snapped. "In fact, I'll send you on your way."

With a swift, smooth move, he drew his gun, raised it, and fired. Krieger's head jerked back as a black hole appeared above his right eye. He went straight down to the ground, like a bundle of sticks somebody had dropped.

The suddenness of the violence didn't seem to take the others by surprise. Lame Wolf looked at the dead man for a moment, then shrugged and said, "Well, I suppose we don't actually need him anymore, do we?"

"We sure don't," Greendale replied as he thumbed a fresh cartridge into his Colt to replace the one he'd just fired.

"It was a rhetorical question," Lame Wolf muttered.

"I don't care what it was." Greendale pouched the iron. "I just want Roosevelt to hurry up and get here so we can get this over with. For now, let's move Tiny closer to what's left of that damn trading post. At least it's still givin' off quite a bit of heat."

By the time the riders who had abducted Alice and Kermit stopped, the young woman had learned several things about them. She knew their names from hearing them address each other: her captor was called Oscar, the one who had Kermit draped across his horse's back was Nate, and the third man, who seemed to be the leader, was John. The other two did what he said.

Apparently, John was also the most intelligent of the trio, judging by how he spoke. Oscar talked in a dim-witted rumble, and Nate just repeated and agreed with whatever Oscar said. Alice knew she was being judgmental, but she didn't care. She and her brother had been kidnapped by a bunch of louts.

Not that Greendale and the others had been superior intellectual specimens. At least Tiny and Lame Wolf had been fairly well-spoken, and Tiny could read, although he seemed to prefer those low-class dime novels. Or perhaps that was just all the Dutchman had on hand. It wasn't like there was much actual culture to be found anywhere in the Black Hills.

Alice wished they had never come here. She knew that her father wanted to do a favor for his old friend Mr. Bullock, and there had been no reason to believe that the journey would be dangerous, but if Alice could go back and change things, she would refuse to come and would tell all the others that they shouldn't, either.

Too late for that now. Too late for anything except trying to survive.

When the three riders stopped, Oscar shoved Alice off the horse. She hit the ground feetfirst and tried to keep her balance, but she failed and sat down hard. Kermit tumbled down beside her, landing with a pained grunt. She grabbed him and pulled him to her.

"Are you hurt?" she asked.

"No, I just twisted my leg a little when I landed. It's nothing to worry about."

His voice was still strong, as if he were determined not to show any of the pain or fear he must be feeling, but she knew her brother well enough to know how scared he was. She was aware of that, too, because she felt the same way. She put her arm around his shoulders and held him close against her.

The three men dismounted. John said to the captives, "You two just sit there while we let these horses rest and figure out what we're gonna do next."

"I don't hear nobody comin' after us, John, and I've been listenin' for that," Oscar said. "How come they didn't come after us?"

"Yeah, how come they didn't come after us?" Nate added.

"I don't know, but be thankful for small favors," John said. He looked around. "I wonder where the hell we are."

Alice wondered the same thing. Since the night was clear, millions of stars were visible overhead, flooding the hills with their silvery illumination. A quarter-moon floated in the sky, as well. With that much light, Alice could make out the figures of the three men, the horses, and Kermit beside her.

They were surrounded by slopes that she knew were covered with thick forest, even though the trees blended into a black blur. The men had halted their horses in a narrow valley. Alice wasn't very skilled at estimating distances, but she thought the valley couldn't be more than half a mile wide. Smaller stands of pine littered its floor, and boulders that must have rolled down here hundreds or even thousands of years ago from the looming slopes up above had formed rocky mounds.

"We've come several miles from the Dutchman's," John said, as if he had reached a decision. "We'll make camp here, inside that ring of rocks."

He pointed to a ragged circle of boulders about a hundred yards away.

"We can build a small fire in there so we can warm up and boil a pot of coffee," he went on.

"But if they're lookin' for us, that'll help them find us," Oscar objected.

"No, the rocks will shield the fire so it won't be visible

except from up close," John said before Nate had a chance to echo Oscar's words. "And before anybody gets close enough to spot it, we'll hear 'em coming."

"Well, maybe. I reckon it's worth a try." Oscar rubbed his gloved hands together in an attempt to warm them. "If we don't have a fire, we'll all be chunks of ice by the mornin', includin' those two."

He jerked his head toward Alice and Kermit.

"Come on," John said to the youngsters, motioning with his hand. "On your feet. You can walk that far."

Alice's belly hurt from lying over the horse the way she had, and she felt a little sick at her stomach from being in that position, too. Kermit probably didn't feel any better. But just as with their previous set of captors, they had to cooperate for now . . . until a chance to escape presented itself.

That same thought must have crossed John's mind, because he added, "And don't go gettin' any ideas about making a break for it. If you try, we'll catch you, and you'll sure as hell wish you hadn't done it."

"We're not going anywhere," Alice muttered as she got to her feet. She reached her hand down to Kermit to help him stand. "Come on."

She pulled him up, and they began trudging toward the ring of boulders. The three men, leading the horses, followed closely behind them.

"Once we've warmed up a mite and got some coffee in us, you're gonna tell us just what it is about you kids that makes you so valuable," John said. "I don't reckon a smart man like Gus Greendale would have carried you off from Deadwood if he didn't figure on gettin' a good payoff out of the deal."

Oscar chuckled and said, "I can tell you one mighty good reason a gal who looks like that is valuable."

"Yeah." Nate let out a snickering laugh that made Alice's skin crawl. "She's worth a whole heap, all right."

Kermit's hand tightened on Alice's. That helped her not give in to despair, but despair was never far off. She knew she and her brother were still in great danger, but she had hoped that with these new captors, she wouldn't have to worry constantly about being molested, as she'd had to with Hank Singleton.

If anything, that threat had become even worse now, because John didn't seem to have the same iron grip on his partners that Gus Greendale did. Greendale had Lame Wolf and Tiny backing up his orders, too, and even though Oscar and Nate had done what John told them so far, they also outnumbered him. Alice knew she couldn't depend on him to save her if the other two decided to have their way with her.

"Don't worry, Alice," Kermit said quietly, as if he knew what she was thinking. "Father's not going to let them get away with this."

Alice wished she could believe that. But as much as she admired her father and knew his capabilities, Theodore Roosevelt was only one man.

If he was going to rescue them, he would need to have plenty of help . . .

Chapter 27

"You should have woken me," Seth Bullock said the next morning when Frank, Conrad, and Hunter told him about the fire they had seen in the distance.

"You couldn't have done anything about it," Hunter said. "Didn't see any point in bothering you."

Conrad smiled and added, "Actually, he said that an old-timer like you needed your rest."

"Old-timer, is it?" Bullock said with a scowl.

Frank said, "Don't worry, I reminded him that he's damned near as old as we are."

"I have a young soul," Hunter responded dryly.

"Sure you do," Bullock said.

They had moved back into the trees to build a small fire, cook breakfast, and brew a pot of coffee. With the sun up, the fire wouldn't be visible, and the trees would disperse the smoke from it.

A short time earlier, Conrad had used one of the spyglasses to check on Roosevelt and saw that the President was doing the same thing, fixing himself some breakfast, so the four unlikely guardian angels had a little time to spare this morning.

Also, Conrad had searched for any sign of the man who

had been following Roosevelt the day before but hadn't spotted him. The Easterner had either given up, or else he had found himself a good place to go to ground for the night.

Conrad didn't believe they were lucky enough for that potential complication to have resolved itself, so he figured the man was still around somewhere and would be dogging the President's trail.

After finishing breakfast and getting ready to ride, Bullock went to check on Roosevelt again and came back to report, "Teddy's on the move. If that fire you fellas spotted actually was the Dutchman's place, then we're a little closer than I thought we were. Ought to be there by the middle of the day."

"We'd better climb down off this ridge and get a little closer to the President, then," Hunter said. "There's a place not far from here where we can do that."

Bullock nodded. "I was about to suggest the very same thing."

Hunter took the lead again. After a while, they came to a defile that nature had cut into the face of the cliff. It provided a path down off the ridge, although a steep and rocky one. The men had to dismount and lead their horses as they descended. It was slow going.

"As long as this is taking, Teddy's going to get more of a lead on us," Bullock grumbled.

"Can't be helped," Hunter said. "Anyway, we'll make it up. I know a shortcut that ought to get us to the Dutchman's just about the same time he gets there."

"I hope you're right."

"When it comes to the Black Hills, I nearly always am."

Bullock didn't argue with that sentiment.

When they reached the bottom, they mounted and rode hard toward a seemingly unbroken line of hills. Roosevelt's route would take him through a pass that lay a mile or so to the north.

"I've never come this way before," Bullock said. "Are you sure we can get through, Hunter?"

"I'm positive," Hunter replied, then added, "unless there's been a bad rockslide or something since the last time I've visited these parts."

"So you're *not* sure?"

Hunter grinned and replied, "Well, let's just say I'm hopeful. Most of my life, that's been enough to get me through."

"There's more than just you riding on this," Bullock reminded him, then went on, "I'm sorry, Hunter. I know you're as aware of the stakes as we are."

"Shoot, Seth, you're just worried about your old pard's family. I didn't take any offense."

"Well, I appreciate that." Bullock leaned forward in the saddle. "What's that I see up ahead?"

Hunter's grin widened. "That's our way though, just like I hoped it'd be."

Conrad didn't see anything at first, but then he made out a dark, vertical line in the face of the bluff ahead of them. As they came closer, he realized it was a narrow crack, wide enough only for a single man on horseback. And even that would be a tight squeeze if the hombre was big enough.

"Wait a minute," he said. "You're sure that goes all the way through, Hunter?"

"Like I said, it did the last time I was in these parts."

Frank asked, "How long is it?"

"About half a mile, I'd say. It twists and turns a mite, so it's hard to be sure."

"If we get in there and it's blocked part of the way through, it'll be pure hell trying to back the horses out, single file. That's liable to take a long time, and the President's bound to reach the Dutchman's quite a while before we do."

Hunter nodded and said, "I know. I never said it wasn't a gamble. But if we can make it through, this way will get us there ahead of him, and we can get ready for whatever trouble he's gonna run into."

Frank looked at Bullock and asked, "What do you say, Seth? You're calling the shots on this little expedition."

Bullock considered for a long moment as they continued riding toward the crack, then said, "I reckon we've got to risk it."

"Then let's do it," Frank said with a decisive nod.

Conrad agreed. Life was full of gambles. That is, if you were living it the right way . . .

Buddy the coyote went first, trotting easily between the towering stone walls, seemingly unbothered by the way they loomed over him. Hunter Buchanon entered the narrow passage next. His broad shoulders brushed the walls on both sides. Bullock followed him into the cleft, leading one of the pack horses, then Frank leading the other pack horse, and Conrad brought up the rear.

Even though the sides ran pretty much straight up and down, the crack was so narrow and the walls so high that they seemed to lean inward, as if at any second they might slam together for all eternity, crushing the puny men and horses trapped between them. That thought made Conrad's skin crawl. He tried to banish the itchy feeling, but he couldn't quite manage it.

That half-mile Hunter had mentioned was going to seem a lot longer.

The first few turns were just easy bends, but then the group came to a sharper crook in the path. They didn't have room to dismount, so Hunter had to urge his horse on through. The animal made it. Since Hunter was the biggest of the men, that meant the others could get through, as well.

The sun was well up by now, but not much of its light penetrated down into the cleft. A gloomy perpetual twilight that didn't do anything to improve Conrad's mood or his taut nerves cloaked the passage.

Finally, after what seemed like at least an hour, a bright column of sunlight appeared ahead of the men. It was the end of this harrowing shortcut. Relief went through Conrad as he realized they had made it.

They emerged from the cleft onto a slope that ran down to a fairly broad valley. The ground looked flat from up here, but Conrad knew that once they got down there, the terrain would be more rugged than it appeared.

As they reined in, Hunter pointed across the valley to the northwest and said, "The Dutchman's place is about two miles that way. It won't take us long to get there. We ought to be an hour or so ahead of the President, so we'll have a chance to get the lay of the land."

"Let's keep moving, then," Bullock said with a note of impatience in his voice. "We might be able to round up Greendale and his gang and rescue Miss Alice and Kermit before Teddy even gets there. That would mean there wouldn't be any danger for him."

That sounded good to the other three. They let the horses rest, but only for a few minutes before nudging the animals into motion again.

They rode down into the valley with Hunter still leading the way. Buddy bounded on ahead of them, darting out of sight now and then as he spotted something in the brush that caught his interest, probably some wild animal. He came back a few times with his muzzle bloody, licking his chops, making it evident that he had nabbed a rabbit or some other prey.

Now that they were riding almost side by side, Conrad said to Hunter, "I still don't see how you managed to tame a wild animal like that."

"Who says I tamed him?" Hunter responded with his

customary grin. "Bud pretty much does what he wants. If that goes along with what *I* want, then everything's good. If it doesn't, then I'm just outta luck. But he's his own boss, don't ever make any mistake about that."

As Conrad had figured, the valley floor had plenty of ups and downs, marked as it was by hills and ridges and gullies. When they came to a creek, Hunter said, "This stream runs right by the Dutchman's. We could follow it, but then they'd be liable to see us coming. Better if we cut across country, even though the trail will be rougher."

"I don't want Greendale knowing that we're anywhere around," Bullock said. "So I don't care how rough the trail is." He paused and added with a grim note in his voice, "Chances are, it won't be any rougher than what those children have gone through so far."

The others knew he was probably right about that.

There wasn't an actual trail the way Hunter took them through the valley. They had to make their way up and down sandstone bluffs and force their mounts through thick brush that clung and clawed at horses and riders alike. It wasn't as nerve-wracking as following the crack in the earth that seemed as if it were about to close up on them, but it *was* arduous. Conrad felt sweat break out on his forehead and on his torso under the sheepskin coat and flannel shirt. The chill in the air turned that sweat cold and made it even more uncomfortable.

At last, Hunter lifted a hand in a signal for them to stop and then motioned for them to dismount. The other three men understood the need for silence from this point on. They tied the horses to saplings, slid Winchesters from saddle boots, and then went ahead on foot, sliding down into a dry wash and then proceeding along it until Hunter gestured for them to climb out.

That wasn't the last of the climbing. Hunter started up a

steep ridge. Frank, Conrad, and Bullock followed him, being careful not to dislodge any rocks that might roll back down the slope with a clatter.

A few moments later, they reached the top. Hunter took off his hat before he poked his head up. The others followed suit. As they eased up a little more so they could look down the opposite slope, Hunter whispered, "There it is, boys. The Dutchman's."

Only it wasn't.

Instead of the old trading post, all they saw was a tumbled-down collection of burned ruins. Here and there, a tendril of smoke still rose from the charred remains. A stone chimney stood at one end of the debris, but the conflagration had blackened the crude slabs of rock.

The adjoining corral was destroyed, too. The charred poles looked like black lines on the ground. No horse carcasses were visible, so evidently any animals quartered in the enclosure had escaped the smoke and flames.

No human bodies could be seen, either, except for one that lay *inside* the smoldering ruins—but that corpse wasn't burned. It sprawled facedown among the ashes, not far inside one of the mostly collapsed walls.

"Hell's bells," Hunter breathed. "Whoever that fella is, he didn't die in the fire. He'd be burned up if he had. Somebody *pitched* him in there after the fire was out."

"And he had to be dead when they threw him in," Bullock said, "or else he would have scrambled back out to get away from the hot ashes."

"Maybe not if they had guns on him and he knew they'd shoot him if he did," Frank said. "I've known human buzzards lowdown enough to torture a man that way. But I don't reckon that's very likely. I think you're both right, they tossed his body in there after he was dead and the fire was out."

Conrad asked, "You think that's the Dutchman?"

"Could be," Hunter replied. "He used to be a big, strapping fella, but the last time I came through this way, the years had wizened him up a heap. I figured I'd stop and buy a drink, but he took a potshot at me, yelled and cussed in German, and stepped out to shake his fist at me. I figured I didn't need that sort of aggravation, so I just yelled back at him a little and rode on." Hunter shook his head and added regretfully, "He was an unpleasant son of a gun, but he didn't deserve whatever happened to him down there."

Frank said, "The question now is, where are the men who killed him?"

"You mean Gus Greendale and his bunch," Bullock said. "It figures they're the ones who did it. But I don't see any sign of them."

In fact, the burned-out trading post and the area around it appeared to be completely deserted. Bullock had taken his spyglass out of his saddlebags and tucked it in his coat pocket before climbing this ridge with the others. He pulled it out now and extended it.

"I'm going to risk taking a better look," he said as he lifted the tube to his eye.

He peered through the glass for a long moment, shifted the telescope, and studied the scene some more. When he finally lowered the instrument, he said, "I can make out some scuffed areas around the ruins that are probably the tracks of horses and men, but there's no telling how long they've been there."

"Somebody had to be here last night," Conrad said. "That place didn't burn itself down, and the fire didn't start from lightning."

"Over there across the creek, where the trees are thick and there are some rocks, too, there are places where men could hide and keep their horses out of sight."

"You think that's where Greendale moved to after the trading post burned, Seth?" Hunter asked.

"Might be," Bullock allowed. "I didn't actually see anybody moving around, mind you, but that doesn't mean they're not in that thicket. The thing of it is, there's not any other good cover very close to the building. When Krieger built the place, he cleared out most of the trees and brush around it. The Indians were still troublesome enough in those days that he wanted to be able to fort up and defend the post if he needed to."

"Maybe we should split up," Frank suggested. "A couple of us could work our way around to the west, cross the creek a ways upstream, and then come in behind those trees."

Conrad said, "That sounds like a job for you and me, Frank."

"No, I know this country better than any of the rest of you," Hunter said. "You and me will go, Kid." He chuckled. "We'll leave these two old-timers up here to rest a spell longer before the ball opens, if it does."

Frank and Bullock just glanced wryly at each other and didn't waste the time or energy to remind Hunter that he was practically the same age they were.

"What if we discover that the kidnappers are gone, and they've taken the President's children with them?" Conrad asked.

"Then we'll pick up their trail," Bullock answered without hesitation. "I'm not turning back until those youngsters are safe."

"None of us are, Seth," Frank said quietly. "But it's possible that after the fire, Greendale decided to move the rendezvous somewhere else. He could have left instructions down there for the President to find, somewhere Mr. Roosevelt would see them."

Bullock nodded slowly. "Could be. But my gut tells me

this is still where they plan to have the showdown. Only one way to find out." The legendary former lawman looked back and forth between Conrad and Hunter. "Good luck, boys. Go find those children . . . and the no-good varmints who stole them."

CHAPTER 28

Conrad and Hunter slid back down the slope to reclaim their horses. They mounted up and Hunter headed west with Conrad right behind him. Buddy trotted along in front, as usual.

"Is that coyote any good for trailing?" Conrad asked.

"Well, he's not exactly a bloodhound, if that's what you mean. Like I said earlier, he sort of does what he wants. But sometimes he acts like he understands what I'm saying, and I can get him to do a few things." Hunter looked over at his companion. "You ever hear of an old mountain man called Preacher?"

"Yeah, I have," Conrad said. He didn't add that he had heard many stories of Preacher's exploits from Smoke Jensen, who had shared quite a few of those adventures with the old mountain man.

"I ran into him once," Hunter mused. "He had this big cur that he just called Dog, and I swear, that critter understood every word Preacher said to him. And Preacher seemed to know what Dog was thinking, too. I never saw anything like it. It was the same way with his horse, too. You know what he called the horse?"

"Horse?" Conrad said. It wasn't actually a guess, although he made it sound like one.

Hunter slapped his thigh and laughed. "That's right. Craziest thing."

Conrad didn't say anything. His father had a dog called Dog, too. It made sense to Frank, so Conrad wasn't going to argue about it.

Hunter shook his head and went on, "I wonder whatever happened to ol' Preacher? He must be dead by now, as old as he was when I crossed trails with him."

"Yeah, must be," Conrad said, although he wasn't convinced of that. According to Smoke, Preacher hadn't paid a visit to the Sugarloaf in several years, and considering that Preacher had to be at least a hundred years old by now, it made sense to assume he had passed on somewhere, probably up in the high country he loved so much.

But Smoke hadn't been convinced of that. According to him, Preacher's age had seemed frozen in time. For many years, he had looked and acted like he was in his late sixties, still vital and active despite his weathered countenance and the silver in his hair and beard.

"Besides," Smoke had added when he was spinning those yarns to Conrad in the parlor of the ranch house at the Sugarloaf, "I've been told several times that Preacher was dead, beyond a shadow of a doubt, and then later he turned up hale and hearty with some explanation of how he survived. So I'll never really believe that old pelican has crossed the divide unless I see his carcass with my own eyes."

If that policy was good enough for Smoke Jensen, Conrad thought, it was good enough for him, too.

The conversation was an enjoyable one, but Conrad and Hunter didn't allow it to distract them from the business at hand. After they had ridden for a mile or so, Hunter turned north again.

"We're well out of sight of the Dutchman's," he said. "We can cross the creek and start working our way back east."

"We need to be careful," Conrad said. "We can't let Greendale and his bunch spot us, if they're there."

Hunter just gave him a look, as if questioning the need for Conrad to even say such a thing to him.

Conrad shrugged. "Never hurts."

"From what I've heard about Kid Morgan, you never were the cautious type."

"That was a long time ago." The smile that passed quickly across Conrad's face was wistful. "Well, maybe not all that long in actual time. But it seems like a whole heap of years."

"Like I said, it ain't the years. It's the miles."

They rode on in silence after that. A short time later, they came to the stream and splashed across it. The water had to be icy, coming down from the mountains the way it did, and flowed fairly fast as it swirled around the horses' legs, but it was only a couple of feet deep and the bed was rocky, easy to ford.

The two men headed east, taking pains not to skyline themselves and sticking to the trees as much as they could. Just as Conrad's instincts told him they were approaching the Dutchman's again, Hunter slowed, confirming the younger man's hunch.

"It's not far now," Hunter said quietly. "Let's swing north a ways and circle in behind them."

"Assuming they're there."

"Seth said his gut told him they are. I'll believe Seth Bullock's gut 'most any day."

From what he had seen of Bullock so far, Conrad shared that assessment.

A short time later, Hunter reined in and motioned for Conrad to follow suit. They dismounted, and once more taking their Winchesters with them, cat-footed forward. A long, shallow ridge of piled up stone slabs appeared before them. Hunter pointed. They were in for another climb, and again they would have to be careful not to dislodge any of the smaller rocks or let their rifle barrels strike any of the boulders and make a racket.

As they were climbing, a gust of wind even colder than what they had been experiencing all day blew against Conrad's right shoulder and tugged at his hat. He paused and turned his head to gaze toward the northwest.

The sky overhead was still mostly clear, a deep, brilliant blue broken only by a few wisps of fluffy white clouds. But to the northwest lay a low line of blue-black clouds, barely visible over the wooded hills.

Conrad tapped Hunter's shoulder and pointed. The big man shrugged and nodded. It looked like a storm was blowing down out of the mountains, but there wasn't a thing in the world they could do about it.

Better to concentrate on something they could control, Conrad told himself . . . like the Winchesters in their hands.

They reached the top of the ridge. A stone slab about a dozen feet wide and at least fifty feet long lay at an upward-angled slant right in front of them. Conrad and Hunter carefully laid their rifles on the rock and then pulled themselves up onto it as well. On their bellies, they crawled slowly and silently toward its other edge. Again they took their hats off before they risked a look.

The thicket of trees and brush Bullock had mentioned ran from near the creek all the way to the base of the ridge where Conrad and Hunter had taken up their positions. Conrad knew that a number of lower, rounded boulders lay between the trees and the creek, although he couldn't see them from where he was.

Trees grew on the creek's far bank, too, but they were spread out more, and beyond them was a stretch of open ground that sloped gently up to the burned-out trading post, some fifty yards from the stream.

Conrad studied the scene intently, then leaned closer to

Hunter and breathed into the older man's ear, "I still don't see anybody around here."

"Just wait," Hunter whispered. "Keep your eyes on the trees . . . there!"

Conrad caught his breath. He had seen movement in the trees, too. It was brief, just a flicker and then gone, but now that he knew where to look, he focused his gaze there and a moment later he saw a hand lift to brush at what looked like an ear.

Or was it? If that was an ear, something was wrong about it. Misshapen, maybe . . .

Conrad stiffened. He was looking at what was left of an ear, after part of it had been cut or shot off.

He went cold inside, colder than the gusts of wind moving through the valley.

As a teenager, he had been abducted by outlaws who demanded ransom from his mother for his safe return. During his captivity, they had mutilated his ear. Ever since then, he had worn his hair on the longish side to conceal that, at first out of vanity and then, as time passed, simply out of habit. He was long past the point where he really cared what anybody thought about his appearance.

But seeing the deformed ear of the man hiding in the thicket made Conrad's mind go back to that harrowing time in his life. He had come close to dying several times, and he had never been more frightened.

Of course, that was also when he had met Frank Morgan for the first time and discovered that the famous gunfighter was actually his father, and that had changed the course of Conrad's life in many ways . . . most of them good, but some not so much.

Conrad drew in a deep breath, forced those memories out of his head, and returned his concentration to the present. His only concern right now had to be for a couple of youngsters who were also experiencing the terror of being kidnapped by evil men.

"I see one of them," he whispered to Hunter.

"There are at least two more. And I think they've got the horses back here at the base of the ridge. I thought I heard one of 'em moving around a minute ago."

"Any sign of the Roosevelt kids?"

"Nope. But if they're down there, they're probably being kept with the horses."

"You reckon we can get down this side of the ridge without giving ourselves away?"

"Looks like we might have to try—" Hunter began, then broke off and reached over to grip Conrad's arm. With his other hand, he pointed out into the valley.

Conrad saw the same thing Hunter had just spotted: a lone rider, leading a pack horse and heading toward what was left of the Dutchman's place.

President Theodore Roosevelt.

Conrad recognized the outfit the President was wearing, as well as the rider's stocky but powerful figure. Roosevelt sat the saddle well, too, as befitted the man who had led the Rough Riders. Conrad had no doubt it was him.

Roosevelt reined in abruptly. Conrad had a hunch the President had just spotted the burned-out ruins of the trading post. He could only imagine what must be going through Roosevelt's mind right now. The man had expected to find his stolen children here; to be greeted by that charred rubble must have sent all sorts of dread rampaging through his mind. He had to be wondering right now if Alice and Kermit had died in that blaze.

Staring at the ruins wouldn't change anything. After a moment, Roosevelt urged his mount into motion again and rode slowly toward what was left of the Dutchman's.

Hunter Buchanon whispered, "If those varmints are gonna make a move, they're bound to do it soon."

"They'll make a move," Conrad said. "They wouldn't have dragged the President all the way out here just to let him ride away. They'll have all their attention focused on him now, so this might be our best chance to get down there and come up behind them."

Hunter nodded in agreement and said, "Let's go."

Gus Greendale's pulse thundered with hatred in his head. All those long days and longer nights he had spent behind the towering gray prison walls had honed his hate to a razor-sharp edge.

And there stood the object of that hate, less than a hundred yards away. Why, from here he could put a bullet in Teddy Roosevelt's head, Greendale thought.

But where would be the satisfaction in that? Sure, Roosevelt would be dead, and in that instant before all awareness fled, he might even have a pretty good idea of who had killed him and why, but that wasn't enough.

No, he had to suffer more first, and Gus Greendale knew exactly how to make him do it.

Roosevelt had ridden to within twenty feet of the ruins and dismounted. Now he stood there, holding his horse's reins, as he stared at the devastation. After a long moment, he raised his eyes from the burned-out trading post, lifted his head, and looked around, wary, like an animal sensing a threat nearby.

"What are you waitin' for?" Hank Singleton asked from behind the tree where he was hidden, a dozen feet to Greendale's left. "Go ahead and shoot him!"

"Not yet," Greendale said.

"Don't forget about the money," Lame Wolf called softly from his hiding place on the other side of Greendale. They had left Tiny back with the horses. As the day went on, the giant's skin had taken on more of a grayish hue. He insisted he was all right, but Greendale figured he was dying.

"The money's bound to be in his saddlebags or on that pack horse," Singleton said. "Let's just kill him and be done with it." A wolfish grin spread across his angular face. "Hell, if we time it right, we can all shoot him at the same time. That seems fair, don't it?"

"Not yet," Greendale said again.

And with that, he stepped out from behind the tree and started walking toward the man he had hated for so long.

Chapter 29

On the other side of the valley, Frank Morgan and Seth Bullock had continued watching from their vantage point to the south of the old trading post. They had seen Roosevelt approaching from the east.

"That's Teddy," Bullock said quietly. "I'd know him right away from how he sits the saddle."

"He's seen what's left of the Dutchman's," Frank said as Roosevelt reined in.

Grimness etched trenches in Bullock's face as he said, "I hate to think of what must be going through Teddy's mind right now. He's afraid Alice and Kermit are dead."

"We don't know they aren't."

"I won't believe it," Bullock snapped, with a shake of his head. "We're going to find a way to save those youngsters. Greendale wouldn't have killed them."

"More than likely he wouldn't have meant to, but they could have died in the fire anyway."

"We didn't see their bodies in the ruins."

"Might not be able to from here," Frank said, "if they were burned so bad nothing's left but bones."

Bullock had no answer for that.

Roosevelt rode on and stopped again, closer to the ruins. He dismounted and seemed to be studying them, as if trying to figure out exactly what had happened here. He stayed that way, motionless, for a few minutes, and then looked around.

A heartbeat later, Frank saw a man step out of the trees on the far side of the creek and stride toward the President.

"Look!"

"I see him." Bullock extended his spyglass and lifted it to his eye. "I never laid eyes on Gus Greendale, but that fella matches his description." He hurriedly closed the telescope and started to get up. "We'd better get down there—"

"Hold on," Frank said as he put a hand on Bullock's shoulder. "We don't know where the kids are. If they're still alive and we go rushing in, it could put them in danger."

"But if that's Greendale, Teddy's in danger now! Greendale could start shooting at him any time."

"I don't think Greendale's in a rush. He's waited fifteen years for his revenge on Roosevelt. He'll want to linger on that."

"I sure as hell hope you're right," Bullock muttered.

"Howdy there, Teddy," Greendale called as he came to a stop at the creek. "It's been a while."

Roosevelt had spotted him right away and stiffened at the sight of him. He started to lift the Winchester in his hands but then stopped the motion.

"That's right," Greendale shouted mockingly. "You don't want to kill me just yet, do you? Not until you know where those kids of yours are."

Roosevelt started toward the creek, his sturdy, muscular legs moving like pistons to drive him along.

"You . . . you scoundrel!" he burst out. "You rapscallion! Kidnapper of innocents! By God, sir, they don't come any lower than you!"

"You can harangue me all you want," Greendale said as Roosevelt came to a stop on the creek's southern bank and glared across the fast-flowing stream at him. "That don't change the fact that I've got something you want. Two somethings."

"I brought the money you demanded," Roosevelt barked. "I'm prepared to turn it over to you as soon as you've returned my children."

"Not so fast now. We're old friends, and it's been a mighty long time since we've seen each other. More than fifteen years, in fact."

"I know how long it's been," Roosevelt said.

"Do you know what it was like for me, spendin' those years locked up? Maybe I'll tell you. Maybe you ought to just stand there and listen while I tell you what each and every one o' those damn days was like."

Roosevelt regarded him coldly and said, "Spew whatever venom you'd like, man. Just give my children back to me."

"In due time, in due time." Greendale grinned and then licked his lips, as if he were enjoying a delicious meal. "And I reckon I won't bore you with a lot of talk about my time in prison. I figure you'd rather hear about those youngsters of yours and how *they've* been spendin' their time lately. That gal of yours is a pretty one, sure enough. Feisty, too. No matter what we done to her, she never lost her spirit or her fight. And that little brother of hers watched every bit of it."

Roosevelt's normally ruddy face turned pale with horror and rage.

"You monster!" he said. "You're vermin, Greendale, absolute vermin! You always have been."

Greendale's grin turned ugly. He cocked his head a little to the side and said, "Now, see, talk like that is a real burr under my saddle, Teddy. You think you're so much better than me and my friends. Back in the old days, you paraded around the Black Hills like you were a king or somethin'! Acted like it was your right to have your men shoot poor Hubert and ol' Amos and have the rest of us locked up."

"You were outlaws. I was simply doing my duty as a law-abiding citizen."

Greendale went on as if he hadn't heard what Roosevelt said. "Well, you ain't a king, not even now. You may be President, but out here, that don't mean a damn thing. Out here, what counts is who's got the gun . . . and who's willin' to use it."

Roosevelt's jaw jutted out defiantly. "If you intend to shoot me, get it over with. But you should know that if you do, the army will come in here and scour the hills until you're found and brought to justice. You may have your revenge, but you'll soon lose your life."

"Well, maybe that's a trade I'm willin' to make," Greendale said.

The two men stood on opposite sides of the creek, glaring at each other, as long, tense seconds ticked past. Finally, with a slight crack in his voice that showed how uncharacteristically close he was to losing control, Theodore Roosevelt said, "In the name of heaven, man, do what you like to me. The money is in one of the packs. Just let my children go."

Slowly, Greendale shook his head. "You know, Teddy, there's a part of me that almost wants to do that. But I can't."

"For God's sake, why not?"

"Because if you were to go up yonder to the Dutchman's and root around in the ashes for a while, you'd find what's left of 'em."

The howl that burst from Roosevelt was a primal sound, the cry of an animal in enormous pain, a cornered beast with no way out. And as that cry echoed back from the hills, Theodore Roosevelt jerked his rifle to his shoulder.

Conrad and Hunter slid over the edge of the massive stone slab and dropped a few feet to the next one lower down. They moved quickly now, less concerned as they saw one of the kidnappers emerge from cover and approach the creek.

"What the hell is he doing?" Hunter asked as he and Conrad continued their descent.

"Looks like he wants to have a talk with the President," Conrad said. "You think that's Greendale?"

"More than likely. From what Seth's told me, he's the one who forced this showdown in the first place."

They came to a spot where the piled-up slabs of rock ended at a slope covered with much smaller rocks. About forty feet wide, it slanted down to the thicket at the bottom.

As they paused, Hunter said, "There's no way we can get down there from here without making a racket."

A shot suddenly blasted from the creek. "No time to worry about it now!" Conrad said as he leaped out onto the talus and started to slide.

Hunter didn't hesitate. He bounded after Conrad, and a second later, both men were careening down the slope toward the trees with showers of rocks and gravel flying through the air around them.

In the midst of all that commotion, Conrad thought he heard the distant crack of a rifle, but he couldn't be sure. And there was no time to worry about it as he and Hunter reached the bottom of the slope and came out of their slides into stumbling runs that carried them into the trees. Conrad hoped he didn't bash his brains out against one of the trunks before he regained control of his momentum.

Somewhere close by, horses neighed in shrill alarm. With that sound to guide them, Conrad and Hunter caught their balance and plunged ahead. Hunter gripped his old LeMat, while Conrad had filled both hands, the right with his Colt, the left with the broom-handle Mauser.

Abruptly, they broke out into a clearing. The horses were there, tied to a rope strung between tree trunks. So was an enormously tall and broad black man with bloody bandages wrapped around his barrel chest. Obviously, he was wounded, but he didn't let that stop him from planting his feet, raising guns in both ham-like hands, and blazing away at Conrad and Hunter.

Hunter yelled and dived to the side as slugs whipped past his ear. Conrad let his momentum carry him forward a little more as he dropped to one knee and thrust both guns out. Shots rolled from them in a racketing, deadly tide. Muzzle flashes ripped through the gloom in the thicket. From his belly, Hunter triggered the LeMat's lower barrel, and the charge of buckshot exploded from the muzzle with a roar.

The giant rocked backward as bullets and buckshot pounded into his chest. Fresh bloodstains bloomed like crimson flowers on the bandages. Arms like the trunks of small trees sagged. He staggered to one side, then back the other way as he struggled to lift the guns again.

Conrad was about to put a bullet through his head when the horses, spooked by the noise and the sharp bite of powdersmoke, lunged against the rope to which they were tied, broke free, and stampeded right over the mortally wounded man.

More guns barked from the direction of the creek. That had to mean Roosevelt was alive but still in danger.

As Hunter surged to his feet, he called to Conrad, "I don't see the kids!"

"They're not here!" Conrad said. "But we have to help the President!"

Hunter nodded. They charged through the trees toward the creek. They hadn't gone very far when Conrad spotted a man kneeling behind a tree and firing a rifle. He saw the mutilated ear and knew this was the man he had seen earlier. The kidnapper must have heard them coming, because he whirled around, and the rifle spouted flame and smoke at them.

Conrad triggered the Mauser twice. The semi-automatic

pistol spat lead. One of the bullets ricocheted off the Winchester in the man's hands, but the other punched into his throat and knocked him back against the tree he had been using for cover. He dropped the rifle and clapped both hands to his throat, but he couldn't stop the blood that fountained out. He leaned against the tree for a second with the bright red stuff flooding over his fingers, then slid down to the ground and toppled onto his side.

Bullets ripped through the air from their right. Hunter returned the fire, catching a glimpse of a darting, buckskin-clad figure who moved at an awkward but incredibly swift pace. Hunter grimaced as he realized he couldn't see his target anymore. The other kidnapper was gone, and Hunter didn't know if he had hit the man or not.

Silence descended on the thicket as the last of the echoes faded. Conrad realized that no more shots were coming from the creek.

Had the President survived?

Moments earlier, Theodore Roosevelt had realized that he was too slow. The butt of his rifle smacked into his shoulder and the barrel began to rise, but as the Winchester came up, he saw that Gus Greendale already had his rifle leveled and was about to fire. Roosevelt stood no chance of beating him to the shot.

Greendale suddenly jerked backward just enough to make the barrel of his Winchester climb a couple of inches. The bullet that erupted from it as his finger jerked the trigger screamed across the creek and flew several feet above Roosevelt's head. Roosevelt had no idea what had caused Greendale to react like that and miss an easy shot . . . until he heard the distant sound of a rifle shot somewhere behind him, far enough away that it had lagged behind the bullet's arrival.

Across the creek, Greendale dropped his Winchester and stood swaying as he pawed at his chest with one hand. Blood welled between his fingers. His eyes seemed unfocused, but then his gaze fastened on Roosevelt and he rasped, "You . . . you four-eyed son of a . . ."

Without finishing the curse, he pitched forward and landed with the upper half of his body facedown in the creek. The water around him took on a pinkish tinge as blood from the wound in his chest spread through it.

More shots exploded from the trees and bullets screamed through the air around Roosevelt. He wasn't out of danger yet, so he couldn't afford to dwell on what Greendale had said about Kermit and Alice dying in the fire. He threw himself onto the ground, propped himself on his elbows, and started shooting back at the kidnappers still hidden in the trees.

Several hundred yards away, a few moments earlier, Frank Morgan had lowered the rifle he held. A thin wisp of powdersmoke still curled from the Winchester's muzzle.

Seth Bullock looked at him and said, "I thought you were famous for using a handgun."

"Just because a man's known for using a Colt, that doesn't mean he can't use a long gun, too," Frank said. "And with your friend Teddy in such a predicament . . . well, there just wasn't time to miss."

As a fresh volley of shots roared from the trees on the other side of the creek, Bullock leaped to his feet and said, "He's still in a heap of trouble! Come on, we need to get down there!"

* * *

Bullets still clipped through the branches and thudded into the trunks of the trees in the thicket. Conrad and Hunter took cover as best they could. Conrad could tell the shots came from across the creek, which meant that the President had to be the one responsible for them.

With his back pressed to a trunk, Conrad risked leaning his head a little to the side and shouted, "Mr. President! Mr. President! Hold your fire! It's Conrad Morgan!"

"And Hunter Buchanon!" Hunter bellowed, joining in.

The shots ended. After a moment, Roosevelt called, "Mr. Morgan? Is that you?"

"Yes, sir! One of the kidnappers is dead, and the other's gone! What about Greendale?"

"Dead," Roosevelt replied flatly. "Are . . . are my children in there?"

With the danger of being drilled by a friendly bullet ended, Conrad swung out from behind the tree and strode forward. He hated to be the one to give Roosevelt the news, but as he stepped into the open and saw the President on the other side of the creek, struggling to get up, he said, "No, sir, I'm afraid there's no sign of them."

"Merciful heavens," Roosevelt muttered as he made it to his feet. Then he stiffened and went on, "Who's that?" as he looked past Conrad.

A glance over his shoulder told Conrad that Hunter had emerged from the thicket as well. He said, "That's Hunter Buchanon, Mr. President. He's a friend."

Hunter stepped up beside Conrad, pinched the brim of his hat as he nodded, and said, "It's a plumb honor to meet you, Mr. Roosevelt, sir."

"Thank you for your help, Mister . . . Buchanon, was it?"

"Yes, sir."

Roosevelt took a deep breath and then asked, "Where is Seth Bullock? Nothing has happened to him, has it?"

"No, sir," Conrad told him. "In fact, I think that's him heading this way now, along with my father."

Roosevelt turned to look at the two riders moving at a fast lope across the valley toward the Dutchman's.

"Bully!" he exclaimed. "Thank the stars that Seth is all right." Then a haunted look came over his drawn face as he turned to Conrad and Hunter. "You're sure the other kidnappers have been dealt with?"

"Well, one got away," Conrad said again, "but I don't reckon he's much of a threat on his own."

"Very well." Roosevelt drew in a deep breath and heaved a sigh. "Greendale told me that I . . . I would find my children in the ruins of the old trading post. I must go and find out if that's true."

Chapter 30

Hunter stepped into the burned-out shell of the trading post behind Roosevelt and said, "Be careful, Mr. President. With this cold wind blowing, the ashes should be pretty well cooled off, but there could still be a few hot spots here and there."

Roosevelt ignored him and continued stomping around. Gray clouds of powdered ash rose around his feet as he searched for the remains of his children.

Hunter hunkered on his heels next to the body that lay facedown, not far inside one of the collapsed walls. He took hold of the corpse and rolled it onto its back. The face was burned some from the heat of the ashes, but he recognized it.

Hunter lifted his head, looked at Conrad, who stood outside the ruins waiting for Frank and Bullock to get there, and called, "It's the Dutchman, all right. Looks like somebody shot him in the head, and since it wasn't any of us, I'm betting on Greendale. He was snake-mean enough to have done that when he didn't need Krieger anymore."

"Don't reckon we'll ever know for sure what happened," Conrad said, "but you're probably right."

Frank and Bullock rode up, leading the pack horses.

Without dismounting, Bullock nodded toward Roosevelt and asked, "Is Teddy all right?"

"He's not wounded," Conrad said, "but Greendale told him the kids are dead and that the bodies are in what's left of the trading post."

Roosevelt had charged all through the ruins. His trousers were completely gray from the layer of powdered ash that covered them. He swung around toward the others, threw his arms out to the sides, and exclaimed, "They're not here! I've looked everywhere! They're simply not here!"

"Might be hard to be certain of that, Teddy," Bullock said gently. "If they were buried underneath something—"

Roosevelt held up hands blackened from pawing through the devastation.

"There's nothing big enough left to conceal them," he insisted. "I've looked everywhere in here, I tell you! There's no sign of them."

"Then that's good news," Frank said, "because it means that wherever they are, there's a chance they're still alive."

"But where can they be?"

"Greendale could have hidden them somewhere around here," Conrad suggested. "I don't believe for a second that he actually intended to turn them over to you in exchange for that ransom money, Mr. President."

"Nor do I," Roosevelt agreed. "They were never anything other than instruments of revenge for that horrible man." He paused, took off his pince-nez, and wearily scrubbed a hand over his face. "We have to find them."

"We'll start scouting for tracks right now," Bullock said. He glanced at the sky. "We'd better be quick about it, too, because it looks to me like there might be some snow in those clouds moving in."

Roosevelt shuddered visibly. "If those poor children are caught in a blizzard—"

"We'll try not to let it come to that. Come on, Frank, let's see what we can find. Hunter, you're a good tracker. You should join us."

"I'll fetch my horse," Hunter said. He jerked a thumb across the creek. "It's back over yonder."

"I'll come with you," Conrad said, "and gather up the gang's horses, along with any weapons and ammunition I can find. It never hurts to be better armed."

They waded back across the creek while Frank and Bullock split up and began riding slow circles around the Dutchman's place, looking for tracks that might indicate where the children had gone. Despite Bullock's reassuring words to Roosevelt, the likelihood of them being able to pick up the trail was pretty small, Conrad thought, especially with their time limited by the potential snowstorm rushing down from the northwest.

Conrad and Hunter were approaching the thicket when a sudden shrill yipping caught their attention. As they stopped in surprise, a ghastly apparition stumbled out of the trees with Buddy nipping at its heels and tugging at a trouser leg. Conrad was shocked to recognize the massive black man he had figured was dead after being shot to pieces and trampled by stampeding horses.

The giant still lived but was in terrible shape. The bandages around his torso were sodden with blood, so wet that it seemed impossible he could have a single drop still flowing in his veins. His left arm hung limp and was twisted unnaturally where it was broken in at least two places from being stomped by the horses. His face was battered and bruised until it looked more like a mound of broken basaltic rock than a human face. The wheezing and rattling as his bullet-torn lungs struggled for air could be heard above the chuckling of the creek.

And yet still he moved, putting one foot in front of the other as he came toward Conrad and Hunter.

"Good Lord!" Hunter exclaimed as he dragged the LeMat out of its holster. "We'd better shoot him again!"

Conrad caught hold of Hunter's wrist.

"Wait," he said. "I don't think he can hurt us, the shape he's in, but he *might* be able to talk."

"And tell us what happened to the kids," Hunter responded, catching on to what Conrad meant. "You're right. Better be careful, though, just in case he *does* try something."

The two of them split up, veering apart so they could approach the giant from different angles. They kept hands on gun butts so they could draw and fire quickly if they needed to. The giant made no threatening moves, however; in fact, he didn't even seem aware of their presence as he plodded forward.

He took a few more steps before his eyes rolled up suddenly in their sockets. He pitched forward, crashing to the ground like a felled tree. Conrad tensed, figuring that death had finally caught up to the man, but then he heard the wheezing breaths continue.

He hurried forward and said to Hunter, "Let's get him on his back. Maybe he can still talk."

Hunter motioned Conrad back and dropped to a knee beside the giant.

"Let me roll him over," he said. "You get a gun out and watch him for any tricks."

"I think he's too close to dying to try anything," Conrad said, "but I'll keep an eye on him anyway."

He unleathered his Colt while Hunter grasped the giant's shoulders and, with a grunt of effort, rolled him onto his back. The man lay there, his bloody chest rising and falling in a slow, irregular rhythm. After a few seconds, his eyelids began to flutter. He opened his eyes but didn't seem to see anything.

Hunter leaned forward so that he was more in the giant's

line of sight and said, "Are you there, mister? Can you hear me?"

The bleary eyes focused a little. "Who . . . who are . . . ?"

"My name's Hunter Buchanon," Hunter replied. Conrad didn't figure the name would mean anything to the giant, but it might allow more of a connection between them and help keep the man conscious and coherent. Hunter asked the most important question. "Where are the President's kids?"

"Gus? Gus?" The dying man's voice rose and became more urgent. *"Gus?"*

"Gus is gone, friend," Hunter said gently. "He's not here anymore. He left you behind, so why don't you tell me where I can find those young'uns?"

"Lame . . . Wolf? H-Hank?"

"All gone. It's just you, friend. Do you remember the children you had with you?"

"Alice and Kermit," Conrad quietly supplied the names.

"Alice and Kermit," Hunter repeated as he leaned closer. "A girl and a boy. You remember them? Where are they?"

"Never meant to . . . to hurt them," the giant rasped. "I thought maybe . . . maybe I could get G-Gus to let them go . . . after we settled the score with . . . with Roosevelt . . ."

"Did you let them go?"

"No, they . . . they ran off . . . but the others . . . got them."

"The others? What others?"

"From . . . D-Deadwood . . . Gus hired them . . . They weren't supposed to . . . come with us . . ."

It was obvious the man was slipping away. He had hung on longer than Conrad expected him to. Conrad knelt on his other side and said, "You mean the men who staged that fight with you?"

Amazingly, the giant smiled. "It wasn't much . . . of a fight."

"But they have the children now?"

"M-Maybe . . . Probably . . . Kids ran off . . . across the

creek . . . P-Perry and the others . . . went after them . . . toward the mountains."

Hunter and Conrad exchanged a glance. Hunter said, "Northwest, more than likely. Gives us a place to start, anyway."

Conrad nodded and said, "What's your name, mister?"

"W-Wendell," the giant forced out. "Wendell . . . William . . . W-Wilkerson . . . but everybody called me . . . Tiny . . . Been a long time . . . since anybody asked—"

He stopped short and his chest rose one more time as he drew in a deep breath. Then it fell as that breath came back out in a long, rattling sigh, and Conrad knew it would never rise again.

"A place to start," Conrad said with a grim nod. "And there's no time to bury him or the Dutchman."

"Maybe we can come back later," Hunter said, "and put up markers for both of them. I reckon both of 'em were pretty sorry specimens to do the things they done, but . . . hell, they were human folks."

"That's right," Conrad said as he rose to his feet. "Let's grab those horses, join up with Frank and Mr. Bullock, and see if we can pick up that trail heading toward the mountains."

Once again, he had abandoned his friends, Lame Wolf thought bitterly as he limped along a faint game trail that led back east from the Dutchman's place. It left a bad taste in his mouth as it stirred up those old memories of slipping out of the trading post the night Hubert and Amos had been killed and the other members of the gang captured.

They all claimed they didn't hold any grudges against him for escaping that night, but Lame Wolf didn't know if it was true. How could they not resent the fact that he still had his freedom while theirs was lost?

But this was different, he told himself. Gus and Hank and Tiny hadn't been captured today. They were *dead.* And Lame Wolf couldn't have prevented their deaths or done a damned thing for them by hanging around and getting killed, too. So it only made sense to put this misbegotten misadventure behind him and move on. It was a shame that none of them would get any payday out of it, but that was how things worked out sometimes. He was good at surviving, living a hardscrabble existence. He had plenty of experience at it . . .

Lame Wolf followed the trail between two humps of earth covered with brush and rocks but stopped short as he heard the unmistakable sound of numerous guns being cocked. His breath caught in his throat. The brush on both sides of the trail crackled quietly as rifle barrels thrust through it and pointed at him.

Moving very slowly, Lame Wolf raised both hands and said, "I'm not looking for any trouble, boys, and if you're planning to rob me, I'm afraid you're going to be very disappointed."

"Nobody's going to rob you, redskin," a man called from around a nearby bend in the trail. A moment later, two riders came around that bend and reined in so they could glare at Lame Wolf.

Both men wore suits and fancy hats and had the look of Easterners. The man on Lame Wolf's right was shorter and stockier and at least had a look of competence as he held a revolver pointed in the Indian's general direction. His face was broad and beefy and he had a neatly clipped, graying brown mustache.

The other man seemed as out of place in the Black Hills as a flower hat on a pig. His face was pale and pasty and egg-shaped. In fact, the man's whole head reminded Lame Wolf of an egg. His chin receded and his eyes bulged out, and when Lame Wolf looked at him, he had the same sort of feeling he did when he turned over a rock and uncovered a bunch of squirming maggots.

And yet the man carried himself as if he were in command here, and rightfully so. Arrogance radiated from him like heat from the sun.

Lame Wolf turned his attention back to the other man. Recognition jolted an exclamation out of him.

"I know you," he said. "We met you on that hill outside of Deadwood a few nights ago."

"That you did, redskin," the man agreed. "My name is Ambrose Neill. You may not have known that, but your boss did. Where *is* Greendale?"

"Dead," Lame Wolf replied heavily. "So is Hank Singleton and, I strongly suspect, Tiny."

A look of alarm appeared on the egg-man's face. "What about the brats?"

"The Roosevelt children?" Lame Wolf shook his head. "I don't know. They got away from us last night, but I think some other fellows grabbed them while they were trying to escape."

"Other fellows?" Neill repeated. "What other fellows?"

"Some that Gus hired back in Deadwood to help us." Lame Wolf saw the fury building on the egg-man's face, darkening the unhealthily pallid skin, but he was into his explanation now and didn't see any way of stopping it. "Gus figured they, ah, followed us so they could try to cut themselves in on the deal if they got a chance. And last night, they did."

"So what you're saying," the egg-man demanded, "is that you've ruined *everything*!"

The last word came out in a roar of rage. The egg-man pawed under his heavy coat, as if trying to find a gun.

"Hold on, hold on," Neill said hurriedly. He reached over and put a hand on the egg-man's arm. "We can fix this."

"I don't see how," the egg-man fumed. He glared down

at Neill's hand until Neill removed it from his arm. "Our men don't have the Roosevelt brats anymore, and the plan is ruined without them."

"But *somebody* has them. All we have to do is find them before Roosevelt does, and we can carry on."

Lame Wolf spoke up again. "The President didn't come alone. He has friends with him. At least two that I saw." He paused, then added, "Men good with guns."

Neill waved that away. "I never expected Roosevelt to follow orders and come alone. I'm sure he planned all along to double-cross us." He looked over at the egg-man. "It's fortunate that you brought along enough men to deal with such a problem, Senator, and even more fortunate that you caught up with me so that I can lend you a hand as well."

Senator? Lame Wolf thought. That hideous egg-man was a senator? Who would be foolish enough to select such a slimy specimen to represent them?

Not that it mattered now, he added to himself. The arrival of Neill and this other man from the East meant there might be a chance to salvage something from the scheme that had fallen apart. With that in mind, Lame Wolf said, "I can help you find them."

Neill's interest visibly quickened. "You can?"

"I know which way they went," Lame Wolf said with a solemn nod. In truth, he didn't know if the children's captors had continued in that direction, but he was going to cling to that hope, anyway.

What else did he have?

"But we must hurry," he went on. He pointed to the northwest and the clouds building over the Black Hills. "There will probably be snow by nightfall. It will cover any trail they may have left."

"Well, then, what are we waiting for?" Neill snapped. He

raised his voice and called, "Get your horses. We're moving out."

The egg-man—the senator—said, "You're awfully quick to give orders to men working for *me*, Neill."

"I just want to find those children and get on with our revenge against that damned Roosevelt, Senator."

That seemed to mollify the egg-man somewhat. He didn't say anything else as half a dozen men emerged from their hiding places in the brush. Three of them were dressed in Eastern garb like Neill and the senator. Lame Wolf didn't actually recognize the other three, but he knew the type: drifting hardcases who, more than likely, had been hired back in Deadwood to provide extra muscle and guns. All six had cold, brutal faces and looked perfectly willing to kill, as long as the price was right.

They were also the sort who might gun down an old Indian with a bad leg just for fun, Lame Wolf told himself. He would have to be careful. He figured that if Neill and the senator got what they wanted, they wouldn't hesitate to dispose of him just to simplify things.

Lame Wolf wasn't going to let that happen, but first there was the matter of finding Alice and Kermit Roosevelt . . . and with a storm blowing in, that might not be easy . . .

Chapter 31

Frank, Hunter, and Bullock were all good trackers. Conrad wasn't bad, although he didn't have as much experience as the older men. Still, he had lived a wandering, precarious existence for several years, and there had been times when his life depended on his ability to follow a trail. So all four men were confident that once they found the tracks they were looking for, they wouldn't lose them.

Theodore Roosevelt had some experience along those lines himself, although he deferred to the abilities of his companions. He was so relieved to hear confirmation that his children *hadn't* died in the blaze that consumed the trading post, it seemed to be difficult for him to think about anything else.

Of course, they had no way of knowing yet if Alice and Kermit were still alive, but at least there was a chance that was true.

With what Tiny had told them before he died, they were able to locate the tracks of three horses heading northwest. Frank studied the sign intently for several moments before saying, "Looks like one of them might be carrying double. Hard to be sure. Can't tell about either of the others."

"Alice is practically a grown woman," Roosevelt said.

"She could be on the horse that might be carrying two people. Kermit is rather on the slender side, so I can see how it could be more difficult to determine if he's with them. For the time being, however, I'm going to assume that they have both children."

Bullock said, "That's about all we can do. That and pray."

Hunter knelt beside the coyote and scratched his head. "Buddy, you reckon you can follow the scent those varmints left? Right here, Buddy, smell that. Find 'em, boy! Find 'em!"

The coyote just looked at him.

"Well, it was worth a try, I suppose," Hunter said with a shrug.

"Let's go," Bullock said. They all swung up into their saddles and rode out.

Buddy dashed on ahead. Hunter grinned and said, "See, he was just waiting for us to get started good. Didn't see any point in making the effort until he knew we were gonna follow him."

None of the others argued with him, but Frank and Conrad smiled slightly. Roosevelt and Bullock were too grimly intent on their mission to bother.

The clouds continued moving in, hungrily gobbling up the blue sky overhead. It wasn't long before they swallowed the sun itself. Gray gloom settled over the darkly wooded hills, and that gave the already chilly wind even more bite.

Conrad tugged his hat down and tightened the throat of his sheepskin coat. He was bringing up the rear. Frank and Hunter were in front, right in the teeth of the wind, followed by Roosevelt and Bullock, the two old friends riding side by side, and then Conrad leading the pack horses and keeping an eye on their back trail.

He wasn't expecting anyone to be following them—there shouldn't be anybody back there except that lone member of

Greendale's gang who had gotten away—but instinct kept the skin on the back of his neck prickling anyway.

Or maybe it was just the cold. Roosevelt had told them that the only member of the gang unaccounted for was a semi-crippled old Indian called Lame Wolf. Conrad didn't think they had much to worry about from him.

Once the clouds settled in and completely covered the sky, it didn't take long for the first snowflakes to begin falling. They were light and scattered, swirling down here and there from the looming gray clouds. The temperature was right around freezing, Conrad judged from the way the flakes melted as soon as they hit the ground. But the mercury was dropping, and if it fell much farther, the snow would begin to stick, especially if it started coming down harder.

That was what happened. The snowfall increased, the air got colder, and patches of white began to appear on the ground. Some flakes had already begun to collect on tree branches. The storm wasn't bad yet . . . but it could get that way, and Conrad was convinced that it would.

"We're going to lose the trail," Roosevelt fretted.

"Maybe not," Bullock tried to reassure him. "The snow won't start to cover the tracks for a while yet. We don't know how far ahead of us they are. They probably didn't keep traveling all night. More than likely, they made camp somewhere, and it's possible they didn't move on today because the weather was threatening. Why, it could be that we're within a mile or two of them right now."

"Do you actually believe that, Seth?"

"I believe it's possible," Bullock said, "and there's only one way to find out if it's true or not."

"That's right, Mr. President," Frank said over his shoulder. "Best thing for us to do is keep moving while we still can and make up as much ground as possible. When you're faced with trouble, it's usually smart just to go straight ahead, right on through it."

Roosevelt sighed and nodded. "That's always been my philosophy as well, Frank."

So far, the snow hadn't been heavy enough to affect visibility, but as Conrad lifted his eyes toward the hills in front of them, he saw that their contours had gotten blurry. It was hard to make them out, and he couldn't see the mountains in the distance at all anymore.

He hoped that the men holding the Roosevelt children had enough sense to find a safe place to get in out of this storm, if they hadn't already.

Their captors were arguing again, which made Alice nervous. If a fight broke out among them, she was afraid the older man, John Perry, would be killed. So far, he had persuaded Sheehan and Poore not to molest her, arguing that she was bound to be worth more in the long run if they left her alone, even though they didn't know who she and Kermit really were and hadn't figured out what to do with them.

She had overheard the other two talking about how they ought to forget about trying to ransom her. Their idea was that they ought to just have their fun with her, then find some whorehouse they could sell her to. That way they could get something out of the deal.

The boy, in their opinion, was pretty much worthless. They could shoot him in the head and leave him, and at least the scavengers would get some use out of him.

Perry had managed to head off that talk so far, but Alice knew it was only a matter of time before the other two got tired of listening to him.

They were already annoyed with him. Right now the argument was about the weather. Perry had insisted that they stay where they were until they figured out their next move. Alice had been glad for that, since it meant her father might have an easier time locating them, but then the weather had changed and the friction between the three men grew worse.

"We should've found us a better place to hole up," Sheehan insisted in a loud, angry voice. "Maybe a cave or something."

"Yeah," Poore agreed. "A cave."

"We're mostly out of the wind, here in these rocks," Perry said. "That's worth something, ain't it?"

Sheehan snorted. "Yeah, until the snow drifts four feet deep in here. What're we gonna do then, John?"

"Maybe it won't snow that much." Even as Perry said that, he didn't sound as if he actually believed the words.

"Look how hard it's comin' down already!" Sheehan said.

"Yeah, it's really comin' down," Poore added.

That was true. The air was filled with swirling, dancing white flakes. Under other circumstances, the scene would have been pretty, Alice thought as she sat huddled against one of the rounded boulders alongside Kermit, with a blanket draped over both of them.

The snow had started to collect on the ground in places, forming a thin layer of white. It melted when it hit the blanket because of the warmth that came through it from their bodies, but then the cold wind froze that moisture, creating a crust of ice that crackled faintly every time they moved.

"Well, it's too late to find somewhere else now," Perry said as he faced the other two men. "This place is better than no shelter at all, which is what we're liable to wind up with if we go wanderin' around in a snowstorm."

Sheehan glared at him for a moment longer, then turned away, muttering something.

"What was that?" Perry asked.

"I said, our mistake was listenin' to you in the first place,"

Sheehan snapped. "And lettin' you think you were in charge of this business."

"Following Greendale and his gang was my idea, wasn't it?"

"Yeah, but what's it gonna get us?" Sheehan waved a hand through the falling snow. "Froze to death, more than likely!"

"Why don't you have another cup of coffee?" Perry suggested. "You'll feel better if you do."

He nodded toward the fire they had built in the lee of a boulder that bulged outward enough to shield the flames from the snow. Poore had spent quite a bit of time that morning collecting firewood, and he had enough piled nearby to keep the blaze going for a long spell. Maybe not for as long as they were going to be stuck here, though.

"All right," Sheehan said grudgingly. "Come on, Nate."

For a change, Poore didn't immediately do what somebody else told him to. Instead, he stood there with a frown on his usually dull-witted face. He had even closed his mouth, which hung open most of the time.

Perry saw that and said, "What is it, Nate?"

"I thought I heard somethin'," Poore replied. He looked around as the creases in his forehead deepened.

"Heard what?"

"A horse, maybe."

Sheehan said, "You just heard one of our horses, more than likely."

Poore shook his head. "No, it was out yonder somewhere." He gestured vaguely into the falling snow, indicating the valley that ran to the east.

"I don't hear anything," Perry said. "You just imagined it, Nate."

Sheehan abandoned the idea of getting another cup of coffee and said, "Maybe he did and maybe he didn't. Maybe Greendale and the rest of his bunch have finally gotten around to coming after us. We'd better get ready for trouble."

"I really don't think they'd be out lookin' for us in weather like this," Perry insisted.

"I tell you, I heard somethin'," Poore said sullenly. He pushed his bottom lip out. "I ain't a damn idjit, no matter what you think, John—"

That was when a gunshot, muffled slightly by the snow, blasted somewhere close by and a chunk of Nate Poore's skull flew off, taking some blood and brain with it in a grisly pink explosion. His knees buckled and he went straight down.

Sheehan bellowed a curse and lunged toward the rifles they had leaned against one of the rocks. He got a gloved hand on a Winchester barrel and started to jerk the weapon up when more shots crashed. Bullets thudded against Sheehan's bulky figure. He wore a thick coat, but it wasn't thick enough to stop any of those slugs. The shots drove him back against the boulder. He bumped into the other rifles and knocked them over.

Sheehan dropped the Winchester he had grabbed and clutched at his chest. As he did so, another bullet smacked right through his hand and drilled on into his heart. He fell, twisting as he did so, and landed on his back. His sightless eyes stared up into the storm. Snowflakes settled onto them, but he never blinked.

At the first sound of the shots, Alice had grabbed hold of Kermit and clutched him tightly to her. There was no place for them to hide, but thankfully, the bullets all seemed to be directed toward the men on the far side of the ring of rocks. Of course, ricochets were always possible.

The gunfire stopped as abruptly as it began, leaving a startled John Perry on his feet. He had his hand wrapped around the butt of his gun, but he didn't pull the iron as a man stepped out of the swirling snow and pointed a rifle at him.

"Better not, friend," the stranger said.

Perry let go of the gun like it was blistering his fingers. He stuck both hands in the air and said, "D-Don't shoot."

"Not unless you do something stupid," the stranger said. He had come closer, so that Alice was able to get a better look at him. She was stunned to see that he wore an overcoat, a dark suit, and a derby. He would have looked more at home on the streets of Washington than here in the middle of the Black Hills.

More men followed him out of the storm. Two of them were dressed similarly to the first one, while the other three looked like cowboys. No, not cowboys, necessarily, Alice thought. Outlaws. They reminded her of Gus Greendale and Hank Singleton.

A couple of the newcomers checked the bodies of Sheehan and Poore, making sure they were dead. The man who had the rifle pointed at Perry asked, "Is there anybody else around here?"

"No," Perry said. "Just . . . just me. And those kids."

One of the other men wearing a derby walked across the camp and stopped in front of Alice and Kermit. They both peered up at him in confusion. She should have been happy that they'd been rescued, Alice thought, but somehow she was still afraid.

Perhaps these men *weren't* here to rescue her and her brother. Perhaps once again, things had just gotten worse . . .

"Are you children all right?" the man looming over them asked. He sounded as if he were looking for information, not that he actually cared about their welfare.

"Yes," Alice managed to say. "We . . . we haven't been injured. We're just cold . . . and frightened."

The man nodded. He turned his head and called over his shoulder, "They're here."

A moment later, three more men walked into the camp in the rocks. Two of them were also dressed like Easterners, but Alice's heart slugged as she recognized the third man. He was Lame Wolf, the old Indian who belonged to Greendale's gang.

He appeared to have switched allegiances.

Then Alice's pulse raced even faster as she realized she knew one of the other men, as well. She had seen him on a number of occasions and even been introduced to him a couple of times. And every time she'd been forced to take his hand and smile at him, her skin had crawled, as if she had accidentally picked up a particularly loathsome creature.

Even so, the sight of him shocked an exclamation out of her.

"Senator Pulsipher!"

He stepped forward, smiling, and said, "That's right, my dear. Under the circumstances, I'm sure you're very happy to see a familiar face."

The man with Pulsipher chuckled and said, "I don't know, Senator. The young lady doesn't look all that happy to me."

The politician's smile vanished, replaced by a cold, hateful, arrogant smirk.

"It doesn't matter," he said. "I have them now, and soon . . . very soon . . . their father will be mine to command." Pulsipher looked around at Lame Wolf. "You. Indian! Is there a better place we can wait out this storm?"

Lame Wolf nodded. "Yes, I know a place not far from here. A cave. We ought to be comfortable there."

"Well, don't just stand there. Lead us to it."

Without waiting for orders, the man standing over Alice and Kermit reached down, grabbed the blanket, and whipped it off them. He took hold of Alice's arm and pulled her roughly to her feet. One of the other men hauled Kermit upright.

Alice hated herself for doing it, but she screamed as fresh terror welled up inside her.

"Shut that little tramp up," Pulsipher ordered. Alice's

captive tossed his rifle to one of the other men and clapped that hand over her mouth. He dragged her across the camp. Alice tried to struggle, but she was too weak and cold, and despair had settled into her soul, just as cold as the wind that sent the snow dancing through the Black Hills.

Chapter 32

A few minutes earlier, Lowell Hammersby would have said it wasn't possible for him to get any colder than he already was, but he would have been wrong. When he heard the young woman's scream, the last of the still-flowing blood in his veins turned to ice.

He was leaned forward in the saddle, hunched over, his head lowered against the wind. His gloved hands were clamped tight around the saddle horn. At least, he thought they were. He couldn't feel them much anymore. But when he looked at them, they were still there, holding in place the reins he had wrapped around the horn so they wouldn't slip from his numb fingers.

In response to that unexpected scream, a scene played out in his mind as if he were watching it on a stage at a theater back in Washington. The dashing hero—himself, of course—rushed in and surprised the villains who had kidnapped the beautiful young heroine and her brother. With a thunderous volley of deadly accurate shots from his revolver, the hero dispatched all the miscreants except for their evil leader. Then, tossing the empty weapon aside disdainfully, the hero engaged the gang's mastermind in a furious exchange of fisticuffs that ended with the villain's utter, humiliating defeat.

Whereupon, naturally, the beautiful young heroine threw

herself into the hero's arms and showered him with kisses of gratitude, kisses that swiftly became something even more urgent and passionate . . . and then, thankfully for discretion and propriety, the curtain swept down, leaving the hero to bask in the glory of his triumph . . .

"D-Don't be a d-damned fool," Lowell Hammersby said aloud through chattering teeth. "You're n-no h-hero."

But he *was* stubborn, otherwise he never would have been able to follow Senator Warren Pulsipher, the hired toughs Pulsipher had brought with him from Washington, and the hardcases he had hired in Deadwood before setting out on the President's trail, all the way out here into this wilderness.

Hammersby had been lucky, too, and he knew that. Not only was he not a hero, he wasn't a frontiersman by any stretch of the imagination, either, and yet he'd been able to follow those men and not get caught. He had survived on the scanty rations he had bought hurriedly in Deadwood before setting out on a rented horse. He had slaked his thirst at the various streams they had crossed. He was filthy, hadn't shaved in days, and ached in every muscle of his body.

But he was here, watching the enemy, just as he had observed when Pulsipher's group caught up to the other man who'd been following Mr. Roosevelt. A few times, Hammersby had been close enough to overhear snatches of conversation, and he had heard the stranger referred to as Neill. Evidently he held some sort of old grudge against the President, too, just like that outlaw Greendale.

Greendale was dead now, and the sole surviving member of his gang had joined forces with Pulsipher and Neill. And *that* had been a stroke of luck for the President's enemies, because the old Indian had been able to lead them in an alternate route, around their original destination, so that they were ahead of Conrad Morgan and the other men who'd set out to aid in the rescue of the children.

It was quite an elaborate web, composed equally of strands of happenstance and evil design, and it had brought them all here . . . to a frozen hell.

At least Miss Alice and young Kermit were still alive. From his vantage point on a hill more than a quarter of a mile away, Hammersby had seen that. He had watched the brutal murder of two of the current set of kidnappers. The third member of that trio was still alive, but he was a prisoner now, too, with his hands tied behind his back.

They were all getting ready to leave, Hammersby realized. The snow was thick enough that he was having trouble seeing now. He had to get closer. As the men put Alice and Kermit and the other captive on horseback and then mounted up themselves, Hammersby nudged his horse into motion. It plodded down the hill. Enough snow had coated the ground that the horse's hooves left tracks in it as he started across the broad valley toward the rocks.

The snow was a blessing in disguise. By the time Hammersby reached the former camp, the others were gone and he couldn't see them anymore. But the tracks their mounts had left were still visible, even though the snow was starting to fill them. If he didn't waste any time, Hammersby told himself, he would be able to follow their trail and find out where they were going.

And what he would do after that, he had no idea, he realized as he and his horse disappeared into the storm.

The snow was a little disorienting, but despite that, the cave was right where Lame Wolf thought it was and he was able to lead the others straight to it.

It was at the top of a rocky slope that angled down for a couple of hundred yards. An equally rocky bluff rose above it, too steep and lacking in hand- and footholds for a man to climb down. Some scrubby pines topped the bluff. With an open field of fire in front of it, a few men could hold the cave against an army.

Lame Wolf hoped it wouldn't come to that . . . but when you'd been audacious to kidnap two of the President's children, there was no telling what might happen.

In the beginning, Lame Wolf had gotten mixed up in this scheme out of a desire for both revenge and a nice ransom payoff, but during the course of the afternoon he had realized that Senator Warren Pulsipher didn't seem to be all that interested in either of those things. Neill wanted revenge and money, sure, but Neill was working for Pulsipher. In the end, it would be the senator who pulled the strings and called the shots. Lame Wolf's instincts told him that Pulsipher was an absolutely odious man, the sort who gave all politicians a bad name, but he was also stubbornly determined to get what he desired.

Lame Wolf wasn't quite sure what that was, but he figured if he stuck with this bunch, he would find out sooner or later.

The cave was fifty feet deep, maybe forty feet wide at its mouth and a little wider than that at the back, since the walls angled out slightly. Boulders had tumbled down from higher on the slopes and landed on the narrow ledge in front of the cave, providing several good positions for riflemen to be posted to hold off an attack.

The space was big enough and the ceiling high enough that the men were able to bring the horses inside. They herded the animals into a rear corner, then a rope was tied to outcrops in the rock walls and strung across at an angle to form a makeshift corral. The rope would serve to hold the horses there unless they got too spooked.

The prisoners were put in the other rear corner, tied hand and foot. Lame Wolf was a little surprised that Pulsipher had allowed the man called John Perry to live; Perry seemed to have no further value to the senator.

But that was none of Lame Wolf's business, he reflected as he hunkered on his heels beside the fire he had built and soaked up some of the warmth from the flames. There was a good supply of firewood in the cave, as well as rocks arranged into a fire ring, courtesy of previous pilgrims who had stopped here. In a place as far from civilization as this, travelers who took advantage of any shelter tried to leave it in good shape for the next fellow who came along.

Pulsipher and Neill walked over to the fire and extended their hands toward it.

"Roosevelt ought to be along later today or tomorrow," Neill said. "Assuming, of course, he doesn't freeze to death first."

"I don't want that to happen," Pulsipher said. "Roosevelt's no good to me dead."

Neill pursed his lips in thought and said, "Now, see, when you looked me up, Senator, you talked me into joining forces with you because you promised I'd have my revenge on that man."

"And you assumed that meant killing him?"

"Well, what was I supposed to think?"

Pulsipher chuckled. "If you kill Roosevelt, that's it. It's over and done with. I'd prefer to punish him and make him suffer for a long time. What better way to do that than to render him powerless? To turn him into a puppet . . . a puppet whose strings will be firmly in *my* hands?"

"And you'll do that by threatening his children?"

"Of course. He'll follow my orders, do whatever I tell him, or else his precious brats will die. *I* will be the true ruler of this country!" Both of Pulsipher's hands clenched into fists. He shook them in front of his chest and his lips twisted into an ugly snarl as he went on, "For a man with Roosevelt's pride, such a fate will be *hell on Earth*!"

Pulsipher sounded mad, Lame Wolf thought, and apparently he wasn't the only one to get that impression. Neill frowned and said, "I know what he did to Greendale and myself, but what did he ever do to you to make you hate him so?"

Pulsipher's head lifted. "He doesn't agree with my political stance," he said, "and he doesn't respect me!"

"And for that, you—" Neill stopped short and raised both hands, palms out. "No, no, forget it. That's your right, and without your money, none of this would have happened."

"And don't forget that," the senator snapped. "You'll just have to be content with getting your revenge on Roosevelt the way I've planned."

"Fine, fine. Whatever you say, Senator."

Pulsipher jerked his head in a nod and stalked away. He crossed the cave to stand in front of the prisoners. Clasping his hands behind his back, he rocked back and forth slightly as he smirked malignantly at Alice, Kermit, and Perry.

Still warming his hands at the fire, Neill moved a little closer to Lame Wolf and said so quietly only the Indian could hear, "He's crazier than an outhouse rat."

"I cannot argue with you, Mr. Neill," Lame Wolf replied, equally quietly.

"Well, all I know is that things may get rather hectic when the President shows up, and if Roosevelt happens to catch a bullet . . . accidentally, of course . . . such things happen, don't they?"

"I would not want to be the man who fired the fatal shot and robbed Senator Pulsipher of his most ardent desire."

"Neither would I," Neill said, "but would you risk it for a thousand dollars?"

Lame Wolf turned his head enough to look up at the other man. "Are you offering that?"

"Maybe. Keep it in mind, should the opportunity arise."

Lame Wolf nodded slowly and turned his attention back to the fire. He didn't believe Neill for a second. The man would get him to kill the President, then pay him off with a bullet. Lame Wolf could see that happening.

But a thousand dollars was a lot of money, and if there was even a chance that Neill was telling the truth . . .

He would have to think about that, Lame Wolf decided, and he might not ever have the chance anyway.

The way the snow was falling and the wind was howling out there, Teddy Roosevelt might not ever get here. He might wind up a frozen carcass, somewhere in the Black Hills.

The five men stood so that the horses blocked the wind a little while they talked.

"I won't turn back, and I won't stop," Theodore Roosevelt declared. "My children are out there somewhere, and I won't abandon them, no matter how bad the weather gets. Would any of you men do such a thing, if you were in my position?"

"Finding a place to hole up until the storm blows over isn't the same as abandoning them, Teddy," Seth Bullock said. "We'll still be on their trail."

"A trail that will be gone forever by then!"

Frank said, "It won't be any help to those youngsters if you freeze to death, Teddy. What Seth says makes sense." He paused, then added, "Although, if I'm being honest, I reckon I'd feel the same way you do if I was in your place."

He glanced at Conrad. He had risked his own life plenty of times for his son, and Conrad had returned the favor.

Hunter spoke up, saying, "I've seen plenty of storms like this, and I don't figure it's gonna turn out to be a full-bore blizzard. Probably won't get more than five or six inches of snow out of it by morning, and it'll be gone. We can push on then, and we'll be more likely to find what we're looking for."

"I've spent time in this region as well," Roosevelt said stubbornly, "and you can't be sure the storm won't be worse than that, Mr. Buchanon. Today may be our only chance to catch up to the scoundrels who have abducted my children. I say we push on, now that the horses have rested."

"Wouldn't hurt to let them blow a little while longer," Bullock said.

Roosevelt glared at the suggestion, but he said, "Very well. Ten more minutes, and then we resume our search."

Hunter looked around and said, "Where'd Buddy get off to? I haven't seen him in a while."

"Neither have I," Frank said, "but I'm sure he's not too far off. He seems pretty devoted to you, Hunter . . . which is something I never thought I'd be saying about a coyote."

Hunter grinned. "Yeah, he's something special, all right. I—" He stopped short and raised his head. "Is that him yipping that I hear?"

Conrad said, "I don't hear anything except the wind. Maybe that's what you . . . No, hold on a minute." He frowned. "Maybe I *do* hear something, but I'm not sure it's that coyote of yours."

Hunter walked around the horses, saying over his shoulder, "I'm gonna go check."

"I'll come with you," Conrad offered. He had to hurry to keep up with Hunter's long-legged strides.

The snow was a couple of inches deep now and still falling fairly heavily. That white layer covered the ground where the two men walked. They hadn't gone very far when Conrad spotted something bounding toward them, a dark shape against the snow.

"That's him, isn't it?" Conrad said.

"Yeah." Hunter lifted his voice. "Buddy! Hey, Bud!"

Buddy appeared to be fine as he ran up to them. Hunter reached down with a gloved hand to pet the coyote, but Buddy snapped at him, causing Hunter to jerk his hand back and exclaim in surprise. Then Buddy caught hold of Hunter's trouser leg with his teeth and tugged on it.

"What's got into you, Bud? What in blue blazes are you doing?"

Buddy growled a little as he pulled on Hunter's trouser leg. He let go of it, ran off a few yards, then whirled around and dashed back to grab at the fabric with his teeth again.

"If I didn't know better," Conrad said, "I'd swear he's trying to get you to follow him."

"Yeah, it sure seems like it."

"Has he ever done that before?"

"Nope. Something's got him riled up, for sure." Hunter looked over at Conrad. "Maybe we'd best go see what it's about."

Conrad nodded in agreement.

"Go on, Buddy," Hunter said to the coyote. "Show us what's got you excited."

Buddy turned and ran off into the snow again. Hunter and Conrad trotted after him. From behind them, Frank called, "What are you doing?"

"Buddy's found something," Conrad shouted back. He didn't know if that was actually true or not, but for the time being that was what he was going to assume.

With the snow falling thickly through the air, it was difficult to see very far, but anything dark was going to stand out against the white, so it wasn't long before Hunter said with excitement in his voice, "Isn't that a horse up there?"

"Looks like it," Conrad agreed. "There's a man on it, too."

The horse was about fifty yards away, trudging slowly toward them. The men broke into a run. Conrad could see the rider hunched over in the saddle, swaying back and forth.

"That fella's in a bad way," he said to Hunter. "Maybe hurt or wounded."

"Yeah, he—There he goes!"

The rider had toppled out of the saddle, falling limply to the ground. The startled horse danced off a few steps to the side and then stopped. The fallen man hadn't moved by the time Conrad and Hunter pounded up to him a few moments later.

Conrad dropped to a knee beside the man while Hunter hung back a little in case of a trick, although that didn't seem at all likely.

"I don't see any blood on the snow," Conrad said. "Maybe he's just mostly frozen."

The man lay on his side. Conrad rolled him onto his back, and as he did, surprise went through him like a punch in the gut.

Of all the men he would have expected to come across, covered with snow and unconscious in the middle of the Black Hills, Lowell Hammersby probably would have been the last on that list . . .

Chapter 33

"I d-don't think . . . I'll ever b-be warm again," Hammersby said through chattering teeth as he leaned toward the fire Frank had built. They had cleared the ground for the fire by sweeping the snow away with their boots. The layer of the white stuff was still thin enough to do that.

"You will be, Lowell," Roosevelt said as he hunkered next to his young assistant. "Just think about Washington in the summer, and how hot it is then! Once you're back there, you'll be wishing for this weather, eh?"

From somewhere, Hammersby summoned up a faint smile. "I don't think so, Mr. President. But you could be right."

His voice sounded a little stronger now that he'd started to thaw out some, Conrad thought. Hunter had checked Hammersby's fingers and didn't find any signs of frostbite, which was good. They hadn't taken a look at his toes yet, though.

"Now," Roosevelt said crisply, "where is this cave you mentioned, the one where those scoundrels are holding my children?"

"I . . . I'm not sure I can lead you back there. I wasn't thinking that far ahead. I just hoped you were somewhere close behind them, Mr. President, and that I could find you."

Hunter said, "I reckon it was Buddy who found *you*. That was a stroke of good luck. As for leading us back to that cave where the gang holed up, you may not have to worry about that."

All the others looked at him. Roosevelt demanded, "What do you mean by that, Mr. Buchanon?"

Instead of answering the question directly, Hunter asked, "Was that cave at the top of a bare slope, with the face of a bluff rising above it?"

"Yes, that's right," Hammersby said. "How did you know?"

Seth Bullock said, "You've been there before, haven't you, Hunter?"

Hunter nodded. "I've been all over the Black Hills. I spent a night in that cave once, eight or ten years ago."

"Can you find it again?" Roosevelt asked.

"Once I've been to a place, I can go back to it." Hunter waved a hand dismissively at the falling snow. "Even in weather like this."

Hammersby started to stand up. "Then we should go. There's no time to waste."

"You should warm up more, Lowell," Roosevelt said.

Hammersby shook his head firmly. "No, sir. I don't want Miss Alice and Master Kermit in the hands of those villains for one more second longer than necessary. There's no way of knowing what that . . . that traitor might do!"

The news that Senator Warren Pulsipher apparently was behind the plot against the President had shaken Roosevelt and surprised the other men. Conrad wasn't really shocked, though, remembering what his initial impression of Pulsipher, gleaned from Roosevelt's comments, had been.

"You're right," the President said now. "Pulsipher is a madman if he believes he can get away with threatening my children. We must deal with this as quickly as possible."

"I agree. Now, if someone would be kind enough to help me back onto my horse . . ."

"It'd be my honor, Lowell," Conrad said as he took Hammersby's arm to assist him. Sometimes you found courage and heroism in places where you wouldn't expect to . . . like in the heart of a man such as Lowell Hammersby.

"It's impossible, I can tell you that right now," Roosevelt said as he handed Seth Bullock's telescope back to his old friend. "An attack up that slope would be suicide. They would mow us down."

"That's how it looks to me, too," Bullock said.

The six men were hidden in a screen of trees several hundred yards away from the slope leading up to the cave. Hunter had led them here unerringly, just as he'd claimed he could. But now they had run into what seemed like an immovable obstacle, and to make matters worse, the light would begin to fade in another hour or so.

Frank took that into account as he said, "Maybe we'd be better off waiting until night. We could slip up there in the darkness."

"They'd see us coming against the snow," Conrad said. "We'd never make it all the way to the cave."

Hunter rubbed his bristly chin and said, "There might be another way."

All eyes swung to him.

"What we need is to get in there amongst 'em before they know we're there," he went on. "We know there's nine enemies in that cave, counting that senator fella. If, say, me and Conrad and Mr. Morgan could get in there, we'd be outnumbered, sure, but I reckon we're all worth at least three of those varmints apiece."

"I agree," Conrad said. "But how do we get there?"

Hunter pointed. "There are trees up on top of that bluff.

We could circle around where they wouldn't see us, tie ropes to the trees, and then go down them until we're able to drop right in the big middle of that bunch and start cleaning 'em out."

"They'd hear you coming down the bluff above them," Bullock objected.

Roosevelt frowned and said, "Not if all their attention was focused on a distraction."

"What did you have in mind, Teddy?"

"I've led charges up hills in the face of great odds before, you know."

"Now hold on," Bullock said. "Just a minute ago, you were telling us that a charge up that slope would be suicide."

Roosevelt shrugged. "There's risk involved, certainly. But what man won't run a few risks for the sake of his children?"

Frank said, "You know, it might not be quite as risky if you and Seth and Lowell stampeded the horses up the slope first. Once the light starts to fade, those fellas in the cave won't be able to see as well, and they might not realize all the saddles are empty. You three can keep your own mounts and follow the other horses, and maybe by the time you got to the top, we'd have things under control and the youngsters would be safe."

"It might work," Conrad said, "but there'll be a lot of lead flying around, Mr. President."

Roosevelt waved that away. "It's our best chance."

For a moment, the others all considered it. Then, slowly, each man nodded.

"One change," Bullock said. "I'm coming with you and going down that bluff to the cave."

"Aw, Seth," Hunter began, "you're too—"

"Don't say it," Bullock warned him. "If you and Frank can do it, so can I."

Frank clapped a hand on Bullock's shoulder. "I'll be happy to have you siding our play, Seth."

"So will I," Conrad added.

"It's settled, then," Roosevelt said. "And if you're moving on foot and staying out of sight, it's likely to take some time to get in position, so you'd better start now."

"That's what I was thinking," Hunter said. "We've all got ropes, boys. Grab 'em and let's get moving."

The plan was a pretty simple one: Conrad, Frank, Hunter, and Seth Bullock would signal Roosevelt from atop the bluff when they were ready to make their move, then Roosevelt and Lowell Hammersby would mount up and drive the other horses up the slope in front of them. The men inside the cave, believing themselves under attack from the front, would open fire, and the shooting would cover any sounds the four rescuers made descending the bluff on their ropes. When they were close enough, they would drop down among the kidnappers and cut them down mercilessly.

"Take Pulsipher alive if possible, though," Roosevelt had requested. "I want him to face justice in a court of law, just as Greendale and Neill did originally."

Hammersby had revealed Neill's identity to the President, who remembered the incident in New York that had led to the former policeman's arrest and imprisonment. The whole thing made sense now, although Pulsipher's involvement was still rather murky. According to Hammersby, though, he was the one who had orchestrated the whole thing in the first place, for whatever reason he might have had.

Now, as the grayness that cloaked the valley thickened with the approach of an early night, Conrad and the others were in position on top of the bluff. Getting here had been a long, tiring hike and then climb, but it could have been worse, especially if the snow had been deeper. There was enough of the stuff on the ground to turn the world white around them, but it wasn't difficult to walk through.

They tied the ropes they had brought with them to tree trunks, making sure the knots were secure. When the ropes were dropped over the edge, the other ends reached to just above the cave mouth. It was unlikely any of the guards who sat behind boulders on the ledge in front of the cave would look up and notice them, but it wasn't out of the realm of possibility. The sooner the four men made their move, the better.

Hunter broke a branch off a tree and wrapped some cloth he had brought with him around one end of it. He had to strike a couple of matches before the makeshift torch caught on fire, but as soon as it was burning, Hunter held it above his head and moved it back and forth. That was the signal they had agreed on with Roosevelt.

Hunter continued waving the torch for a minute, then tossed it onto the snow to gutter out. They hadn't wanted to risk having Roosevelt send a return signal, so all they could do now was wait and see if the President launched the distraction.

"Damn, what if he didn't see it?" Hunter muttered as they stood there, holding the ropes they would use for the descent.

"I know Teddy," Bullock said. "He was watching for it. It's just a matter of time—"

Suddenly, a clatter of hoofbeats, some shouts, and several gunshots rose above the sound of the wind. Men down in the cave yelled in alarm. Muzzle flashes winked in the gloom as Roosevelt and Hammersby fired above the heads of the horse they were driving in front of them. The kidnappers began shooting back at them.

"Now!" Seth Bullock said.

The four men backed over the edge and started walking down the face of the bluff, going hand over hand on the ropes, bouncing slightly away from the rock wall as they pushed off with their booted toes. It was a dangerous descent—one slip could prove disastrous—but it was quick, too, and in a matter of moments they were perched right above the cave mouth. The guards were about a dozen feet below them.

The men exchanged glances in the swirling snow and then pushed out one final time and let go, dropping straight down onto the ledge.

They didn't aim for the guards; landing on top of a man like that meant too much of a risk of getting tangled up, maybe breaking a leg. Instead they landed between the boulders where the guards were posted.

Conrad drew both guns as he fell. As he landed and his knees bent to take his weight, he fired the Colt and the Mauser at the same time. The bullets ripped into the guards on either side of him, both of whom died likely not having any idea what had just happened.

At the same time, Hunter shot the third guard, while Frank and Bullock charged deeper into the cave, which was lit by the campfire the kidnappers had built.

"Kill them!" a man screeched. Frank recognized him as Senator Pulsipher from Hammersby's description. "Kill the brats, too!"

A stocky man with graying brown hair, in Eastern clothes, lunged toward the Roosevelt youngsters. That would be Ambrose Neill, and Frank had no doubt Neill would kill Alice and Kermit just to obtain some manner of revenge on the President. He swung his gun in Neill's direction but held off on the trigger when Seth Bullock darted forward, into the line of fire. Bullock left his feet in a diving tackle, wrapped his arms around Neill's legs, and brought the man crashing to the ground. They began rolling from side to side, slugging away brutally at each other.

A bullet whipped past Frank's head. He saw a buckskin-clad Indian running toward the prisoners. The Indian flung another shot in Frank's direction that made him crouch. He pulled a knife with his other hand as he dropped to his knees beside a cringing Alice Roosevelt.

Frank was about to risk shooting the Indian, even though he was awfully close to the children, when a man who also seemed to be a prisoner suddenly threw himself at Alice. His hands were free somehow, and one of them also held a knife that he aimed at Alice's neck.

Before that deathblow could land, the Indian drove his knife into the man's side. The man fell away from Alice and tried to fight back against the Indian, but the buckskin-clad man struck again and again with his knife. He had dropped his gun during the struggle, however, and the other man suddenly scooped it up. Flame lanced from the barrel. The Indian was thrown back as the slug struck him, but he had already done enough damage with his knife. The other man dropped the gun he had just fired, groaned, and rolled onto his side. A spasm went through him as he died.

Out on the ledge, Conrad and Hunter had each dropped to a knee as a storm of lead howled around them. Three more gunmen charged them, firing as they came. Conrad felt a bullet tug at his sleeve, and Hunter's hat flew off, drilled by one of the shots.

Then a fresh volley raged from the guns held by Conrad and Hunter, and would-be killers jerked and stumbled as bullet after bullet pounded into them. Their movements became a macabre dance as momentum carried them forward. Guns slipped from suddenly nerveless fingers. The hired killers pitched forward, dead before they plowed face-first into the rocky ground just a few feet away from Conrad and Hunter.

A running figure darted past Conrad, whose eyes stung from the clouds of powdersmoke that filled the cave. Despite that, Conrad recognized him as Senator Warren Pulsipher, who was trying to escape like the rat he was.

Pulsipher had only taken a couple more steps, however, when he was met by a powerful fist that came out of the snow and smashed into his face, knocking him backward.

President Theodore Roosevelt loomed out of the gathering darkness and strode determinedly toward Pulsipher, who scuttled away from him with a panic-stricken look on his egg-shaped face.

That panic abruptly vanished, replaced by cunning viciousness, as Pulsipher jerked a pistol from under his coat and leaped to his feet.

"Now at least you'll die, you . . . you damned *Republican*!" he cried.

The crack of a shot punctuated Pulsipher's shout. Conrad had been about to fire, but somebody had beaten him to it. He glanced over and saw Lowell Hammersby standing behind and to one side of Roosevelt. The aide held a smoking rifle in his hands.

Pulsipher staggered, dropped his pistol, and moaned as he looked down at the spreading bloodstain on his shirtfront. He pawed futilely at it with one hand, then dropped to his knees. He fell forward, caught himself on his other hand, and raised his head to stare at Roosevelt.

"It . . . it should have been me," he gasped. "I . . . I'm the one who should have—"

"Been running the country?" Roosevelt snapped. "I pray to God I'm long dead before the likes of you ever occupy the White House, you worm."

Pulsipher whined, collapsed the rest of the way onto his belly, and twitched a couple of times before lying still.

"I'm sorry, sir," Hammersby said. "I know you wanted him taken alive, but I couldn't stand by and let him shoot you."

"If you hadn't done it, Lowell," Conrad said, "I was about to."

"Yeah, me, too," Hunter added.

Roosevelt sighed. "I suppose it's better this way. The spectacle of a sitting senator being put on trial for kidnapping, conspiracy, and heaven knows what else . . . well, it wouldn't have been good for the country."

"Mr. President," Frank said. He shepherded a pair of blanket-wrapped figures forward. Alice and Kermit, freed at last, rushed into their father's arms. Roosevelt, crying unashamedly, caught them up in a tight embrace, as if he never intended to let them go again.

Seth Bullock stepped up alongside Frank with a gun in the ribs of his prisoner, a battered-looking Ambrose Neill. "Looks like you'll be headed back to prison, mister," he said.

Neill sighed. "I suppose. But perhaps one of these days, things will change. And if they do . . . I'll be remembering *you*, too, Mr. Bullock."

Roosevelt looked around at the others, and with uncharacteristic emotion, he said, "I . . . I can never repay the debt that I owe you men. My deepest thanks will never be enough."

"Well, you ought to thank that fella over there while you can," Frank said with a nod toward the Indian, who sat with his back propped against the cave wall. "He saved Alice's life for sure just now, and probably Kermit's, too."

"But . . . but he's one of the men who kidnapped us in the first place," Alice said.

"Maybe so, but that other fella was about to kill you when the Indian stopped him."

"Lame Wolf," Kermit piped up. "His name is Lame Wolf. And the other man is John Perry."

With an arm around each of his children, Roosevelt went over to where Lame Wolf sat and said, "I'm told I owe you my thanks, sir."

The old Indian smiled up at him and said, "You remember me . . . Teddy?"

"I most certainly do. You rode with Gus Greendale."

"Yeah. I've done some . . . pretty bad things. But I never . . . killed a kid . . . or stood by while one was hurt.

Found out just now . . . that I still couldn't." The front of Lame Wolf's buckskin shirt was soaked with blood, and it was obvious that he was fading fast. But he forced himself to go on, "A while ago . . . I saw Pulsipher talking to Perry . . . saw the senator slip him something . . . Reckon it had to be a knife . . . so Perry could cut himself loose . . . and kill the kids if it all went wrong . . . No telling what Pulsipher promised him . . . Anyway, Perry had to know . . . he probably wouldn't come out of it alive." A hollow laugh came from the dying man. "Hell, none of us . . . come out of it—" A choking cough silenced him for a moment, then he looked up and, instead of finishing what he'd been saying, he told Roosevelt simply, "I'm sorry, Teddy."

Then his eyes closed and his head fell forward, leaving silence in the cave except for the crackling of flames in the campfire.

CHAPTER 34

Deadwood

"Will there still be a celebration, Mr. Bullock?" Kermit asked.

"Of course there will," Bullock replied. "Folks here in town don't know what happened out there in the hills." He looked around the table in a private dining room in the Bullock Hotel. The remains of a lavish meal were spread across it. "Nobody except the folks who are here this evening know the truth."

"And that's the way it shall remain," President Theodore Roosevelt added in a firm voice from the head of the table. "There shall be no mention of this unfortunate misadventure in the press or in the history books. It would serve no purpose for the American people to know that their leader has been gallivanting around pursuing outlaws and kidnappers and renegade senators. *Especially* renegade senators from the opposing party. Good heavens, some of the opposition newspapers would publish stories making it sound as if *I* were the villain and that wretched Pulsipher the hero!"

His wife reached over and rested her hand on his as she said, "Now, Theodore, you don't need to get all wound up and deliver a political speech tonight."

"Of course not, my dear Edith," Roosevelt agreed. "Instead, this is an occasion for being thankful. And so . . ." He looked around the table at the men sitting there, interspersed among the children. "Thank you, Conrad. Thank you, Frank. Thank you, Hunter. Thank you, my old friend Seth. And you . . ." His gaze settled on Lowell Hammersby. "Thank you, my great and good friend Lowell, because without your gallantry, we might not have ever found that cave in time."

Hammersby looked embarrassed. "I'm, ah, just glad I could be of assistance—"

"I'd say you saved the day in more ways than one, Lowell," Conrad told him with a smile.

"And you even did it without losing any fingers or toes to frostbite," Hunter added.

"Well, it was that coyote of yours who led you to me," Hammersby pointed out. "So I suppose he's a hero, too."

"Oh, yeah, sure he is," Hunter agreed. "Just don't tell him. He's liable to get a swelled head about it."

That brought laughter from everyone around the table. When that died down, Roosevelt said, "I don't suppose you've reconsidered my offer of that cabinet position, have you, Conrad?"

"I'm afraid my answer is still no on that, Mr. President," Conrad replied. "I have some mines back in Colorado to get to."

As well as a beautiful young woman with thick blond curls and a fast gun hand, to boot, he added to himself. It would be good to see Denny again.

And as he thought about her, he wondered for the first time what it would be like to spend the rest of his life with Denise Nicole Jensen.

That was a question for another time, Conrad told himself. Tonight, despite the cold outside, was for basking in the warmth of a family reunited. It didn't matter who they were, or how powerful and important the head of that family was.

All that mattered was that they were together again, joined in the love they felt for each other.

Conrad glanced across the table at his father, who smiled and nodded at him, almost as if Frank knew what he was thinking. This adventure might have drawn to a close, but somewhere down the trail another was liable to be waiting.

It was hard to dodge trouble for very long, when your name was Morgan and you packed a fast gun.

Chapter 1

"I declare it's darker'n the inside of a dead man's boot out here!" exclaimed Dad Clawson.

"It ain't dark over here by the fire," countered Dad's younger cow-punching partner, Pete Driscoll.

"No, but it sure is dark out here." Dad—a short, bandy-legged, gray-bearded man in a bullet-crowned cream Stetson that had seen far better days a good twenty years ago—stood at the edge of the firelight, holding back a pine branch as he surveyed the night-cloaked, Bear Paw Mountain rangeland beyond him.

"If you've become afraid of the dark in your old age, Dad, why don't you come on over here by the fire, take a load off, and pour a cup of coffee? I made a fresh pot. Thick as day-old cow plop, just like you like it. I'll even pour some of my who-hit-John in it if you promise to stop caterwaulin' like you're about to be set upon by wolves."

Dad stood silently scowling off into the star-capped distance. Turning his head a little to one side, he asked quietly in a raspy voice, "Did you hear that?"

"Hear what?"

"That." Dad turned his head a little more to one side. "There it was again."

Driscoll—a tall, lean man in his mid-thirties and with a

thick, dark-red mustache mantling his upper lip—stared across the steaming tin cup he held in both hands before him, pricking his ears, listening. A sharpened matchstick drooped from one corner of his mouth. "I didn't hear a thing."

Dad turned his craggy, bearded face toward the younger man, frowning. "You didn't?"

"Not a dadgum thing, Dad." Driscoll glowered at his partner from beneath the broad brim of his black Stetson.

He'd been paired with Clawson for over five years, since they'd both started working at the Stevens' Kitchen Sink Ranch on Owlhoot Creek. In that time, they'd become as close as some old married couples, which meant they fought as much as some old married couples.

"What's gotten into you? I've never known you to be afraid of the dark before."

"I don't know." Dad gave his head a quick shake. "Somethin's got my blood up."

"What is it?"

Dad glowered over his shoulder at Driscoll. "If I knew that, my blood wouldn't be up—now, would it?"

Driscoll blew ripples on his coffee and sipped. "I think you got old-timer's disease. That's what I think." He sipped again, swallowed. "Hearin' things out in the dark, gettin' your drawers in a twist."

Dad stood listening, staring out into the night. The stars shone brightly, guttering like candles in distant windows in small houses across the arching vault of the firmament. Finally, he released the pine bough; it danced back into place. He turned and, scowling and shaking his head, ambled back over to the fire. His spurs chinged softly. On a flat, pale rock near the dancing orange flames, his speckled tin coffeepot, which owned the dent of a bullet fired long ago by some cow-thieving Comanche bushwhacker in the Texas Panhandle, gurgled and steamed.

"Somethin's out there—I'm tellin' ya. Someone or some-*thing* is movin' around out there." Dad grabbed his old Spencer repeating rifle from where it leaned against a tree then walked back around the fire to stand about six feet away from it, gazing out through the pines and into the night, holding the Spencer down low across his skinny thighs clad in ancient denims and brush-scarred, bull-hide chaps.

Driscoll glanced over his shoulder at where his and Dad's hobbled horses contentedly cropped grass several yards back in the pines. "Horses ain't nervy."

Dad eased his ancient, leathery frame onto a pine log, still keeping his gaze away from the fire, not wanting to compromise his night vision. "Yeah, well, this old coot is savvier than any broomtail cayuse. Been out on the range longer than both of them and you put together, workin' spreads from Old Mexico to Calgary in Alberta." He shook his head slowly. "Coldest damn country I ever visited. Still got frostbite on my tired old behind from the two winters I spent up there workin' for an ornery old widder."

"Maybe you got frostbite on the brain, too, Dad." Driscoll grinned.

"Sure, sure. Make fun. That's the problem with you, Pete. You got no respect for your elders."

"Ah, hell, Dad. Lighten up." Driscoll set his cup down and rummaged around in his saddlebags. "Come on over here an' let's play us some two-handed—" He cut himself off abruptly, sitting up, gazing out into the night, his eyes wider than they'd been two seconds ago.

Dad shot a cockeyed grin over his shoulder. "See?"

"What was that?"

Dad cast his gaze through the pines again, to the right of where he'd been gazing before. "Hard to say."

"Hoot owl?"

"I don't think so."

The sound came again—very quiet but distinct in the

night so quiet that Dad thought he could hear the crackling flames of the stars.

"Ah, sure," Driscoll said. "A hoot owl. That's all it was!" He chuckled. "Your nerves is right catching, Dad. You're infecting my peaceable mind. Come on, now. Get your raggedy old behind over here and—" Again, a sound cut him off.

Driscoll gave an involuntary gasp then felt the rush of blood in his cheeks as they warmed with embarrassment. The sound was unlike anything Dad or Pete Driscoll had ever heard before. A screeching wail? Sort of catlike. But it hadn't been a cat. At least, like no cat Dad had ever heard before, and he'd heard a few during his allotment. Night-hunting cats could sound pure loco and fill a man's loins with dread. But this had been no cat.

An owl, possibly. But, no. It hadn't been an owl, either.

Dad's old heart thumped against his breastbone.

It thumped harder when a laugh vaulted out of the darkness. He swung his head sharply to the left, trying to peer through the branches of two tall ponderosa pines over whose lime-green needles the dull, yellow, watery light of the fire shimmered.

"That was a woman," Driscoll said quietly, his voice low with a building fear.

The laugh came again. Very quietly. But loudly enough for Dad to make out a woman's laugh, all right. Sort of like the laugh of a frolicking employee in some house of ill repute in Cheyenne or Laramie, say. The laugh of a prostitute mildly drunk and engaged in a game of slap 'n' tickle with some drunken, frisky miner or track layer who'd paid downstairs and was swiping at the woman's bodice with one hand while holding a bottle by the neck with his other hand.

Dad rose from his log. Driscoll rose from where he'd been leaning back against his saddle, reached for his saddle ring Winchester, and slowly, quietly levered a round into the action. He followed Dad over to the north edge of the camp.

Dad pushed through the pine branches, holding his own rifle in one hand, his heart still thumping heavily against his breastbone. His tongue was dry, and he felt a knot in his throat. That was fear.

He was not a fearful man. Leastways, he'd never considered himself a fearful man. But that was fear, all right. Fear like he'd known it only once before and that was when he'd been alone in Montana, tending a small herd for an English rancher, and a grizzly had been prowling around in the darkness beyond his fire, occasionally edging close enough so that the flames glowed in the beast's eyes and reflected off its long, white, razor-edged teeth it had shown Dad as though a promise of imminent death and destruction.

The cows had been wailing fearfully, scattering themselves up and down the whole damn valley . . .

But the bear had seemed more intent on Dad himself.

That was a rare kind of fear. He'd never wanted to feel it again. But he felt it now, all right. Sure enough.

He stepped out away from the trees and cast his gaze down a long, gentle, sage-stippled slope and beyond a narrow creek that glistened like a snake's skin in the starlight. He jerked with a start when he heard a spur trill very softly behind him and glanced to his right to see Driscoll step up beside him, a good half a foot taller than the stoop-shouldered Dad.

Driscoll gave a dry chuckle, but Dad knew Pete was as unnerved as he was.

Both men stood in silence, listening, staring straight off down the slope and across the water, toward where they'd heard the woman laugh.

Then it came again, louder. Only, this time it came from Dad's left, beyond a bend in the stream.

Dad's heart pumped harder. He squeezed his rifle in both sweating hands, bringing it up higher and slipping his right finger through the trigger guard, lightly caressing the trigger.

The woman's deep, throaty, hearty laugh echoed then faded. Then the echoes faded, as well.

"What the hell's goin' on?" Driscoll said. "I don't see no campfire over that way."

"Yeah, well, there's no campfire straight out away from us, neither, and that's where she was two minutes ago."

Driscoll clucked his tongue in agreement.

The men could hear the faint sucking sounds of the stream down the slope to the north, fifty yards away. That was the only sound. No breeze. No birds. Not even the rustling, scratching sounds little animals made as they burrowed.

Not even the soft thump of a pinecone falling out of a tree.

It was as though the entire night was collectively holding its breath, anticipating something bad about to occur.

The silence was shattered by a loud yowling wail issuing from behind Dad and Driscoll. It was a yapping, coyote-like yodeling, only it wasn't made by no coyote. No, no, no. Dad heard the voice of a man in that din. He heard the mocking laughter of a man in the cacophony as he and Driscoll turned quickly to stare back toward their fire and beyond it, their gazes cast with terror.

The crazy, mocking yodeling had come from the west, the opposite direction from the woman's first laugh.

Dad felt a shiver in Driscoll's right arm as it pressed up against Dad's left one.

"Lord Almighty," his partner said. "They got us surrounded. Whoever they are!"

"Toyin' with us," Dad said, grimacing angrily.

Then the woman's voice came again, issuing from its original direction, straight off down the slope and across the darkly glinting stream. Both men grunted their exasperation as they whipped around again and stared off toward the east.

"Sure as hell, they're toyin' with us!" Driscoll said tightly, angrily, his chest expanding and contracting as he breathed.

"What the hell do they want?" He didn't wait for Dad's response. He stepped forward and, holding his cocked Winchester up high across his chest, shouted, "What the hell do you want?"

"Come on out an' show yourselves!" Dad bellowed in a raspy voice brittle with terror.

Driscoll gave him a dubious look. "Sure we want 'em to do that?"

Dad only shrugged and continued turning his head this way and that, heart pounding as he looked for signs of movement in the deep, dark night around him.

"Hey, amigos," a man's deep, toneless voice said off Dad and Driscoll's left flanks. "Over here!"

Both men whipped around with more startled grunts, extending their rifles out before them, aiming into the darkness right of their fire, looking for a target but not seeing one.

"That one's close!" Driscoll said. "Damn close!"

Now the horses were stirring in the brush and trees beyond the fire, not far from where that cold, hollow voice had issued. They whickered and stumbled around, whipping their tails against their sides.

"That tears it!" Pete said. He moved forward, bulling through the pine boughs, angling toward the right of his and Dad's fire which had burned down considerably, offering only a dull, flickering, red radiance.

"Hold on, Pete!" Dad said. "Hold on!"

But then Pete was gone, leaving only the pine boughs jostling behind him.

"Where are you, dammit?" Pete yelled, his own voice echoing. "Where the hell are you? Why don't you come out an' show yourselves?"

Dad shoved his left hand out, bending a pine branch back away from him. He stepped forward, seeing the fire flickering straight ahead of him, fifteen feet away. He quartered to the right of the fire, not wanting its dull light to outline him, to make him a target. He could hear Pete's spurs ringing, his boots thudding and crackling in the pine needles ahead of him, near where the horses were whickering and prancing nervously.

"What the hell do you want?" Pete cried, his voice brittle with exasperation and fear. "Why don't you show yourselves, darn it?" His boot thuds dwindled in volume as he moved farther away from the fire, spurs ringing more softly.

Dad jerked violently when Pete's voice came again: "There you are! Stop or I'll shoot, damn you!"

A rifle barked once, twice, three times.

"Stop—" Pete's voice was drowned by another rifle blast, this one issuing from farther away than Pete's had issued. And off to Dad's left.

Straight out from Dad came an anguished cry.

"Pete!" Dad said, taking one quaking footstep forward, his heart hiccupping in his chest. "*Pete!*"

Pete cried out again. Running, stumbling footsteps sounded from the direction Pete had gone. Dad aimed the rifle, gazing in terror toward the sound of the footsteps growing louder and louder. A man-shaped silhouette grew before Dad, and then, just before he was about to squeeze the Spencer's trigger, the last rays of the dying fire played across Pete's sweaty face.

He was running hatless and without his rifle, his hands clamped over his belly.

"Pete!" Dad cried again, lowering the rifle.

"Dad!" Pete stopped and dropped to his knees before him. He looked up at the older man, his hair hanging in his eyes, his eyes creased with pain. "They're comin', Dad!" Then he sagged onto his left shoulder and lay groaning and writhing.

"*Pete!*" Dad cried, staring down in horror at his partner.

His friend's name hadn't entirely cleared his lips before something hot punched into his right side. The punch was followed by the wicked, ripping report of a rifle. He saw the flash in the darkness out before him and to the right.

Dad wailed and stumbled sideways, giving his back to the direction the bullet had come from. Another bullet plowed into his back, just beneath his right shoulder, punching him forward. He fell and rolled, wailing and writhing.

He rolled onto his back, the pain of both bullets torturing him.

He spied movement in the darkness to his right.

He spied more movement all around him.

Grimacing with the agony of what the bullets had done to him, he pushed up onto his elbows. Straight out away from him, a dapper gent in a three-piece, butternut suit and bowler hat stepped up from the shadows and stood before him. He looked like a man you'd see on a city street, maybe wielding a fancy walking stick, or at a gambling layout in San Francisco or Kansas City. The dimming firelight glinted off what appeared a gold spike in his rear earlobe.

The man stared down at Dad, grinning. He was strangely handsome, clean-shaven, square-jawed. At first glance, his smiling eyes seemed warm and intelligent. He appeared the kind of man you'd want your daughter to marry.

Dad looked to his left and blinked his eyes, certain he wasn't seeing who he thought he saw—a beautiful flaxen-haired woman with long, impish blue eyes dressed all in black including a long, black duster. The duster was open to reveal that she wore only a black leather vest and a skirt under it. The vest highlighted more than concealed the heavy swells of her bosoms trussed up behind the tight-fitting, form-accentuating vest.

The woman smiled down at Dad, tipped her head back, and gave a catlike laugh.

If cats laughed, that was.

There was more movement to Dad's right. He turned in that direction to see a giant of a man step up out of the shadows.

A giant of a full-blooded Indian. Dressed all in buckskins and with a red bandanna tied around the top of his head, beneath his low-crowned, straw sombrero. Long, black hair hung down past his shoulders, and two big pistols jutted on his hips. He held a Yellowboy repeating rifle in both his big, red hands across his waist. He stared dully through flat, coal-black eyes down at Dad.

Dad gasped with a start when he heard crunching footsteps behind him, as well. He turned his head to peer over his shoulder at another big man, this one a white man.

He stepped out of the shadows, holding a Winchester carbine down low by his side. He was nearly as thick as he was tall, and he had a big, ruddy, fleshy face with a thick, brown beard. His hair was as long as the Indian's. On his head was a badly battered, ancient Stetson with a crown pancaked down on his head, the edges of the brim tattered in places. He grunted down at Dad then, working a wad of chaw around in his mouth, turned his head and spat to one side.

Dad turned back to the handsome man standing before him.

As he did, the handsome man, lowered his head, reached up, and pulled something out from behind his neck. He held it out to show Dad.

A pearl-handled Arkansas toothpick with a six-inch, razor-edged blade.

To go along with his hammering heart, a cold stone dropped in Dad's belly.

The man smiled, his eyes darkening, the warmth and intelligence Dad had previously seen in them becoming a lie, turning dark and seedy and savage. He turned and walked over to where Pete lay writhing and groaning.

"No," Dad wheezed. "Don't you do it, you devil!"

The handsome man dropped to a knee beside Pete. He grabbed a handful of Pete's hair and jerked Pete's head back, exposing Pete's neck.

Pete screamed.

The handsome man swept the knife quickly across Pete's throat then stepped back suddenly to avoid the blood geysering out of the severed artery.

Pete choked and gurgled and flopped his arms and kicked his legs as he died.

The handsome man turned to Dad.

"Oh, God," Dad said. "Oh, God."

So this was how it was going to end. Right here. Tonight. Cut by a devil who looked like a man you'd want your daughter to marry. Aside from the eyes, that was . . .

As though reading Pete's mind, the handsome man grinned down at him. He shuttled that demon's smile to the others around him and then stepped forward and crouched down in front of Dad.

The last thing Dad felt before the dark wing of death closed over him was a terrible fire in his throat.

CHAPTER 2

"You think those rustlers are around here, Pa?" Matt Brannigan asked his father.

Just then, Tynan Brannigan drew his coyote dun to a sudden stop, and curveted the mount, sniffing the wind. "I just now do, yes."

"Why's that?" Matt asked, frowning.

Facing into the wind, which was from the southwest, Ty worked his broad nose beneath the brim of his high-crowned tan Stetson. "Smell that?"

"I don't smell nothin'."

"Face the wind, son," Ty said.

He was a big man in buckskins, at fifty-seven still lean and fit and broad through the shoulders, slender in the hips, long in the legs. His tan face with high cheekbones and a strawberry blond mustache to match the color of his wavy hair, which hung down over the collar of his buckskin shirt, was craggily handsome. The eyes drawn up at the corners were expressive, rarely veiling the emotions swirling about in his hot Irish heart; they smiled often and owned the deeply etched lines extending out from their corners to prove it.

Ty wasn't smiling now, however. Earlier in the day, he and Matt had cut the sign of twelve missing beeves as well as the horse tracks of the men herding them. Of the long-looping *devils* herding them, rather. Rustling was no laughing matter.

Matt, who favored his father though at nineteen was not as tall and was much narrower of bone, held his crisp cream Stetson down on his head as he turned to sniff the wind, which was blowing the ends of his knotted green neckerchief as well as the glossy black mane of his blue roan gelding. He cut a sidelong look at his father and grinned. "Ah."

"Yeah," Ty said, jerking his chin up to indicate the narrow canyon opening before him in the heart of west-central Wyoming Territory's Bear Paw Mountains. "That way. They're up Three Maidens Gulch, probably fixin' to spend the night in that old trapper's cabin. The place has a corral so they'd have an easy time keeping an eye on their stolen beef."

"On *our* beef," Matt corrected his father.

"Good point." Ty put the spurs to the dun and galloped off the trail they'd been on and onto the canyon trail, the canyon's stony walls closing around him and Matt galloping just behind his father. The land was rocky so they'd lost the rustler's sign intermittently though it was hard to entirely lose the sign of twelve beeves on the hoof and four horseback riders.

A quarter mile into the canyon, the walls drew back and a stream curved into the canyon from a secondary canyon to the east. Glistening in the high-country sunlight and sheathed in aspens turning yellow in the mountain fall, their wind-jostled leaves winking like newly minted pennies, the stream hugged the trail as it dropped and turned hard and flinty then grassy as it bisected a broad meadow then became hidden from Ty and Matt's view by heavier pines on their right.

The forest formed the shape of an arrow as it cut down from the stream toward Ty and Matt. That arrow point crossed the trail a hundred yards ahead of them as they followed the trail through the forest fragrant with pine duff and moldering leaves.

At the edge of the trees, Ty drew the dun to a halt. Matt followed suit, the spirited roan stomping and blowing.

Ty gazed ahead at a rocky saddle rising before them a hundred yards away. Rocks and pines and stunted aspens stippled the rise and rose to the saddle's crest.

"The cabin's on the other side of that rise," he said, reaching forward with his right hand and sliding his Henry repeating rifle from its saddle sheath.

Both gun and sheath owned the marks of time and hard use. Ty had used the Henry during his town-taming years in Kansas and Oklahoma, and the trusty sixteen-shot repeater had held him in good stead. So had the stag-butted Colt .44 snugged down in a black leather holster thonged on his buckskin-clad right thigh.

The thong was the mark of a man who used his hogleg often and in a hurry, but that was no longer true. Ty had been ranching and raising his family in these mountains for the past twenty years, ever since he'd met and married his four children's lovely Mexican mother, the former Beatriz Salazar, sixteen years Ty's junior.

He no longer used his weapons anywhere near as much as when he'd been the town marshal of Hayes or Abilene, Kansas, or Guthrie, Oklahoma. Only at such times as now, when rustlers were trying to winnow his herd, or when old enemies came gunning for him, which had happened more times than he wanted to think about. At such times he always worried first and foremost for the safety of his family.

His family's welfare was paramount.

That's what he wanted to talk to Matt about now . . .

He turned to his son, who had just then slid his own Winchester carbine from its saddle sheath and rested it across his thighs. "Son," Ty said, "there's four of 'em."

"I know, Pa." Matt levered a round into his Winchester's

action then off-cocked the hammer. He grinned. "We can take 'em."

"If this were a year ago, I'd send you home."

Again, Matt grinned. "You'd try."

Ty laughed in spite of the gravity of the situation he found himself in—tracking four long-loopers with a son he loved more than life itself and wanted no harm to come to. "You and your sister," Ty said, ironically shaking his head. He was referring to his lovely, headstrong daughter, MacKenna, who at seventeen was two years younger than Matt but in some ways far more worldly in the ways seventeen-year-old young women can be and more worldly than boys and even men.

Especially those who were Irish mixed with Latina.

Mack, as MacKenna was known by those closest to her, was as good with a horse and a Winchester repeating rifle as Matt was, and Matt knew it. Sometimes Ty thought she was as good with the shooting irons as he himself was. Part of him almost wished she were here.

"You're nineteen now," Ty told Matt.

"Goin' on twenty," Matt quickly added.

"Out here, that makes a man." Ty jerked his head to indicate the saddle ahead of them. "They have a dozen of our cows, and they can't get away with them. They have to be taught they can't mess with Powderhorn beef. If we don't teach 'em that, if they get away with it—"

"I know, Pa. More will come. Like wolves on the blood scent."

"You got it." Ty narrowed one grave eye at his son. "I want you to be careful. Take no chances. If it comes to shootin', and we'd best assume it will because those men likely know what the penalty for rustling is out here, remember to breathe and line up your sights and don't hurry your shots or you'll pull 'em. But for God sakes when you need to pull your head down, pull it down!"

"You know what, Pa?" Matt asked, sitting up straight in

his saddle, suddenly wide-eyed, his handsome face showing his own mix of Irish and Latin, with his olive skin, light brown hair which he wore long like his father, and expressive, intelligent tan eyes.

"What?"

"A few minutes ago, I wasn't one bit scared," Matt said. "In fact, I was congratulatin' myself, pattin' myself on the back, tellin' myself how proud I was that I was out here trackin' long-ropers with the great Ty Brannigan without threat of makin' water in my drawers. But now I'm afraid I'm gonna make water in my drawers! So, if you wouldn't mind, could we do what needs doin' before I lose my nerve, pee myself, an' go runnin' home to Ma?"

He kept his mock-frightened look on his father for another three full seconds. Suddenly, he grinned and winked, trying to put the old man at ease.

Ty chuckled and nudged his hat up to scratch the back of his head. "All right, son. All right. I just had to say that."

"I know you did, Pa."

Ty sidled his mount up to Matt's handsome roan, took his rifle in his left hand and reached out and cupped the back of Matt's neck in his gloved hand, pulling him slightly toward him. "I love you, kid," he said, gritting his teeth and hardening his eyes. "If anything ever happened to you . . ."

Feeling emotion swelling in him, threatening to fog his eyes, he released Matt quickly, reined the dun around, and booted it on up the trail.

Matt smiled after his father then booted the roan into the dun's sifting dust.

Ten minutes later, father and son were hunkered down behind rocks at the crest of the saddle. Their horses stood ground-reined twenty feet down the ridge behind them.

Ty was peering through his spyglass into the valley on the saddle's other side, slowly adjusting the focus. The old trapper's cabin swam into view—a two-story, brush-roofed, age-silvered log hovel hunkered in a meadow on the far side of a creek rippling through a narrow, stony bed.

The cabin was flanked by a lean-to stable and a pole corral in which all twelve of his cows stood, a few chewing hay, others mooing nervously. Five horses milled with the cattle, also eating hay or munching grass that had grown high since the place had been abandoned many years ago. That fifth horse might mean five instead of four men in the cabin. One man, possibly whoever was buying the stolen beef, might have met the others here with the cows. Ty would have to remember that.

A half-breed named Latigo He Who Rides had lived there—an odd, quiet man whom Ty had met a few times when he'd been looking for unbranded mavericks that had avoided the previous roundup. He had never known what had happened to He Who Rides.

One year on a trek over to this side of the saddle he'd simply found the cabin abandoned. It had sat mostly abandoned ever since except when rustlers or outlaws on the run used it to overnight in. It was good and remote, and known only by folks like Ty who knew this eastern neck of the mountains well.

Rustlers had moved in again, it looked like. Ty had a pretty good idea who they were led by, too. A no-account scoundrel named Leroy Black. His brother Luther was probably here, as well. They were known to have rustled in the area from time to time, selling the stolen beef to outlaw ranchers who doctored the brands or to packers who butchered it as soon as the cows were in their hands.

Knowing the Blacks were rustling and being able to prove it, however, were two separate things.

The Black boys were slippery, mostly moved the cattle at night. They were probably working with their cousins, Derrick and Bobby Dean Barksdale. The Blacks and Barksdales made rustling in the Bear Paws and over in the nearby Wind Rivers a family affair. That they were moving beef in the light of day meant they were getting brash and would likely get brasher.

Ty grimaced, his cheeks warming with anger. Time to put them out of business once and for all.

Ty handed the spyglass to Matt hunkered beside him, staring through a separate gap between the rocks. "Have a look, son. Take a good, careful look. Get a good sense of the layout before we start down, and note the fifth horse in the corral. The odds against us likely just went up by one more man. We'll need to remember that."

"All right, Pa." Matt took the spyglass, held it to his eye, and adjusted the focus. He studied the cabin and its surroundings for a good three or four minutes then lowered the glass and turned to his father, frowning. "They don't have anyone on watch?"

Ty shook his head. "Not that I could see. They've gotten overconfident. That works in our favor."

"We gonna wait till dark? Take 'em when they're asleep?"

Ty shook his head. "Too dangerous. I like to know who I'm shooting at." He glanced at the sun. "In about an hour, the sun will be down behind the western ridges. It'll be dusk in that canyon. That's when we'll go. Knowing both the Blacks and Barksdales like I do, they'll likely be good and drunk by then."

Matt nodded.

Ty dropped to his butt and rested back against one of the large rocks peppering the ridge crest. He doffed his hat, ran a big, gloved hand brusquely through his sweat-damp hair. "Here's the hard part."

"The hard part?"

"Waiting. Everyone thinks lawdogging is an exciting profession. Truth to tell, a good three-quarters of it is sitting around waiting for something to happen."

"Good to know," Matt said. "In case I ever start thinkin' about followin' in my old man's footsteps."

"Forget it," Ty said, smiling. "You're needed at the Powderhorn. That's where you're gonna get married and raise a whole passel of kids. We'll add another floor to the house." Suddenly, he frowned, pondering on what he'd just said. "That is what you'd like to do—isn't it, Matt?"

A thoughtful cast came to Matt's eyes as he seemed to do some pondering of his own. Finally, he shrugged, quirked a wry half-smile, and said, "Sure. Why not?"

Ty studied his oldest boy. He'd always just assumed, since Matt had been a pink-faced little baby, that the boy would follow in Ty's footsteps. His ranching footsteps. Not his lawdogging footsteps.

Now he wondered if he'd made the wrong assumption. His own father had assumed that Ty would follow in Killian Brannigan's own footsteps as a mountain fur trapper and hide hunter. That they'd continue to work together in the Rockies, living in the little cabin they shared with Ty's hardworking mother halfway up the Cache la Poudre Canyon near La Port in Colorado. Killian Brannigan had been hurt when Ty had decided to go off to the frontier army and fight the Indians and then, once he'd mustered out, pin a badge to his chest. One badge after another in wide-open towns up and down the great cattle trails back when Texas beef was still being herded to the railroad hubs in Kansas and Oklahoma.

Those years had been the heyday of the Old Western gunfighter, so Ty, too, had had to become good with a gun.

Despite what Ty had said to Matt about lawdogging being three-quarters boredom, it had been an exciting time in his life. While he'd visited his parents often, he'd never regretted the choice he'd made. Being a mountain man and working in tandem with his mountain woman, Ciara Brannigan, pronounced "Kee-ra," had been his father's choice. Killian and Ciara had both been loners by nature and had preferred the company of the forests and rivers to that of people. While Ty had loved his parents and enjoyed his childhood hunting and trapping and hide-tanning alongside his mother and father, he'd been ready to leave the summer he'd turned seventeen.

And leave he had.

Now he realized he should have known better than to assume that his own son would want to follow in his own ranching footsteps. It wasn't a fair assumption to make. And now Ty wondered, a little skeptically as he continued to study his son, if he'd been wrong. He hoped he wasn't, but he might be. If so, like his own father before him, he'd have to live with the choice his son made. That time was right around the corner, too, he realized with a little dread feeling like sour milk in his belly.

He just hoped Matt didn't make Ty's own first choice. He didn't want his son to be a lawman. He wanted him to stay home and ranch with Ty and the boy's mother, Beatriz.

Time passed slowly there on the top of that saddle.

The sun angled westward. Deep purple shadows angled out from the western ridges. Birdsong grew somnolent.

Ty kept watch on the cabin. While he did, two of the four men came outside, separately and at different times, to make water just off the dilapidated front stoop. Another came out to empty a wash pan. That man came out the cabin's back door a few minutes later to walk over to the corral and check on the cattle that were still mooing and grazing uneasily. That was one of the Barksdale brothers clad in a ragged broadcloth coat and floppy-brimmed felt hat. He wore two pistols on his hips and held a Winchester in his hands.

On the way back to the cabin, he took a good, long,

cautious look around. Then he reentered the cabin through the back door.

While Ty kept watch, Matt rested his head back against a rock, tipped his hat down over his face, and dozed.

Finally, Ty put his spyglass away and touched his son's arm. "Time to go, son," he said. "Sun's down."

He picked up his rifle and looked at Matt, who yawned, blinking his eyes, coming awake. He wanted to tell the kid to stay here, out of harm's way, but he couldn't do it. Matt wouldn't have listened, and he shouldn't have. He wasn't a kid anymore. He was almost twenty and he was part of a ranching family. That meant he, like Ty, had to protect what was his.

Ty hoped like hell they got through this all right. If anything happened to that kid, his mother would never forgive Ty and Ty would never forgive himself.